CW00693253

About the Book

The Girl in the Water is a work of fiction. Any references to historical events, real people, or real places are used fictitiously. Other names, characters, places, and events are products of the author's imagination; any resemblance to actual events, places, or persons, living or dead, is entirely coincidental.

September 17, 2022 :: First Edition

Published in Canada by
Nummist Media :: Halifax, NS
nummist.com

☐ ISBN 9780995287853 (paperback)
■ ISBN 9781738788651 (hardcover)
☐ ISBN 9780995287846 (ebook)

Cover art by Janet Howse
Book design by Joseph Howse

Dedication

To my family and Pat McLarney,
who remind me, Life is a mighty force.

Cast of Characters

Listed in order of first mention:

Nadia (Nadezhda) Mikhailovna a scholar
Nastya (Anastasia) Mikhailovna Nadia's older sister,
    an artist
Ida Ivanova Nastya and Nadia's friend
Johnny (Jaan) Nastya and Nadia's friend
Gramma Ninel Nastya and Nadia's paternal grandmother,
    a veteran
Katya (Yekaterina) Lvovna Nastya and Nadia's mother,
    a factory worker
Misha (Mikhail) Pavlovich Nastya and Nadia's father,
    a shipping clerk
Grandpa Pasha (Paavo) Nastya and Nadia's paternal grandfather,
    a veteran
Grandpa Lev Nastya and Nadia's maternal grandfather,
    a schoolteacher
Tolyan a hooligan
Giorgi Licheli a detective
Cherny Gramma Ninel's cat
Pierre/Petrushka (Robespierre) Gramma Ninel's warhorse
Kio a leader of partisans
Galya Gramma Ninel's youngest sister
Anton Igorevich Yahontov a psychiatrist
Andrei an orderly
Yuly Lvovich Babich Gramma Ninel's neighbour
Petya a radio operator
Sokolov an officer in Naval Aviation

Sergei Sverdlov a detective
Anya Vladimirovna Sverdlova Sergei's wife,
        a childcare worker
Rosya Lekht Yuly's cousin
Manya a childcare worker
Fenya (Agrafena) Petrova a detective
Marat Petrovich Fenya's older brother,
        a manager and photographer
Pyotr Marat and Fenya's father,
        an optical engineer
Avel an informant
Yuri a custodian of a library
Fraydel Yuly's daughter
Minah Yuly's wife
Tentser Fraydel's cat
Gramma Marusya Nastya and Nadia's maternal grandmother
Igor Igorevich Yahontov a psychiatrist
Cosmos / Tentser II a cat of changing circumstances
Oleg a doorkeeper
Kazimir a barbecue operator
Sveta (Svetlana) Kazimir's wife
Wayne/Pricey (Gawain Price) a merchant mariner

I: Swept Away

1: Daydream

Call her Nadia; her parents did.

She never once dreamt of lions but there was a time, as a colourless childhood advanced into benighted adolescence, when foreign candy and shortwave radio seemed the stuff of dreams. She and her elder sister Nastya and Nastya's friends Ida and Jaan collected the candy wrappers. Their rainbow colours had no parallel in the blocks of crumbling tenements that looked like sullied wedding cakes, picked over by all and sundry hands in an atmosphere of sweat, smoke, secrecy, and dubious libations. Hunger, sated briefly—that was a wedding party.

Jaan styled himself "Johnny". He was the one with the shortwave radio, which he had put together in a shed on a country road somewhere, from parts he scrounged on his truant expeditions by commuter rail. He was pleased to lecture the youngest, Nadia, on the workings of the device and the role of the ionosphere in shortwave propagation. Nastya and Ida were more excited by Johnny's plan to resurrect a motorcycle he had hauled from a bog.

Lecturing Nadia was one thing but Johnny was not one for chitchat. Nastya never got much out of him when she gushed about the man he would be: an engineer, a scientist, a cosmonaut, a radio anchor, a motorcyclist-adventurer.

"I'm nobody's worker and nobody's hero," Johnny scoffed at Nastya one time.

Ida took a different tack. One summer, day after day, she voiced a daydream about finding a new place to go—instead of the shed in nobody's hayfield, a beach between nobody's forest and nobody's sea. On the high sand dunes, even higher pine trees would give them shade and the breeze would fill their lungs with salt and pine as it rolled the

3

water and the branches and the sand. They could be "just happy, just us," in such a singular landscape of straight and waving forms.

"A change could be good," even Johnny admitted at last. The motorcycle was not starting; it had not started since their grandparents went to war. He had sweat in his eyes, greasy gashes on his hands, he stank unbearably even to himself, and he was beginning to imagine that the shed was being watched.

Anyway, the hayfield had become infested with ticks that year, so Nastya and Nadia were ready to support a change.

As if she had already chosen the spot from a library of survey photographs, Ida led them all to it the following day. It was far. They had only two hours of late afternoon to enjoy there but they agreed it would be a fine place to return. "If only we could camp for a night or two and spend the whole day... Hmm," Ida sighed and by then, all four were living in a daydream.

A youth event in a farther town afforded a pretext to be away. Johnny used connections to falsify their attendance.

On the first evening, around their campfire on the beach, they experimented with lightly roasting a few foreign candy bars in their precious wrappers. This had been Nadia's idea, she had emptied her secret stash, and she was proud to make this contribution to the illicit party. They laughed like mad as they tried to lick molten chocolate from the singed rainbow foil.

Nastya passed around a bottle of Vana Talinn rum liqueur. "Not for you, Little Hedgehog," she said to Nadia.

They climbed the dunes to watch the sunset. At the last light, Ida said, "Hmm, I'm going down again. I need a moment."

She went walking East, her feet straddling the tideline in a kind of dance. As she got farther, Johnny reached into his pack for something else he had scrounged—a pair of large binoculars.

"What's she doing?" Johnny crowed.

Even without binoculars, it was plain enough that Ida was stripping, tossing her clothes to the wind, and then wading out into the surf. Johnny's optics just gave him the best view.

"Stop that!" Nastya said.

"Why?" asked Johnny. "I'll share if that's the problem; here, look." He held out the binoculars but it was Nadia who reached for them. "Not you."

This second refusal stung unexpectedly. Nadia lay back and chose to ignore it all in favour of scanning for Venus and Mercury in the western sky.

"Is she drowning herself?" Johnny asked. "No. False alarm."

Nadia drifted off to the sound of the wind in the pines. She was tired from the day's travel and sun and earlier swimming (in bathing suits) and staring into the fire and eating chocolate, along with tons of mussels they had gathered and bread from home.

The stars were many when Ida returned with most of her clothes. Nadia was awake to hear her say, "I lost my neckerchief." Nastya made chitchat about all the places they could look for it tomorrow. That put everyone to sleep.

The next day, supplies ran out and there was little appetite for mussels alone. "Are you alright to gather mushrooms without me?" Nastya asked her sister. "I did promise Ida I'd help her find her neckerchief."

Being excused from that errand suited Nadia well enough, so she spent the morning in the pine forest. She knew from their grandmother what was poison and what was not. The old woman had survived among partisans.

The party got back together for lunch on the beach. There were plenty of mushrooms, as well as clams that Johnny had dug. He was showing Nadia another of his recent scroungings—a portable radio—and they were about to string an antenna up the dunes when Nastya and Ida arrived with a red neckerchief full of red-and-gold cloudberries. By luck, they had found both and thought they made a pretty presentation to share between sisters and friends.

Nastya and Ida laid the fire as Nadia and Johnny strung the antenna and tuned in a faint crackle of rock and roll. They were less well equipped than in the shed and hayfield, where they had hidden a splendid antenna by stringing it along a rotten fence. "*En tout cas*," said Nadia, putting on airs of an international scholar, "*l'ionosphère fonctionne mieux la nuit.*" She got a little smile from her teacher. He was good with languages, on account of his shortwave listening.

They baked the clams and seared the mushrooms with rocks in the fire; the cloudberries they ate raw. The feast was briny, earthy, and tart.

Everybody sat, sated. They were hot from their labours and the fire, sun, and sand, and a diet newly rich in molluscs.

The wind had died down. The radio reception was improving just a little.

A distant freighter passed from East to West.

They lay burning. Nadia read a book of Chekhov's tales. Nastya embroidered little cloudberries on Ida's neckerchief. Ida took Johnny's binoculars and studied an island a good kilometre away—just more dunes and pines, pines and dunes, but captivating to her. Johnny was at a loose end.

"I can swim there," Ida said.

"You can't," Johnny informed her.

"You'll have to stop me."

The binoculars went down in the sand. Ida was on her feet, striding out to sea, and—once more—stripping on the way.

The other three sat up. Nastya rested her sewing in her lap and appeared unable to breathe. Nadia placed a bookmark in Chekhov and put him away in her satchel.

Ida, now thigh-deep in water, was bending to throw it on her face and back. From below her shoulder blades, down to her buttocks, she was crisscrossed by red and purple stripes; she had taken a beating for something lately. The deepest wounds were C-shaped—a buckle—while her upper back bore a more diffuse bruise, faded to yellow, where she had probably been held down. *Doesn't that hurt?* Nadia wondered about the salt. Ida did not show it. She finished splashing herself and just kept wading deeper.

Johnny tensed, stood up, and tensed some more.

Up to her breasts in the surf, Ida paused to unbraid her long hair—blond, which seemed whiteish against her burning face and neck—and then she dove headlong against a surge. Rolling back a little and then forwards in fierce strokes, she made her way out to sea.

"She'll drown," Johnny said, as if to cue the hero to action. Finding no man but himself, he stripped to his shorts and raced after her.

Now in deep water, Ida rolled over in a wave and started to backstroke. She was a good swimmer and Nadia thought there was no need to panic as yet.

Johnny was not closing the distance.

The daydream ended, for some of them, within the next couple of minutes, which can be a long time to swimmers. The wind picked up again fast. Ida, on full display, went under in a swell. Johnny kept paddling after her like mad and went under in the next one.

They came up together choking. That awful sound blew ashore and further covered up the crackling rock and roll.

The wind lulled a little and they got to shallow water before the next big swell. Linked shoulder-to-shoulder, sputtering all the way, they marched ashore.

Pair of fools, Nadia thought. Ida was actually coughing out a laugh. Her clothes, except the neckerchief, had washed out to sea. Johnny looked back out there as if unsure he were wise to have left the depths.

What Nastya thought was in her eyes. She was crying.

"Nastya?" her sister asked.

"We're leaving," Nastya rasped. "I was wrong to bring you here."

2: Suitcase

That autumn, when Ida got an abortion (and Nadia was not supposed to know), it was the end of the fellowship of four; the sisters' parents made sure of that much even if they had not made sure of much till then.

Their father, Misha, and mother, Katya, pulled strings to relocate the family from the Baltic to the Black Sea.

(He was a shipping and receiving clerk. She was a factory worker.)

Misha's colleague from Odessa suggested to him that it was a fine city, sure to be edifying for the girls. Odessans are famous as practical jokers.

The grandmother would stay. "I made a promise to Misha's father," she said, "and anyway, dears, the South would never suit me. I'll take the long winter nights with the long summer days."

They stuffed their lives in one suitcase apiece, Nadia's being the smallest. She had little besides books and clothes. There was a formal photograph: grandmother and granddaughters. It showed the old woman in a wooden chair with little Nastya and Nadia standing by her knees and her husband's mariner's cap in her lap. There was the candy wrapper collection. There was a leftover length of antenna wire that had served as a bookmark. To Nadia's regret (if hers alone), there was nothing as a keepsake of Ida.

They travelled two days and nights by train via Leningrad, Moscow, and Kiev. Nastya and Nadia had never travelled overnight, nor such a distance. The dormitory car had fifty-four bunks, with sheets spilling into the corridor. On one side, each grouping of four shared a little table, not big enough to spread a newspaper. On the other side, the bunks were in twos with no tables. The toilets were locked whenever the train got near a city, in order to create a "sanitary zone" where no waste was flushed.

People chitchatted, wandered, chitchatted with somebody new, nibbled and drank, wandered, shared their nibbles and drinks, lounged, slept, played cards or chess, changed their socks, opened windows, waited for the toilets, took potions for indigestion or a cough, closed windows, and looked for missing socks.

The world unfolded. The world got warmer. The world stank of socks. Everything brushed together; every sense was overwhelmed by pickled herring, pickled men, shirtless men, farts, and foul breath.

Nadia barfed in the cavernous Kiev station in the middle of Night II. This drew attention to her family and then a tramp tried to sell them a bronze ring. "Gold?" he asked. "Something fine in gold for a girl's hand?"

Enticed to look, Nadia thought, *That's pretty. He's rubbed it till it's bright. Poor, dirty fingers and a bright ring with X's cut into the face.*

"Go away!" hollered Katya, throwing herself between her nauseated younger daughter and the tramp. "Go away or it's you who'll pay!" The tramp moved on without a word.

Nadia felt regret (a distraction from her discomfort, at least). Had that ring been a keepsake? She thought the tramp misunderstood the ring because it looked to her like a gift a girl would give, rather than one she would find flattering from a man.

"Let's go," whispered Misha. "Katya—Mama—girls, let's go."

"Come on, Nadia," Nastya said, "hold on to my arm. Papa, take our cases, please."

They continued on to Odessa in a car recently vacated by another fifty-four people, shifted from various states of unconsciousness.

Nadia begged to lie in an upper bunk and to have the window open so she could feel the updraught. The neighbours bitched about it and chastised Katya as a madwoman of a mother; the girl would die of cold. "I'll shut the window if you stick your tongues in it!" Katya hissed. "Anyone who isn't blind drunk can see my daughter is sick from this stuffy air. Whose fault is that? You, you hustle alongside like parrots on a perch and you echo your great-grandmothers' wisdom and for all your preening, all you do is shit and stink up the air! Die of cold in autumn, wrapped in blankets on a train? Let me tell you, her grandmother was a partisan! Tell them!"

"As my wife says, we would prefer to have the window open."

The train is going in circles, Nadia thought—or perhaps she said it aloud but no one heard. She was burning. She tried to ask Nastya for water, ask Nastya to read to her, ask Nastya for anything but no words would come out.

A conductor thrust his way down the shaking corridor. He bellowed threats and everybody shut up.

On the bunk below Nadia, Nastya was holding her breath in an effort not to sob.

Rocked to sleep, Nadia felt a little relief again. She dreamt of a sand dune and pines, Venus and Mercury, and in her dream she woke in the night as she felt on her face something hot, which was ash. It had blown from a cigarette Ida was smoking. "Bad luck," said Ida. "Here," and Ida offered the cigarette to Nadia. Had something like that been real?

3: **Transformations**

Odessa afforded them better housing: a detached cinderblock home with five rooms and a little garden. The outside door opened onto a kitchen with a gas stove. To the right was a shower room; ahead was a family room. Off the family room were two bedrooms with three beds.

This home was on a street corner next to a small park with a seesaw and a disarmed T-34 tank. Street cats frequented the park (the tank being a hot seat in the sun), the roofs of houses (likewise), and every part of Odessa, especially the waterfront. Street dogs were also common around wastelands, including the unkempt corners of big parks.

Misha had a long, daily walk to his work at the docks. He also took long walks alone in the evenings. Sometimes, he befriended a particular cat or dog. Occasionally, he would take his daughters out to meet such a friend but his wife would have nothing to do with that.

On other occasions, Misha would take his daughters to naval air-shows and he would point out the types of planes by name. The girls got him a book on Naval Aviation for his birthday, so they all became quite expert.

Katya took every opportunity to send her daughters to youth events pertaining to the arts and culture. She considered these things essential to their Odessan edification. Nastya was considered good at drawing and crafts, Nadia at literary recitals in multiple languages.

"The girls are transformed," Katya wrote in a letter to a work-friend up North. She never got a reply.

Katya was a person who believed wholeheartedly in transformations. Daily—even hourly—she seized upon some newfound goodness or badness in a drama with an audience of one. She would fly to the Moon; she would die of oppression; could no one see that it was so? She would honour her father (a teacher, dead of a heart attack), for a life of extremes was the burden of the educated worker.

The transformative school that Katya's father might have founded (had he not died of exhaustion at his middling post) was nothing like the latter-day Odessan school his granddaughters attended. Katya never asked about the school's realities and was never told.

Within their first term, Nastya and Nadia saw a teacher attacked in the schoolyard. A gang of boys was squatting by the wall, on either side of a door, and when this teacher stepped out, one boy called, "Now!" They grabbed chunks of masonry and flung them at her from both sides. Hit on the head, she moaned and staggered back in a strange, abstract form: flailing arms, gaping face, bloodied hair, floral dress. She retreated back through the threshold and slammed the door on the boy-kingpin's hand.

"Cunt!" he wailed in pain. "Filthy whore! Fuck! Fuck! I think she broke it!"

A rival jibed, "Tolyan thinks she broke it."

"Dear Comrades, we've suffered the heavy loss of Tolyan's cock."

There was more of that and a scuffle. Like a ball of fighting cats, tumbling into more cats, the scuffle threatened to become a general schoolyard brawl.

Police sirens were approaching, *Ba-woo-ya, ba-woo-ya*.

The Tolyan gang fled over the fence and out of sight. A minute later, the streets echoed with either firecrackers or gunshots.

4: Such Hosts

Two years later, Gramma came South to visit. She arrived in a cold snap, a week before the winter break. Nastya was finishing her first term of higher education and Nadia was about to turn sixteen.

Gramma was on an evening train, so Misha, at the end of the work-day, was supposed to go straight from the docks to the station to wait for her. Katya had planned it that way; meanwhile, she was cooking and the girls were getting the house ready.

At one point, Katya went out to dump vegetable peels in the garden. When she re-entered, she found Gramma sitting on her big suitcase, near the stove. The old woman was breathing soup steam and listening to her granddaughters, who had not yet noticed her; they were bustling about, chitchatting and laughing, in the family room and their bedroom.

"Gramma!" Katya greeted her. "Girls, come!"

"Hello, dears. I slipped in when you had your backs turned."

The old woman was welcomed with kisses. Without getting up, she touched Nadia, Nastya, and Katya in turn. Gramma's hands had changed in the last two winters; her fingers had become crooked and knotty. Pine trees grow like that on the rocky cliffs in Crimea. (On summer vacation, the family had even sent Gramma a postcard of such a tree.)

"Gramma," said Katya (squeezing in between her and the stove to give the soup pot a quick stir), "you must be tired. Did you stay the night in Moscow with your friend, the archivist?"

"No. I think I am more a trial than a friend to her."

"How can you say that? You two are always writing each other."

"Well, I'm writing requests that she obliges when she can. Anyway, I went via Vitebsk, not Moscow."

"You should have gone via Moscow. It's faster. You must have tired yourself out, coming all that way on slow trains—day, night, day, night…" (Vegetable peels rained into a bucket as Katya spoke and peeled.)

"No, it was fine, dear. I've travelled that route many times by night."

"When was that, Gramma?"

"When we blew it up." With a grunt, Gramma shifted herself off her suitcase. "I do wonder, though, whether Nastya and Nadia might show me our bedroom and then the new shower and toilet you've mentioned in your letters, and where is my son, anyway?"

A potato dropped to the floor. "What?"

"My son. He wasn't at the station and I had your address from your letters, so I came on my own to surprise you."

"He's probably with a cat or a dog," Nadia said. (Till then, she and Nastya had stood attentively near the threshold of the family room.)

"You might have to explain that, dear."

Nastya interjected, "Papa is always nurturing animals he meets on his walks. He loves them to distraction."

"Dear, a distraction is what men do love."

Just as Misha's mother said this, he slipped into the house with sweat on his brow. He wore a smile that only added to his fevered look.

"Mama—Gramma," Misha panted—"missed you by minutes. Got your message from the Station Master when I arrived. He was taken, couldn't say enough about you, told me you saved his father's life in the War!"

"Oh, the nice Station Master," said Gramma as she got another kiss. "He thought his father and I must have met at some point. I wasn't so sure."

"I've had…"

"Where were you?" Katya enquired as she sliced a large potato in two.

"Yes, I'm telling you, I've had the most remarkable encounter of my own today. That's what made me late."

"A remarkable encounter, do tell. I haven't had one for years."

He wheezed and then managed to speak more clearly. "A young detective came to the docks today." As this announcement settled, all were quiet, save the bubbling pot. "He's coming to dinner tonight."

"I hope he's cooked something," Katya said. The words were her usual fare but her voice sounded strange.

"Why is a cop coming to dinner?" Gramma asked.

"A young detective, Mama." Her son assured her, "He's a new kind. He's very attentive to the truth of things. I helped him … with some things he needed to learn about the docks."

"I hope he's paying for that," his wife said. She tossed the last of the week's potatoes in the pot. This one seemed to have a bit of extra force behind it and the pot spat back, far enough that the scalding spray was felt by more than one person in the poky kitchen.

"No, it's not like that. Just trust me, this is a person we want to know. He could be a good friend to us."

"What's he like, Papa?" Nastya wondered.

"I would call him a serious sort of man, about twenty-five, not yet thirty, tall, very neat, clean-shaven, with dark hair and dark eyes. What else about him?"

"Does he prefer cats or dogs?" Nadia asked.

"What's his name, Papa?"

"His name is Giorgi, Nastya. Nadia, you'll have the chance to ask him anything at all and find out whether your questions puzzle even a detective."

"You know, dear," said Gramma to Katya, "it's hit me that you're right. I am tired. The company would be too much for me, so I'll go straight to bed."

"What about this food?"

"Just keep it warm and have the children bring it in after you've all eaten. I've had nibbles all the way here, from the people on the train." Leaving the kitchen and looking for the bedroom, Gramma said, "When I was young and hungry, I starved. Now I'm old and have no appetite, they feed me all the time."

"This way, Gramma," Nastya said as she led the old woman by the hand. "Nadia, would you bring Gramma's suitcase, please?"

The case was heavy. *She's got the old bombs in here.*

The sisters showed their grandmother the bedroom, then showed her the way back through the family room and kitchen to the toilet, and finally got her placed in the bedroom once more. Meanwhile, Katya had told Misha to go change his shirt, so he crossed paths with his mother and daughters in the family room as he headed to the other bedroom. Then, on his return to the kitchen, Katya pronounced her judgment: "No, it's no good. You'll have to shower." His mother was, at that time, still in the toilet, so he waited alongside his daughters, who were waiting to guide his mother.

"Goodnight, goodnight, goodnight, goodnight," Gramma bid each of them in turn as she left the toilet.

"No, we'll get you settled first," Nadia said. *I gotta see what's in the trunk.* However, she was to have no satisfaction, for Gramma just wanted the big suitcase put out of the way in a corner with a spare blanket over it.

"...to keep out the damp. How humid it is! Oh, I'm sure you've heard enough out of me for one night. Thank you, dears. Go meet ... whoever it was, Georgian name, my son's new..."

(Gramma fell asleep in the middle of giving this instruction. Nadia eyed the case for a moment before following Nastya out.)

Misha took his time in the shower. The design was a wet room, vented by a pipe-hole through the cinderblock wall. If one stood on tiptoe to look through the pipe, the garden and street were clearly visible. The whole system did much to contribute to the home's dampness and draughtiness. However, the shower did have a water heater in it, so it was one place to get warm on such a night and, unlike the stove-front or bed, it was a place to be alone.

The shower left him sleepy—and ahead would be an evening of talk, food, and wine, all repurposed from the occasion of his mother's arrival to the occasion of introducing Giorgi. For just a moment, Misha wondered why he was bothering to upend the family's plans but that question seemed to go the way of the steam or of a cat's nocturne.

Taking the clean shirt down from a hook by the pipe-hole, Misha found that the steam had improved it; it almost looked ironed. "Better," said Katya when he emerged. She tasted the soup, straightened his collar, and called, "Nastya, Nadia, what are you doing?"

"Finding some things to entertain Papa's friend," Nastya replied from the family room. "I have my sketchbook…"

"Good!"

"…and Nadia is going to read from…"

"*Crime and Punishment*?" Nadia proposed.

"No, something romantic," her sister said.

"*Anna Karenina*?"

"That might do. Let's look for a scene…"

Thus, they all prepared a scene of their own, the best they could muster: a steamed shirt and straight collar; potato soup and Soviet Champagne; sketches and a recital of famous prose; and a grandmother already abed, so one could say, "Ah, we must speak softly because Gramma is sleeping; she's just had a tiring journey."

Giorgi showed up with a loaf of brown bread and bottle of Moldovan red wine. He was in uniform and, himself, looked a bit like a slim, dark bottle with a red wrapper around his cap. Katya was quick to wrest the gifts from his hands ("Nadia, put these in the centre of the table") and lower the coat from his high shoulders ("Nastya, hang this in Papa's and my bedroom"). The hat went the same way as the coat.

Next, Katya started to raise her hand to wipe soup steam from her brow. Giorgi interpreted the gesture as a proffered hand, which he clasped in both his hands as he made a kissing motion over it in the air. He proceeded to wring Misha's hands and, finally, bow to the "young ladies" as they re-entered the kitchen.

"Well," Katya said as if presenting a mystery, "why are we all standing here? We have a much nicer room…" (She hesitated to gesture towards it.)

"…just through here," Nastya finished.

"Hi," Nadia said belatedly. Giorgi looked at her, nodded, and went through to the family room, where the round table was set for dinner.

A room like this would fain be a pocket kingdom, its damp floral wallpaper an impregnable defence. Shortages and fear, along with the living memory of famine and terror, could not sag (thin limbs and all) into the sofa like a shirtless Banquo's ghost. Spring could put Winter forever in the grave, sealed by flowers and more flowers, sewn up with grass that sprang through vegetable peels, and sated at last by libations of potato soup and wine.

"How nicely the young ladies have set the table with the meal their radiant mother made."

"Do sit," Katya bade their guest.

They dined, with much chitchat. At least, the family offered chitchat to Giorgi; he marvelled at it (especially anything Katya had to say); and the evening progressed as a superficial exhibition of their lives, made to seem more colourful by the appearance of this stranger as a black backdrop.

They all had their fill of potato soup and brown bread. They mopped the floral bowls with the crusts. By that time, the bottle of Soviet Champagne was depleted and the Moldovan red had been un-corked to give everyone a try. (It would get used up soon enough over the holidays.)

"You were kind to bring the wine," Katya said. "You must have rushed to get it, before Comrade Gorbachev bulldozed the vineyard and closed the store at seven. Happy holidays, Comrade Gorbachev."

"Ha," said Giorgi.

Then came a lull.

"It seems," said Misha, "owing to the suddenness of our friendly gathering, Giorgi, I have not allowed my wife time to prepare a dessert."

Giorgi raised his hand and was on the point of declaring his own fault in the matter and the lavishness of the hospitality under these or any circumstances, when Katya spoke up: "We're saving the sugar, eggs, and butter, Misha."

"For what?"

"A cake."

"A cake?"

"Can the detective help you?"

"A birthday?" Giorgi ventured. "One can scarcely believe the ladies are ageing but…"

"Yes," Misha laughed, "our Nadia turns sixteen!"

"Sixteen on Tuesday," Katya said.

"Congratulations!" Giorgi toasted, "May the young lady's wishes all come true!"

"A cake will do nicely," said Nadia. "Thank you, Mama."

"Nadia is our prodigy," Nastya told their guest. "One day she'll be on the radio, maybe the stage or the screen! You should hear her read Tolstoy!"

"I insist on it," Giorgi said. "She mustn't be shy."

"Alright, she mustn't be shy," Nadia consented, "but she must find her place in the book. Why doesn't Nastya show you her sketches first?"

They performed the little show. Giorgi said he had never seen the Crimean coast evoked so well in charcoal, nor heard such a rendition of Kitty's heartbreak when Vronsky danced with Anna at the ball. The sisters thanked him, gave a bit of an encore at everyone's insistence, and eventually packed off to bed with soup and bread for Gramma.

They could hear further snippets of the conversation, especially when its timbre deepened, and they struggled not to snicker at the tipsier-sounding bits.

"Tell me," said Giorgi, "what way did you travel to Crimea?"

Katya answered that they sailed overnight on the best and oldest cruise liner, the *Admiral Nakhimov*. She and Misha danced on deck while below, in the theatre, the girls watched the best and newest action film, *The Detached Mission*. They did not usually watch such fantasies about machine-gun-toting musclemen fighting Americans in the jungle but it was a vacation, after all.

"That sounds like a good night on the *Nakhimov*," Giorgi concluded, "but if you stay with her five nights, she goes to Georgia! That is because it takes five times as long to get a girl in Georgia. Ha."

Katya did not stay up much longer. She said, "Giorgi, feel free to keep my husband as long as you like but when you're done, don't forget to send him in to fetch your hat and coat."

Giorgi rose and bowed to the "dear lady".

Misha assured her, "We won't forget, thank you."

Katya disappeared into her and Misha's dark bedroom and shut the door. Giorgi sat down again. Misha was squinting in the manner of a man who has forgotten his aim. Giorgi glanced around the room.

Misha raised a finger. "One thing you won't find," he said, "is a television. When we moved here, Katya said, we'll all find better things to do."

"May one ask…?"

"Well, the *Nakhimov* and then there was a tutor, Galician girl, ended up moving to Poland." Misha flexed his nose.

Over their drinks, the pair chitchatted for a while about transportation, geography, and boxing.

"I won a gold medal, in school," Misha confided.

Giorgi raised his glass. "A scholar!"

"No, no, a boxer. They called me Yellow Bear, for my hair. I'm starting to lose a little of that now—a little. I was all ready to make my comeback at the Moscow Olympics but I quit when another bear stole my fame—another bear, Olympic Mishka, the mascot, the cartoon character."

"Ha." Giorgi glanced at the bottom of his glass before moving on to a serious statement. "Nadezhda Mikhailovna has true wit," said he, speaking of Nadia to her father with great formality. Of the other daughter, he added, "Anastasia Mikhailovna has a warm soul."

"Have they?" asked Misha as he refilled their glasses. "I suppose you must be right. You're the detective, my friend."

"You're the father. Oh, to your health! That's my last because I have more work ahead of me tonight and you've already been more generous than I deserve, you and Yekaterina Lvovna. Such hosts! Thank her for me."

"You're going already?"

"I must."

"You don't want to tell me more … about either of my daughters?"

"Another time … my friend."

5: Dresser

Katya pretended to be asleep when Misha came to get the hat and coat.

Later, when Misha was in bed and snoring a wine-ful snore, Katya slipped away to sit at a little dressing table with a square mirror. There lay her husband's cigarette case and lighter. They were a set, made of stainless steel, embossed with a scene of the sea and a seagull on the case and a lighthouse on the lighter. She had given him these as an anniversary present in the early years. He kept hand-rolled cigarettes, lately of Bulgarian tobacco, in the case. She lit one and, in its faint light and the moonlight sliced by bars on the window, she studied her face in the mirror. She pulled her hair back, found no change in the grey temples, and wondered whether she and her daughters should all wear their hair in loose, brown curls—maybe for Nadia's birthday.

The cigarette tasted awful. If honey and flowers could go sour, they had done. She had no idea who got him started on this garbage—not, she hoped, some woman well acquainted with Bulgarian sailors and the haunts and ways of street cats.

She kept smoking it anyway and wondered how it would look with dark red lipstick and the curls, if she had curls, if she had lipstick.

6: Complicated Things

The following week, on the last day of school before the break, Nadia was walking home when a police car slowed down beside her to match her speed. She lowered her eyes towards the frosty pavement and kept going. A vaguely familiar but greatly formal voice called out, "Nadezhda Mikhailovna … please, will you get in?"

The Coachman of Death, had he been stopping for a fare, might have received a reaction like hers.

"Forgive me, I startled you!" Giorgi said as he popped out of the car. "Do you remember me—Giorgi, your father's friend? You didn't recognize me, startling you like that!"

"Sure!" *Fuck!*

With a black-gloved hand, he pressed the black peak of his cap. He had knocked it as he rushed from the car. "I noticed you walking there."

"I noticed you driving there!"

"Ha."

"Was it that you had a message for my father?"

Of course, it was not that; he had wanted to drive her home. She decided to oblige. By the end of the short drive, she was "Nadia" to him.

Over the holidays, Giorgi became a recurring and spontaneous visitor. He would stop for a single drink and a little nibble; then, he would tell the whole family of his certain belief that Nadia would enjoy accompanying him on an errand he was running (sometimes by foot, sometimes by car).

Nadia was reading Shakespeare (her birthday present) and she had misgivings about her family's willingness to humour this cop of a Petruchio. Nastya and their parents were agreeable with him. Their grandmother kept silent, to the point that Giorgi apparently believed she was a mute. He would always wring her arthritic hands and say something like, "Your smile warms us, Gramma. No words could be more precious than that."

Nadia tried her best to prepare neutral topics of conversation for her outings at Giorgi's side. She scrounged material from every corner of her life—but never too much from one place—and posed questions that bordered on the absurd.

One evening between New Year's and Christmas, they walked to a recreational part of the waterfront. This was not far from her home. One just had to cross the park and go down a set of broad, unsupported concrete steps—nothing to compare to the Potemkin Stairs but a fine vantage point in its own way. The plateau gave way to a pink evening sky with inky clouds. Below, the sand of the long, flat beach looked grey because of snowmelt but the piers and seawall were caked in nodes of polished ice. These caught the low-lying light and it seemed as if giant, wet, pink roses were dripping into the sea.

Few people saw this. At this time of year, romantic ideas focused more on hot drinks and *The Nutcracker*, less on walks by the sea.

At the foot of the big stairs, Giorgi stopped at a kiosk to buy an evening newspaper with blocky headlines and a pack of Prima cigarettes with the fancy white script on the red box. That was his errand. He put the cigarettes in a pocket, leafed through the paper, stuffed part of it in his belt, and left the rest with the vendor.

They walked along a pier and back. They went down a little stairway in the seawall to a deserted patch of beach. She picked up a conch shell, bigger than her fist by half, and peered inside—sand. Bouncing it from hand to hand, she leaned against the wall and squinted into the setting sun. Giorgi smoked as he, too, looked out to sea. They stood there a long time in silence.

After finishing his cigarette and letting it fall to the sand, Giorgi turned away from the sunset to face Nadia. Below the little brim of his peaked cap, his dark eyes seemed to be photographing her piece by piece. She found herself at close quarters between him and the seawall.

"My father thinks highly of you," Nadia blurted. *No, that's a wrong turn.* "He worries about us, though, about Nastya and me. A father should worry about his daughters, shouldn't he?"

"How so?"

"I mean, today, things can get complicated for young people, can't they?"

"Do you ... or Nastya ... have some experience of that?"

You presume. "No. Let's talk about something else." She bounced the conch shell to Giorgi, slipped past him, and climbed the stairs in the seawall.

He followed her but kept a little distance now as they walked back. "What else did you want to discuss?"

"Your experience, I suppose—of young people."

"What do you mean by that?"

"I mean, in your profession, you know people's problems."

"Go on. You have something particular in mind. I understand you that far, Nadia."

Careful to avoid any details, Nadia mentioned that there had once been rumours of a boy at school who went truant and did strange things in strange places—a scrounger, a loiterer, but not a violent boy. How would such a case be punished; could he educate her on that point?

"Truancy from school, petty delinquency?" Giorgi asked himself. "Oh, depending on his age and the committee's findings in his case, he could be sent to either a psychiatric hospital or a reformatory. The education at our reformatories has an excellent reputation. Oh, they might have him digging potatoes or they might make him a painter or, who knows, a politician? We call it all productive labour. He won't be shot."

Pondering the implications of her latest line of questioning, he added, "I don't chase truants. I ... do other things. Of course, we have no organized crime in Odessa. I make sure it stays that way."

"That's a great responsibility," Nadia said. *We're both too quick at this,* she thought.

He brought her home.

That night, in Nastya and Nadia's room, the sisters whispered about the happenings of the day. The pair of them were sharing Nadia's bed while the visiting grandmother snored in Nastya's.

" 'Of course, we have no organized crime in Odessa,' " Nadia echoed in a *sotto voce* rendition of her admirer's Georgian accent. " 'I make sure it stays that way—with my high boots and my high belt and my hat so high it wipes Comrade Stalin's arse in Heaven!' "

"Shh! Shh! You're horrible! He's a…" (Nastya was struggling to contain her hysterics) "…good man! Papa says he's a … good friend to us! Remember, Nadia, he's your…" (but whatever he was supposed to be to Nadia was swallowed in a snort).

"I know!" Nadia's farce had become unstoppable. "When he thinks about our wedding night, he has to pull up his belt—higher than ever—to make room for his cock!"

"Stop it!"

"That's what Comrade Stalin tells him!"

"You'll get us both in trouble!"

"Of course, you're right, Stalin says that too!"

Nastya held a pillow to her little sister's face. This was a protocol they had between themselves. A moment later, Nadia stopped shaking and touched her sister's shoulders in a kind of hug. They had calmed down, it was again safe to breathe, and they lay in the dark in their cold, dank room.

There was silence.

When had Gramma stopped snoring?

7: Banishment

The next day's blow-up happened on a geographic scale. Before breakfast and without explanation, Nastya and Nadia were banished to the park. That scarcely mattered, insofar as their grandmother's hollering reached a good distance beyond the four walls that surrounded her and her direct target, their parents.

This was around dawn. The morning was not freezing but it was smoggy. A tramp lay motionless on a bench. He had a newspaper over his face and a bottle near his hand, which dangled to the ground. Nadia and then Nastya sat on the seesaw, which was wet with dew. As they heard the harangue, they seesawed in the spirit of performing senseless labour.

Not every word was audible but the main points were clear.

Nadia was unfit to be courted or married. Try to push her into it and she could well destroy lives—not least, her own dear life.

Nastya was in no position to be a protector to Nadia.

Misha and Katya did not see their children as they really were. Misha, for that matter, scarcely saw anything at all and Katya saw too much of herself in everything.

A strange man in uniform did not brighten an old woman's holidays.

After expounding these points, Gramma lowered her voice. She, Misha, and Katya were negotiating something.

The neighbouring houses had remained quiet and unlit. Everyone was probably listening on the sly.

On her end of the seesaw, Nastya was weeping. "You've ruined your chance, Nadia."

Nadia said nothing. *Don't be hysterical,* was her first thought. *Oh, I don't know. I guess I have really made shit for us this time. Poor Nastya.*

Actually, at that moment, their father was taking the worst of it. His wife had broken ranks and she was railing at him for all the feckless matches ever made by Man. (Her father had introduced them in the days when Misha was the best boxer in the school.)

Katya having scored a point of her own, everyone hushed again. The sky was growing pale. Neighbours put on lights and made a clatter as they cooked their breakfasts or pretended to do so.

The tramp got up and stumbled away in a meandering path that followed other bottles, trash bins, and cigarette butts.

At last, it was Katya alone who came to the sisters in the park. Her eyes were red like Nastya's. "Eat," the mother said; "I have bread and cheese for us. Then, you're going to show me Papa's cats and dogs. We can save some of this for them if you like."

They crossed the park, went down the concrete steps, and took the direction opposite to Nadia and Giorgi's last walk. Near a pavilion, in the rubble shoring up a seawall, lived a colony of cats. "The small, grey, striped one is a favourite of Papa's," Nadia said.

"Yes, I see him. Him?" Katya asked.

"Yes."

They gave crumbs of bread and cheese to the cat.

"You can pat him, Mama," Nastya said.

As if willing herself to touch a hot stove, Katya did. "Alright," she whispered, "let's sit somewhere here." She took a place on the seawall. Nadia sat beside her. Nastya stood nearby and cuddled the cat.

"Do you miss Estonia, Nadia?" Katya asked.

"Sometimes."

"I thought so. You're going to spend some time with Gramma up there."

"Oh. What about Nastya?"

"No, she has to stay at her studies here."

Katya kissed Nadia on the shoulder, stood, emptied the last crumbs from a coat pocket, left them for the cat, and then turned to walk back.

Nastya put the hungry cat down beside the food and then speechlessly followed Katya.

Nadia looked at the cat eating crumbs, the coast with its ice now melting fast, and her mother and sister walking away.

To be separated from Giorgi was a relief. To be separated from Nastya was a punishment Nadia had never imagined—not in her life. They seemed to have dredged up such a cruelty from the history books.

8: Payphone

Gramma lived on the outskirts of Tallinn in an antiquated apartment block, which had been hastily erected after the War, shoddily renovated under Khrushchev, and utterly neglected ever since. Her flat's greatest luxury was a coal stove, which had been installed when the building was converted from communal living quarters to single-family units. A toilet and shower were still shared with neighbours on the same floor—the eighth floor, up a staircase with broken lights.

If Gramma had ever called in a favour, it was not to get prime housing.

There were two rooms and no balcony. The main room had one window, which leaked. Gramma's bedroom was windowless.

Nadia slept on a sofa in front of the stove. The rest of the main room's furniture amounted to a table and pair of chairs near the window.

A sink, in a corner, looked lost and alone, like a child standing with a drooped head in a rainstorm.

A good deal of space was taken up by kindling and coal. The old woman carefully managed the supply, so the place stayed warm, albeit sooty.

A black cat, by the name of Cherny, shared the sofa with Nadia at night. By day, Cherny went hunting for vermin in the building and the grounds. If one did not inspect Cherny at the door, her catch could end up under the sofa.

On the whole, Cherny's hunting was a benefit to the building's sanitation, so Cherny had probably saved human lives. Gramma, in turn, had saved Cherny's life many times with injections, powders, disinfectants, and lancets.

A lifetime ago, Gramma had been a veterinarian. When she mentioned names from the War, most were horses' names. She had a special fondness for a black-and-white gelding named Robespierre, also called Pierre or Petrushka. He was, she said, one-eighth Arabian and nine-eighths strong of heart. (This was, perhaps, the most sentimental thing Gramma ever said.) She mentioned that once, in a night and a morning, she and Pierre rode almost two hundred kilometres to escape "something".

The big suitcase went in Gramma's room and was never completely unpacked. Every week or two, a stack of papers arrived in the mail and Gramma filed them in the case. Other times, she took papers out, studied them, burned some in the stove, and put the others back. Most days, she wrote a letter to Moscow—to her friend, the archivist.

After school, Nadia would meet up with Gramma at the post office or in a queue at a store and they would take a bus back to the apartment from there. Encrusted in winter sludge, the Ikarus bus would splutter up to the curb and fill its jowls with shivering people. Gramma would be afforded a seat. Generally, others had to stand. The slow trip featured a view of snowy roofs in disrepair. Gothic tiles atop limestone masonry, corrugated iron atop hundred-year-old boards, and asbestos cement atop cinderblocks had all become equals.

Arriving back at the building after dark, they would climb the eight flights of half-lit stairs with whatever they had in their bags—at best, a great deal of mail and a few groceries, though sometimes nothing but Nadia's books and homework. The neighbours occasionally left nibbles and kindling at Gramma's door and the old woman saved a portion of everything, so she and Nadia could always manage a supper, however meagre.

Gramma had no telephone in her flat. (She refused to speak on a phone, ever.) There was a payphone on the ground floor. After supper, Gramma would get out a pencil and little notebook, take account of the money and supplies, and sometimes give Nadia coins for a phone call. Nadia would go back down the eight flights (and make an echo with her hurried steps) and feed the coins into the cold, steel phone box in the draughty lobby. The lightweight discs of aluminum-bronze and copper-nickel-zinc fell with a dull clack.

1,500 kilometres away, Katya would pick up the receiver of a carrot-coloured phone in the floral-patterned family room. She usually had a lonely spiel: Nastya was studying late at the library, Papa was out drinking with Giorgi, "so it's you and me at home tonight, my young one, my soul. What are you reading? Tell me something beautiful from it."

Another time, it was worse: "I'm all alone, my soul. I'm all alone. I'm all alone. What are you reading? Tell me something beautiful from it."

Then, one night, it all turned upside down. "My young one, hello, hello. … I'm not alone tonight. I'm so happy you've called before… Oh, first, I should explain. You know how tired I've been. The quotas at the factory are impossible; the forewoman is a tyrant; she's turned the others against me with this malicious gossip; don't ask me to repeat it. Anyway, Giorgi has been so kind. He said … the stress is making me ill, so he took me to see the wonderful doctor whom all the detectives see and the Doctor has prescribed a month's rest for me at the wonderful sanatorium where the detectives take their rest—you know, the ones who suffer injury or fatigue. Giorgi will drive me up because he wants to go anyway to visit his colleague, who is suffering a long-term case of… What? Oh, it started as a back injury and now he's fatigued from the pain. Giorgi will drive me up early tomorrow morning, so he's here on the sofa tonight. What are you reading? Tell us something beautiful from it."

After that conversation, Nadia climbed the stairs in dull, weary footsteps. She found Cherny on the landing, went with her into the flat, and sat opposite Gramma at the table. Gramma was writing a letter. Nadia spent some time arranging books, pens, and sheets of paper on her side of the table. She had an essay to finish. *Concentrate, concentrate,* she told herself.

Without looking up from her letter-writing, Gramma said, "Go on, dear, say what's on your mind. Talk."

"Are your letters something about Grandpa?"

(His name was Paavo but he was Pasha to his wife and Grandpa to the granddaughters who never met him.)

"Yes."

That was illuminating. Nadia penned a paragraph in her Astronomy paper on the search for extraterrestrial radio transmissions, felt Cherny weaving back and forth around the table legs and skirt-clad legs, and heard a whimper of wind under the window. *Soon, I'll break into tears or chitchat like Nastya.* "How did you meet him, Gramma?"

"I recruited him, in a way. My unit was cut off and we came North. Well, that was a mistake in many ways. We had no friends here and we soon had difficulty feeding ourselves, let alone mounting a resistance. My Captain told me, 'Go and watch the farms around here and find some boy of eighteen, who may be dodging the German draft, who lives alone with his mother and sisters. See that they have livestock. You are a woman of twenty-two and an animal doctor, so you can get their sympathy and trust.'

"My Captain spoke that way. I called him Kio (like the illusionist—well, Kio the Elder to you, dear) because he could plan for something to be there and then, magically, it was. Thinking back, I suspect he had done his own reconnaissance before telling me what I should find.

"Now, when I found my match all on my own, I was quite proud of myself. Being proud of myself, I played the role with conviction and I had no difficulty in begging a hot meal from the mother, birthing a calf with the sisters, and, like an ingenue, catching the boy as he watched me from his hiding place. There he was, an open secret, the son and brother they were hiding from the German draft, and the way he was looking at me an even more open secret still, and I swore to them all I'd never betray him. Then, I confided my secret to them.

"They could hardly refuse to help us then.

"First, it was food. Then, it was siphoning off petrol for bombs. Finally, he couldn't be apart from me, so he fought by my side. We got other recruits through him, too.

"For Pasha, I believe it was all for love. Our victory left him empty-handed, without his old country, but empty-handed and in love, so then it was my turn; how could I refuse? After the War, we married, had Misha, and stayed in the North. Then, one day, your grandfather disappeared."

The old woman put a kettle on the stove and Nadia went back to her paper on alien radio chitchat.

The following week, the mail contained a priority letter from Odessa. Gramma and Nadia opened it on the bus. "Dearest Gramma, Dearest Sister," it began with great formality.

The bus hit a pothole and the words seemed to fly everywhere. Nadia leaned closer to Gramma's shoulder.

A rear wheel hit the same pothole and the words scattered again.

Gramma tried to fold up the letter in her clumsy and painful hands. "Perhaps we should read this at home."

Nadia's chest felt tight. The old woman's voice, normally so calm or so resolute, had just then betrayed a hint of disaster.

Nadia seized the letter and scanned the next words: "Giorgi and I are married. Are you surprised? I believe I am! All so suddenly, after Giorgi came back from getting Mama settled into her rest at the sanatorium, Papa began to feel old and wistful and said the two of us should be giving him grandchildren! 'Let's get you married right away and surprise Mama when we go up to visit her.' Giorgi said, 'I agree,' and I laughed and said…"

The bus lurched again and Nadia relinquished the letter. She felt dizzy and knelt beside Gramma's seat. Other passengers rippled around them.

"Nastya loves you—you above all," her grandmother told her—"but Nastya needs to be married. She'll be a good wife and good mother. You'll have a little nephew or niece soon enough—far less trouble than a husband and child of your own if you ask me."

I didn't. "I don't like to think of her with him. I hate him."

"Then be glad you aren't his."

"If I had been…"

"…she might have married another just like him. That's one short-age we don't have. Shh. You and I have a great deal in common."

9: Letters

Letters kept coming and going. As Gramma continued her long ex-change with the Moscow archivist, Nadia became a prolific correspon-dent to Nastya. All these letters were a form of traffic in hope and desperation, sustained in private acts of writing and rewriting, reading and rereading, sometimes on the page and sometimes in memory, steal-ing sleep in the night and concentration in the day. Thoughts of a letter are as close as a baby in the womb.

Gramma got sick at the end of February, had a slow recovery, and fell behind in her correspondence. Nadia brought letters and parcels back from the post office and left them on top of the suitcase for Gramma to process later.

All this time, the world and the school were full of news. The Mir space station went into orbit and got its first crew. (Nastya sent cuttings of colour photos from a magazine. She opined that the men were brave but the decor was bad, despite rumours of it being designed by a woman. Perhaps, Nastya quipped, it was the woman's revenge against men who painted kitchens green and white.) Meanwhile, the 27th Congress ap-plauded Gorbachev's plans to outlaw nuclear weapons, counteract im-perialism with sober thinking, and accelerate the country's socioeco-nomic development into the coming millennium, in keeping with the dynamic vitality that is inherent in Marxist-Leninism.

On a slushy day in March, Nadia came home to find her grand-mother sitting with a letter in her hand. The paper, in her arthritic grip, seemed inextricable and harmful, like a nail in a knot of a tree. The old woman had let the stove go out and she was doing nothing about the leaky window, which she normally would have stopped with a rag.

"What's in the letter, Gramma?"

"News from Moscow, if you can call it news."

"What news?"

"A record of your grandfather has been found, if you can call it a record, if it was really found."

"He is dead, is he, Gramma?"

"Yes, dear, these forty years—probably within days of our last breakfast. You know, as a small child, Misha had big ears and after breakfast, Pasha kissed Misha on the ears and kissed me on the neck. He would do that in front of all the other families in the apartment. Then … he went."

Gramma continued, "The letter tells me he was arrested, later executed. The accusations and other … details … are no longer known. Recently, he was rediscovered and rehabilitated as part of a major review of the archives. Medals for him might be forthcoming."

"Maybe in another forty years."

"Yes, if all goes well."

"I'll make us tea and you can tell me more news." Nadia went about stopping the leak, rekindling and feeding the coal stove, and getting a kettle on.

When Gramma spoke again, she was thinking of times before Misha's birth. "That must be all of us dead but me. Only, my youngest sister, Galya, nobody could remember seeing her there when the Germans hanged our families. On the other hand, nobody saw her afterwards."

Grandmother and granddaughter were sitting in the two padded wooden chairs by the round wooden table, near the leaky window that clattered as the sleet hit it. The furniture was small and it enforced a compact arrangement of one's body and glass of tea. Gramma said, "I suppose, in the South, you would have been able to get lemons more easily for your tea."

"A bit more easily." They sipped tea that had no lemon. "Do you want me to try to get some next time? I don't mind queuing."

"No, I don't like lemon in my tea."

"Honey?"

"If you can find any." They sipped tea that had no honey either. "What ever happened to that boy?"

"Mmm, what boy, Gramma?" For a moment, Nadia was unsure whether *that boy* might be of Gramma's generation or her own.

"The one who could find anything—the Estonian who called himself something English."

"Jaan—Johnny?"

"Mmm."

"I don't know what happened to him."

"Then, there was the girl—Ida. I liked her." They sipped tea that had no cloudberries. "I don't hold anything against a girl with German grandparents. People are so foolish."

"I liked Ida too."

"You don't know what happened to Ida?"

"No…"

"We should find out. That can be our private project."

This proposal did not quite ring of Ida's old promise—to be "just happy, just us" on a sand dune under Baltic pines—but Nadia agreed.

10: No Horse

Now, in the evening before bed, Gramma would drink a mixture she prepared for herself. She said it was to help her sleep, on account of the lingering cough from her recent illness.

Gramma's sleep was troubled by more than a cough.

The first time the howling woke Nadia, she thought for a moment it might be Cherny in agony. A cat can cry like that when expecting to die. Then, she realized it was coming from Gramma's room. Rushing in, Nadia tripped over Cherny (who had run alongside her), tripped over the suitcase, and added to this banging and howling by shouting, "Gramma, wake up!"

"Fuck off!" the unconscious woman barked in reply. "This horse can't be left. Hand me your pistol."

"Gramma, there's no horse!"

"There is! There's … a fucking StuG III down the lane and I won't leave this horse. Hand me your pistol."

"Gramma!"

Nadia had to grapple with the old woman to wake her.

"What? Oh, dear. I had a dream."

"I'll make tea."

"No, I'll go back to sleep. Take Cherny. I've terrified Cherny."

After a hush, something could be heard scurrying inside the walls. They had woken the building.

ii: Ida's Mill

The search for Ida was complicated by Ida's innate bad luck. Ida's innate good luck would also come into play.

Ida had been an orphan. Not long before befriending Nastya at a new school, Ida had been released from a boarding school to go live and work at a millhouse that made cider. Nadia knew this much and had a vague recollection of the millhouse by a river. She, with Nastya, had been there just once. Ida had not been in a position to play hostess at the place, nor had she even pilfered cider for her friends. Beyond the requirements of her placement there, Ida never touched cider.

Thus, Nadia spent a drizzly Spring Break looking for a cider mill to match a memory. On the afternoon of the last day in March, a Monday and (as it happened) the day when the weather reluctantly started to improve, she found it and she spoke with a forewoman who had come out for a smoke in the yard.

"Hello, can you help me, please?"

"What's the trouble?"

"I'm looking for my friend, Ida Ivanova. Does she still work here?"

"Ida! No but let's not forget her," the forewoman said. "She was a crazy girl. She made up nutty stories—fairytales, lies, any excuse for sneaking off." The words fell like ashes from her puckered lips. "Are you one of her excuses? Haven't I seen you before?"

"I visited here once. I was only a child then."

"So you're old and wise now?"

"I'm trying to find a friend I've lost, that's all."

"If it moves you along, I suppose I might as well tell you. They took her to the nuthouse, where she belonged."

"No, that can't be."

"Old, wise, and a doctor, are we? Well, they did. She did nothing but laugh and weep for two days before they finally came. Nobody else could sleep and I have the workers' safety to consider. You wouldn't know about my responsibilities, though, would you?"

"Please, when was this?"

"More than a year ago. Harvest, our busy time."

"Where did they take her?"

"How should I know? I've told you, I have my own responsibilities, running a mill if you don't mind."

The forewoman walked off. On her way, she chucked the remains of her cigarette in the river.

Nadia watched the building a while longer. She wondered what Ida's life had been in all those hours apart from chasing daydreams.

The sun came lower and shone through the budding apple branches onto the brown river. A crew of workers (most of them Nadia's age or just a little older) came out to load crates onto a flatbed truck, a round-snouted piece of Army surplus on six wheels, with a pattern of dusty chevrons running round the rubber. There was an apple painted on one door and a red star on the other. Nadia remembered seeing Ida drive the truck the time before. Now, a big foreman was stretching his legs out the driver's side (the apple's side). He stepped onto the sideboard and gazed back through the flatbed's wooden slats as the loaders filled it. Bossing and berating his juniors, he rolled up his sleeves to show his thick forearms, though he himself would do no lifting. He wore a wide belt with a polished brass buckle that caught the late afternoon light like a pale cider. He stared at her and she decided to leave.

12: Ida's Tower

Gramma and Nadia tracked Ida to a place known as the Narva Psychiatric Hospital No. 3 Named After Doctor I.A. Yahontov. The late, eponymous Doctor Igor Antonivich Yahontov had not only made a name for himself in psychiatry but had also fathered a line of other doctors and Party members. One of the progeny, Doctor Anton Igorevich Yahontov, now held the post of Chief Physician up there at No. 3.

No. 3 was housed in a Teutonic, limestone tower with a modern, red stucco facade. Colloquially, it was known as the Ruby Palace. Gramma and Nadia had received a booklet with a photograph of the building, which stood on a cobblestone street lined with golden maple trees "like Rideau Canal in Ottawa, Canada," as the caption singularly described it. They had secured an appointment to visit No. 3, see Ida, and speak with Anton Igorevich.

The booklet, with text and photographs by Anton Igorevich, revealed the marvels of life inside No. 3. The text was trilingual in Russian, English, and French. The photographs showed blissful patients (unisexually styled in hospital gowns and short-cropped hair), sitting on plush furniture and playing chess and smiling up at the staff who served them their pills—or else luxuriating in peat baths or radon baths, or taking repose in the sunroom after electroconvulsive therapy, or receiving sympathy and insight from Anton Igorevich in his parlour.

Nadia spotted mistakes in the English, the French, and even the Russian. She conceived of this Doctor Yahontov as a man of narrow reading.

On the train to Narva, Nadia studied a map book and made notes in a journal as Gramma looked out the window and reminisced.

"We're near a place called Sillamäe," Gramma said at one point. "Around here, the Germans had a network of concentration camps. They forced the Jews to mine something. I must think, dear. Hundreds of German engineers came up to supervise it—shale oil, maybe something else. I should remember because we captured one for questioning."

"I can't find Sillamäe on the map."

"Even so, I suppose someone still uses the place."

They arrived at the station and, being too early for their appointment, they walked to the banks of the River Narva. The reservoir was letting out the April floodwaters so, looking South, they could see the brown and white cascades around Kreenholm Island, where the factory complex churned out textiles behind its 19th-century brick walls. To the North, Hermann Castle (on the West bank) and Ivangorod Fortress (on the East) overlooked the haunches and girders of the Friendship Bridge.

For seven hundred years, people had been building megastructures to control this river. Still, every spring, the river rushed to the sea.

They left the river and made their way to the tower of No. 3. All the while, Nadia was carrying a quilt of colourful birds and flowers, folded up and stuffed in a potato sack for protection. The quilt was a gift for Ida.

Outside the Ruby Palace, the red buds of the maples were just starting to burst into green. "Green maple, yes, curly maple, / Yes, curly, carved," Gramma trilled a song from the past.

The stucco was less red than the photo had shown and more like the mixed colours of a handful of rough rubies. The storms had dirtied and discoloured it unevenly and, in places, hail had chipped it away to reveal the limestone underneath. This Ruby Palace, like the ruby bearings in a watch, endured a strange relationship with Time.

They climbed the stone steps, which were concave from centuries of wear, though no one else was walking them at that moment.

Gramma leaned against the wall to catch her breath. The stucco made a faint cracking sound.

Nadia knocked on the tall, oaken door, which had a brass knocker in the shape of a wheat wreath beneath a sickle, hammer, and star.

They waited. They got no hint of No. 3's inner workings. There were no windows on the ground storey.

Nadia swung the wheat wreath harder. The wheat might as well have been real wheat, for all the good it did to swing it at tools and stars.

Now what?

"Maybe they'll come out on the hour," Gramma said.

A series of scraping sounds hinted that procedures were being applied to the door. A peephole, behind a little grate, slid open and shut. A bar, bolts, and locks shifted out of the way. The hinges squealed.

A woman, younger than Gramma but older than Nadia's mother, pulled open the door, squinted at them, and parted her lips. She wore a white frock and cap, keychain, and stethoscope. The latter marked her as more than a nurse; she was a physician's assistant. She checked her wristwatch.

Nadia began to introduce Gramma and herself.

"I know," the assistant said. "Come in." She opened the door wider and beckoned for the visitors to enter. They came into a large, cool hall, two storeys tall.

At the centre of this entrance hall stood a block of white marble. The top of it was carved as a bust of Lenin at double life size. His gaze and chin were slightly raised and stripes of sunlight fell across him from on high, for the hall was crowned by a row of window slits.

At the far end, past Lenin, the hall tapered towards an inner gate of steel bars.

The assistant sealed the oaken door and then pointed to a white, steel bench along the white, plastered wall. "Sit. The nurse will come to us when she has her patient ready."

"Thank you, Comrade," Gramma said.

"Of course, Comrade."

Gramma and Nadia sat. The assistant paced to the inner gate and back to the front gate, checked her watch, paced to Lenin, and brushed Lenin's scalp. Dust swirled up into the sunbeams. She brushed his nose and chin.

The assistant squinted at the window slits and again parted her lips. Then, she came to sit beside Nadia and touched Nadia's wrist.

"What is it you're doing, Comrade?" Nadia asked.

"Shh," said the assistant, squinting at her watch.

Does she have bad eyes and feel her way, like a mole? She's sweaty.

"Your pulse is rapid and shallow. You look pale. Are you well?"

"Very well, thank you, Comrade. We had a brisk walk before we came."

"I will have an orderly bring you tea and jam when you are settled inside."

"You mean, while we're visiting Ida?"

"Of course, Comrade."

"Ida will like that, I'm sure. We would share food, as children."

"You may remind her of that."

"Yes, why not?"

"Her appetite has been poor."

Gramma stood up. She had seen a young nurse approaching the chokepoint of the inner gate from the other side. This young woman wore a white frock and cap, keychain, but no watch or stethoscope. A pair of locks turned and the gate swung into the entrance hall. That was when Nadia realized it: the inner gate was mounted backwards, so it was a point of inversion, past which the inside became a second outside, and the true interior, the sanctum, was nothing but a waiting room with Lenin—that promisor of eventual perfection.

The assistant placed a hand on Nadia's shoulder to stop her from standing. "Your bag, Comrade—the nurse will search it."

The nurse had a quick step and was already reaching into the potato sack on Nadia's lap. "That's a quilt for Ida," Nadia said as the nurse teased it out and squeezed each square. "We thought she'd like the birds and flowers because…" (*I'm babbling!*) "…when we were children…" (*I sound mad!*) "…we'd gather mushrooms and berries…" (*It's nonsense!*) "…and see all kinds of pretty things." (*It's idiocy! Where is the language of Tolstoy?*) "All the good things in life are simple. That becomes easy to remember when one is wrapped in old patches that have turned to feathers and petals of every heavenly colour, every comfort and warmth, in the undulating threads of the sun."

Easily and silently, the nurse refolded the quilt and put it back in the sack.

The assistant, who had been squinting, said, "I see you are a true friend of hers." Still handling Nadia's shoulder, she walked her towards the open gate. Gramma and the nurse followed.

They were past the gate, locked in, beyond a bend, and walking up a ramped, white corridor when Gramma announced, "I could do with that tea and the chairs in your booklet, Comrades."

The assistant proposed to send the nurse ahead to fetch an orderly to bring a wheelchair to wheel Gramma the rest of the way up.

"Well, dear Comrades," Gramma puffed, "I rode to Berlin on the gun mantlet of a T-34-85, with my thighs around the barrel, and you can imagine the laughs the boys got from that—twenty of them around me on the turret and slopes—so I suppose, now, a wheelchair can't be the worst blow to my pride."

The assistant's squint and parted lips had turned into a gawking stare. The nurse scurried onwards, making the pale patterns of light and shadow flicker as she passed by electric sconces and window slits.

Gramma trilled patriotically, "The armour is hard, and our tanks are fast, / And our men are full of courage!" She was seized by a dry coughing fit, so fierce that it pushed her tongue past her lips.

The assistant left Nadia's shoulder, went to Gramma's, and studied the old woman's convulsions. "Unfasten your grandmother's brooch." Nadia put down the sack and obeyed the instruction. The brooch was a floral piece with a silver filigree vine and enamel blossom. The vine pricked Nadia's nervous fingers. As she took it off and Gramma's blouse came loose and the coughing fit continued, a canteen fell out and hit the floor, *glunk*. The assistant applied the stethoscope to Gramma's chest, Gramma gestured towards the canteen, Nadia grabbed it, unscrewed it, and pressed it against Gramma's lips as the assistant struggled to keep the stethoscope tube free from entanglement.

Gramma took a sip, made a sound like a horse, and managed to bring the fit under control.

The assistant finished listening. "You have bronchitis."

"Do I rattle like a draughty stovepipe?"

"That's one way of putting it, Comrade."

"Let's do me up. This sight would have destroyed morale, if the boys had seen the future." With clawed fingers, Gramma accepted the brooch from Nadia but pushed away the canteen. "This brooch was my mother's. She gave it to me on my graduation. I have nothing else of her—of any of them. Did you lose family in the War, Comrade? You must have been a child."

The assistant said nothing.

"So many children grew up in orphanages," Gramma continued. She had done up her blouse and now she accepted the canteen from Nadia. "Go on, Comrade. The rest is for you. You must enjoy a drink at night. It's good kirsch—hard to come by."

The assistant took the canteen, smelt the distillation of cherries and their bitter-almond pits, and screwed it tight. She took the potato sack, handed the quilt to Nadia, and wrapped the canteen in the sack for herself.

Soon, the nurse returned with an orderly—a lean, young man who looked as if he struggled to keep his strength up. As he wheeled the chair to Gramma, he wore a plaintive expression on his sunken face. She told him, "If I had a steak, I'd feed it to you, for both our sakes."

"We can dream," the orderly said.

"Well, while you do, push."

The nurse, since her return, was carrying a paper cup half full of water. She said to the physician's assistant, "I have the patient's pills ready but I wasn't sure whether you wanted me to wait."

"No, we'll do her medicine. These people won't mind."

They passed one landing. "The baths are on this level," the orderly said to Gramma. "The patients' quarters are next up. That's where I'm taking you first. Then, the machines are the floor above that and the staff quarters are up top. That's where I'll take you later, to see the Doctor."

"If they put you in a suit and black pencil tie, you could guide foreigners," Gramma said.

"Oh, I hope I do meet the Canadians when they come!"

"What?"

"That's enough, Andrei," the assistant said.

"Sorry, Comrade."

Andrei finished propelling Gramma to the second landing and he helped her out of the wheelchair. There were several steel doors on the landing. The nurse approached one of these, checked its peephole, and then opened its padlock, bar, and deadbolt. The assistant entered first and beckoned for the visitors and nurse to follow, while the orderly waited outside.

Beyond the threshold was the plush room that had featured in the booklet. Alone in there, Ida was sitting sideways in an overstuffed armchair, with her understuffed limbs dangling over the chair arms. She wore a hospital gown rolled up above her knees and elbows. Her wrists were bandaged. Her slippers were on her hands. Her shortened hair was brushed forwards and back, away from a bald spot on the right side of her scalp. She was gazing across the room at a television, which had just decried the bombing of Libya and was about to praise the May Day preparations in Kiev and the plentiful rain in Byelorussia.

The nurse rushed to straighten Ida in the chair, unroll her gown, move the slippers to her feet, and brush some hair over the bald patch. "She wasn't like this when I left her!"

"She likes to make us look bad," the assistant said, "but in the end, she can only hurt herself. Isn't that right?" (The question was for the patient.)

Nadia went to kneel by Ida's chair, to spread the quilt across Ida's lap, and to stroke Ida's hand and brow. "Ida, Ida." Ida's skin felt dry and smooth—even impermeable—like a piece of bone china on a shelf. Her face, gaunt and pale, was as impassive as any mask. "Yes, it's me: Nadia, Nastya's sister. All this time I've missed you, Ida. I was two years in Odessa and now they've sent me back, just me, to live with Gramma. It was fate because, with Gramma's help, I've found you."

Ida's blue eyes probed Nadia's green.

"She would seem sluggish," said the nurse, "were it not that she moves when our backs are turned."

"Administer the standard dose," the assistant ordered.

The nurse took four hexagonal, grey pills from her frock pocket. She pressed a pill and a sip of water, alternately, into Ida's mouth until all four were gone.

"What are those?" asked Nadia as she lent a hand to brace Ida's head upright.

"Medicine," said the nurse.

Gramma had been witnessing every act and verse but no one, except perhaps Ida, was at a vantage point to read the old woman's face. Gramma was leaning on another armchair, opposite Ida's. Between them was a tea table, with no tea as yet but with a chess set arrayed for battle. Gramma had no intention of sitting for a game but she said,

"You are a survivor, dear."

The assistant checked her watch and told the nurse the time. "Write it down. What did you do with your own watch, anyway?"

The nurse made a note in a pocketbook and she mumbled an apology that made no mention of the places a wristwatch might go: a boyfriend's bedside; a manhole missing a cover; the coat lining of a pawn broker or fence.

"Comrade," said Gramma to the assistant, "I wonder whether you could put in a word with the Doctor for us before we go see him. Come, let's you and I discuss it while the girls have their visit." They slipped out to the landing.

The nurse lingered. "Have you swallowed those, hmm?" she interrogated the patient. Ida remained stoic. The nurse pressed more water upon her and Ida made a sequence of gulps in her sinewy throat. The nurse prodded Ida's lips and cheeks before deciding that the pills had gone the way of the water. "Good, you will let us make you better after all."

To Nadia, the nurse added, "If anything happens, press the button by the door." The nurse left and the deadbolt turned.

Ida took hold of Nadia's hand and spat three pills into it. Nadia pocketed them. Ida took her hand again and expelled some remnants of the fourth pill in an acidic puddle. Nadia, still on her knees, shuffled away to wipe her hand on the underside of the other chair.

Ida kicked off her slippers, tucked the quilt under her feet and thighs, and smoothed the upper part of it over her abdomen and breasts. She traced the patches with her fingers as she gazed at the chessboard.

"Black or white?" Nadia asked. She got off the floor and into the chair.

Ida did not reply in words. White was already on her side and she leaned forwards, still clutching the quilt tightly to her chest in her left hand as she made her gambit with her right. She palmed the two white rooks and stacked them in E5, near the centre of the board.

Nadia advanced king's pawn to E6, so it stood at the foot of the great tower.

Ida lifted her upper rook and, with it, captured the sacrificial pawn at E6. She laid the pawn flat, like a lintel, across the two white rooks. The pawn's head lay at E6, towards the black king.

Nadia was inclined to throw another pawn at E6 but, in gestures,

Ida proposed an alternative: queen to F6, king's bishop to D6, and king to E7, to surround the head of the prostrate pawn. Nadia accepted this friendly suggestion.

Ida tumbled the white rooks or (as they seemed) the posts of the black pawn's sickbed. The black bishop also fell but the black king and queen, in their crowns with white topknots, only trembled. Ida mouthed some words.

"What is it?" Nadia asked.

Ida tried again and again to make her face work. Nadia was able to half read, half hear, "I'm falling from his tower. I'm falling in his machine."

The deadbolt turned again. Ida grimaced and shrank back into a more tightly quilted pose. When she saw it was Andrei coming through the door, she turned to watch the television. It was showing bombed-out, dusty streets and reciting a letter of condemnation.

"I have the tea," said Andrei as he manoeuvred a trolley across the threshold and pulled the door shut by hooking it with his foot, "and the jam." He made it sound like a significant pairing: the Tea and the Jam.

Andrei slid the chess set aside and, in its place, he set down an aluminium tea set, along with a pair of tea glasses in aluminum holders, embossed all around with wheat wreaths, sickles, hammers, and stars. "I hope it makes you feel better, Ida," he said as he poured the steaming, jam-dark tea through a strainer into her glass. He motioned, *More jam?* There was an aluminum bowl of it—blackberry.

Ida glanced away from the television and Andrei took this as *Yes.* He stirred a heaping teaspoon of extra jam into her tea glass. She stuck a hand and bandaged wrist out from the quilt to take it. Holding the glass motionless, Ida stared down into it and watched the globs of blackberry sink.

Andrei was serving Nadia. She declined the extra jam. He could leave it with her; she would serve Ida more as needed—*in accordance with the laws of fluid dynamics.*

Before leaving, Andrei gazed at Ida and told Nadia, "She has better days. The Doctor is making her better."

The television, though its volume was low, talked over Andrei. As meekly as possible, he crept out and turned the deadbolt.

Nadia lifted her wreathed and sickled glass and breathed in the steam, which mixed with the scent of vomit on her hand. She sipped the syrupy and astringent fluid. "I suppose this is to blacken our tongues so everyone knows we're the serpents."

A faint smile flitted across Ida's lips and she took a swig as a man might do from a beer stein, fast, without seeming to mind that the tea was hot. She got a brief charge, as well as a purple upper lip, and she used it to puff a clear and simple question: "Do you smoke?"

"No," Nadia replied. *What can I say on this topic of interest?* "Down in Odessa, Papa started rolling Bulgarian tobacco, which Mama hates as only Mama can. If she were here, she might find a way to compare it all at once to this tea, a bazaar after dark, and a troupe of fallen women."

"She would."

"Then, Giorgi smokes Prima cigarettes. He's Nastya's brand new husband and a cop, of all things—oh, sorry, a 'young detective,' Papa says."

"Is he strict?"

"He's ... insinuating. I don't like him. That's what got me banished."

"Oh, Nastya," Ida muttered. That was the end of her charge.

Nadia went on to share the news of Katya's retreat to a sanatorium, Gramma's and Cherny's home-treated ailments, and the death of Grandpa Pasha. Ida managed a few nods. *Am I boring her with chitchat?* Nadia took the glass from Ida's hand and Ida slipped into a simulacrum of Sleep. *Is all this from the half a pill she didn't puke?*

Wondering whether to leave (and how), Nadia eyed the red button by the door. She decided not to press it.

A while later, the deadbolt turned and Andrei pulled the door open for Gramma. Ida did not stir much. Gramma, already on her feet, was pointing back to the wheelchair and telling Andrei, "See what you can do; it's the right wheel that seizes," and she left him studying the problem as she did an orbit of the armchairs. She paused once to analyze the chess game and again to feel Ida's bald spot. "Steady, dear," she whispered. Circling back to Nadia, she said, "Dear, come and let's be at our best."

Nadia touched her mouth, then touched the quilt, and softly spoke whatever words of kindness came to mind. She left with the misgiving that perhaps she had brought nothing in or out except a few memories of a stoic clown.

On the landing, a nurse was emerging from another door. Nadia caught a glimpse of an un-plush room, windowless, with steel beds on which silent patients sat or lay. Some were in straight jackets. Some were strapped down. The nurse carried a metal bin that clunked hollowly as empty syringes rolled around inside. She bolted and barred the door, rummaged in her frock pockets, found a used paper cup, crumpled it, and chucked it too in the bin. She rummaged again, found a key, locked the padlock, repeated the whole process for the door to the plush room, and then headed upstairs.

Andrei finished his inspection of the wheelchair. "All ready," he said and they were off, albeit at a pace that lagged behind the nurse's footsteps, unseen but still heard until she clanged through another door.

As they passed the third-floor landing, the lights flickered. Andrei reverted to a more talkative mode. "I feel sure the Doctor will make Ida better soon."

"What makes you sure of that?" Gramma asked.

"Oh, he has to. I overheard him say, 'The patients must be better by the time the Canadians come.' "

"I've never met a Canadian," Gramma said. "What makes you expect this delegation?"

"They're coming all this way to study the Doctor's research—his machine—but I shouldn't try to tell you about that. I'd only get it wrong."

"Would you?"

"Oh, yes. Anyway, you don't need my version. You'll be seeing the Doctor himself in a minute!"

They arrived at the fourth and final landing, which was the most inviting landing insofar as the doors had no padlocks, bars, or deadbolts on this side. Andrei parked Gramma's wheelchair by a window slit and he pressed a red button by the endmost door.

The peephole slid open and shut. Andrei took two steps backwards.

Doctor Anton Igorevich Yahontov pulled open the door to his parlour and stepped out of its lamplight to say, "Dear Comrades, welcome. We welcome visitors here." He circled round to personally take hold of the wheelchair's handles.

Gramma stood.

Yahontov chuckled and feigned surprise. "What's this? Have we made you walk, Comrade?"

"Only from the train station, Comrade Doctor," Gramma replied, "and that much was in my power."

"We should train Andrei to drive the ZiL for our honoured guests."

Andrei opened his mouth but not fast enough.

Gramma said, "That would be too much for us, Comrade Doctor."

"My little joke, Comrades. Come in. Andrei, goodbye."

Yahontov's parlour was as the booklet had pictured it, except that Gramma and Nadia stood in for the archetypal solace-seeker. A pair of brass floor lamps occupied the two corners nearest the door. An overstuffed sofa stretched along one wall. Opposite it was a long, short window that offered a somewhat restricted view overtop the maples towards the river. A far corner of the room had a stand for a skeleton, with the skull-top sawn off to reveal a pink plastic brain. The last corner had a stand for a world globe, with a red pin in Ottawa. Between the skeleton and globe was a fireplace, surrounded by slate tiles, with bookshelves above the mantle for the works of the Doctors Yahontov. The floor was of petrified oak, covered with an exactly centred Turkish carpet where the Chief Physician's mahogany desk separated his high-backed mahogany chair from two short-backed ones for his visitors. They all sat.

"Dear Comrades," said Yahontov with his hands in the air as if clasping an invisible orb, "let us examine the case." He placed his thick fingertips on a folder on his desk. Then, he flipped it open, spun it around, and pushed it towards the visitors. "These photographs..." (he spread them out with his fingers) "...show my patient's wrists after a recent suicide attempt. This was a serious attempt. She is a careful planner. One thinks she is dreaming but she is planning. This time, she stole a key to the janitor's closet, she stole a razor from the man's supplies, and she waited to be sent for hydrotherapy. There is always a female attendant with her at the hydrotherapy but this time, my patient colluded with another to have her attendant called away to some fictitious emergency. Then, very steadily, she cut herself and put her wounds in the water. By the time the whole deception was discovered, the loss of blood was very great. Had she not received a transfusion within minutes, she would have died. You can see, also, the wounds became infected. This complication occurred because it was the peat bath hydrotherapy. She may have had in mind that the dark peat water would conceal the blood. Even when discovered, she protested, 'What blood? What blood?' and struggled to hide her wrists in the water. Now, as we speak, her wounds are healing better. With time, the scars will be faint. I have replaced her hydrotherapy with a course of shock treatments, using a new machine developed by myself and my engineering colleague in Leningrad. She is receiving the safest and most effective shock therapy in the world. We are even working to export this system to America, to Canada. Once, her case would have been considered incurable, a doomed life, but today, there is hope for so many like her. For now, know that she is in the right hands. Would a sane woman do this with a razor?"

"Comrade Doctor," Gramma replied, "let's not quibble over what a sane or insane woman would do with a razor."

Yahontov flashed a lemony frown. "She also stole bleach. If she hadn't cut herself, she would have swallowed bleach."

"I saw a farm girl drink pesticide, in the War," Gramma recalled. "I saw many suicides and attempts and killings and cruelties and every kind of man, woman, beast, and machine. I was our medic, Comrade Doctor."

"How interesting. I may have read your story somewhere."

"Have you? Let me suggest to you, Comrade Doctor, since your incurable patient is doing better, it could do you no harm to turn her over to an old medic for grandmotherly care. The newspapers might like that story ... even in faraway Canada."

"She is young. I can see merit in home care, providing that the moral environment is good." Yahontov looked at Nadia.

"I'd be Ida's only friend. What harm could I do?" Nadia asked. *What harm?* She wanted to weep for the cost of this transaction, for its indignity to her grandmother. *Nobody has seen more of life than this kind of old woman. The giving of it and shedding of it and the nursing and hard-grafting of it was hers, so in recompense she would be silenced, cornered, and used. Now we glimpse a final act to come.*

"Indeed." Yahontov addressed Gramma again: "As for her medications, I would require that my instructions be followed strictly."

"I understand that."

"Yes. One does feel pity for these orphans. What good could come of taking the offspring of defective elements and throwing them all together? Here, we maintain separations. She has not been exposed to pathological obsessions of a political character and such should be avoided—all her life, if possible—because she does have guile, which could endanger her and harm society if ever she were to see herself as a martyr to a cause."

"We just sit around and talk about tea," Nadia offered. "There's not much cause to be martyred in that."

Yahontov closed the file. "I am satisfied with your answers. This interview of ours has served its purpose. I am releasing my patient to your care."

A sort of ceremony ensued. Yahontov asked Gramma and Nadia to stand by the globe. Would Gramma be so gracious as to point to Berlin and would Nadia be attentive to the old woman's gesture? He took a Praktica camera from his desk, set the aperture of the 50mm Tessar lens to f/2.8, and photographed them like that.

Next, they were required to return to the entrance hall between the inner and outer gates. Gramma walked, as she said it was easier on the way down. The physician's assistant did all the paperwork with Gramma and then left them with Lenin to wait and wait. As they sat on the bench, far beneath the window slits, Gramma turned to hold Nadia's head in a hug and to whisper in her ear, "They are listening."

They conversed about the kind of tea they should have with Ida when they got back.

"Cloudberry?"

"You're dreaming! Where would we get any, this time of year?"

The assistant returned with an echoing clang of the inner gate. Ida was not with her. "She has no clothes."

"Didn't she come with any?" Gramma asked.

"Never mind," Nadia interjected. "We have my sweater and ... the quilt we gave Ida can be a skirt."

"How is the nurse to dress her in that?" the assistant asked.

"You can pin it with Gramma's brooch."

"People will take one look and send her back."

"Please, have pity!"

Whether affected or not by Nadia's plea, the assistant took the items and disappeared back through the inner gate.

Gramma fingered the empty space where she had worn the maternal relic—the floral brooch of silver filagree and enamel.

When the assistant returned, she had with her a big orderly, pushing Ida in a wheelchair. "You may take her," the assistant said, "and these medications and instructions from Doctor Yahontov." She thrust a paper bag at Gramma.

The orderly kept rolling Ida forwards. The assistant went to unlock the outer gate. Ida sat in audience to the handover of herself as if it were a minor scene in a minor movie. She had hospital slippers on her feet and, as the scene neared its climax, she drummed half a tune against the footrests of the wheelchair. Nadia and Gramma practically had to catch her as the orderly lifted her out of the wheelchair, past the gate, and onto the steps.

The rare release was done. The gate slammed shut.

"Come, come," Gramma said as she and Nadia frogmarched Ida down the steps, "we can sit in the park round the corner." Ida stared, tear-blind, at the cool sun of springtime. They moved her, like a gelatin sculpture, into the park, where pigeons and chessmen-come-to-life might have finished her if they had had a mind to do so. A woman led her children out of the park as Gramma, Ida, and Nadia collapsed in unison onto a bench. "Come, dear, let's make sure your skirt is done up properly." Gramma inspected it. The brooch was nowhere to be seen—just a simple hospital pin. "Yes, I see, everything is done up expertly."

The old woman sucked a few breaths into her broochless bosom. She had an elated and morbid look, as if it had finally come time to pull all the grenade pins and charge to her death.

Nadia kissed Ida hard on both cheeks. Ida tasted of peat. "You're coming home with us, Ida. What do you think?"

Still dripping tears, Ida was starting to giggle. She tried to say something; it came out garbled.

"What?" Nadia tried to interpret: "Persians are leading you on?"

Ida shook her head, a matted mess of cropped blond hair. She tried again.

"Partisans are leading you away!"

Gramma waved the paper bag. "Very soon, dears," she puffed, "we will go to the beach and throw Comrade Doctor's pills in the sea."

II: Mother of Millions

1: Shock Therapy

A long time later, in the middle of a night of broken dreams, Nadia served Ida a glass of tea and asked a question about Yahontov's machine.

"Oh, I didn't have the privilege of seeing the machine in action," Ida said. "Watching is for visiting Canadians. No, they strapped me down and knocked me out with a couple of needles before they flipped the switch. They never said exactly what they meant to do and, of course, it made no difference to tell them I didn't want it. I got their pet idiot, Andrei, to tell me what he knew, which wasn't much. They were electrocuting my brain to make my memories 'better', he said. I think they did blow some bits out of there, enough to make me unbelievable, you know. Then, other bits are still there but they burnt the colour out.

"There was one time, I'd pissed off the Witch and I think she messed with the injections so I didn't really go to sleep but I couldn't move and couldn't breathe and it hurt inside me everywhere, the shock, you know. I pissed myself.

"They burnt the colour out." Ida looked at the debris in the bottom of her glass and finished, "Somehow, I've got to feel things again, you know."

2: Right Arm

They had had a long way to go, already, before they could talk over tea between nightmares.

On the night they first hauled Ida back to the outskirts of Tallinn, Nadia believed Gramma would die at the foot of the stairs. The old woman collapsed in a choking fit and unhooked the payphone's receiver on her way down.

Ida, still supported by Nadia on the other side, glided to the bottom step and slumped against the bannister there. A shiver ran up the stair rail, a mouse trap sprang somewhere, Cherny shot up a wall, and a wire came loose, so the lobby's last functioning lightbulb began to flicker. Ida started whimpering and clawing at her bald spot and quilt squares as her spooked blue eyes shot a scene of flickering horror: a rescue gone wrong; a wingèd saviour, in phantom flames, choking on the smoke of her own body.

Nadia grabbed the receiver. A sign on the payphone promised that the emergency number was free. This was a lie and it refused to ring, for want of a coin.

Nadia bent to search Gramma for money but the old woman rasped, "No! Get Yuly Lvovich! You can trust Yuly."

(Yuly Lvovich Babich was another longtime resident of the eighth floor. He had something to do with fish farming and had given them a tin of sturgeon caviar at Passover, though Nadia had not known him to be a person close to Gramma in any sense except an apartment number.)

Gramma added, "A list about Cherny is in the medicine cupboard."

Nadia ran. Somewhere on a dark landing, she almost slid, so she decided to slip off her shoes (a tired, old pair of brown leather flats that had been suitably nondescript for the hospital visit). Soon after that, she stepped on the sprung mousetrap. The wire jabbed the soft part of her sole. Running, running, running, she tried to think of Ida showing no pain.

When Yuly Lvovich got a knock on his door, he was already up to answer it, in striped pyjamas and running shoes. "What, what?" he asked and he got a breathless account of Gramma's plight as he peered through baggy eyes into the hall from his doorway. "Alright. Whose blood is that?"

"Mine, just my foot. Please hurry, she asked for you!"

"I'll get her medicine." Yuly left the door ajar and was back in a moment with a bottle of kirsch. He brushed past Nadia and ran downstairs. She kept not far behind him, though it seemed an entire night within a night before they arrived in the flickering light of the lobby.

"My God!" Yuly Lvovich moaned. "What happened here?" (He had a habit of bringing God into things and this was a difference between him and Gramma but she was in no state to even cough her objections now.) "Who is she?" he wondered about the gaunt, purple-lipped, bald-patched, bandaged, quilted, and quaking young woman who hugged the bannister as he rushed past. "Up!" He lifted Gramma, pressed her spine against the wall and her shoulder against the phone box for support, and administered kirsch from the bottle. He got a face-ful of it coughed back at him.

"Always the gentleman," Gramma growled.

Nadia edged in to take over the role of physical support to Gramma. Yuly shrugged, wiped his face, and went to sit on the stairs, where Ida took hold of the bottle and drank. "Ah, fuck," she gasped.

Yuly Lvovich raised his eyebrows, took back his bottle, and capped it.

"Cherny..." said Gramma.

"I'll check on Cherny!" Yuly snapped as he stood and waved his free hand. "God forbid we forget Cherny while you and ... this one? ... are dying here!" He stomped upstairs into the darkness to search for the black cat.

Ida pointed to the dangling receiver. Gramma pulled it up by its coils (by wrapping these around the knots of her fingers), then she gripped it, and she slammed it down onto the hook.

Nadia led Gramma to the bottom step and sat her down, on the opposite side from Ida. Nadia herself took the middle.

They were all half asleep when Yuly Lvovich returned to say, "Cherny is fine. I used the spare key and put her in your bedroom. That way she won't get out when you ... three? ... go in. Up!" He locked arms with Gramma and Nadia. Nadia locked arms with Ida. The bannister (on Ida's side) and the wall (on Gramma's) braced the line.

Of that night, Nadia's remaining impressions were scattered. Yuly Lvovich had a strong right arm. He stayed long enough to get a fire going in the stove and to make sure Nadia soaked her foot in alcohol (though not, this time, his kirsch). He left after saying, "She's snoring away in there and Cherny is telling me to go drown in a fire." Was that really the turn of phrase? Nadia remembered it that way. She and Ida slept end-to-end on the sofa under the quilt and sometime in the night, Nadia found herself hugging Ida's feet to stop the kicking.

3: Another Day

The next day, as the first light entered the window like an ink stain washing away, Gramma rocked Nadia's shoulder to wake her up. "You have school."

"Right." Nadia rolled away from Ida and sat on the floor at Gramma's feet. Gramma started pulling Nadia's hair straight back to make a tight bun. "Gramma, no, I'll do that. Your poor hands…"

She dismissed this with a weary whisper: "I've seen worse … chopped by a sabre."

"Should I stay to help with Ida?" Nadia asked as she ran her eyes along a sprawling, bandaged arm.

"No, she'll sleep away the morning at least. You can try to get some things for her on your way back. She'll need a lot of juice."

"She hates apple juice."

"Get birch juice or anything sweet, also tomato juice. Get condensed milk, salt, nuts, sausage, and bread." Gramma fed the coal fire.

"Brown bread?"

"Yes. I have bandages and disinfectant but if you see more, get them. You can decide what else she needs for her person."

Cherny cried to get out.

Nadia stood up and found that her foot still hurt. She hobbled to the door and released Cherny into the hall. Out there, the blood trail was gone and two items stood near the door: a block of Druzhba processed cheese in foil and a vial of brilliant green dye (renowned for its antiseptic, antifungal properties). Nadia brought these in and placed the cheese in the centre of the little table. "A gift of friendship," she murmured.

Gramma was making tea. Nadia reached past her to get to the cupboards for a rump of black bread, a jar of pickled cucumbers and tomatoes, plates, knives, spoons, and an eyedropper. She set the table, then sat on the floor to apply drops of dye to her foot, and finished by putting the dye and eyedropper away in the medicine cabinet. Gramma served the tea. She and Nadia breakfasted on bread, cheese, pickles, and tea while Ida slept in the heat from the stove.

Nadia packed her books, as well as a travel clock (from the table) so that she could be sure to keep time with the buses and stores. She shouldered her satchel, kissed Gramma, straightened the quilt over Ida's feet, grabbed a shopping basket at the door, and left to catch the bus.

On her way past the payphone, she remembered that she had to call her mother at the end of the day. Katya would be waiting by the phone in her room at the sanatorium. (That month, there had already been one devastating occasion when Nadia forgot to call at a promised time.) *What can I tell her about Ida? Nothing?*

Ahead of her, she had a long day's struggle to think of her lessons—not of sleep, food, queues, and Ida. At one point, a teacher warned her that she was letting everyone down today. She was watched, from the classroom walls, by a set of printed faces: the brand new "Glory to the Women Workers" woman with her headscarf and roses and skyscrapers and big brown eyes in broad strokes of the watercolour brush; the "You Should Know Much in Order to be Useful to the Country" woman, stencilled in blue in front of her brown chalkboard of formulae and her cyan railroad bridge; the grinning farmers embracing cows and wheat sheaves; the grinning gas worker in hardhat and mitts who strode (almost danced) across the gas works yard as his sports jacket flapped in the wind; and a painting of Lenin that was surprisingly intimate (as far as such things go), with him in a blue tie with white dots and standing at a table with a red tablecloth, whereupon he had a saucer, tea glass, and spoon, as well as the papers he was fingering as he gazed at an unportrayed audience while parting his lips almost in a smile as if he had just said something witty, and his left hand (up to the wrist) in his trouser pocket, in the manner of an Everyman who, at some point in his workday, adjusts his sweaty drawers. She was letting them all down today and she had a long way to go towards her life's quota in the eventual perfection and she did want to learn and she was not supposed to be wasting life by picturing people naked, people screwing—be they Party leaders, cops, or orphans.

She threw up in the washroom at lunchtime. She was unnerved by a pattern that was becoming hard to miss and the pattern was not eventual perfection; it was multiple banishment and, in each banishment, a new pretence to add to the last. Tonight, she would telephone her mother. Besides, she imagined so many ways to lose Gramma, who kept a list about Cherny in the medicine cupboard, and Ida, who was scarcely back.

At the school cafeteria, Nadia got an extra bottle of tomato juice. *Just one extra won't raise questions here.* She sat on her own and ate soup made of processed cheese and stared at a wall of white bricks and tried not to cry. A bitch came by to ask whether Nadia was missing her Mama and whether her Gramma was still alive to ride the buses with her.

After school, Nadia sat on a secluded park bench to check her foot. The green dye still coloured it but the wound was tender and she squeezed a bit of clear fluid from it. She should have brought the green stuff with her. Anyway, the foot was a small problem, an inconsequential pain.

She did the rounds of the stores—strings of people, passing empty shelves. *We've made markets into museums. "Here is the refrigerator where butter used to be. Line up and see. Stick your hand in and feel the cold. Over here we have a cleaver and bones. On this board, you may read the per-person allowances, which reflect last night's ancient beliefs about the Coming of the Shipment today."*

She picked up a tall, dented can of stewed pork, which the butcher had placed on display among the bones. She got a bag of rye buns. She wandered into a copse of birch juice jars—the three-litre big ones, stacked tall. Some people said such a cheap, plentiful, and colourless juice must be fake, mere sugar-water, but Gramma attested that it was birch and Gramma was from Byelorussia, after all.

Near the birch, the rust-red tomato was to be found in similar jars.

"Black marketeers don't snap these up," Nadia muttered to herself as she loaded a jar of birch and a jar of tomato into her basket.

She searched for toiletries, found few, despaired, and went to the checkout.

Carrying her book-bag and the basket of jars and other things, she crossed the market's empty parking lot and sat at the bus stop. The evening was still light but getting cool, enough to raise the hairs on her sore forearms as she rubbed them and thought of Ida. She noticed a man slowly pushing a food cart on the other side of the street so she crossed and bought a bag of hazelnuts from him. A young woman there, about Ida's age or Nastya's, was pacing along the curb and tugging at her overalls and sweater and craning her neck at passing cars.

A side street gave a glimpse of the harbour and the traffic at sea.

After a moment's hesitation, Nadia went up to the overall-tugger and asked, "Excuse me, have you got any smokes? I'll pay."

"Uh, what kind of smokes?"

"Any kind." *Oh, stupid Nadia.* "I mean, any cigarettes."

"Okay."

They came to a deal: five cigarettes for the last coins in Nadia's pocket. The older girl watched as Nadia hid the cigarettes at the bottom of a pencil case in her satchel.

The one-off supplier muttered, "Lucky you, something to hide." The cars kept passing. "Okay, I'm busy, so…"

Nadia returned to the bus stop and rode home with a sore foot, tired arms, and aching head and stomach. She found Ida sitting (half kneeling) on the sofa, with her hair wet and combed like a politician's, in a wave over hollow baldness. Ida was studying a newspaper, which lay in pieces all over the sofa. She was freshly bandaged about the wrists and she wore a pair of Nadia's pyjamas, which were too short for Ida but (in her current condition) a little bit baggy.

"Cheers, Mate," said Ida with renewed powers of speech. "Your Gramma… Ah…" (she yawned) "…went for a shower. Stove's hot."

"I got presents for you."

"For me? Well, you have made me the luckiest Ivanova alive."

Nadia placed the shopping basket on the table and came to the sofa with her satchel. Ida kicked off some news-sheets to make room. Nadia sat, mirrored Ida's half-kneeling pose, and dug out the pencil case.

"Nice pencils," Ida murmured as Nadia started to bring out the contents. "Nice cigs, oh, oh. I think they're foreign. Look at that filter, like gold. You…" (Ida shook her head) "…are a maiden too good for this world."

Nadia fetched a matchbox and saucer from the cupboard and lit Ida's cigarette. Ida smoked, stared at the stove, stared at the newspaper on the floor, and turned to Nadia to offer her the cigarette.

"No, it's for you," Nadia protested. "Well, one puff." She choked on its taste of ash and menthol. *Does that girl on the curb smoke these to cover the smell of her breath?* She began to wonder whether the smoke might send Gramma into another coughing fit.

When Ida had finished the cigarette, Nadia chucked it in the stove, packed the rest away, rinsed the ashes from the saucer, opened the window, and put her satchel in its usual place under the table. Battling like a matador with a bull of smoke, she waved the quilt to circulate some air and, at last, she returned the quilt to Ida and shut the window again.

"Hello, dears," Gramma announced herself. The old woman approached the table, inspected the shopping basket, and said, "I see you got canned stewed pork."

"Yes."

"Just like the War."

"Is it?"

"Plenty of birch juice and tomato…"

"Yes."

"Was there any condensed milk?"

"I don't think. I don't remember."

"Never mind." Gramma attempted to open the jar of birch juice.

"No, Gramma, let me."

"I'll go get something for the can." Gramma went into her room and shut the door.

Ida yawned vocally, stretched until her elbows popped, and got up to bring three glasses to the table. "Birch juice, birch juice," she chanted sleepily as she sat and watched, like a reveller awaiting a midnight fountain show. Then, underneath Nadia's hands, there came a sound like the croak of a metallic frog as the vacuum seal broke and the lid came off. Nadia poured. Ida downed a glass and a half and her face seemed to wake up more properly.

Nadia, too, had a drink of the light syrup that had the sweetness and smoky sharpness of a damp forest.

Gramma returned with a pocket knife, which her own hands could not open. Nadia took it and tried to puncture the can but the knifepoint kept slipping.

"I can do that," said Ida as her blue eyes greeted the blade.

Nadia grunted and took another jab, blunting the knife-tip and failing again to breach the pork's tin tomb.

"You do it, I do it, or we starve, Little Paw," Ida tsked.

"Save us, Dearest Smartass." Nadia relinquished the knife.

Ida smiled, gripped the handle, laid the blade flat against the table, hammered it with the can until it was straight, whisked it against the rim in a show of sharpening it, plunged it through the lid with a mighty stab, and wrenched it round to cut the lid away. Salty, spicy, fatty, porky juice splashed on the back of her left hand (the one gripping the can) and she licked it. "Hmm-hmm-hmm, needs something." She seized the bottle of tomato juice, uncapped it, and started pouring it into the stew as she stirred with the knife. "I have skills."

"That might be enough tomato, dear," Gramma said as she pawed Ida's elbow.

"Okay, however you like it," Ida acquiesced. "Let's dish out." She pushed the dripping knife across the table to Gramma and then waited with clasped hands.

"Clean that and fold it, would you?" Gramma asked Nadia. "I'll heat this, shall I, dears?" she added in a whisper.

An acidic, spicy scent filled the flat and mixed with the backdrop of coal and menthol as the meal got cosy in a saucepan. Nadia rinsed the knife and attempted to buff it with a towel. *This heirloom has an admirer, so…*

The old woman drank a bit of birch juice and declared it genuine.

Nadia gave up on her polishing. She watched, from behind, as Ida's hair began to dry and as Ida snuck a peek beneath her bandages.

Having pocketed the knife, Gramma started serving the pork-tomato stew into bowls. A knock came at the door. Nadia answered it; it was Yuly Lvovich. "What in God's name is the hammering in here?" he wanted to know.

He's spent fifteen minutes deciding whether to come over and ask that.

"No cause for concern," Gramma said. "We were just having a little trouble opening a can."

Yuly raised his eyebrows. Nadia made room for him to step inside.

"Does he want some?" Ida asked Gramma.

"No, I don't think it's his type of food," Gramma replied.

"Doesn't he like tomato?"

"Who says I don't like tomato?" Yuly asked.

"We're having stewed pork topped with tomato juice," Gramma said.

"Oh, well." Yuly went to check on the stove fire.

"Thank you for the cheese and green stuff," Nadia said. "I put it on my foot this morning—the green stuff; we had the cheese with breakfast."

"Oh, good." He moved on from the stove to check the cupboards. "I can always get you green stuff. We put it in the fish ponds to kill algae."

Ida brought her bowl and spoon over to the sofa and sat with the quilt over her legs. "Warmer over here, good and warm," she chattered. "That window is draughty. I can seal it for you tomorrow if you have rope and wax. I can seal jars or anything with rope and wax and it'll be airtight." She scooped meat and juice into her mouth and sucked air between her teeth as if she were both eating and smoking the seasoning: pepper, garlic, bay leaves.

Gramma and Nadia began to eat at the table as Yuly toasted a sandwich of rye bread and processed cheese against the grate of the stove.

"Young man, come sit by me," said Ida to the old fish farmer. "Didn't you try to get us drunk last night?"

Yuly sat, filled his cheeks with a large bite of the hot sandwich, and tapped his fingers on his knee and his sneakers on the floorboards.

"I'm Ida. I can tell you're shy like me."

Yuly laughed a sighing laugh through toasted cheese and he gave her a sideways handshake across the sofa's divide. "Ida, I'm Yuly."

As Nadia chewed her last bite of the pungent mush, she rummaged in her satchel for the travel clock, a little red-and-white speckled toy of a clock, with rust around its seams and a bell that hung askew like a flirt's beret. Being only the size of a small child's palm, it spent much of its existence being dwarfed by the nearest object, be it a glass or a jar or a can. Also, it kept poor time. Thus, it was a clock that asked to be picked up and babied. Nastya and Nadia used to play with it when they visited Gramma.

"I'm ten minutes late," Nadia announced.

"That made me sleepy," Ida was saying about the food. "Hmm, are you keeping a guy waiting? You could push it longer than ten."

"Mama is waiting for my call."

"Well, then, you know best. Where's your phone, anyway?"

"Downstairs. Bye."

As a reminder to Ida, Gramma added, "Remember, dear, you noticed it last night."

"Oh, that phone." Ida's shoulders twitched.

Nadia was halfway out the door (and Cherny had run in to jump on the arm of the sofa) when Yuly asked, "Have you got enough phone money?" This came to Nadia as a guilty reminder of how she had come to be skint at the street curb. "Take this and tell your mother I remember teaching her husband to fish, before her father or some teacher taught him to swing his fists. Tell her God bless."

Gramma told Yuly, "I'll pay that back to you later."

Nadia accepted the coins and ran downstairs with them in hand. *Damn foot, ow, ow, ow.* She got there and paid into the machine.

"My young one, my faithful soul," Katya answered the phone on the first ring, "you remembered to call when you felt me longing for the softness of your voice."

"Mama, of course I remembered. I'm here."

"You're here. Every minute, you're here. Let me tell you about our day here, yours and mine. At dawn, the seabirds were singing as we started our morning run along the causeway, out to the island with the observation tower where the band plays on the balcony at dinnertime. The acoustics over the water are perfect and we can hear them on the mainland, even from our own room, when you and I dine in here. Anyway, this morning, we jogged to the observation tower, which is also a communications tower, and we went in to rest in the lobby on the swinging basket chairs under the wind chime chandelier. Then, Petya, the young radio operator, came down from the mezzanine to say, 'Yekaterina Lvovna, you seem in excellent form this morning and you've saved me a trip to the mainland. Your son-in-law has just radioed to inform you that he and your daughter are aboard a special flight to Kiev, so today she will not telephone you until 13:15 hours, when she will be settled in their apartment there.'

"You can imagine the questions that entered my mind but Petya swore he knew no more than he had already said.

"Well, we jogged back to the mainland, you and I, had breakfast under the colonnade, and went to the radon baths. (The radon is is always so soothing after our long run.) Then, it was turning drizzly outside so we stayed in and played ping-pong with Lieutenant Colonel Sokolov of Naval Aviation. We had lunch with him (because he said he'll be sad when I go home next week and he'll hear no more of you and me) and afterwards you and I went up to our room to wait for Nastya's call.

"At 13:10 hours, Nastya rang. I said to her, 'What's this about you and Giorgi and a special flight to Kiev and an apartment there?' I said, 'Even Lieutenant Colonel Sokolov hadn't known of a special flight today to Kiev and he's in Naval Aviation, so spill it! What's the news?' "

"Mama…"

"I'm getting to the important part, my eager one."

"Hold on, then. I have to put more money in." *Clack. Clack. Clack. Clack.*

"Ready?"

"Yes, Mama, go on."

"Then, Nastya told me. There has been an occurrence at the Vladimir Ilyich Lenin Nuclear Power Plant."

"Where is that?"

"Near Pripyat."

"The River Pripyat?" Nadia remembered Gramma's stories of the vast and wild Pripyat basin—its sedge marshes, its thickets of birch and pine, the call of countless birds at dawn's light and wolves by moonlight, a place where men felt safest on horseback, so Himmler sent his SS Cavalry there (near the start, in summer 1941) to test the methods of massacre. The Germans must have imagined the swamps as bottomless; they thought it might be efficient to drown all the women and children by chasing them there but, in the end, instead they shot most along with the men. Villages burned and the birch remained like slender ghosts in singed white clothes that clung to pallid limbs. To these images, Nadia struggled to add *an occurrence at the Vladimir Ilyich Lenin Nuclear Power Plant.*

Katya clarified, "The city Pripyat, named for the river. It's near another city called Chernobyl, near Kiev. The whole city of Pripyat is being evacuated to Kiev—and maybe Chernobyl will be next."

"Something awful must have happened."

"Yes, I believe it's big and Giorgi has a role to play. He's made a great impression as a Junior Lieutenant. His Captain and even his Major recognized that they relied on Giorgi's contacts in the case of the Israeli smugglers. Anyway, with the occurrence to investigate and the evacuation to manage and order to be kept when people panic as we know they do, there is so much happening in Kiev that officers are being brought in from across Ukraine and the Inspector, the Major, and the Captain are bringing Giorgi as an aide.

"Let me tell you something else about the Major's fondness for Giorgi. On the plane, when Nastya got worried about missing our morning call, the Major overheard her and Nastya was afraid she was embarrassing Giorgi in front of him but it was the Major who said that Giorgi should go to the cockpit and have the pilot send a radio message to the tower. He said, 'Let him send a message to his family. Now is the time.'

"That sounds a bit like a promise, don't you think? This is Giorgi and Nastya's start. By the time they are parents, Giorgi could be a full Lieutenant. As you can imagine, Nastya is in ecstasy. Now, about the apartment…"

"Mama, the money…"

"Yes, I asked and a full Lieutenant would make…"

"The phone money!"

"I'll wait while you put in some more."

Clack. "I'm out. Sorry. You'll have to tell me the rest next time."

"Yes. I wonder whether it will make the news. You never know, they might show Giorgi, he being such a tall officer."

"Mama, we don't have a television…" … *nor do you, at home, remember?*

"No, Gramma doesn't like electronics, does she? Anyway, Nastya told me she's sending you a letter today from their new address. May they be safe, you be safe, and the letter be safe on its way. If my love could only be your shield… Next time, you must tell me something beautiful you've read. Your hunger for knowledge would make your Grandpa Lev so proud. Just don't forget to feed your whole self. You're young and…"

Nadia interjected her love as the line went dead. Coinless, she trudged upstairs to share bits of the news before all might fall into weary sleep. Perhaps Yuly, who seemed to sleep so little, might fish for scaly rumours in the night. Perhaps the coming letter from Nastya would cast light into dark waters. *Is Nastya safe? What can I tell her about Ida?*

4: Weather

That week, black rain fell in Byelorussia and the forests of white birch began to die.

5: Report

A day passed without the arrival of Nastya's letter.

Ida reiterated her idea about getting rope and wax to seal the window. She also wondered whether Yuly, as "an able young man", could obtain foreign newspapers for Nadia to translate aloud. Ida was anxious to know "what odds they give us, outside," and, in this, she seemed to exhaust herself again.

60   II: MOTHER OF MILLIONS

At day's end, Yuly could only repeat the official announcement from the nine o'clock TV news: five sentences introducing an accident, a damaged reactor, a remedy, assistance, and an investigative commission.

Katya was not answering the phone.

The next afternoon, Nadia got the letter at the post office and she read it on a packed bus where people were too busy whispering about the news to notice her and the words in her hands.

"Little Hedgehog, hello," Nastya greeted her.

"Life would seem so much simpler if, today, you and I were walking in the forest and collecting marsh marigolds for your hair. Can those days return? My dream is to have a daughter and place her hand in yours.

"By now, you will have heard Mama's version of events. I am fearful and she is blind to it. Perhaps I am to blame for saying too little but Giorgi believes it must be this way and I have said more than he would like me to say.

"The Major has a strange sense of humour about the situation. He says, back in '79, Brezhnev gave him and his first wife a memorable vacation to the base in Herat, Afghanistan, and now Gorbachev wants to be even more generous to him and the new wife.

"We are three couples sharing these large rooms that seem to be less like an apartment and more like a set of boudoirs attached to a private bar. The higher-ups would hold functions here but, in the present emergency, it's housing for visiting detectives and their wives. Right now, it's four in the morning, the men have got off their first shift, and the Captain has puked everywhere. I've just helped his wife scrub the carpet and she assures me it is not the drink, which he normally holds well, but that he was surely poisoned by radiation in Pripyat this afternoon.

"The Inspector is elsewhere. He keeps telephoning here and we try to stop the Captain from answering, he is so agitated, so ill.

"I hear Giorgi typing a report as the Major is dictating to him. What things they have seen, had to do, and had to tell the people there! I cannot repeat what I hear. Perhaps you will hear some version of it on the news.

"My poor Giorgi is a good man and brave. How badly a gallant man is used! I wish I had the faith to pray for him.

"As for Mama, can you help her somehow? I don't know what to do, being stuck here in Kiev for the indefinite duration of the crisis and inquiry, while she is due to go back to Papa next week. You listen to her and I ask you to consider, what kind of welcome awaits her on the factory floor now? Giorgi has pulled strings to extend her rest once and he cannot again. The Doctor has hinted (cruelly, for what does he know of Mama's life?) that too much fondness for rest, rest from the ordinary life, might look like sluggishness and malingering. You must somehow help her return to reality. Her heart is full of nothing but you.

"I hope that Gramma is well and that you can remind her of your responsibility to get back to Mama soon.

"I love you through all my days and nights," and she signed it with a little sketch of a hedgehog sitting with a wolf pup.

"P.S. We are told to shower frequently, that it might wash away radiation we have absorbed from the atmosphere or from our men."

Nadia folded the letter back into its envelope, held it to her chest, closed her eyes, and let the bus rock her as she tried to imagine the words she would put on paper that night—a sisterly reply, followed by a scholarly lab report about an oscilloscope and harmonics—but none of that till she brought a decent dinner home.

6: Ticket

They struggled and straggled and, in fifty days, came several ways to the end of spring. When a lifeline frayed and could have snapped, they tried to splice words and acts to make another. Each thin deliverance seemed to bring all things to the brink of depletion.

Still, they hoped to regroup in summer.

Giorgi got a full Lieutenant's second star and Nastya got pregnant. Giorgi said, the first star to ever rest upon his shoulder was his "rose of a wife"; the second would be their "petal of a child".

They invited Nadia to come visit them in their own Kiev apartment as soon as exams were over. From the bounty of Giorgi's new wages, the offer included a second-class train ticket for a bunk in an enclosed compartment.

Nadia took more than her usual time to reply. Nastya's follow-up letter said, Nadia must be burying her head in her books and doing her utmost to excel in her exams but, in her next free moment, would Nadia briefly send word about her plans so that Giorgi could buy the ticket?

Also, would she be rejoining Mama and Papa in Odessa after the visit to Kiev?

There were complications that remained unknown to Nastya and Katya, let alone Giorgi and Misha. The "private project"—bringing Ida home—had outstripped the economic wherewithal of all involved. Gramma's pension was meagre. Nadia had never yet earned a wage. Ida, soon after fixing the window seal and compiling a preliminary file on the nuclear fallout, had resolved to escalate her efforts. She scanned the newspapers for postings, sliced them out neatly with a knife, got her official documents in order, and showed up at the recruitment offices of various factories. She herself knew that her stamina and concentration were shot but, in a workplace, who could tell? Ida, as well as anybody, might have started a career and looked forward to receiving the designated pay rises, apartment, and medals as the years rolled by. At least, she might have put money in her pocket to pay for a friendlier summer.

There were, however, complications. For every good story Ida might tell, her documents insinuated something else.

She was an ethnic German. She had gone to a boarding school for orphans. When she worked her way out of that place, then, at her next and final school, she started flunking courses—including "Foreign Language (German)". Although her "Physical Training" and "Geography" were "Good", her "Human and Society" was "Very Poor". Nobody ever got "Very Poor", what had she possibly done? Then, she fell off the map, with no diploma and no recent activity in her labour booklet, so where had her goodness with geography got her? The obvious thought was, to the clink or the nuthouse.

To remove doubt, Ida dressed for these interviews as she would dress for the factory floor, in baggy pants and a shortsleeved shirt, and her scarred forearms were there to see and, for good measure, she flexed a bit of muscle.

Time and again, she was told that she could not even be considered. The words, in some cases, might have meant that her interviewer was looking for some consideration from her. She gave none but said, "Thank you all the same," and got a bus to the next one or, if she was done for the day, she went to the Old Town and wandered around till she found a derelict house in which to sit on the damp floor and have a smoke or, if she had no smokes, to smash the boards on the windows, as any glass was long since smashed to slivers.

She would shadow-box.

She would trace the long, old splits in a post and beam of Gothic timber. She would hug the diagonal brace, hoist herself up, hook her legs around it, and hang upside down, sometimes with her fingertips brushing the floor if it were a low beam or she stretched her shoulders to popping.

Whether sitting or hanging, she would close her eyes and listen to the creeping drip of water and, to this metre, she would snicker and whisper descriptions of the people she had met that day (interviewers and applicants and bus-riders, tramps, and kids), descriptions for Nadia's amusement when they would talk at night from opposite ends of the sofa, after Nadia finally shut her books and left them at the table.

One evening, Yuly Lvovich questioned Ida about the job search and told her, "I only wish I could help, Ida. They never liked me or my papers either."

Late that night, on her way down the hall to the toilet, Nadia overheard Yuly and Gramma arguing in Yuly's apartment. He was saying, "We have to bribe someone to hire her—anything! If she can't get herself hired here, she'll get picked up for the latest work assignment from Hell. They'll probably send her to join the set of Germans in Kirghizia, where some nomad can carry her off tied to his horse to be his fourth wife. That, or they'll tell her: here's your chance, work abroad, come cook and clean for our boys in Afghanistan. Pick your favourite; maybe he'll keep the rest of the Army off you."

"I didn't know you were the expert on women and horsemen and war."

"No, forgive me, in your day, I was safe in the Gulag. What a blessing there's gold in Kolyma."

"Enough of this, it's no use."

"God knows, I try! There must be something I can do, Ninel!"

"Oh, say a prayer, why don't you?" Gramma snarled and she opened the door and walked straight past Nadia.

Nadia met Yuly's eyes as he shut his door.

The following evening, Yuly visited after dinner. He said he had come to bring Ida a different newspaper, this one in Estonian, which, he supposed, Nadia might be able to translate for her. Why a job posting in Estonian should do well for Ida, he did not say. He hung around and gave Gramma a lot of silent looks.

Nadia chose this moment to speak of the invitation from Nastya and Giorgi. She finished by saying, "I haven't decided what to do."

"Haven't you?" asked Gramma.

"No, I mean, I'm not sure the timing is right. I might just be in the way. What do I know about pregnancy?"

"That's a poor excuse, isn't it, dear?"

Yuly muttered, "You'd've been a harsh judge in that manger."

Ida just scratched Cherny's neck.

Nadia tried again. "If you say it's poor, Gramma, fine, but I don't know where or how I'm best used."

Gramma balked. "Do you entreat me to tell you how a person is best used?"

Wide-eyed, Nadia replied, "Not if you don't want!" She turned to Ida and asked, "Should I ask Nastya whether you can come too?"

"I don't know," Ida said. "I think Nastya and I fought last time we saw each other. I mean, it's not that I mind, I'm sure it was a fair fight."

"Can it have been so bad?" Gramma asked.

Nadia wondered, *Does she mean, can it have been worse than Nastya and me?*

"Oh, it can," Ida said. "Honestly, I don't remember, it could've been."

Could've been blood all over the walls, Nadia thought. She had not been there. Nastya had kept her away from Ida towards the end.

"This is academic, anyway," Gramma objected. "Dears, the invitation is for Nadia and we have no money for Ida to go on holiday in Kiev."

"Maybe I shouldn't go," Nadia said.

"Why," Ida asked, "have you forgotten something too?"

"I mean, I could be looking for work here, like you."

Yuly's brow had furrowed. He raised his hand and said, "I would like you both to go. This Giorgi can buy a ticket for Nadia. Well, I can buy one for Ida. She can stay with my cousin, a very respectable woman in Kiev—God knows, too respectable for my company but she'll be good to Ida. All it takes is a little flattery, Ida, and..."

"You do too much for us," Gramma protested.

Yuly countered, "I do this for my sake. Ida can do something for me in Kiev. Ida, I want you to visit a gravesite for me, place a pebble for remembrance."

"Young man, I'll place a boulder if it does you good."

"Surely," Gramma pointed out, "you could just as easily go your-self."

"It would be less pain and more joy if Ida went for me."

"Then I can't object," Gramma said, "but I'll pay it back to you."

Now, Yuly's face went red. "Can you accept so little of me?" he wanted to know. "Ida, Nadia, please." He walked out without another word.

"Why do you treat him like that?" Nadia decided to quiz her grand-mother. "Do you think we're better than him, we're pure?"

"How dare you!"

Oh, that got the great liberator where it hurts.

"There is a great deal you don't know," Gramma added as she, too, walked out.

7: Eulogy of the Waffle Iron

After another day of job-hunting (in which the Estonian newspaper brought her no luck), Ida stopped at Yuly's apartment, accepted his offer, and let him introduce her by phone to his cousin, Rosya Lekht, whom he had already briefed.

Ida continued down the hall and announced her plans. She was going to try her luck in Kiev, at least for a spell.

Gramma took this nonchalantly. For dinner, she fried up some potatoes and sausages, with extra for Ida, and served them with heaps of sour cream. "They'll expect a fuller figure in Kiev, dear."

Ida bowed her head over her meal. She seemed overcome by some combination of exhaustion and reverence. As if memorizing the smell, she just breathed for a minute. Then, she began to take slow bites, to yawn, and to rub her watering eyes. "I'll be gone," she murmured, "before the bay leaves are fringed in red."

That evening, Nadia wrote to Nastya to accept the invitation. For the first time, Nadia's letter included a message for Giorgi: "Tell the Lieutenant, thanks for the upgrade and let's make the most of this arrival. I expect him at the station with his stars on."

Between then and their departure, Ida bought new, foreign clothes from a black marketeer in the Old Town. Yuly had given her money for this purpose. Showing her haul to Nadia in the night, Ida explained,

"He says I'll do well to look stylish for Rosya. He says she'll like to be associated with a cool youth."

To this end, Ida had procured a pair of blue jeans and two long-sleeved flannel shirts. One shirt was red-black-and-yellow plaid with buttons; the other was buttonless black-and-white horizontal stripes. "I think they wear these at their cottages and these on their yachts," she said of the plaid and the stripes, respectively.

Nadia admired the feel of the denim and the cotton flannel. "All this and a ticket too..."

"My ticket is for the dormitory car but yes," Ida said.

"You'll be the belle of the dormitory car, is all I can say. You'll be the one to know in Kiev before you even get there."

"That should please Rosya ... maybe." Ida put the clothes away in a canvas army backpack, a shabby old thing that she had bought as her travel bag. "I have to adjust to the idea of what people might want to do to me now. I've read of girls stabbing other girls for jeans."

"I didn't see that in Odessa."

"Maybe in Kazan. Anyway, if your Gramma is right (and she's seen more of the world than anyone else I know), in Kiev, it's all about fat boobs."

"I'm not sure she said that exactly."

"She implied it."

"I'm sure it's not all about fat boobs."

"You've all been nothing but kind."

"Now you really are talking nonsense."

On the morning of their departure, the quilt was the last thing to go into Ida's pack. Gramma saw them to the door of the apartment; Cherny, with the air of battered propriety that old felines have, saw them to the door of the building.

What is my grandmother all about? Nadia asked herself. *Is it her life's work to rescue people, to catalogue us in her trunk, dig us up from oblivion, feed us sausages and birch juice, intertwine us under a quilt on a sofa by a coal stove, tell us "Fuck off!" in her nightmare as she shoots a dying horse, and then, one day, throw our questions back on us as she gives us the shove? Cherny knows her best. Who am I?*

Instead of Gramma, it was Yuly who accompanied them to the station. When they got on a bus or off a bus, he insisted it was his job to hoist Nadia's little suitcase and Ida's lightly packed army bag, which both seemed like dolls' luggage in his big arms. They all chitchatted. He told silly jokes. They laughed.

The last thing they asked Yuly was about his work. "Young man, how come you're still at the fish farm?" Ida wondered.

Nadia added, "Why aren't you retired like Gramma?"

"Oh, I get so many benefits," Yuly sighed.

He waved them off towards Leningrad in the rising heat of mid-morning.

For this first leg of the journey, they were together in a seating car. As the train entered Narva, Ida shut the curtains.

Early in the evening, they switched trains in Leningrad. Nadia found her compartment empty but for herself. She thought about her mother's time alone in a bedroom in the sanatorium. Nadia had phoned home to Odessa the night before, promised to visit there after Kiev, and listened to a novel variation from Katya. She (Katya) wished that Lieutenant Colonel Sokolov of Naval Aviation would come meet her for lunch in the factory cafeteria so that all her coworkers and especially the forewoman (ever her chiefest tormentor) could see that Katya had such a connection; dare she say, such a friendship?

Hot and bored and overtired from recent nights of study and coordination and packing, Nadia slept away the speediest part of the journey.

Early in the night, while switching trains in Moscow, Ida and Nadia met up. They discussed the fullness of one car, the emptiness of the other, and a daring plan. Sometime before midnight, Nadia would unbolt the gangway door on her side. At midnight, Ida would sneak up, switch cars, and tap at the door of Nadia's compartment, which would be marked by a tassled bookmark, tied to the handle.

Later, when the tapping came, Nadia was already on her feet. She opened up (making Ida squint as light spilt into the corridor) and she pulled Ida's arm to hurry her into the compartment.

Nadia recovered the bookmark and fastened the bolt as Ida appraised her new surroundings. "Four bunks for the two of us?" Ida whispered. "Well..."

"Well...?"

"...you've made me the luckiest Ivanova alive."

Nadia stretched out, her head towards the dirty brown curtains, and she kicked her socks off. "How?" she played it out further. "How do two spare bunks make you lucky?"

"How?" Ida echoed. She shook the bedrail of the bunk above Nadia. "You watch how." She chucked her socks at the foot of the bed atop Nadia's, then turned and shook the other bedrail. "Strong, good and strong."

"You'll be gentle, won't you?"

Ida chortled, "No." She turned towards the door, took a moment to feel the train's sway in her knees and stomach, then grabbed both bedrails, leapt, swung, flipped, and hung upside down, facing Nadia and the curtains. Ida grinned (a bit breathlessly and nauseously) as the train tossed her like a pendulum at sea.

"I've lived for this," Ida rasped.

Presently, Ida's face got red and she let herself sway upright and drop to her feet. With swimming eyes, she gazed down at Nadia.

"Nosebleed," Nadia gave the alert.

"Hmm-hmm, yes." Ida pinched her nose as blood streamed copiously down her chin and across the black and white stripes of her flannel shirt. "Hmm-hmm, I die a free woman."

"Here," said Nadia, sitting up and digging under the bunk for her suitcase, "I have a fresh pair of socks…"

"Don't boast."

"…so you can mop up your gore."

Ida accepted the socks, put them on her hands, and squeezed her bloody nose with one as she wiped her chin and stripes with the other. "Muh."

Nadia also got out a collection of Ibsen's plays (in translation) before shoving her case back under the bunk. She reclined and read a little as Ida bled.

"Muh."

"Sit and I'll read to you."

Ida took the bunk opposite and listened to the opening of *Hedda Gabler*—a nice house, a return from a voyage, sleeping in. "Where's this?"

"Norway."

"When?"

"A hundred years ago."

Ida listened to some more. "Where's Brabant?"

"Belgium."

"Hmm-hmm-hmm. Your Mama made such good waffles. Didn't she say she used a Belgian recipe?"

"Oh, of course," Nadia said as she bookmarked her place. "Beat the whites and the yolks separately; fold them into the batter at the end."

"Give the waffle iron's eulogy one last time."

Nadia cleared her throat. " 'All progressive mankind mourns the loss of a dear friend that was big and square with shiny plating, that died shooting sparks. Our consolation is that Brezhnev lives on.' "

Ida laughed. "Muh."

Nadia closed her eyes and let her left hand dangle into space. She had lost track of her own voice; it was rambling in her head or in the forest of pines and oaks beyond the rails; it was announcing the news or humming a lullaby. She had no feeling of whether her lips were open or closed but she remained vaguely aware of movement and sound, as well as a stale smell and flickering light.

Through a blood-soaked sock, Ida squeezed Nadia's fingertips. "Got any smokes?"

"No."

"You want me to flick the light off?"

"Yes. I have an idea. We'll be passing through Bryansk, express."

"Are you asleep?"

"No, I'm telling you my idea."

"Oh. I mistook it for a dream idea."

"No. Flick the light off, open the curtains, and hang upside down like before. When we pass through Bryansk, I'll flash the light and we'll cause terror on the platform—visions of a blood-spattered woman, hanging upside down."

"You are an artist."

They executed the prank.

"Do you think anyone saw?" Ida asked once they were past Bryansk and she was sitting and nosebleeding some more. "I couldn't see out very well."

"I don't know," Nadia said.

"Worth it anyway. Muh." Ida sighed through all the blood. "To sleep?"

"*Perchance to dream,*" Nadia replied in English.

"What's that?"

"Maybe we'll dream."

"Maybe we're dreaming already."

They slept a little.

The train jolted now and again. Through the rolling darkness, Ida stretched to give Nadia a light kick and asked, "Do you ever wish you'd turn into a cloud of smoke?"

"Why, so you could smoke yourself?"

"I don't know. Maybe your Gramma would know."

"Sleep, if you can."

"Maybe I'm sleeping already."

At dawn, Nadia went to the washroom to wash out the socks. She came back with wet socks and offered to wash Ida's face and lend her a sweater.

"Sure."

Having opened the window in Nadia's absence, Ida was staring out at the fields of proverbial golden wheat and black earth, damp with mist and dimly lit by a sun still below the horizon, below the rows of plump deciduous trees that divided the farmland into its administrative units.

Ida sat and pulled off her shirt. Nadia went to shut the curtains.

"Leave it open," Ida told her. "Oh, preserve the Nation, the farmers might see me in my bra. I'm dying for air."

"Yes, alright."

"It smells like wet bread."

As she attended to her friend, Nadia imagined a poster: at dawn, the farmers hugging the cows and wheat sheaves as the stencilled train rolled across the landscape, Ida in its window, Ida gloomy upon waking, bloody-nosed Ida in a bra, Ida still underweight in the shoulders, the unyielding shoulders that could bear her weight aloft. Perhaps Lenin would be in first class with a witticism on his lips.

Ida kept staring past Nadia, out the window, as Nadia scrubbed away the crests of dark, crusted blood.

"Fields," Ida whispered with a minimum of movement, "are depressing."

"You want the curtains open, yes?"

"Yes."

"My great grandparents were all farmers," Nadia said.

"My great grandmother was a German from Switzerland, allegedly."

"I wonder how they all felt about the fields at our age."

"When I was seven (allegedly seven)," Ida continued, "I remember my first lucky break. They were deciding which of us to make into school kids and which to make into retards. The school kids went to the boarding school and the retards went someplace else. They gave me lots of hints where I'd be going. Then, up rose my hero: Manya—mawkish, spineless, obedient Manya.

"Manya hadn't been working at the orphanage long but the senior staff figured her out fast. Manya wanted to be the children's loving angel but she was incapable of refusing an instruction, so they made a game of having her deliver punishments. They had her lock me in the cold room for four days and she cried and cried but she did it. After that, I think she thought she owed me.

"Manya hauled me before a committee and she read a letter that was allegedly my mother's dying instructions for me. My great grandmother was allegedly a Red Cross nurse who came to the prisoner-of-war camps and stayed on to nurse the People after the Revolution. Manya told me to tell the committee, if I got an education, could I grow up to be a good and peace-loving and useful person like my great grandmother Ida, the namesake my mother chose for me?

"You can believe, at seven, I wept and begged and swore I could.

"The committee decided I was not quite a retard, I could go to the boarding school, and I could have my mother's letter. I thanked them all and swore the letter and the school would make me good.

"I'm sure they extracted some price for me from Manya—her obedience in administering ten other kids' bad luck."

Nadia asked, "Did the letter mention any other family?"

"No, a mother and great grandmother were all I got. My mother or Manya, as the case may be, was not a prolific writer."

"What happened to the letter?"

"I'm keeping it in the left cup, over my heart. I don't remember, do I?" Ida shrugged or maybe just flexed her shoulders. "If my Red Cross great-gramma was real, I wish she'd've stayed in Switzerland ... or at least gone back there to have her kid. She'd've had a choice, wouldn't she?"

"Which sweater do you want?"

"The blue." Ida accepted the pale blue sweater and pulled it over her head. Nadia restored a degree of symmetry to Ida's hair, which had grown back with roundness, enough to start covering the tops of her ears. "How do I look?"

"Like my beautiful friend."

"Hmm." Ida got up. "Time for us to split."

"You have Nastya's phone number?"

"Yes."

"And I have Rosya Lekht's phone number."

"Yes. When you're settled, when the time's right, we can all meet up. I can congratulate Nastya and meet her Lieutenant and hear about the ways they'll spoil their baby."

They parted with a hug and alternate cheek kisses. "I love you," Nadia said.

"Take care, Little Paw." Ida opened the door a crack, checked that the passage was empty, and scrammed.

Afterwards, Nadia realized that the bloody, striped shirt was still on Ida's bunk, along with the damp, bloody socks. Away they went to the bottom of Nadia's suitcase, where she hid them doubly by putting them inside her flattened satchel. While repacking, Nadia discovered an unexpected book tucked away amid the others: *Great Expectations*, with a slightly worn cover that had gone soft in the corners. Inside, Yuly had written a sort of blessing for her.

Not in a reading mood, Nadia tidied the sheets where Ida had been and then lay down again on her own bunk.

Tonight, we'll each sleep in a place we've never been.

A few hours later, the wet-bread smell of the wheat fields gave way to a smoggy Kiev morning in the Dnieper valley. The train began to sigh and groan into the station. A conductor knocked at the door, checked her ticket, and added, "Stay in your compartment. We will be delayed disembarking."

What's that about?

The train stopped and Nadia waited. Finally, there came a different knock. Nadia answered it to find a cop—a Private—raring to enter. Quite unlike Giorgi, this one was plump-cheeked, plump-breasted, fair, and not tall.

The Private squeezed into the compartment and said, "This is a search." She ran her hands over Nadia and then under all the bunks.

Oh, no, what is this nightmare?

Crouching, the Private pulled out the suitcase and snapped its latches open with her pink, painted nails. She lifted the lid, looked inside at the first layer—Nadia's books—and flicked through all the pages with her thumbnail.

She'll find the bloody shirt. We're for the Kirghiz, wives 4 and 5.
"Excuse me," said Nadia, "do you know Lieutenant Giorgi Licheli?"

The Private looked up. "Yes, he's here, on the platform."

"I'm his sister-in-law."

"Nadia, good morning." The Private shut and latched the case and sprang to her feet like a new toy. "I'm Fenya. The Lieutenant is training me."

"I'm sure he's full of praise."

Fenya stifled a burble. "That's the Lieutenant's way, certainly. He talks of your sister and mother like film stars."

What does that mean?

"I've met your sister," Fenya added. "She's kind. She told me we're not so different because we're the same age and we're learning from the same man."

"Thank you for sharing that, Fenya." Nadia stooped to take her suitcase in hand.

Fenya affirmed, "You may go. He's waiting for you."

Moments later, Nadia stepped out onto the platform. She recalled the first time she had transited Kiev, the night she had puked and met the tramp with the brass ring. This seemed as if it could have been just a few hours earlier, instead of two years and three seasons ago.

Then, Giorgi, looking pale in his black uniform, stood tall before her. He looked different than at Christmastime—heavier under the eyes and thinner around the mouth. She stepped within arm's length of him and stared up into his face. He ventured a faint smile and waited for a proffered hand or perhaps a hug. Getting neither, he patted her atop both shoulders. "Nadia," he said, "here we are, meeting for the first time as brother and little sister."

"Hi. How's life?"

"Normal," Giorgi asserted. "Nastya makes my 'normal' into joy."

"She works at that." *Whatever else has changed, we're still both too quick at this.*

Giorgi said, "I do hope your trip was restful. We heard a strange report from the Bryansk station … but never mind, you are here."

"Strange report?"

"I would not be surprised to find it was a prank by hooligans."

"Do you have to deal with that often?"

"More often than you might imagine, Nadia."

"I'm sorry to hear that. Your talents should be better spent."

"Normally, they are. Do you mind if we wait here for a few minutes?" Giorgi rolled his neck as he looked this way and that.

"I don't mind…" …*you giraffe in boots and starry epaulets and a ribboned hat to hide your horns.*

Fenya finished her sweep of the train and then she approached, entering the long shadow cast by Giorgi's shoulders in the midmorning light.

"Nothing, Lieutenant," Fenya reported.

The dormitory car was emptying now.

Giorgi nodded. He asked Nadia, "Have you met Agrafena Petrova?"

"Yes, Fenya and I just met."

Fenya asked, "Shall I drive you to your apartment, Lieutenant?"

"Yes. No, only Nadezhda Mikhailovna. I have somewhere else to be."

Nadia asked, "Is Nastya waiting at home?"

"Yes, she is feeling the first hardships of motherhood in the mornings."

"Oh, right."

"Fenya is becoming an excellent driver. Soon she'll be chasing the crooks all over Kiev—*bang, bang,*" Giorgi chuckled. He looked more exhausted than if he himself had just given birth. "You'll be safe with her, safe as if … safe as if you, too, were still in the womb. Ha."

"Lieutenant, can I get anything for your wife on the way?"

"No, no, it's Nadia she wants, post haste. I believe, next to motherhood, sisterhood must be the most beautiful of bonds."

"I have a brother," Fenya stated.

The mention of this brother seemed only too banal at the time. Nadia thanked Giorgi, followed Fenya, and scanned the platform in vain for a glimpse of Ida with Rosya Lekht. Most of all, though, Nadia felt sudden joy—a turn of luck, almost a glimmering expectation of triumph—that she was headed to see Nastya and that she and Nastya would be alone at their moment of reunion.

8: Renovations

Fenya had a sharp left turn and a lot to say about Kiev. She was especially voluble about the Kiev Arsenal Factory, where her father and brother worked. Her father, Pyotr, had engineered lenses for the Space Programme since its early days. Her brother, Marat, was a manager in Consumer Optics. Consumer products were sure to be the future of the enterprise—indeed, of the country. Had Nadia heard of Kiev photo cameras for professionals and serious amateurs? Kievs were the answer to Sweden's Hasselblad cameras, the ones the Apollo astronauts had used on the Moon. Last year, Marat had taken a summer course in photography in Gothenburg, where Hasselblad had its headquarters. The Swedish models, the women, had incredible clothes and bodies. Fenya had found the pictures and made Marat tell her all about those women, their lives. They were always in the sun, they drove and sailed just for fun, they sang anything by ABBA. The male models were good-looking too, really trim, but a lot of them were fags. You had to look hard to catch any of those in Kiev. The Arsenal Factory was serviced by the Arsenalna metro station, the deepest in the world.

"We have long summer days in Estonia, too," Nadia said as she eyed the apartment towers alongside the freeway and fingered the handle of her suitcase in her lap. "I guess it's like Sweden that way."

"Then Marat would love it. Are you artistic, like your sister?"

"No, not me."

"You should've let me put your suitcase in the back."

"No, I have handkerchiefs in here in case my nose runs."

"If you're sick, I can pick you up something for that."

"No, it's probably the wheat pollen. I suppose it blows in from the countryside and collects in the valley."

"I never thought of pollen doing that," Fenya admitted. "We get smog. I can close my window if you want."

"No…" …*please just drive.*

"We're almost there, anyway. You do look tired, Nadia. Maybe I should come up so I can help your sister and you."

"No, you have your duties."

"Well, I'd be letting the Lieutenant down if I didn't ask."

"Thank you for thinking of us, Fenya."

They were off the highway and cruising the folded streets between the towers and little parks. Fenya seemed a bit lost. After a few minutes, she pointed at a playground where metal mushrooms sprang from the sand. They had curly, white stalks and dented, red caps, starting to fade to pink. "Kids here will draw all their mushrooms like that," Fenya said. At this landmark, she turned and pulled up to a building much like the others.

My life is not going to be what I thought it would be, Nadia told herself matter-of-factly as she exited the cop car. The words caught her by surprise. Meanwhile, she had to assure Fenya that Fenya need not guide her from the curb to her sister's door.

Fenya drove away with a flutter of pink nails out the window.

Nadia pressed the proper buzzer, got a muffled greeting on the intercom, and rode up in a narrow elevator with faux wood panels.

Nastya greeted her sister with a crushing hug and kisses, as well as declarations by lamplight, for the entryway was lit by a pendant lamp with a rosy pink shroud of translucent plastic. ("Little Hedgehog, look at your eyes—so grown up, so pretty, so hungry for everything! You'll devour that suitcase of books in no time and then what'll we feed you?") At Nastya's invitation, Nadia sat on a stool to untie her shoes. "Go on." All this was followed by an announcement: "I've been saving some news since yesterday so you can be first to hear."

"It's twins," Nadia guessed.

"No! I've got my education back on track." (She had taken special leave to accompany Giorgi to Kiev.) "I've been accepted to the Kiev State Institute of Culture this fall."

"That sounds prestigious. What'll you learn; what'll you be?"

"I'm in the cultural-educational track. I'll be able to lead leisure programmes or design parks or curate a museum."

"Then you'll have Mama showing up at your work every day."

"She'll say she's checking it out for when you come."

"I might be there." Nadia kicked off her shoes and her train-musty socks. She cracked her toes. The parquet floor felt polished and well-swept underfoot. "You can give me the tour ... of here."

"Good, yes. We're making it home. Come see."

The entryway forked left and right around a wall-mounted coat rack, which was painted with dolls' faces to keep an eye on the entrants. Nadia followed Nastya left to a pair of bedrooms. The one nearer the entry, the guest room, was smaller with no window; it had probably been a closet. Most of it was filled by a narrow bed, which, however, was wider than a sofa or a train bunk and more tidily made up, in a rather formal blanket with pink flowers and dark leaves on a crimson background. Nadia left her suitcase in there. The larger bedroom had a window, a bed for two, and a pile of components for a crib. "Giorgi wants to build it," Nastya explained. "His family were once woodworkers, did you know?"

"No, he never said."

They moved on to the other fork, past the coat-rack dolls again. The bathroom was first on the right. The fixtures were of lichen green, the backsplashes were white tile, and the wallpaper was a pattern of snowflakes, forever falling as if on a frozen forest below. The tub was narrow but of full depth and it had a flexible hand shower. Everything was polished to a rare standard. Even the grout looked clean.

I shouldn't have chucked my socks on the floor, Nadia thought and she darted back to the entry to pocket them while Nastya was picking lint from the grate of a ventilation duct.

Next, the right fork led straight on to the kitchen. Here, the floor was brown tile set diagonally. The sink, backsplashes, and plaster were grey. The countertops were birch plywood with orange laminate and the cabinets were likewise painted orange. A window lit up the white rectangularity of a new Minsk-10 refrigerator and electric stove.

"I wanted the kitchen to be anything but green and white," Nastya said. "This is our most finished room. Well, it should be, we've spent a month on it—ourselves, every day for my part. People say, 'Why did you want to finish the kitchen first?' and I say, 'Because it's for me,' and Giorgi says, 'Because it's for her.'"

"Should you really be pushing yourself so much?" Nadia asked.

"Sure, it's good for me, it makes me happy. Anya comes by and helps. That's the Captain's wife. She's become a friend."

"What is she like?"

"Thoughtful. Calm. 'Measured' might be the word. She's in her thirties. She and he have been together a long time but they can't have children. He isn't well, especially now." Nastya took a clean, damp cloth from the sink and started wiping counters.

"What is Fenya like?"

"Fenya, the Private?" Nastya glanced out the window. "What should she be like?"

"I don't know. I was under the impression she comes around to help out too."

"Oh, she pops her head in on an errand from Giorgi, when he's out working odd hours."

That's an interesting pattern.

"Come on," said Nastya as she rinsed the cloth and placed it back in the sink, "more to see." With a damp grip, she took Nadia by the hand.

The last stop—the culmination of the tour—was the main room, off the left end of the right fork. Thus, it occupied the central-windowside position, between the left fork's master bedroom and the right fork's kitchen. One-third of the main room had originally been a balcony but the previous occupants had enclosed it.

There was open space in the middle of the room, maybe for standing and chitchatting with drinks in hand, maybe for dancing, *click-click-stomp, click-click-stamp* on the parquet. A boombox stood on a little cabinet against the wall. Nadia went over to play the tape already in it. Alla Pugacheva's mezzo-soprano voice overflowed the boombox with longing as she sang about an act of blowing it all on one romantic gift: "Million, million, / Million, scarlet roses…"

Nadia switched it over to FM radio, where students were being interviewed about summer plans: to join a collective farm on the steep banks of Lake Baikal; to spread goodwill to Mongolia as part of a construction brigade; and other picturesque joys of labour. She switched it off.

"This is a nice set, Nastya."

"I thought you'd think so." Nastya confided, "If you ask Giorgi nicely and promise to use headphones, he'll probably lend you some confiscated tapes. I'm sure Kiev has something more to your worldly taste."

Oh, so under the coat, he takes all genres. "Good to know."

There was a dining table for six, crammed into the corner of the enclosed balcony so that three of the chairs were unreachable. "When we have a party," Nastya explained, "we pull it out a bit and all squeeze in. Of course," she laughed a little, "we—Giorgi and I—we end up sitting with our backs to the concrete posts." With her nails, she rapped one of the former doorposts of the former balcony. She wore a wedding band of rose gold, with a mirror polish that begged to be shown on an enclosed balcony.

Nastya has long nails now—not much good for holding a needle or charcoal. Superior for picking lint.

The enclosed balcony extended past one of the former doorposts, all the way to a former windowpost. The space in-between was a nook with a rosy pink sofa facing a black-lacquered coffee table and a built-out window. A white bookshelf divided the nook from the dining area and its shelves housed an assortment of police manuals, nuclear engineering documents, sketchbooks, cultural-educational textbooks, and natural mementos of the Baltic, the Black Sea, and the Caucasus Mountains. On a midlevel shelf sat a carrot-coloured phone, identical to the one in the family room in Odessa. Nadia pointed to it.

"The direct line to Mama," Nastya said. "Well, Giorgi also uses it for his work. If he can't get away from the phone, he can at least answer it on the sofa and I can bring him coffee and he can look at my sketchbooks."

"When you're a curator," Nadia said, "you might have to keep the coffee away from the artwork."

"Oh, no one is more careful than Giorgi about things like that. He never leaves a spot on anything."

And yet you are with child. "Are you happy here?"

"We have fun…" Nastya rolled her eyes a little and added, "…a lot of fun." She ran to the washroom and threw up.

May I do that after you? "Oh, Wolfie, you're … barfing a lot, Giorgi says."

"He said that?" Nastya asked into the bowl.

"No, no, he said," (Nadia put on her *sotto voce* Georgian murmur as she held her sister's hair back), " 'She is suffering the first hardships of motherhood. Things do get very hard for mothers, also hard for fathers.' "

Nastya snorted and groaned. "Stop, you've made me puke through my nose."

" 'I cannot stop. Your pukes are roses.' "

"Guh-guh-guhluh." Pumped dry, Nastya sank back onto her haunches. With watery eyes and a drippy nose and a vomit-scented sigh, she stared up at her sister. "Gramma didn't change you."

"History will judge." Nadia flushed the pukes. "Want to go lie down? You look green … and white."

"I wouldn't mind lying down." Nadia helped her to the master bedroom as Nastya continued, "You could open the window here and in the kitchen and the two by the dining table and … unless you want to go unpack or take a bath first … get me a bottle of fizzy lemonade and a chocolate bar and a pomegranate. Get yourself anything you'd like."

For her own part, Nadia decided not to eat until later. She served her sister and closed her in. Then, Nadia got her satchel from the suitcase, took it to the bathroom, blasted the bloody shirt and socks with the hand shower, and left them to soak in the sink. She swept Ida's blood down the tub drain and, at last, ran herself a bath and lay in it for an hour.

As the water rose around her, Nadia noticed it was yellow. This was no trick of the light or the green tub; it came as pale yellow from the pipe and it pooled as bright yellow below. She lay in it all the same.

A little later, over lunch in the kitchen, Nastya remarked on the nice shirt that Nadia had hung out to dry on the towel rack by the radiator.

"Oh, it's not mine. I borrowed it."

"I thought it was a bit long for you." Nastya added a thick layer of horseradish to a ham-and-coleslaw sandwich. "You haven't picked up a sailor, have you?"

"Did Gramma tell you? Look, it's embarrassing, he can't apply for a flat. We're living on Gramma's sofa until his divorce comes through in Cuba. He's gone there now to make it final, he left me his shirt as a love token. We're just lucky that Gramma accepts us, it's true love."

"Oh, shut up. Keep your secrets if you like," Nastya said as she munched on burning horseradish. "Here, I got a transit map for you." (She produced it from a drawer.) "I thought you might want to go out this afternoon."

"Thanks. Shall we go somewhere together?"

"Not today. I have to check in with Anya. She may need me to cover for her this afternoon."

"Cover what?"

Nastya lowered her voice. "She runs a kind of service for families … ones who don't want to send their kids to the regular nurseries. The regular upbringers aren't great. You might not remember but I do, you crying when I walked you to nursery in the mornings. Anyway, Anya works at a nursery that exists on paper; in reality, it's just her taking kids in her home. She collects the regular salary as if she worked at a nursery, plus money changes hands privately, you get it? Now, with

Sergei (the Captain) being so ill, she tries to get away to be with him when she can, to go with him to his medical appointments or just bring him a home-cooked meal. They'll have a picnic in a park somewhere so he gets a break from his work. I cover for her."

"Does she pay you for it?" *Our mother made me ask.*

"Well, she contributes materials to our renovation. Nadia, I couldn't take money. Besides, it teaches me what my responsibilities will be and these kids are basically good, basically happy kids, they're from good families. They're just not as clever or cute as you were."

"Well, there's no substitute for love," Nadia said as she opened the map.

Nastya nodded and squinted out at the bright midday.

Nadia chewed a bite of her own sandwich and imagined the depths of the Kiev metro as she touched its lines on paper. She had never been in a subway. She had seldom even been in a basement—only when the school or the apartment block held a civil defence drill. "Where should I go?" she asked Nastya, in order to get a second opinion after Fenya's.

Nastya shrugged and kept looking out the window. Then, quite abruptly and matter-of-factly, she said, "Kiev is haunted, if you ask me. You're going to feel it wherever you go. The architecture in the city centre is as grand as anything, I suppose. There's the Monastery of the Caves, with the monks' relics and catacombs, if you want to see how the millennium started; if you want to see how it's been ending, there's the All-Union Lenin Museum with stuff from his life or, if you go the other direction, the Mother Motherland, she stands atop the Museum of the Great Patriotic War and it's a place of incalculable sorrow. Can you imagine a mother who has seen twenty million of her children die? She's past even knowing their names." Nastya's eyes shone; she appeared to be headed for a huge, morbid cry. She smothered it. "Well, I suppose we have a few memorials still in us but those are the two big new ones in the last five years."

"How long will that all take to see?"

"Oh, a full day even if you started early. Maybe today you should just go book-hunting. Some of the metro stations have a regular book market or library nearby, I've marked them. Then, on a Sunday, you can see what people sell in Frunze Park. You'll find more there but the prices are high, so it's a good place to trade." Nastya laughed a little and added, "We got my cultural textbooks there. Giorgi was out of uniform, of course, but we got a great price when he said, 'I must count my money,' and he reached into his pocket and took out his badge with everything else. Afterwards, I made him promise not to embarrass me like that again. He said he hadn't intended it."

"Book-hunting sounds perfect for me," Nadia said. "You leave it to me to curate your baby's collection because nobody will sell you anything good if you strong-arm them like that. Leave it. You'll feel more at home with your soul."

Nastya laughed a little more and sniffed back phlegm, perhaps tinged with puke, masked by horseradish.

"Anyway," said Nadia, "I want the job of reading bedtime stories. I suppose I have to learn Georgian to honour your baby's heritage."

"I suppose I do too. Now you've really got me worried."

They finished lunch and washed the dishes. Nadia went to get her satchel, along with money and books, *to read, perchance to trade.*

They rode the narrow elevator with the faux wood panels. *So many places,* Nadia reflected, *smell like melting grease.*

Outside, Nastya pointed Nadia in the direction of the bus stop and then they parted ways. Anya's building was not far so Nastya would walk. Nadia wished her a good afternoon with those kids of good families.

At the subway station, people were hustling to return late to work, after spending lunchtime in queues for the shops.

A fast escalator—so long and steep that it hid its ending—echoed with announcements as it carried Nadia down to cool, breezy halls adorned with columns, arches, chandeliers, and mosaics. Day-old rain-water wafted on the cold blasts of air. So did piss.

She wheezed. Everyone was wheezing, all in one's stride.

Aboard the car, a man in a suit stumbled from one handrail to the next and admonished his fellow passengers. That bag was overpacked and in the way. That boombox was a nuisance. A girl might at least comb and dry her hair.

A lad threw a fake punch at the back of the man's head for a laugh.

Nadia was relieved to get out of that clammy abyss, though the way back up seemed twice as long. The mugginess of the June day hit her when she got outside. There would be more rain to come, to be tracked on muddy shoes, to go stale in the depths again.

Across the street, there was a cultural centre with a library and a bookstore on the ground floor. Upstairs, it had a small cinema and small gallery and some kind of offices. She stood in the entry hall between the library, the bookstore, and the stairs. She studied a sign with a map of the place (as if a map could speak and tell her how to ascend to a career in those offices) and she glanced around, through glass doors, at the main desk in the library and the sales counter in the bookstore. There was a librarian, a middle-aged woman with rolled-up sleeves, big cheekbones, big hair, and an ever-drifting expression beneath her makeup, as if she were sucking lemons and roses, alternately. She had a disconnected phone beside her on the desk; its wire terminals hung in the open. Across the way, there was a sales clerk, a young man with a moustache, who periodically adjusted the strap of his wristwatch. He had scarcely any expression—perhaps just a touch of flusteredness. He had a phone on a shelf behind him.

There's fate, Nadia supposed, *and what a joke fate plays. Fate surely has a taste for the torrid as well as the absurd.*

She decided to enter the bookstore. Behind the glass, she met the familiar smell of a forest of paste and pages.

"Do you trade used books here?" Nadia asked at the counter.

"Yes," said the young man, choosing his words, "we do, on the usual terms. If you want to buy a book and you can't find it new, we might have it used but the price will be the same as if it were new. If you want to sell a book, we will take it on consignment and offer it for sale at the standard price, as if it were new; then, if it sells, we will take a ten percent commission and the ninety percent will go to you, but you have to come in to pick it up."

"Thank you, that's as I thought," Nadia said.

"Do you have a book to sell?"

"Perhaps not today. I am looking to buy a book for a child."

He nodded. "We do trade a lot of used books for children. I suppose they outgrow one and move on to another."

"Do you suppose husbands and wives do the same thing?"

"Perhaps." After a couple seconds of silence, he pointed and said, "The children's books are over there, near the back, some new, some used."

"Thank you."

She followed the directions to an area where the shelves were shorter and the musty smell seemed more childlike somehow.

Maybe here I look tall for once.

Nadia found a slightly battered early edition of *Uncle Styopa: Policeman*, with half-familiar verses and illustrations, featuring none other than Styopa, the colossal cop, the genial gendarme, whose giant stature was a boon to anyone in need of a three-metre hero. "He with a cockade on his hat, / He with an overcoat beneath a belt," he was the one who put a stop to the vandalistic rampage of a little hooligan in a toy store; then, Styopa fixed a traffic light too.

Nearby was the latest *Uncle Styopa* book (one Nadia had never seen), in which the massive man had retired to become a snappy dresser, a sporty guy, who clowned around by riding a donkey, yet he wore his naval medals over his tennis shirt and, happily, he was on hand to fish a kid out of the sea when a family's day of fun quite nearly went wrong.

Reckoning that Nastya's child would get enough of all that already, Nadia put the Uncles Styopa back on the shelf.

I'll never look tall.

Roaming, she came to a bin at the back of the store, where the smell was mustiest of all. She rummaged. Mostly, it was a mess of flaking paper, a desiccated bog of compacted, broken books that nobody would have bought at the obligatory full price, if at all. They included puzzle books, two hundred pages each, with all the answers filled in. There was a manual of playground games, with stains of tomato juice maybe. After she struck the local interest books about the lives of kids and youth on this or that collective farm, as told in their own words, with photos by somebody or other from Kiev or Kharkov, she was nearly ready to give up. Then, she discovered a children's edition of Pushkin poems, entitled *Mermaid, and Other Fairytales.* The cover was blue linen, faded but hard-wearing, and debossed in gold with a stylized mermaid. This spirit had a cascade of parallel curves for her three metres of hair, lank from the river water. Her eyelids and lips were open as mournful crescents; she wept triangular tears and bared triangular teeth. She had concentric circles for her boobs and nipples.

As Nadia saw things, mermaid boobs were a fair enough alternative to giant policemen, so she picked up the book and browsed its pages. They were populated with brightly coloured poster-paint illustrations, many of them full-page or double-page spreads bleeding to the edge, all setting in relief the passionate words of Pushkin. "Good," Nadia decided aloud. *This is good, Nastya's child can grow with this.*

She paid the young clerk for the book, he asked whether it was for her child, she said no, and then she wandered over to the library to sit and read. There was a big fan that cooled the readers, fluttered the pages, and circulated the sweatiness and mustiness.

Nadia set her satchel atop her table and spread out a few books including the newfound *Mermaid* and *Great Expectations*. She read the first three pages of the latter—an orphan visiting a graveyard in a marshland and meeting a hungry, menacing tramp. "And you know what wittles is?" She did not. She stopped to go fetch a copy of the *Oxford English Dictionary*.

The hours passed away as she made slow progress through this dialect and the materials, the happenings, the imaginings of a boy's life on the Kentish marshes, a boy turned upside down and shaken to see what might fall out.

While Nadia sat and read, a man with a book trolley clattered around the library, in and out of the stacks and the reading area. He was pulling items from the bookshelves and periodical racks by the fistful, each time leaving a hole in the delicate, musty continuum. Sometimes, he would get a piece of paper from his shirt pocket, lay it out on the trolley to study it, and cross things out with a pencil. At last, when his cart got heavy, he took a break, cleaned his glasses with a scrap of newsprint, and strolled over to read the titles of Nadia's books.

Behind the square glasses, he was a lean man of perhaps fifty, with wavy, grey hair, small ears, and a soft yet insistent voice.

"Mermaid," he muttered. "Did you just recently land?"

"I'm visiting Kiev," Nadia replied. "What do you do here?"

He grinned with a scant set of tarry teeth. "I make the place look pretty. Today, I'm taking out filthy old papers." He unfolded a newspaper and pushed it in front of her. "Look at this," he told her. "Tell me what you see in this picture."

"That'd be the May Day parade, here, this year."

"The caption tells you that. Tell me what you see, there…"

"If it's a puzzle, give me a minute."

"…or what you don't see."

"I see there's hardly anyone in the reviewing stands—no one presiding over the parade."

"That's right. Five days, five days after nuclear meltdown, the bastards didn't cancel the parade. They buggered off to save themselves—got chauffeured to the cottages, I bet—and left the rest of us no wiser, singing songs of gratitude in the streets because, just like in the olden days, our masters are so good. Look at that girl in the tunic with the flowers in her hair, that could be you, they'd have you walk through radiation just to get your smile on camera for the day." He twisted his face and looked as if he wanted to bite the newspaper. Instead, he folded it and slid it into Nadia's satchel. "Take it for yourself, Mermaid, a souvenir. I already have my copy."

"Thank you."

He was leaving with his cart, while the librarian was approaching with a frown. Nadia gave her a questioning look and the woman returned to her desk.

Soon after that, Nadia decided it was time to go. She got to the subway station at rush hour. Bags and baskets added to the crush, as people made a final attempt at shopping on the way home. A few old dears (early to rise, early to queue in their advancing years) had hoarded big loads of groceries in prams or else in sacks they practically had to drag. They roamed the halls and cars to offer this and that for sale. "Swindler!" a pockmarked man shouted at the back of one such woman. She just kept moving while humming an unrecognizable tune.

By the time the doors opened onto Nadia's final stop, she was resolved to attempt a breakout. She did manage to duck and weave her way ahead of many of the wayfarers while hugging her satchel to her chest. The bottom half of the escalator was empty. She decided to run up it until she reached the clump of people.

As she stepped off, into a junction where another onrush of mankind surged between escalators and underpasses, something made Nadia stop. Her blood was pounding from the dash and the noise. The arched halls echoed with babble and barter and footfalls, erratically, like a bubbling soup her mother might make, full of furiously-chopped chunks rising to the surface. "Nadezhda," the voice of the station seemed to say, a hollow call as if across deep water, the unbottled sigh of all worn-down and fed-up commuters going home—home to what?—perhaps to an object of yearning—a word, a meal, a bottle, a body—or else to the yearning on its own. "Nadezhda."

She looked around and saw it was her lofty brother-in-law, calling her name over everybody's head. She locked eyes with him and leaned against a pillar as he closed the distance. He held a mix of seven roses—two red, three peach, two pink, all double-wrapped in orange paper inside brown paper, tied with a slim, orange ribbon. "I bought these for Nastya," he burst out almost boyishly. "These grannies selling flowers, they know when and where to catch a man. They're at parks at lunchtime, stations in the evening, theatres at night, and hotels in the morning. Ha."

"You are *drôle*. Did you grab anything liquid too?"

He touched his face. "No, we do have a bottle of wine at home but Nastya is not drinking now."

"No, of course, that was silly of me."

"Nothing of the kind." They began to move along towards the surface. "We—you and I—can have a drink after dinner."

"Okay, thank you."

"Please, you must feel at home."

"You've got a nice flat, you've worked hard," Nadia told him.

"Nastya will renovate us to paradise." They were approaching the bus stop in a haze of golden rays and diesel, giving her a sense of cinematic conclusion to a disorienting day of transportation. As she imagined the epilogue (*Nadia became a devoted aunt, reading mermaid stories and absorbing radiation*), Giorgi went on, "People say, 'Why did you want to finish the kitchen first?' and I say, 'Because it's her plan. Don't try to boss an artist!' "

The bus ride stifled the conversation, such as it was. Giorgi appeared acutely conscious of a need to shelter the flowers, as well as his hat and head, from knocks and bumps and decapitation. He looked queasy by the time they got off. They passed the beaten-up mushroom sculptures. They rode in the grease-scented lift.

The light flickered, the elevator's motor growled, and Nadia's chest tightened.

The electricity stabilized, the lift kept moving, and Nadia exhaled.

At the door to the flat, Nastya greeted them with extravagant kisses, first on Giorgi's lips ("My hero") and then Nadia's lips likewise ("Little Hedgehog"). The coat-rack dolls, with simpering eyes and mouths, looked down on Nadia's mortification.

"Close your eyes," Giorgi told Nastya. She did so. (Nadia took this opportunity to sit on the stool and remove her shoes.) Giorgi placed a hand over Nastya's eyelids, produced the bouquet from behind his back, and pressed it into Nastya's outstretched hands. His face wrinkled a little around his eyes. "What do you think you have?"

"Would it be roses?"

"How many?"

"Would it be seven?"

"I can't surprise you anymore!"

Nastya giggled and then opened her eyes and shrieked a little as Giorgi spun her around.

Nadia, barefoot again, took her satchel and dirty socks into her room. She had decided to save the gift of the storybook for another time.

"What is this dress?" Giorgi was asking.

"I borrowed it from Anya. Do you like it, a bit more summery, do you think?"

"Yes, yes, orange is your colour. How thoughtful Anya is."

"She is, she is. Go on, get your boots off and put your slippers on. Go sit in your nook." *Clomp, clomp. Scuff, scuff, scuff.*

Nadia sat on the narrow bed, pressed her feet against the wall for exercise, and occupied herself with unsnarling her sweaty hair. Nastya walked up to the open doorway and said, "Supper won't be long."

"Good, I'll come help."

"Thanks." Nastya adjusted the orange dress around her hips and whispered to Nadia, "One of the little boys puked on mine."

"You should have puked on his teddy or something—a proportionate response."

"I don't think Anya would have approved."

"That's typical. These hard-dealers train us to be soft."

"You belong on the radio somewhere."

They went to the kitchen and finished getting dinner. They pan-fried some new potatoes and onions. From the oven, Nastya took a roasting pan that was filled corner-to-corner by a diamond-shaped flatfish covered in lemon slices. The skin was a mummified colour but, through the gills, one could glimpse moist, white flesh. "This is turbot, the best," Nastya said. "Some of Giorgi's friends in Odessa seized a Turkish fishing boat and they were kind enough to put a few on ice to send to us. This is the last … just when I was getting good at cooking them, too."

Nadia imagined the capture of the boatload of turbot—the latest escalation in a conflict that was, to her, less familiar than the Trojan War.

As a way to get dinner, it smacked of the thinking of Odysseus—perhaps Penelope too.

Nastya was chitchatting about provisions. "Giorgi likes me to get food from away, as much as we can. There isn't always a choice but it's hard to trust anything from around here, no matter how much testing is done. The meat and the milk and the mushrooms from the forest are supposed to absorb it the most. Would you get the fairytale plates from the top shelf in the far cupboard? Giorgi tells me not to climb on a stool."

Easy for him, Nadia thought. She brought down the black plates with painted scenes of warriors on horseback, wizards in flight, councillors whispering in ears of kings, maidens speaking with rabbits, and the like. She left behind an assortment of cartoon plates, architectural plates, Olympic plates, and floral plates. Nastya mentioned the names of people who had given her and Giorgi plates as wedding gifts.

As Nadia came out to set the table, Giorgi leaned over the back of the pink sofa to peek out from his alcove. A cloud of white smoke lingered over his head where his black hat had been. The hat, along with his jacket and belt, were discarded in a corner and he was in grey shirtsleeves with his tie loose, his collar unbuttoned, and dark stains under his arms. He puffed more smoke into the alcove and then asked Nadia, "Will you read us something after dinner?"

"Sure."

Nastya came out with a pair of wooden trivets. One was decorated around the rim with a ring of girl dolls, the other with a ring of boy dolls. She set them in the centre of the table as she said, "My love, smoking before dinner is so bad for your appetite. Put it out and go change your shirt."

"Don't on my account," Nadia said.

"No, Nastya is right. Excuse me." Giorgi butted out his cigarette in a brass ashtray on the coffee table. He got up, collected the bits of his uniform from the corner, and headed off towards the master bedroom. His slippers could be heard scuffing all the way, until he shut the door.

Nastya was adjusting the cutlery and plates to an ideal orientation. She asked her sister, "Would you open the window over there?"

"Okay." Nadia passed through the smoke, imagined it as Ida, and opened the window to let it out into the irradiated heights.

Nastya made two more trips to the kitchen to fetch the frying pan of potatoes (which went on the boy dolls' trivet) and the baking pan of turbot (for the girl dolls' trivet). She nodded. "Drinks."

"Sit, I'll get them."

"The white grape juice, I think," Nastya said. "Mix it half and half with the fizzy lemonade. There's a pitcher in the next cupboard over from the plates."

While acting on these instructions, Nadia noticed the bouquet of roses in a vase on the kitchen window sill. *Should I bring it too? Maybe Nastya thought the table would be too crowded. If I spill it, it's 'Next stop, Kirghizia' for me.* She did bring the vase and the pitcher to the table.

Nastya got up and moved the vase to the nearest window sill.

Just in time for dinner, Giorgi scuffed his way down the hall in a white shirt and white trousers. He had oiled his hair. "What a table, what a fish, what a pair of ladies!" he declared. He tuned in a classical music programme on the radio. Softly, it played the second movement of Shostakovich's *Piano Concerto No. 2*.

Giorgi took his seat as head of the family. Counterclockwise from him were Nastya, Nadia, and then the three empty chairs jammed against the concrete post and the windows.

Nadia began to serve herself as Giorgi did the same for Nastya. Nastya was watching them both and listening to the music—slow, wistful, heartfelt, vulnerable—with a slight smile and slight tears. "That is the sound of a father's love," she said.

"Do you think so, my love?" Giorgi asked.

"Oh, yes," she said, "he composed it for his son—his son my age," she added with a little laugh. "Think of that." She wiped her eyes and turned them downwards to the fish.

They ate a fine meal, one to remember. For dessert, there was a Kiev cake that Nastya had been hiding at the back of the fridge. She confessed that it was baked not by her but by the Karl Marx Confectionary Factory. They munched on the layers of cake and meringue, all coated in chocolate, hazelnuts, and floral frills of buttercream. They drank fizzy lemonade, now with purple grape juice. As their bellies filled, they chitchatted about the history of labour.

Nastya said, "Kiev cake was invented thirty years ago this December, by a girl also named Nadia, who was not much older than you."

"That is humbling," Nadia said around a melting mouthful.

Nastya continued, "She was the assistant to the factory's head biscuit chef, who had screwed up a huge order by forgetting to put the egg whites in the fridge the night before. She helped him cover it up by making a new recipe from everything else they had, which is how we got Kiev cake."

"If we'd all stuck to screwing up biscuits," Nadia said, "we wouldn't be where we are today."

Giorgi let out a single laugh, like a shout, and cake crumbs spattered from his mouth onto Nastya.

You're having the worst luck that way, Nadia thought as her sister picked the bits from the borrowed dress.

Nastya changed the topic somewhat. She wanted to do more baking. She would need more equipment for it. She also wanted a waffle iron.

The conversation died down as the music on the radio stopped and the announcer started uttering platitudes. Giorgi got up and turned it off. "There shall be silence until Nadia reads," said he.

Nadia went to her room, got *The Odyssey* (in translation) from her satchel, and searched for a passage she had in mind. She returned to the table and read it aloud. The heroes got hospitality—a bath and a feast—and then got asked whether they were "pirates, / sea-wolves raiding at will, who risk their lives / to plunder other men?" Giorgi declared that she had captured, in her ardent tone of questioning, the quandary of a man who has realized that he is risking all to aid a stranger. This dilemma seemed, to him, to be an enduring inheritance from ancient culture, with its rigid bonds of hospitality and honour. So much alike were Greeks and Georgians, said he.

There was chitchat about demographics. The town of Tsalka, in the southern region of plateaus and canyons where Giorgi was born, was said to be the only Greek town in the entire country. Notwithstanding, the Greeks of Tsalka spoke Turkish.

"We know a German who speaks no German," Nadia said.

Nastya, with her long nails, picked up the remains of a lemon slice from her fairytale plate. She sucked it and looked at her sister. Nadia said no more. Nastya added, "Yes, the Baltic Germans are quite assimilated."

Nadia bowed her head over the table and burst out laughing. "Quite assimilated!"

Nastya put down the tattered lemon slice and picked a bit of its flesh from her front teeth.

Giorgi said, "I believe I've missed a joke between sisters … but never mind. I enjoy your laughter all the same."

"Sweet Giorgi," Nastya murmured. She stood and started gathering plates. "I'm getting tired."

Giorgi was on his feet to volunteer, "We'll wash the dishes together. Nadia can lie down in the nook with her book. She also seems fatigued."

This arrangement suited everyone.

Sleepily, Nadia browsed the familiar pages of slaughter, enslavement, rape, and plunder, as well as actual affronts to the gods and the unending punishment of being kept from home until one is forgotten. Throughout it all, everybody remained keen on the giving and getting of this and that: a bath, a ritual feast of a barren heifer, a golden keepsake.

Does any of this make a difference? Nadia asked herself. *Does it make it any easier to know one's own heart, much less the heart of another?*

Out in the kitchen, Nastya asked, "Did you order the television today?"

"I ordered the television. I ordered the car. I ordered the baby's car too. Planning is crucial."

Nastya gave him a silly, abrupt laugh like a child ringing a bell. By the sound of it, her nasal passages were clear of puke. "You didn't really order a car?"

"There is nothing real about orders."

Things got quiet out there for a minute. The sloshing of dishwater stopped. The slippers scuffed around a bit on those diagonal tiles. Then, Nastya urged him, "Go to Nadia. Go on. Go on."

Giorgi re-entered the main room with a bottle of sweet Georgian red in one hand and a couple of glasses in the other. Nadia slid away from the bookshelf and sat up to make room for him beside her on the sofa. He sat and filled the glasses. He also conjured a couple of pieces of dark chocolate from his palm.

"To little sisters," he toasted a bit more casually than she might have expected.

"To family." She took a sip and a small bite of the hard but fast-melting chocolate.

They stared out the window at the towers and the dusk. Far below, the last buses were lumbering off to the depots and kids were being called in from the playgrounds. All of that was inaudible.

Nastya came to inform them that she was off to bed but Nadia and Giorgi should continue to have their quiet time together.

The glasses ran empty. Nadia poured herself another half and gestured that she could do the same for Giorgi.

"No, thank you, Nadia," Giorgi said as he shook himself out of muteness. "For several weeks, I've been setting limits for myself. I really must stay alert, with my new responsibilities."

"Lieutenanthood or fatherhood?"

"True wit. Ha. Both. I have never been a man who drinks alone but those nights in Odessa with your father, he likes to celebrate… Forgive me. I would like to explain myself quite differently."

"Why not go on as you started?"

He did not. He said, "Nastya and the job have made me think seriously about what is important, what is for the best."

"That sounds like bitter medicine."

"The medicine is, these days." He pressed the back of his head into the sofa's rosy pinkness, shut his eyes, and rested his legs on the coffee table. His slippered feet hung past the far side. "My boss, he's sick, his medicine is bitter, let's say that. The country is … sick. There is more anger than I have even seen. Way up here, you can't see it maybe but we can down there. We're only beginning to see what it is."

"Are you sick?"

"That is one of the mysteries. Ha."

"Are you likely to be…?" …*to be a sick man, a spiteful man, a most unpleasant man whose liver is diseased? I sincerely want to know.*

"No, I don't think so. I'm simply a tired man, Nadia. My nights on call are endurance training for … my nights on call."

"Get some sleep while you can, Giorgi."

"Yes. I should go to Nastya now." He stood up and tentatively took the bottle of wine.

"Yes, I'm done, thanks," Nadia told him. "I'll go to bed soon too."

"Goodnight, Nadia."

"Goodnight, Giorgi. Thanks for having me here."

"Nadezhda, you are the first and most important guest in this home." Giorgi bowed a little and then shuffled off in his slippers. Nadia heard him put the wine bottle in a cupboard, perhaps a high one. A few seconds later, he was entering Nastya's bedroom on the other side of the nook wall.

As the light declined, Nadia went over to the bookshelf and turned on a lamp—a fluted spire of acrylic glass with a little stainless steel rocket on top like a spearhead. The spire lit up pink. Nadia switched it off and on a few times as she shook with stifled laughter. Round the base was tied a card, illustrated with a scene of a waiving boy-cosmonaut and a docking pair of capsules. The handwritten message said, "The Workers of Yuzhmash give our salute to Heroes!"

Composing herself, she decided to browse Nastya's latest sketches. The sanatorium was there and Mama watching Papa feed a seagull and a rough sketch of a sporting, faceless figure, captioned "Sokolov". More recently, some of the cops and wives had driven to a cottage and gone for a swim in the waves of the wide Dnieper (it would seem). Tucked among these pages was an envelope containing a couple of photo prints. Black and white: a tall silhouette gazed down from a dock onto the sunlit face of a girl grinning up at him; she was wheeling her arms in a blur. "The joyful father- and mother-to-be," read the caption on the back. Colour: The same girl—a brunette with a ring of gold—was scrambling onto a wooden raft; so was another girl—a blonde with pink nails. "A race."

From there, the pages were blank.

Perusing the rest of the book collection, Nadia went into a trance and, around midnight, found herself falling forwards off the sofa with half-dreamt principles of nuclear engineering and park design floating in her head. She tidied up, turned off the lamp, got a pair of hot socks and a hot flannel shirt from the rack by the bathroom radiator, and withdrew to her narrow bower.

The June night hung heavily, the walls were thin, and Nadia lay awake in the unfamiliar bed, which seemed too still compared to the train.

There was soft conversation. Probably it contained passages of great formality. Nastya giggled at something but did not snort.

There was silence, except for a hum that Nadia eventually identified as the refrigerator.

Nadia got up and crept to the kitchen for another piece of chocolate and a cup of milk. (She found only condensed milk, old stock, in a cupboard of canned goods beside a well-sharpened can opener with a distinctive handle: real rosebuds, pink and yellow with little green leaves, entombed in acrylic glass. She diluted the milky syrup with spring water from Georgia.) With her snack, she went to sit on the sofa in the nook once more. This time, she left the light off. The Moon loomed large between two of the towers across the way. By its light, the rosy sofa and carrot phone took on oddly chilly tones.

As Nadia savoured the melty chocolate and dabbled her fingertips in the milk and conjured a memory of Cherny, rain began to cloud the window.

Haunting a sofa seems strange without Ida. Nadia looked at the phone. She had Rosya Lekht's number memorized. She picked up the receiver but then caught herself and put it down again. *What ever are you thinking, Nadia? You've never spoken with Rosya Lekht and here you are, about to make your first impression by ringing her in the middle of the night. "Hello, I'm Ida's sleepless friend." That will really endear Ida to her host.*

Nadia crunched the last of the chocolate, drank up, and lingered by the window awhile before going to wash out her glass. She staggered off to bed and slept with one foot uncovered as the rain poured harder and harder.

9: Wolf-storm

Cherny was away. Cherny had gone to Odessa to slum it with cats who were friends of her caregiver's son.

Honour hath no skill in surgery. Neither hath my father. Nadia was roaming the moonlit piers and boardwalks in search of Cherny among all these poor and doctorless animals.

"Best boxer in the school," countered Grandpa Lev, who happened to be there, reading a newspaper and smoking a cigarette rather than helping *per se* in the search for his daughter's mother-in-law's missing cat.

Lightning struck the mast of an aircraft carrier at sea and it silhouetted a chubby fighter plane, a Yak-38, hovering wobblily over the deck.

A howling wolf of a storm it was, too. A wolf-storm, *ein Wolfssturm*, could be a German word. Who would be a cat or a pilot on such a wolf-storm-night, *so eine Wolfssturmnacht*?

The Yak-38's jet engines kicked the air with a droning roar as if Hell yawned. Then, it shot off into the flashing heights.

There was also sound and motion from another single-man craft, this one down in the water. A little rowboat, fit only for a sleepy river, was struggling against the storm surges. The rower was Grandpa Pasha, in his mariner's cap.

He called for help; he called for Nadia by name.

The boat capsized and Granda Pasha, shouting and sputtering in Estonian, fought to hold onto it as a raft.

One by one, helicopters rose from the carrier's deck and went buzzing over the sea. They swung their searchlights madly in every direction except the right one and Grandpa Pasha, for all his thrashing and gasping, remained invisible and inaudible to the searchers above.

"He's over there, over there, you fuckwits!" Nadia tried to holler at the pilots but she managed only a stifled whisper. She began to cry and pound her hands and wrists against the barnacled iron rail. They bruised and bled.

Grandpa Lev approached her and tried to hug and comfort her. They pressed against each other with a rustling of pages, as if he were a bookcover closing on her. "Don't worry, child, it's in the newspaper, they've rehabilitated him. Everything will be alright."

"He'll drown!"

"I'm not sure I understand you. Why don't we go the theatre? You'll enjoy that. You oughtn't be out on a rough night in a rough place like this."

A caterwaul rose from the rocks in answer to Grandpa Pasha's screams.

"Cherny?"

"They've rehabilitated her…"

"*Elle se noierait;* she would drown," said another man in the tone of a young tutor reciting conjugations for the benefit of his juniors.

"Johnny?"

Grandpa Lev grabbed her bleeding wrists. "Stop this!" he commanded. "We have to leave these men to their work! The search is being led by Sokolov. Now, come with me to your mother. You have to dress for the theatre."

He dragged her off towards the changing rooms overlooking the beach. Her mother was waiting outside the many doors with an outfit for Nadia to wear: a fiery orange ball gown, masterfully recut from a flight suit.

"You're hurting me! Why are you doing this?" Nadia sobbed.

Lightning struck; it leapt from a cliffside railing to the metal roof of the changing rooms and showered down on the balustrades of the piers. The doors behind her mother flashed like kindling as the ball gown took flight in a blast of flames and ash. Thunder and helicopter rotors drowned all cries of life.

10: Beautiful Can Opener

Nadia woke just as Giorgi was headed out the door in the morning. She and Nastya had breakfast together. Nastya was concerned that her little sister might have had a nightmare during the storm. "Giorgi says it's better not to wake a person from a nightmare; it'll be forgotten if it's left."

"I'm fine," Nadia laughed. "Maybe the Lieutenant is right."

"You got yourself some milk," Nastya observed. She took the remainder of the can out of the fridge to put in their coffee.

"Yes, at some point, I did. That's a unique can opener you have."

"Oh, yes," Nastya said, "it was another wedding gift."

"Who gave it to you?"

"One of Giorgi's informants." Nastya sipped her sweetened, thickened coffee and shrugged and added, "He told us, he used to make beautiful can openers in prison to pass the time. He wanted us to have his best piece."

"There's no topping that."

"Yes, no, there isn't. He was so gracious. Avel," she murmured his name.

"Well," sighed Nadia through the heat the coffee left on her tongue, "what do we do today?"

Nastya ran to throw up.

11: Sand Without Sea

On a walk to the playground, Nadia took stock of the summers of her life. There had been sixteen. Now, this seventeenth was starting quite unlike the others. For one thing, she was far from any sea.

She kicked sand into a metal mushroom and listened to the burst of hollow little sounds. On this walk, there was no one but her to hear.

She thought of Ida and salt and Baltic pines.

She wondered whether Nastya and Giorgi had promised each other to be "just happy, just us" as a Lieutenant, a student, and a foetus sharing an apartment in Kiev in a time of fitful renovations and constant radiation.

She wondered at their cinematics—happy sex and roses, enlivened by comic differences to resolve. Nadia scarcely thought Mama and Papa had imparted such expectations of marriage.

She sat on a bench, scooped up a handful of clammy sand, and pelted another mushroom, to the same effect.

She had gone out for a brief, self-imposed exile because she felt she was wearing out the humour of her Georgian voice.

Now, as for the start of this seventeenth summer, it was no start at all. Others her age (some of them) were getting jobs, becoming prodigies of the industrial pastry oven, volunteering in Mongolia, advancing in the ranks of the cadets, or hooking up.

Maybe Ida wants to look for work together. Maybe Ida wants to go out dancing. That seems like a thing to do in Kiev, with her jeans and all.

She wanted to write poetry. Dreams affected her that way. Perhaps she could even get ahold of a typewriter and sell poetic pamphlets for money.

She had to write to Gramma. She had to call Mama. Should she mail a poem to Gramma and recite it to Mama over the line, from phone of carrot orange to phone of carrot orange? *The dream had best stay out of it—or is at least one of them disposed to hear my nightmare?*

How long should she wait before calling Ida? A summer's day seemed long without Ida as an audience, Ida as a co-conspirator, Ida as a knife-edge, Ida as a wisp of bluish smoke.

Maybe Nastya would like to get out for a cultural excursion or to find someplace where she could sketch and Nadia could write. Nadia felt a new responsibility to get her sister away from the centre-stage of lint-picking, rose-arrangement, and recurring pukes.

She rubbed the sand from her hands and walked back to the apartment.

12: Serious Typist

Yes, Nastya did know where her sister might find a typewriter. Giorgi's was in a box on the bottom shelf in his nook.

"I can't think that Giorgi would mind," Nastya reflected. "He's always asking what you write."

"Is he? What do you tell him…?" …*this inquisitive soul, this patron of our arts and letters?*

"Not much."

"Can't he wheedle answers out of you in pillow talk?"

"No," said Nastya as she knelt and brought the black leather box up onto the black lacquered table. For a moment, she looked as if she might puke again.

"Sorry," said Nadia from the sofa, "is that heavy?"

"For a typewriter, not very. You know, when a person tells me something in confidence—whether it's you or Giorgi … or a friend, let's say—I try to be worthy of that trust. I try to keep that person's secret, even if I get only trouble for it, because that is who I am."

"Okay. Sorry."

"How does this fucking thing open?" Nastya wanted to know.

"I think you have it upside down; you want to lift the big half of the box. The little half is cradling the machine like a tray. … The latches might both swing counterclockwise."

"You do it."

Nadia took the box and opened it to reveal the sturdy device in its all-important handsomeness: the gentle bell-curve of the white frame, the black keys like little saddles for fingers, the soft bed of red felt. The top of the box had a pleated red pocket containing a spare ribbon in a blue cardboard package and an instruction booklet made of coarse paper.

"The Lieutenant must be a serious typist."

"Yes, plenty of nights, I hear him at it past midnight and then he starts again at dawn. I'd get more sleep on a farm."

Nadia gestured over the keys and whispered, "What wakeful watchman, fingers flying, sits on sofa, rocket lamp aglow?"

"I can tell you're off to a start." Nastya passed Nadia some paper from the shelf and then got up to go.

"Actually," said Nadia when her sister was halfway to the kitchen, "I was wondering whether you wanted to get out today, maybe do some sketches."

"Where?" asked Nastya as she continued into the kitchen.

"What about those places you mentioned, the Monastery or the Mother Motherland?"

"Come out into the kitchen, we'll talk here."

Nadia parcelled the typewriter back into its box. *Let it sleep; it's unused to daylight.* She went to the kitchen to find Nastya shuffling the plates and wiping the cupboard shelves.

Nastya was saying, "The views are good from the Pechersk Hills, it's a good idea, I just don't know about today. We'd be starting late and the weather is supposed to be shitty all afternoon."

"Well, if it starts to rain, we can go indoors, maybe get tea somewhere."

"No, everyone else will have the same idea. There's nothing so miserable as being stuck in the centre of Kiev in a storm."

"I'd be up for the experience."

"Would you get up on the stool and do the high ones?"

"Only if you promise we'll go tomorrow."

"Fine, we'll leave just after Giorgi in the morning. You must try to get an early sleep. I think Gramma hasn't been making you sleep properly."

"Well, it's not been easy. I've been sharing the sofa with a friend."

"Oh, you and your sailor, of course." Nastya shook her head as she gazed up at Nadia on the stool. "I don't know who is the gold medallist for excuses, Giorgi or you. He should thank you for preparing me for life with an insomniac."

Nadia had little to say after that.

13: Private Line

Her second outing to the library turned into a trudge in the rain. There was a queue at one bus stop, so she decided to walk to another. Her books were safe, since she always kept her satchel waterproofed with a good amount of oil and wax.

The library's custodian (the one with the tarry teeth) made a remark: had she been swimming far? She found out his name was Yuri. The librarian came looking for him and he told her, he was just about to connect her telephone; he had brought the screwdriver and pliers that day.

Nadia spent a long time working on the dialect. She got home late for supper (but Nastya had kept a portion hot in the oven) and she finished off the evening with another bath in discoloured water.

After that, she was sufficiently worn out to try to get an early sleep, as prescribed.

She lay in dreamless darkness. She believed she was tallying columns of words in her head as if they were figures in Gramma's cashbook. The nonsensical work had a captivating quality that competed with lust.

A bell rang.

There was a muffled voice, a scuffle of some kind, and then an insistent knocking accompanied by the same voice but clearer. "Nadezhda, Nadia, someone is calling for you."

"Oh, I'm awake." She scrambled. She answered the door in her pyjamas.

"Did you hear, someone is calling for you?" asked a tall man in a dressing gown with wide cuffs and huge lapels. This robe had a dazzling pattern, like chunks of red and blue wax melted onto icy white wax.

Nastya would have chosen that. "Yes, I heard." Dizzy from getting up, Nadia had to hold the doorframe for a moment. Giorgi steadied her elbow.

Nastya was coming out of her bedroom and adjusting the precarious shoulder straps of her black lace slip. Her brow was creased like rose bark as she asked, "Is it Mama?"

"No, it's not Yekaterina," Giorgi replied; "it's a younger lady, perhaps even a boy; no, a younger lady."

Nadia realized that he was reading her face as he spoke. "Well, alright," she said, "let me go answer it." He let her slip past.

"Who can it be?" Nastya wondered aloud as she followed her sister past the coat-rack dolls. "Not Gramma?"

"No, a younger lady," Giorgi repeated over her shoulder.

Nadia hastened to get around the corners and the furnishings. Giorgi flipped on more lights in the main room.

"Giorgi, no," Nastya protested, "I'm in my nightie!"

"So am I."

"People will see. All it takes is a pair of binoculars..."

Nadia stood by the coffee table and answered the phone as a contest ensued; the lights went off and then on again and off. Phantom colour swatches swam inside her eyes. She sighed and said, "Kremlin on the wire."

Ida's voice was there but she sounded puzzled and far from the phone. A whirring sound covered her up as she said something like,

"What happens now?"

"Ida, hello, are you alright?"

A second later, Ida came across clearly: "I'm here, I'm great. I decided to call you so you wouldn't have to wonder about calling me. I think I left a grim impression on the train that morning."

"Did you? That morning long ago?"

"Hmm-hmm, long, long ago," Ida concurred. "I've been… Rosya, is that clock right? … Time flies. I've been doing some typing for Rosya."

"Typing?"

"Sure, typing."

The lights were still off. Nastya and Giorgi had taken seats on the sofa. They had become quiet and self-contained, like two strangers in an audience as the curtain rises.

Nadia changed her line of enquiry. "What are you doing tomorrow?"

"Hmm, hold the line. … Rosya, do you need me tomorrow? … Sure? … Nadia, I'm free tomorrow."

"Nastya and I are going to the Mother Motherland first thing."

"Okay, good landmark. Shall I meet you there?"

"Yes, whenever you're up, I'm sure you'll still find us there. Nastya was going to do some sketching on the steps."

"Nudes, will it be?" Ida enquired. "Hmm, hold the line. … My friend's sister is an artist. I'm just hearing about her sketches of her husband."

Nadia's heart pounded as she studied her hosts, side-by-side on the sofa, for any sign that they could hear Ida's words.

"Okay," Ida broke off the exchange, "I'll stop kicking and let you sleep. *Her chance to dream,*" she added in speech like English porridge.

"Okay, we'll see you tomorrow."

"Well, let's try."

Ida and then Nadia set down the receiver.

Giorgi asked, "Who is Ida, someone you both know?"

Nastya shrugged. While sitting and waiting, she had picked up the empty brass ashtray to cradle it in both hands. She was rubbing the rim with her thumb-tips to give it a sheen even by moonlight.

Nadia said, "Ida is the German who speaks no German."

"She is 'quite assimilated'. Ha." Giorgi rubbed his wife's back. She looked numb. "Come, my love, you should be in bed."

Nastya stayed put. She was clawing at the pattern inside the ashtray to remove some gunk. She asked, "How long has Ida been in Kiev?"

"She came down on the same train as me. She got her ticket as a gift too. She's being taken in by a woman named Rosya Lekht."

"Well…" Nastya breathed. She put the ashtray back in its place and sniffed the brass and ash on her fingers. Then, she again adjusted her shoulder straps, which had started slipping during the back rub. "Well, it does sound like a turn of fate for Ida. I suppose, then, you told her about my new life too."

"Yes, she wanted to congratulate you on the baby and everything."

"She could have done that on the phone just now. I'm surprised, it's not like her to miss the nearest way."

Nadia shrugged. "I guess she got distracted."

"Right." Nastya got up. "Come on, then, let's all sleep, unless the baby and I the only ones who are still supposed to do that."

Giorgi yawned. He nodded at Nadia and followed Nastya out.

Nadia stayed by the phone for a minute, as if she expected it to ring for a second round, perhaps more private than the first. The towers across the way were mostly dark. Perhaps the residents slept as Nastya would have it; perhaps they watched with binoculars as she would have it not.

Persistent watchers might have seen the light of the refrigerator as Nadia gave up and went for the last slice of Kiev cake.

14: Underestimated People

Mother Motherland was up all night—and still up in the morning—and the Eternal Flame still burned on the neighbouring hill in her high corner of the Pechersk Landscape Park.

The hills (hers and others) formed a lumpy ridge, rising out of a wooded stretch along the right bank of the Dnieper. Bridges, skyscrapers, smokestacks, and the golden domes of the Monastery complex all lay in the hemisphere before her eyes of stainless steel. She held aloft her shield and sword as if they were two banner poles of the sky. Up there, the shield displayed the hammer and sickle and wheat wreath and globe and star. The sword-tip was the second-highest point in Kiev, after the Monastery's cross.

More than twenty storeys below her, her littlest children, the living, walked amidst her bigger children in bronze, her heroic dead, for hers was the suffering of the millions, hers the Liberation, hers the work and food and Cosmos, hers the belief, hers the blood and bones all clad in steel.

As the sisters entered the park, they found themselves wading deeper and deeper into a current of sombre music—a men's ensemble singing the State Anthem. At first, Nadia wondered which hill might be hiding the chorus but then she realized it was a recording. Nastya's and Nadia's guts trembled as they passed through a perimeter of loudspeakers.

"I wonder whether the baby can hear that," Nadia said.

("To labour and heroic deeds he inspired us!" the chorus sang of Lenin.)

"Not yet," Nastya replied. "Hearing is still more than a month away."

"Then you aren't carrying a listening device. Nobody has planted one on you."

"No, Little Hedgehog, we can speak freely."

"When Ida gets here, I'll check her for a wire too. If she's clean, we can go on speaking freely."

"Yes, Little Hedgehog, I'll try with Ida too. Now pay attention. You'll want to tell Gramma all about the monuments in your letter."

The avenue led them down towards a wide tunnel, running through a hill. Atop the hill and a bit to the side of the tunnel, the Eternal Flame was burning gas in a structure like a funnel or an upturned satellite dish. Beside the tunnel's mouth, a concrete bulwark bore a jagged, debossed image of a star.

"All this is the Alley of the Hero Cities," Nastya said. "First, this sculptural gallery depicts the Heroes of the Front and Rear."

They entered the tunnel, which was sunlit through jagged openings in the concrete and the hilltop, and they walked at the base of a bronze frieze. Standing no higher than the bronze soldiers' knees, the sisters gazed up at a mass of rumpled uniforms, clenched jaws, and clenched fists brandishing guns and hand grenades. The grenades were the old kind with a stick handle, like a baby rattle or a stage microphone. One solider was kneeling with a light machine gun braced on his thigh. He appeared to be the People's favourite to touch, for he was getting a good shine on his gun's muzzle and magazine, as well as his outstretched trigger finger and the brim of his cap.

Like other visitors, they moved silently from one figure to another and then one frieze to another. There were partisans, including a kneeling woman in a heavy, rustic dress with a submachine gun at her side. There were friezes of the civilians too. Some of the tall statues were robust workers wielding tools of metallurgy or farming; others were gaunt survivors, raising their fists and grief-stricken faces in defiance of an enemy who could do no more than his worst.

"We're an underestimated people," Nastya stated.

"Are we?" Nadia whispered.

Nastya nodded. She extended her hand towards a statue of a woman standing apart from all others. "She is a mother who has lost her children."

"Did you want to stop to sketch anything?"

"No, further along."

They emerged into a parade ground. To their right was a reflecting pool, arranged around two more clusters of bronze statues. Nastya identified this as the Forced Crossing of the Dnieper. For the moment, it did not catch much of Nadia's gaze because Motherland stood behind it, atop the final rise in the ridge. Stairs led up to one terrace in her hilltop and then another, stopping at the base of her hollow pedestal, where windows looked onto other windows looking onto the vacant sky, all framed in thick slices of concrete, supporting yet more concrete, soaring twice as high again as the earthen terraces before reaching the hem of her gleaming robe. The sunlight, diffused and tinted orange by the morning haze, worked a strange alteration on the coldness and hardness of her folds of stainless steel. Her face seemed stage-lit and her performance as history's most experienced stoic was an enthralling sight from the orchestra seats.

Beside the stairs, the Museum entrance was built into the slope like a bunker's mouth, albeit a large one with glass doors.

A pair of modern tanks, a T-62 and a T-80, were parked at the eastern edge of the parade ground, opposite the Museum entrance. They were painted in bright, floral patterns instead of camouflage. Their gun barrels were raised so as to touch each other in the form of a backlit X. Behind them, nothing was in sight but the sky and the tops of trees that were rooted somewhere downhill.

The sisters headed for the stairs. Nastya pointed out bunches of cut, red tulips lying on marble slabs at the base of the slope—thirteen slabs for the thirteen famous Hero Cities, plus another slab with the inscription, "Glory to the Hero Cities". She said there were flower gardens downhill, past the tanks, and the cuttings would be fresh from there.

The smell of so many tulips got to the back of Nadia's throat—or perhaps the mere idea of them got to the back of her mind—and she felt her face break out in a sweat despite the mildness of the morning. She rubbed her eyes.

"Does it distress you?" Nastya asked.

"Well, about as much as it would," Nadia replied as they climbed the steps. "I feel as if I'm shrinking..." ...*like Alice in Wonderland.*

"Yes, it makes one feel the magnitude of the sacrifices."

"Yes." *The "Drink Me" potion was supposed to taste like cherry tart, custard, pineapple, roast turkey, toffee, and hot buttered toast. Maybe I'm allergic to tulips. England, Holland, teatime, flowers.*

They got to the second terrace and turned to face the way they had come. Nadia asked, "Is this a good place for you to draw?"

"Yes, where better? Think of the young soldiers who crossed the breadth of that river, some of them only on makeshift barges, under artillery fire and aerial bombardment, to face the invader entrenched with rockets and machine guns on hills like these, to liberate the survivors of Kiev and begin the victorious pursuit across the plains behind us. I've seen photos of nurses, too, who made the river crossing to treat the wounded as they kept landing under fire. Come on, let's sit." With tearful eyes but steady hands, Nastya put down her satchel and began to lay out her materials on a short wall that overlooked the slope.

Nadia reached into her own satchel to take out a slim notebook with a red cover of imitation leather. Giorgi had given it to her that morning, from his plentiful stock; he picked up a notebook anytime one was on offer. This one, according to a block of gilded text that sat fatly amidst the red, had come from the offices of the Lottery Commission several years ago. ("When you look at this," Giorgi had told her, "remember, there is no luck. Ha.") The gilt was beginning to fade to grimy black. The inside of the front cover had a notepad with a perforated edge for occasions when one intended to rip out one's words. Beside it, a ballpoint pen was clipped to a slack part of the spine. The rest was a proper notebook with bound pages.

"Are you making notes for your letter?" Nastya asked.

"Yes," said Nadia. On the notepad, she scrawled, "Drink Me / Painting the Roses Red".

For a while, Nastya sketched the northerly view and Nadia wrote in the notebook. After filling a page, Nadia began to feel that the notebook, by fate, had always been hers, never a random castoff from the Lottery Commission or Giorgi. This was how she came to feel whenever she formed an attachment to a secondhand book.

A breeze picked up from the river; it swept through the treetops and across the parade ground. Near the tunnel, a colourful pattern danced in the breeze and caught Nadia's eye. There was Ida, wearing her new plaid shirt of red, black, and yellow. She had left it unbuttoned at the cuffs and around her neck and waist, so it billowed a bit as she stretched with upturned palms to adore the breeze. Her army bag hung from one shoulder. She tossed it aside at the eastern edge of the parade ground, at the foot of another short wall. Then, she charged the tanks, leapt, slapped their gun barrels, and landed on her knees and hands with a roar of laughter and possibly also pain.

People stared. Nastya raised her pencil and clutched it like a talisman as she swung her head towards the startling cry. She squinted. She had not seen Ida nor a cloudberry nor a Baltic pine in almost three years. She had mislaid the memory of screaming cold swims in May or September. She knew nothing of the Ruby Palace; she knew practically nothing of the prison where Avel had made the beautiful can opener. She had not expected Ida to look anything like Avel nor like a feral cat, yet still be alive—lean, shorthaired, and springing, a knockabout clown as always but now in costly clothes.

Still laughing, Ida got up and staggered to the eastern wall to retrieve her backpack. People backed away. She walked a straight path to the stairs, started to climb, but then went down again to look at the tulips on the Hero City slab for Moscow. She picked one up, twirled it, smelt it, and held it against her shirt to see how its centre matched the squares of red, black, and yellow. Finally, she laid it down with the others and attempted to adjust a petal that was coming loose; it broke; she walked away. She fidgeted with the pockets of her jeans and the buttons of her shirt.

Ida ascended to the first terrace, ascended to the second, looked at the sisters, looked up at Motherland, and murmured, "Well... Hmm."

"Why were you laughing?" Nastya asked.

"Hmm, for joy," Ida answered. She grinned, raised her scuffed hands and scarred wrists, crossed her index fingers, and rubbed them against each other with vigour. "Those two tanks look so happy."

Nastya reworked a line in her sketch.

"They've had a long war," Nadia said.

"A long, hard war," Ida agreed. "I'm glad they're free and far from Narva. Hmm-hmm, I should be congratulating Nastya. Come on, Princess, give me a hug. Good for you. Lucky man, lucky baby."

Nastya set aside her sketchbook, got up, touched Ida's shoulders, kissed the air beside her cheeks, looked into her eyes, nodded, thanked her, and sat down again.

Nadia got up next, raised her arms to put them around Ida's neck, and held her cheek-to-cheek as Ida bowed. "Hi again," Nadia said.

"Hi." Ida made an effort to shake or lift or spin Nadia. "Shall we dance?" She answered her own question in the negative: "No, let's not, I've fucked up my back and shoulders."

"You outdid yourself on the train."

"I won't boast."

Nadia let go and announced, "She isn't wearing a wire."

Ida laughed some more. Her face stretched and her eyes looked bright, cool, and constricted, showing a wider ring of blue.

Nastya had flipped to a blank page, where she drew a rough sketch of these two figures. Then, she flipped back through some of her previous work as Ida and Nadia came over. The presentation lingered at the image of a detective smoking on a sofa, with his jacket and stars draped over the back.

"Giorgi, Giorgi, Lieutenant Giorgi Licheli," Ida invoked the man's name, as if he might be coaxed off the page the way a cat is (or is not) coaxed from a secret hiding place. "Nadia told me you'd found your love. Last night, you know, I spoke with him on the phone. He's got a voice... I would say... strong and calm. Your baby can feel safe when Giorgi sings a lullaby. As for how you feel and what he sings to you, well, that, only you would know."

Nastya flipped back to her current landscape. Her eyes glinted and she seemed to search for things that lay beyond the Dnieper Bend, more distant than the hills and crosses, more distant still than the Sun. "He said you sounded friendly," she reported.

"Did he?"

" 'Like a goodnatured person' were his precise words."

"Could he put that on official letterhead?"

Nastya snorted just a little. "Come on, sit between us," she said.

They all sat together, crosslegged, on the short wall.

"Ida is better dressed for this," Nastya said as she adjusted her skirt over her leggings. She settled her sketchbook in her lap to draw again. Then, she added, "It's nice to see you're indulging in clothes."

"Hmm," was Ida's reply. She flexed her chin in a sort of smile.

"You're in German colours," Nastya added.

"Not by design," Ida said. She looked at Nadia. "Have you seen my shirt?"

"Oh…" Nadia began with a nod.

Nastya interrupted, "Perhaps you'll find your love in Kiev."

"Hmm? No, I don't out hold much hope, in Kiev it's all…"

"…it's all about work," Nadia finished. "Ida is here to have her pick of the jobs."

"Plenty of work in the fields," Nastya supposed.

Ida made a face and rubbed the back of her neck. "I was hoping for work in the City," she said. "I was hoping… I don't know… to be less like a bin of tractor parts, less like a bag of potatoes. A job where I could talk, that would be nice."

"Talk about what?" Nastya asked.

"Anything. I could give my ideas about how to make things better, even if it's only little things. What's to lose, if people listened to me?"

Ida got no answer.

"Let me do that," said Nadia, placing her hands on Ida's shoulder blades.

Ida silently accepted the back rub. She continued to wish aloud: "To be a better stenographer, to make a better cigarette, anything."

Nastya was sketching the monument to the Forced Crossing of the Dnieper. The soldiers were crossing the reflecting pool on a jagged, abstract raft. The ones in back were rowing, the ones in the middle were getting ready and then emerging from cover, and those in front were charging up the bank. The forerunner had his submachine raised over his head and he was swinging his other arm wildly; his body was beginning to arch backwards, perhaps in the familiar pose of a man who is shot dead even as he rises to take the lead.

Ida pulled away from Nadia in order to rummage in the army pack.

A duck dove off the sculpted raft and glided into the water. From the concrete wall at the pool's edge, a mother and toddler each tossed a pinch of breadcrumbs. Nastya pursed her lips and began to add these elements to her sketch.

Ida got out a large, vacuum-sealed bag of dates.

Without looking at Ida, Nastya asked her, "What does Rosya Lekht do?"

"She's a scientist," said Ida as she tore the top off the bag. "Rosya's relatives send her these all the time."

"What kind of scientist?" asked Nastya, who shook her head at the offer of the sticky fruit.

"That's good," said Nadia, who had taken one. "I'm drooling."

"A computer scientist," Ida enunciated as she poked at the dates. She was applying a selection process that was uniquely her own. "She has a home computer with colour graphics, a printer, a mouse, the whole frigging party. She's on it half the night, running her codes. I'm learning, well, giving it my damnedest, I haven't slept so badly in years—and not just because of my back—but I can't boast, I'm still a beginner." She leaned close to Nastya's shoulder and added in a low hiss, "It's worth 3,900 rubles."

"You're telling me a story!"

"No. I asked and she told me, 3,900 rubles."

"That's nearly as much as a car."

"Well, Rosya needs it for her work. Of course, not every scientist has one. She's one of the best, so she gets the best."

"She would have to be, all things considered."

"Hmm?" Ida burbled around a date.

"How old is Rosya?" Nadia wanted to know.

"Hmm, forties."

Nastya stopped to flex her hand. Her brow was also working hard. "How do you know her?" she asked.

"She's Yuly's younger cousin."

"Should I know Yuly?"

"Everyone should, he's lovely."

Nastya gave up on questioning Ida and instead cast a quizzical glance straight past her, at Nadia.

Just then, they heard a crisp sound, as if someone in charge had snapped his fingers to bring them to attention.

They gazed down the stairs at a blond man in a light brown suit. *I'll bet he's an Englishman. Yesterday, he misplaced his walking stick; today, he's retracing his steps and so it is, quite by chance, this whole queer business has begun.* He held a slim camera, covered in chrome and black leather, with the name *Kiev* (in English) writ large on the plate above the lens mount. He had a wide, short moustache, which underlined the camera as he held it to his face.

Through flat lips, the man with the camera said, "Don't let me distract you."

He's not English. I am fucking heartbroken.

Nastya obliged the man by going back to her drawing as he continued to shoot.

"Are you talking to us?" Ida asked.

The photographer motioned that he wanted Ida to face sideways like Nastya. Ida stood up, leaned forwards, and motioned with sticky fingers that she did not give a fig.

The shutter kept snapping. Nadia cracked up in nervous laughter.

Nastya took another glance in the direction of the action and she soon set her pencils down. "Stop that!" she ordered. "Think where we are!"

"Exactly," said Ida, "can't we have a solemn moment to ourselves?"

"I know him," Nastya hissed as she pulled Ida down by the arm. "Giorgi and I both know him."

The man let his camera hang by the neck strap and he came up close. He knelt, with his elbow on the wall, and he parted his lips a little as he inspected Nastya's drawing. Nadia noticed that he wore cufflinks of an unusual metal; its ribbed surface looked like grey sand, trodden by birds and flooded with seawater and sunlight.

Nastya said, "This is ... Marat." (He nodded without looking at anyone; he was eyeing the sketch and the actual landscape alternately.) "Marat is Fenya's older brother."

"Who is Fenya?" Ida asked.

"That," murmured Marat, "is a question I have pondered since her birth."

"Riddles, riddles!" Ida chanted. "What is cheaper than steamed turnips?"

"Words are. I hope you haven't decided to dislike me."

"Hmm. Not exactly. I just don't like having my photo taken by surprise."

"That is a pity."

"But that's how it will stay. I see you appreciate Nastya's talent." (Nastya had been smudging clouds with her fingers while Marat and Ida spoke.)

The conversation paused, so Nadia interjected an answer to Ida's earlier question. "Marat's sister Fenya is a junior officer to Nastya's husband Giorgi."

"How precise you are," Marat said.

Nadia remarked to him, "I believe your sister likes to bring you to the detectives' socials as her guest."

"Did she speak of me so warmly as that?"

"No, I saw a couple of photographs you gave to Nastya and Giorgi."

Marat nodded again.

Nastya set aside her sketchbook and supplies and said, "I'm going inside to find a washroom. Could the three of you watch my things?" Without awaiting an answer, she got up, straightened her skirt, and skipped down the steps towards the entrance. As she went, she ran her fingers along the black granite wall, caught some dew, and washed her hands.

"Maybe I should go with her," Nadia reflected. She motioned with a pair of fingers in her mouth.

"I'll go," Ida said. "She and I need to catch up." Ida shouldered the army bag and was sprinting off before Nadia could object.

Leaning over the wall, Marat snapped a photo, which might be captioned, "A chase". He popped a date into his mouth and, like a copycat, wiped his fingertips on the wall. Then, he squinted up at the sky.

"Did you have any particular business with us?" Nadia asked.

Marat got up and paced to Nadia's other side. His eyes turned briefly from the sky to her and then back. "My sister told me to look out for yours, if I was passing this way."

"Why?"

"I believe the mountain-born hero feared for the safety of the inexperienced mother-to-be. Who can blame him, with all the stairs our civilization has built?" Now he was looking at the stairs.

"I believe you're being cheeky," Nadia said.

"Perhaps. No offence intended," Marat said. "The Lieutenant isn't my boss, much less my family, but he makes an intriguing subject. For a few weeks now, I've been studying his life from all angles except, of course, above."

Nadia said nothing but stared into the lens, downwards now, as Marat withdrew onto the stairs to kneel once more. He shot her with Motherland. She had no idea what the caption might be this time.

"Bye," Marat said. "I have a meeting at the Arsenal."

"Should someone follow you to make sure you're safe on the escalators?"

Marat waved with his camera as he ran.

Nadia turned towards the statue and looked up. How might Marat have composed his shot? She saw a seagull gliding on an updraught. She imagined that it had followed a barge all the way from the Black Sea up the Dnieper and then stayed to explore all the high perches over all the crowded parks. With its black, slender face and plump, white body, this gull cut a figure like a royal chess piece and its shining domain was not a sea but a colossus of stainless steel.

Nadia spent a few idle minutes watching the gull and the park-goers below. Then, she decided to gather up Nastya's things and the bag of dates and go into the museum. She donned her sister's satchel and her own, crisscross, shoulders-to-hips, and carried them down the steps at a moderate pace so as not to jostle the contents.

She entered the Museum, a hushed place with soft halogen lights and fine parquet. *This is an atmosphere for Mama. She did her best to have us incubated in places like this, to make us appreciate the intangibles, to give us an inheritance the only way she could. What a melancholy treasure-house is history! How ably a man dabs paint on a canvas for a wall, a cannon for a field, a sign for a barbed-wire fence! Yes, a woman too. Yes, for all the doubts and smiles in the world, a woman is tiger-striped like a man.*

She queued to buy a ticket and to ask where the washrooms were.

The ticket clerk sighed. On a map, she circled a place under the statue's pedestal and downstairs. Her stomach happened to growl as she handed the map to Nadia and said, "You may find a queue there too."

"Thank you."

On her way, she passed exhibits about the Occupation and the suffering of the civilians. There was a prisoner's uniform, stiff with filth, and one could easily imagine an emaciated body lost inside it, big as it was. There was a noose sized for a child.

She passed other exhibits about the sacrifice of the soldiers. The walls were full of personnel photos of the men. Many of them had thick moustaches, in the style of the time.

Below ground, she reached an anteroom before the washrooms. The walls were panelled with mirrors in an approximation of a circle. A young couple were staring at themselves in the glass; the woman fussed with her hair and then with his. He grabbed her ass and kissed her but she soon pulled away, to fuss with her hair some more.

Behold the grandchildren, Nadia thought. *On the other hand, can we assume that our grandparents, too, went at it anyplace they could? If one was to die in a stairway between shelled-out floors or a foxhole in a shattered wood or a steel hull flaming in a field or a gas chamber in the back of a moving-van, then what is the importance of a scene? Only, no mirror stood intact to fix one's hair.*

I know it is more complicated than that.

Nastya burst out of the women's washroom. Over her shoulder, she was berating Ida, who followed close behind.

"Your rudeness to him bordered on sacrilege," Nastya declared.

"Better that than turning him on," Ida replied.

The young couple were no longer looking in the mirror. The man ushered the woman away, towards the stairs, with his hand on her ass.

Nastya wiped her mouth and approached Nadia, who saw tears in her sister's eyes. *Those could be for nausea,* Nadia told herself.

Ida followed and said, "I meant, I thought you'd rather I put him off. I don't care. Next time a man approaches, I'll let your silence be my lead."

Nastya shrugged. She hissed through her nose.

"What shall we do next?" Nadia asked. She seized her sister and her friend by the hand. "Who wants to go up to the observation deck?"

"Hmm. Rosya told me her coworker got stuck in the elevator."

"The elevator is tiny," Nastya said. "Giorgi and I didn't go up."

"Don't tell me the Lieutenant is claustrophobic," Nadia said. She squeezed her sister's hand but got no reply. "No! He is!"

"The world isn't built in my Giorgi's size."

"Hmm-hmm. That settles it. We're going up for your husband's sake."

"How's that?"

"When he hears we all did it, next time, he can't refuse."

"That's patriotism," Nadia agreed.

Nastya laughed a little. "For Giorgi's sake…" She clapped a hand atop Nadia's and Ida's. "Yes, where better? 'All for one…'"

"'One for all…'," Nadia corrected. "'One for all and all for one.'"

"They had great hats," said Ida, remembering the musical miniseries. "Things would be better if your Gramma could still ride around like them."

"Sometimes," Nastya said, "I try to draw her as I imagine her in her youth. Even in a place like this, it's difficult to grasp … how the seconds make Eternity."

Try her bedroom, where the horses die. Try the post office and also here. I don't know where to try, nor where to disappear.

They made their way back to the entrance (to the clerk who was pining away) to buy tickets for the observation deck. Then, with tickets in hand, they proceeded to the third floor, to the Hall of Glory, where they queued for the elevator. Nadia had time to wonder, *Where is our d'Artagnan now, or in what queue is he? Rather, I fear he is alone.*

The Hall of Glory was a tall, circular room with high windows—the ones that looked empty from the outside. The room had a sunken centre, six steps down. Between the columns of windows, thick columns of concrete were covered in golden letters—heroes' names. The concrete slanted inwards towards the ceiling and the distant feet of Motherland. The ceiling was not a full dome but more like the inside of an ornate basin turned upside down, with a gilded mural of heroes and sufferers walking around its sides, in orbit of a giant Order of Victory medal in its centre. This highest honour belonged to sixteen of the top commanders who orchestrated the victories of 1944-45, plus Brezhnev, who became the latter-day face of those victories as a sort of national birthday treat, like a Kiev cake or a memorable outing for himself and the grandchildren to share.

Whatever may be said of heroic deeds and labour, there will be more Kiev cakes, outings, square faces, and kissy faces; we reap these fruits of victory as the birthright of progressive mankind—yet somehow the glory unravels; we need more and more stainless steel, concrete, and flowers of red to keep this project alive, keep housing the couples and foetuses, keep those faces fed and kissing. We're queueing right now beneath a square and full-lipped face of stainless steel—and I'm getting hungry again. If Johnny were here, we might live off the land and string an antenna up this lady to hear the airwaves shaking: radio waves to give us news and music; gamma waves to give us cancer. I'm sure Johnny could scrounge a Geiger counter as well as a radio.

Ida was trying to engage Nastya in chitchat about mutual friends in the present. "Rosya recognized your husband's name."

Nastya looked baffled, as if she doubted her own ability to hear over the echoing crowd. "How?" she asked.

"From documents. She sometimes helps the police when an investigation involves computer systems."

Nastya nodded.

Ida continued, "The critical systems get targeted by saboteurs—terrorists and CIA."

Nastya nodded again.

"Other times, it's just kids messing about."

After a while, they got to the elevator and they squeezed together at the back to make room for an elderly man who stood with a cane in each hand and a nurse holding his elbow. He wore a handful of medals over a loose, mauve turtleneck and he smiled at them through steel dentures and withered lips. He had not been a youth when he defended Motherland. The girls smiled back at him and offered him their salutations but the nurse whispered that any conversation would be a strain for him, on account of his deafness and throat cancer.

O! mercy, Nadia thought. She breathed the stuffy, oily air as her chest shuddered at torments unknown. *Are his real legs still in his trousers or are they at the bottom of the Dnieper?* She began to doubt whether he was really smiling or whether it was just the way the dentures sat.

The girls stopped smiling. The gears hummed around them and the lift climbed at an angle of 75 degrees. After covering the height of a midsized apartment block, it opened onto a metal stairway, too narrow for one climber to pass another except perhaps with an uncomfortable squeeze. The nurse guided the veteran out onto the landing. He handed her the canes, struggled to grasp the stair rails in his shaking hands, and then began to climb in a hunched and halting fashion. The nurse hung the pair of canes over her arm and they clanged on the steps behind her as she also held one rail and steadied her patient with her other hand on his bum. Nastya stepped up to carry the canes.

Four flights of stairs and a quarter of an hour later, all five of them spilled out, sweating, onto the windy observation deck.

An attendant radioed an update to the lower levels: the elderly visitor had cleared the stairs.

The observation deck was a ring of concrete, wide enough for two people to pass, with a short wall topped by a wire fence that rattled as it cut the wind into squares. From the wall, small ledges jutted inwards like the teeth of an internal gear. Between these ledges, huge binoculars stood on steel poles. They were exactly the same as the binoculars Nadia had seen in a civil defence drill, when an air defence officer demonstrated a flak gun.

Nastya gave the old man his canes and he, with the aid of his nurse, made his way to a wooden stool beside one set of binoculars. A child could have stood on the stool to look down into the angled eyepieces but, for a man, it was just a place to sit.

Nastya, Nadia, and Ida went the opposite way and settled around another pair of flak binoculars. Nadia used the binoculars, Nastya took the stool, and Ida climbed up on the ledge.

Nastya squinted into the wind, pulled stands of hair back from her eyes, and lightly wrapped her fingers around the cool wires.

Ida coughed and whispered, "The poor old sod, he was being pushed by a nurse and pulled by the Archangel. I was afraid he'd miss this stop and ride Motherland straight to the depot. Fuck, I'm glad for that breeze. Hmm." The plaid shirt was nearly blowing off her shoulders and its tails were leaping as if a brindled yellow cat were in battle with a brindled red one.

Nadia studied the binoculars. The purple sheen of the coated glass contrasted with the olive green paint. Little by little, she twisted the knurled metal of one eyepiece, looked into it with one eye open, twisted the other, looked with the other eye, and so forth until the two images were properly focused for her eyes. She was rewarded with such a view as she might have had if she were a giant-eyed alien flying over the river.

"What do you see?" Nastya asked her.

"Oh, I see the living rooms of the left bank in great detail. People are slacking off work and wearing their nightclothes."

"I know when you're teasing me, Little Hedgehog."

"I see ... smokestacks that need cleaning, bearing east-southeast, distant ... quite a ways. I'm not sure how to use the distance scale."

Ida had turned her back to the fence, bowed her head, and drawn up her knees. She was sheltering a cigarette and lighter. "I will be pleased to share," she enunciated as she succeeded in puffing smoke. "Rosya let me have some of hers and even her old lighter."

"What else do you see, bearing east-southeast?"

"That's it, just the horizon."

"Do you ever wonder," Nastya asked, "where you'd end up if you got in the cockpit of a plane and flew straight to the horizon and just kept going?"

Ida was still smoking. She flicked some stray ashes from her jeans and then brushed her fingers across the scuffed denim where, earlier, she had fallen on her knees. "Kabul," she muttered.

"What?" Nastya asked.

"Kabul," Ida repeated. "East-southeast from Kiev takes you to Kabul, distant 3,500 kilometres." She puffed. "I'm certified 'Good' in 'Geography'."

"Kabul," Nastya echoed. "Now I know."

Ida shot a glance towards Afghanistan and inadvertently let a few ashes fly into Nastya's hair. Nastya swatted them like midges as Ida asked her, "When your baby grows up, do you reckon the war in Afghanistan will be over?"

"Surely," Nastya said. "Our children and grandchildren will need monuments such as these to remember how great the suffering was in Afghanistan and why we fought a war for progress there. There will be three young Afghan women who are free as we are free, who can spend the day in a park, who have a future." Her voice was as bright and clear as tears.

"Lucky baby," Ida said. She stuck her fingers past the fence to snub out her cigarette on the wall.

A blur of white and black streaked across Nadia's magnified view of the land. She raised her face to see the seagull on another updraught. The bird's shadow, amid a grid of wiry shadows, crossed her and her sister and friend. The thought came to her again, *Where is Johnny now?*

15: Bread for Baby

After their morning reunion at the Mother Motherland, Ida said she had to go do groceries (hers and Rosya's) and make a study of the job postings. Nadia mentioned the library (Yuri's library, as it was in her mind) and suggested that she and Ida should meet there to comb the newspapers another day.

"Well, let's try," Ida said in parting.

Nastya and Nadia peeped into the Museum's cafe but decided that it was expensive and they would go on to the Monastery. Nastya said there were always grannies selling bread and salt, fruit, and small beer at the Monastery. They were artists with bread—indeed, architects with bread; they could make it take any shape at all.

"What about this Museum of Bread?" asked Nadia, who was consulting her map. She answered herself, "I guess it's too far for today."

"Yes," Nastya said, "I believe it was opened in the last five years as well. They've made Kiev a major destination."

"That seems to be true for us…" …*and the population of Pripyat*.

They walked half an hour to the Old Town, where little streets and squares were shadowed by diverse trees, walls of white, roofs of green, and domes of gold. Some of the buildings were recently restored. A Hero City—the likes of Kiev or even Odessa—got a better makeover than Tallinn.

Just past an archway on a cobbled street, a tramp asked them whether they would buy a medal to remember a hero who had fallen on hard times.

"Ignore him, ducklings," a bread-seller told them as she pulled them over to the defensive line that was her table, stacked high with loaves like sandbags. "He flogs a medal every lunchtime so he can fall on a hard time with a different tart each night. You wouldn't take much notice of old men but they have spent a lifetime noticing you."

On closer inspection, the sandbags had floral-patterned crusts.

"Thank you…" said Nadia but, before she could leave, the old woman had pushed a loaf into Nastya's hands, to open a discussion on its crust, its inner softness, its price.

"A traditional rye loaf is very nutritious for Baby," the woman expounded. "Yes, you're starting to rise. For you, duckling, it's free. What's important in these times is to eat well and have faith, isn't it?"

"Yes…"

"Do you want this icon of the Mother and Child?"

Oh, Sister, don't, Nadia pleaded with the sister of her mind.

"I… Yes, alright," Nastya said.

"For you, duckling…" There was a price and Nastya paid it, with the help of a loan reluctantly furnished by Nadia.

There's money gone that I owed to Gramma and she owed to Yuly and "God alone" knows where Yuly got it—farming fishes. I wonder what Yuly would think of Nastya's purchase; Gramma would be hollering at us now.

They also got a little paper cup of salt for dipping the bread, as well as plastic cups of non-alcoholic beer at the next table, which was run by the bread-seller's younger sister.

Nadia pointed out, "We don't need fruit, we still have Ida's dates."

They continued to walk on cobblestones as they slowly emptied their hands by eating and drinking.

When they were out of sight of the hawkers, Nastya reached around her neck to remove the enamel icon on its chain of black stainless steel. She slipped the necklace into her sister's satchel. "Please," Nastya hissed, "take this and keep it for me. Giorgi would think I'm a fool. Please, please don't tell him anything about it."

"Why would I?"

"I don't know. Do you … find it strange, how Marat showed up?"

"Yes."

Nastya nodded and wiped her nose on her knuckles and began to talk about the history of the Monastery, of the monks and gold buried in the caves.

16: Cards of a Different Theme

"I'm sorry there isn't more for supper," Nastya said at the table that evening. "We got to the stores rather late…"

…and we had already spent the grocery money on elevator tickets and an icon.

"Oh, careful, it's hot," Nastya added.

Giorgi raised a hand as he savoured a spoonful of the dish: dates poached in red wine and served in a sauce of caramelized condensed milk with shavings of dark chocolate on top.

(Despite the limited supplies, the cooking had gone smoothly until it seemed practically complete. Then, the water level dipped too low in the pot where they were simmering the can of condensed milk; the can exploded, blowing its lid with a bang like a firecracker; and, as they ducked to shield their faces, it shot globs like molten copper high and wide across Nastya's orange kitchen. Nadia wanted her sister to lie down after the shock; Nastya told her not to be stupid; Nastya would wipe off the stove while Nadia got up on the stool to do the cupboards and ceiling. Half of it had stayed in the can, fit to serve, and they managed to get rid of the rest just before Giorgi came home at half past seven.)

"Make no apologies," Giorgi said. "You have given me this sweet surprise and the anticipation of seeing your sketches."

Yes, and have the photos been developed for you yet?

Later, after hearing Nastya's chitchat about the day, Giorgi added, "Rosya Lekht and Ida Ivanova were kind to give us the dates. To hear that I am known to a computer scientist … is a surprise. Perhaps you will want to invite them here one evening. I will ask Avel about a kosher wine."

When they had finished eating, Giorgi wanted to play cards, a pastime for a Friday night. Nadia cleared the plates while her hosts negotiated the terms of the game.

"Will you be providing the deck?" Nastya asked.

"I will be providing the deck," Giorgi replied.

"Will it be from your world-famous collection of decks?"

"My love, I would not disappoint you."

"Bring it here. I want time to inspect it."

"Perhaps I have it on me." Giorgi pulled a box of cards out of his trouser pocket and emptied it onto the table for Nastya.

"I see, my love, it's very pretty, birds and a royal hunting party. This isn't the same deck as the one in the men's game at the picnic, is it?"

"No, that was a different theme."

"Well, it's only that Anya and I overhead so many admiring remarks about those cards. We said to each other, 'Those men do like pretty cards.'"

"That day's winnings paid for a lot of orange paint," Giorgi recalled. He lit one of his Prima cigarettes. "A distraction can make men play badly."

"Well," Nastya concluded, "I don't see any extra cards here, so you'll have to play a fair game against women tonight."

"I've never played any other kind."

Steamed turnips, Nadia thought as she rejoined them at the table.

"Get Giorgi the ashtray," Nastya said.

Nadia went and returned. She handed him the brass ashtray and he handed her a red notebook and black pencil to keep score. He declared that the grocery money would go to the loser, to spend at the head of a queue.

They played. Giorgi was pleased to teach them some of the lesser known games, which, he said, were popular with prisoners.

At one point, Giorgi mentioned, "I've acquired a deck with an aviation theme, photographs of airplanes with the designations printed underneath. I thought, given your father's interest..."

An electric bell rang, inside a plastic shell of carrot orange, on a bookshelf, in a nook, in a flat, in a high-rise.

Perhaps it is Motherland or the Archangel.

Giorgi got up and answered the phone. After ordinary greetings, he leaned around the corner, put his hand to the receiver, and announced, "There is a man calling."

The Archangel, then.

"He wishes to speak with Nadia."

Tell him I've just gone for a bath. He can kill me with the water.

"His name is Yuly Lvovich."

Could it be bad news about Gramma? Briskly, Nadia dumped her cards, went over, and took the phone. "Yuly, hello, what's happening?"

("Come, Giorgi," Nastya said. "Let's leave Nadia to her call. I'm tired and you're done for the week, so take a bath and come to bed.")

"Hello," Yuly sighed. "Nothing out of the ordinary. Your Gramma and I have simply been talking to pass the evening. She's been talking to Cherny at hers, I've been talking to the television at mine. Am I disturbing you?"

("Bath? Bed?" Nastya repeated. Giorgi nodded, finished inspecting everyone's cards, pocketed the deck, and followed his wife.)

"No," Nadia said, "you're a welcome voice ... though you don't say 'Meow'."

Yuly laughed and sighed. "Tell me what you've been finding to do in Kiev."

She talked about cooking in Nastya's kitchen and making a study of *Great Expectations* at the library and visiting the Mother Motherland with Nastya and Ida.

"You've seen Ida, then. What does she say? How is it with her and Rosya?"

"Ida seems to admire her, to appreciate her generosity."

"Good, thank God for that," Yuly said. "You know, Nadia, introducing any two people is a gamble." Without pausing over this piece of wisdom, he continued, "Rosya said Ida hurt her back, some accident on the train."

"Oh, a bit of a tumble," Nadia said. "She's okay. Ida lands, she bounces."

"Rosya said she started giving Ida some drops for the pain. I mentioned it to your Gramma and your Gramma thinks it's the wrong thing."

"I see. Have you told Rosya?"

"Yes, yes, Rosya doesn't agree."

"What shall I say to Ida, then?"

"Well, just that your Gramma thinks the best thing for it is rest and maybe a bit of liniment and if the pain is bad enough to keep Ida awake, she could have just one shot of alcohol to help her sleep. Of course, I don't know, Ida is not on a farm and she's not behind enemy lines. Rosya might have better medicine."

"Well, a doctor entrusted Ida to Gramma's care and Ida is a human animal, not a computer. I'll tell her Gramma's advice."

"Sure, sure, you're right." He laughed and sighed. "You're like your Gramma when she was your age. You only half see yourself and half of you is a miracle."

"Oh, well, Yuly, thank you…" …*I think.*

"Thank you, Nadia. Look after Ida. Look after your sister. God bless."

"Look after Gramma."

"I try." There was a brief silence. "Sleep well."

"You too. Bye." Nadia hung up and went to the kitchen for a snack. *If we don't get more practical about the shopping, we'll be eating candied rose petals.* While chomping on chocolate and listening to the sounds of bathwater and staring at high-rise lights and picturing Motherland and a foetus and Ida's eyes, she began to wonder about the past. *At my age, Gramma was a Byelorussian farm girl with a set of school medals and a dream to go to Moscow, to the Timiryazev Agricultural Academy, best and oldest of all the agrarian universities in the country, to become one of its youngest graduates. How did Yuly know her then?*

17: Pebbles Out of Place

"Yuly wants me to search the hills." By this reason, Ida persuaded Nadia to accept a complete change of plans and leave the library, though they had only just arrived, Ida a few minutes after Nadia. "Yuly has an old description of a gravesite in the Kiev Hills but he's never been; he doesn't know exactly where it is nor whether there's still a grave to be seen. I'm to place a pebble on it or as near as I can get."

"He trusts you a great deal."

"I hope so. Anyway, I'll be happy enough, exploring the hills."

As Nadia repacked her satchel, she began to wonder whether the library had any historical maps or books that might help in their search. She also gave thought to Nastya's new knowledge of parks and memorials. She questioned Ida about this grave, its date, the person buried there.

Ida replied, "Yuly had a wife named Minah and a little girl, Fraydel. We're looking for the place where Fraydel buried Tentser, her kitty-cat, in August 1940. She sent Yuly a letter and a drawing at the time; he was away."

"What happened to her?"

"Hmm. The following year, Fraydel and her mother quite certainly died. They were still in Kiev when the city was taken."

"I didn't know any of this."

"I know it partly from Yuly, partly from Rosya."

They were stepping away from the table just as Yuri came through the reading area with his book trolley. He looked at them and then in the direction of the front desk and back. "I didn't realize you were here," he said. "Were you leaping in and out of the pages?"

"No," Nadia replied, "just stopping long enough to meet my friend."

"I'm flattered. Oh, you mean her." He grinned, with all his gaps. "Hello, are you a visitor to Kiev too? Maybe you're lost or confused."

"Hmm," said Ida. "Not a visitor, I'm staying … at least long enough to see whether Kiev has a job for me."

"Then you're not a mermaid like this one. Water spirits don't work." He began to enumerate three points on three of his fingers. "Water spirits don't work. Angels don't smoke. Fish don't wear anything but newspaper."

"Well," said Ida, "I've had a bit of luck lately, so I've got good smokes and good clothes. I'm hoping a good job will follow."

"Keep looking," said Yuri. He nodded and rolled along.

They borrowed a book—the Hero City's history in maps and photos—and they went to survey some of the hilly parks, which, 46 years ago, had been wilderness and wastelands on the outskirts. They rode the buses, seized a pair of seats as soon as they could, and talked as quietly as they could, amidst the early shoppers with suitcases and the kids dressed in uniform for summer leisure.

"Doesn't Yuly want some act of remembrance to be performed at a war memorial?"

"No, it's a conversation he and Rosya have had many times. He wants a pebble placed on Tentser's grave. Look, he copied Fraydel's letter for me."

Ida produced a fold of paper from her shirt pocket and handed it to Nadia. Nadia opened it and studied Fraydel's words in Yuly's hand.

"Dear Papa," it began, "I am so sad and sorry. Tentser died today. Mama and I placed him in a green box and we buried him on a hill in the woods. He is under a stone like a pyramid where we scratched his name. We put river pebbles and shells and glass on the sides. We said a prayer. When you come home, I will take you there so you can place a pebble for Tentser too. I love you and miss you. Fraydel."

"O! mercy," Nadia whispered.

"He copied her drawing too and he showed how 'Tentser' can be written. Minah was teaching Freydal languages. She would have been clever like you."

Nadia received this second fold of paper and she opened it to find a pencil sketch, which gave the impression of a sandy slope with spindly pines and a pointed stone. On the margins, the cat's name was written in three alphabets: the Hebrew, Cyrillic, and Latin.

"Do you truly think we can find this?" Nadia asked.

"Who knows? Yuly only asked me to look. This letter made its way 6,000 kilometres to him, literally underground to him, and he says it's the only thing he has to prove he didn't dream her. He thinks there is a reason for it, though he also says the reason won't be what he thinks."

"I don't suppose he and Gramma discuss that dilemma."

Ida shrugged. "Maybe they have ways."

"Maybe," said Nadia. She wondered aloud, "Can two people be so different after all, when they've grown old with their thoughts of all the shorter lives, of cats, of lost families…?"

"Your Gramma didn't lose your father."

"No." Nadia thought of how few words she had shared with Misha since the beginning of the year.

"Let's put these away," Ida said, "and have a smoke."

"Yes, alright."

Ida took back the two sheets of paper and returned them, folded, to her shirt pocket. She was wearing the plaid again that day.

"Oh," Nadia murmured, "I brought your other shirt." She dug it out from the bottom of her satchel and she exchanged it for a cigarette and a flame. She slouched (as much as possible in a straight-backed seat with a metal rail for a neck rest) and she propped up her ankles with her bag (as much as possible without kicking the passenger ahead of her in the ass). She shut her eyes and inhaled smoke deeply as the kids on the bus began to sing a camp song.

("Such joyful laughter / Such flames in the eyes…")

"That's right, Little Paw, smoke, smoke, smoke, it'll help you think better. I need your mind, your focus."

"Sure," Nadia wheezed, "I'm your laser."

("…don't waste a minute / Don't leave time on your hands / Don't leave time…")

"My laser, hmm-hmm," Ida concurred. She lit another cigarette for herself, shifted in her seat, and did end up kicking the singer ahead of her.

("Salute the sun of the Motherland…")

The kid twisted his spine to look at Ida. His ears seemed to retreat from his bony cheeks as she stuck out her lower lip and blew smoke at him.

"Are you a boy?" he asked.

"I'm a lunatic," Ida replied. "Are you a boy?"

He faced ahead and sang.

("It's you that I love above all…")

"I never could stomach the singing," Ida grumbled. "I'd take a beating or forfeit a meal, sooner than learn a song."

("The sun is shining on everyone. / The winter is over.")

"Yes," Nadia agreed, "it's unfair to children; soldiers get earplugs." She was starting to feel nauseous. She rested an ear against Ida's shoulder. Ida twitched. Nadia said, "Sorry, I forgot your pain."

("Georgian, Estonian, Russian, and Uzbek / We're all one great big family / Him, her, you, and me...")

"Does your family have any Uzbeks?" Ida asked.

"No, no, but they probably assume I want one for my birthday—if not my birthday, New Year's or Christmas."

"Hmm, the baby must be coming in the midst of all that. That might save you from unwanted attentions on your seventeenth, you'll be the aunt who was born at an awkward hour, alongside the New Year and Jesus and your parents' first grandchild."

"Go on, make me feel special."

"I hope you at least get your own cake. Your Mama makes such good cakes. There was one... I can come, can't I?"

"If you're not coming to my seventeenth, it's because one of us is dead."

"Hmm. That's alright, then."

They finished their cigarettes and chucked them out the window, onto a deserted curb where a crumbling retaining wall shored up a corner of a park. Where concrete blocks were missing from the wall, some of the rebar was twisted and cut away.

They made the rounds of several parks that day. They got a bit sunburnt. Their mouths were smoky and dry. Nadia threw up in a trash can as Ida laughed. They explored the shadier paths. They saw feral dogs, fire pits, human shit, empty bottles, disposable cups, tins, shreds of plastic, cardboard sheets, empty cigarette packs, needles, rags, and condoms that had been cast off like snakeskins. They saw scattered feathers and swarms of ants around skeletons of birds.

From time to time, they pulled out the drawing and the history book but found absolutely nothing recognizable.

Nadia said, "I don't see any clues leading us to Tentser's Tomb." She gave it this name automatically; it was a factual name. She had read of the Tomb of Cyrus, where Alexander commanded Aristobulus to squeeze through the tiny door; so too had she read of Tentser's Tomb, where Fraydel and Minah put river pebbles and shells and glass as they hoped for Yuly's return.

Yet Asia is wide and the thresholds are small.

"For today, then," Ida said, "let's see the nearest memorial. Rosya will think better of me if I can at least say I've done that much with the day."

"Nastya too. Where is it?"

"There's a place called Babi Yar. Rosya has spoken of it. Most probably, it's where Fraydel and Minah died, along with others in Yuly and Rosya's family."

"Yes, I think we should go there."

They made their way to the bus stop called Babi Yar, on a thoroughfare, near a corner of the park bearing the same name. The ground at the park's edge was grassy and flat, with sandy paths leading through a perimeter of high, leafy trees, as well as shrubs that might catch stray balls. From outside this living wall, the most visible landmark was the top of a television tower.

They followed a path and found that the park's interior dipped to form a low-lying field surrounded by grassy banks. A concrete ramp, like a precipice, jutted out from the nearest bank and, at its tip, a pile of bronze figures was tumbling backwards into the grave. The farther back, the closer they came to nudity as well as death; they were being robbed of their clothes and then their lives.

Nadia and Ida ascended the ramp. At the top, foremost amongst the figures, a soldier and a sailor stood defiantly; they were raising a frantic mother and baby to the top of the pile, to a place of momentary escape from the abyss.

The plaque read, "To Soviet citizens and prisoners of war, soldiers, officers of the Soviet Army shot by German Fascists in Babi Yar, a monument".

The plaque's two readers stood there, forlorn and disconsolate in a moderately popular park in a big city. Some other visitors climbed up for a look and then climbed back down. When Ida and Nadia were again alone on the ramp over the grassy field, Ida spoke again.

"Rosya told me that for 35 years, there was no memorial here. First, there was a brick factory and its wastewater dump. Then, the dam broke and the waste and bodies washed downhill and more people died in the mudslide. Then, there was a landfill to cover it all up again and make the park. Then, there were police to catch any Jews saying prayers. Then, finally, in 1976, the Nation and the Hero City put up this sculpture and plaque."

"What a difference there is," Nadia whispered, "in how a child buries a cat; how a nation … how all progressive mankind buries a child."

"A highway has mileposts," Ida said, "even to go to a swamp or a mountainside. Rosya, she talks as she works at night. She talks and she smokes. She told me, the Fascists used this area for months. They had collaborators too, who came and went. First, they gassed or shot the patients from the psychiatric hospital and dumped them in the ravine. That was the trial run. Two days later, they rounded up and shot the Jews. Then, it was so easy, they went on and on, working their way down a list. Sculptures and plaques never tell you, 'The day before, she was a little Yiddish kid; the day before, she was a locked-up manic-depressive. Her papers and her neighbours said so.' Rosya says there's no shortage of systems to sort us. 'The pre-sort is in aid of the final-sort,' she says. Hmm."

Nadia consulted the book. "Would that have been the Kiev Psychiatric Hospital No. 1 Named After Ivan Pavlov?"

"Hmm, sounds right."

"That's still here. We're only two kilometres away; it's at the other corner of the park. There's a whole chapter…"

Ida stared at Nadia and then at the page. The chapter, "A Garden of Progressive Psychiatry in the Kiev Hills", was penned by one Doctor Igor Igorevich Yahontov.

"Families," Ida muttered.

Nadia shut the book and put it away.

They stood there a minute longer. A breeze had begun to bob the branches in the woods surrounding the field. A flock of sparrows took flight with a sound like pages being fanned by a child's thumbnail. They landed again in the same trees where they started. Beyond the treeline, the television tower pointed skywards like a white rocket with red rings.

"Let's go climb one more hill," Nadia suggested. "Let's end the day somewhere we can remember as just a place you and I were lost."

"Good idea."

They took another bus to a lonely stop at the edge of a light industrial park. Separating it from the forest was a long wall of mixed materials—some segments built of cinder blocks, others of whitewashed brick, others of rusty corrugated iron. They passed through an open gate and some kind of workshop yard, devoid of workers. They followed a trail where flickering sunlight came through the branches of spindly pines. They began to climb a slope.

"I was…" Ida pivoted and walked uphill backwards for a couple of steps before pivoting again. "Thought I heard something. No, it's fine, Little Paw. I was at the Arsenal Factory the other day."

"Oh?"

"Rosya said it's one of the biggest employers in Kiev, so why don't I go there, just play it cool, not come with my papers to ask for a job or an interview, but just ask for a chat about what kinds of jobs they have? Rosya says I need to let people meet me at least once without my papers."

"I see."

"So I did. I talked with a Junior Personnel Manager on his tea break in the cafeteria. I said, I want to know everything about the Kiev Arsenal, I've just blown in from the North, I'm fascinated by the future: computerization and images and light." Ida's hands flew as she spoke. "Then, as we're getting up and I'm wiping up a splash of tea, he says, he recognizes me, he's been trying to place me. He says, didn't I model a few photos for Marat, in Consumer Optics? He says, Marat has ideas about shock advertising, about portraying 'raw young souls'—a way to sell us to the world."

"Are you saying that Marat showed his company a picture of you making a fig at him, as an advertising concept?"

"That seems to be the gist of it."

Nadia started laughing in spite of everything.

"Don't laugh, Little Paw, he's swindling me—and after I told him I didn't like having my photo taken." Ida stopped to scan the trees and light a cigarette. "Do you want one?"

"No, no, not while I'm laughing. No, let's keep an open mind, this could be good for you. Why shouldn't you be admired for being beautiful and free?"

"Because I'm neither of those things. That's only in your eyes, Little Paw. I know how you care."

"Well, I do care but I'm not the only one who cares. Maybe lots of people will care about you one day."

"That'll be the day."

Nadia shrugged and Ida led on, trailing bluish smoke as she climbed.

"Anyway," Ida continued, "I kept it cool with the personnel manager. I thought to myself, I'll get to this Marat later. That's what I did. I came back at the end of the day and I followed him when he left the building."

"No! Then what?"

"Nothing, in the end. I followed him. I was wearing my work clothes and a kerchief so I don't think he recognized me. He met up with this girl cop at a bistro. I guess she was his sister. They had a drink and he gave her an envelope and left. I stayed to watch her. Then, Giorgi showed up and had a drink and a salad with her and he took the envelope and put it in his coat. I recognized him from Nastya's drawings and his voice. Fuck, he's tall in life."

"He is. How did it all seem?"

"Hmm, it was an okay place, I had a half sandwich and a glass of vodka, they put olives in everything."

"How did Giorgi and Fenya seem?"

"Them? A pair of self-absorbed people. They like being cops."

"Anything else?"

"Hmm…hmm, no, beyond that, I didn't twig it. They weren't touching, if that's what you mean. After he left, she stayed on and then there was this other guy, a bricklayer type or a soldier off duty, and she and he had a drink too. That one looked more like a hookup. Then I left them. There was only so long I could make my half sandwich last and I got bored twiddling toothpicks."

"Okay, thanks," Nadia said. "Thanks for telling me. Thanks for looking out for Nastya." She locked arms with Ida and bumped her shoulder.

Ida winced. "Sure, sure, Little Paw."

"Sorry. Did I hurt you?"

"I'm fine, I'm fine." Ida adjusted their locked arms.

They walked. After a pause, Nadia recited Gramma's advice about the back and shoulder. Ida nodded without any expression in her face or eyes.

Has she tuned me out?

"How do you feel about men?" Ida asked.

"Well, it's difficult…" Nadia took a deep breath, puffed out her cheeks, and decided to answer quite honestly, quite plainly, "Sometimes

they're interesting and sometimes they're ridiculous. Sometimes I'm
scared of them."

"Yeah. Yeah, there is variety alright. Not even a factory can turn out
two of a kind, as your Mama would know. I remember she said at one
of your birthdays, the same ingredients, same oven, make a different
cake in different weather." Ida ran her fingers through the pine boughs.
"Not all men are scary. Some are. You can always ask me to advise you
on that part."

"Thanks." *I wish Nastya could have asked. You and I and Mama
and Gramma all, somehow we were gone at a time when Nastya might
have asked.*

"Some of them are just too tall," Ida whispered with smoke as they
strolled uphill arm-in-arm. "Listen now, here's my way of thinking,
Little Paw. You want one who's the same size as you, hmm? That way,
when it inevitably comes to blows, it'll be a fair fight. That's the best
for any young couple and, down the road, it's best for the children too,
to see how a fight should be fair."

Ida pondered her own advice and frowned. " 'Well, it's fine for
Ida,' I hear you say. 'Ida can find a man almost anywhere in the world,
her height is so easily matched, she's well spaced from ankle to earlobe.
Nadia will have to go voyaging below the Equator, in search of lost lands
where the men are shorter than the women and potatoes grow on blue
trees.' Hmm-hmm, no, you have plenty of time to get taller."

To conclude, Ida reiterated, "Always put yourself in a fair fight."

They had come to a vantage point. To the righthand side of their
ascent, the hill abutted on a ravine. Below them was a stretch of aspen
with tall, straight trunks and flat leaves crackling in the breeze. On
another chain of hills, taller and distant, stood a radio tower and a cluster
of apartment blocks. Nadia gazed upon it all with a twinge of fatalism
and depression. She somehow knew that the image of this unremarkable
place had lodged itself in a corner of her mind for a lifetime and she
would remember it on countless occasions of unimportance.

"If I brought a guy up here," Ida mused (more to herself than to
Nadia now), "if I brought a guy … I'd carve our names high up in one
of those trees, where no one would ever find it. I'd carve our names."
Letting go of Nadia's arm, Ida made a sweeping gesture without showing pain. "Then, all the aspen, through their roots, would be invisibly
connected to our names."

"Do you go in for name-carving?"

"Oh, yes, it's the most romantic way to let him know I have a knife."

"Do you?"

Ida did not answer but she murmured, "Aspen, aspen. Date palms."

"What about date palms?"

"Rosya was showing me pictures from Israel. They call the dates 'the meat of the desert'. I want to go there. I'm thinking of emigrating."

"Ida," Nadia mentioned, "you're not Jewish."

"We can't be sure of that."

" 'We can't be sure' doesn't get you into Israel."

"Hmm." Ida took an idle swing at the air and then shielded her eyes as if she were observing the trajectory of something she had flung. She quit it and asked, "What are the Ten Commandments?"

"The laws God gave Moses on Mount Sinai, supposedly."

"I know that, Little Paw. Can you list them?"

"Probably not all. Let me try. There's 'Honour your mother and father.' "

"Fuck."

"Shall I go on?"

"Go on, don't spare me."

" 'Don't kill.' "

" 'Don't kill.' "

" 'Don't steal.' "

"That one is laden with assumptions about property."

" 'Don't do your brother's wife.' "

"Seriously?"

"Yes, something like that."

"Do you reckon that happens much?"

"I guess it must, to be one-tenth of divine law."

"I mean, who wants to do two brothers? Enough is enough."

" 'Don't worship false idols.' "

"Who has time?"

"That's all I remember from Gramma Marusya. She died when I was just little."

"You only got fifty percent."

"Why do you ask, anyway?"

"Hmm-hmm. Rosya said Yuly was noncompliant on one or two Commandments. That was her word, 'noncompliant'."

"One or two?"

"One or two," Ida repeated. "He doesn't have a brother, does he?"

"Not that I'm aware."

"Did Gramma Marusya have brothers?"

"No."

"I wonder what Yuly did. Maybe nothing. Maybe Rosya is just an old gossip, to fill her nights when the computer is being noncompliant."

Nadia tried to picture Yuly, a big man, in scale. How big does a man stand next to a crime or two, a law or two; a stone tablet or two, a computer, a suitcase; Mount Sinai in the far corner of a desert, the Kiev Hills atop the deepest subways, the Kolyma Mountains at the end of a bone-freezing highway; the Seas, Red, Black, and Baltic whose shores entomb the prehistoric dead in sandstone, shale, and amber? *This my hand with pink nails or a golden ring or a bloody sock will rather the multitudinous seas incarnadine.* "I don't know," Nadia said.

"Me neither. I never know."

Do you know what's happened to Johnny? Nadia considered asking.

Ida looked at Nadia and said, "Shall we go?"

"*Allons-y.*"

"*Allons-y,*" repeated Ida as she took her friend's arm again.

18: Stench

Back at the apartment, Nastya asked her little sister, "How was the library? Did you find what you wanted?"

"Good. Yeah."

Nastya kissed Nadia on the cheek but then pulled back and gagged. "You stink like death. You're covered in sweat and smoke."

"Yes, it's stuffy there," said Nadia as she turned to go to her room.

"There's dirt and grass on the ass of your skirt."

"Ida and I sat in a park."

"For very long?"

"I guess a little while. Why?"

"You're sunburnt. You're on your way to looking like a gypsy."

Nadia shrugged and fluffed out her hair a bit. They exchanged a look from opposite sides of the threshold to the converted closet.

"Alright," said Nastya, "go take a bath and get changed before Giorgi gets home. You should call Mama tonight."

19: Smashed Perfume

Nadia rinsed herself off with the hand shower and then ran a bath. Her intention was to have a long soak and to let her mind wander beyond the walls of present cares. As the tub filled, she eyed the contents of the room. Exhaustion gave her a feeling of disappearing into the little things: the fractal branches of the snowflakes in the wallpaper; the ventilation grille's diamonds and X's, popping up behind each other in a staggered pattern like a knit sweater; the immaculate arrangements of mass-produced toiletries.

On a little green shelf in the corner, Giorgi's straight razor was soaking in a glass dish containing green cologne. The liquid let off a clinging, sugary aroma of oranges, sapwood, and moss. More of it was awaiting release from a nearby glass flask with a plastic stopper. The scent and the label identified it as Shipr. *I'm sure Mama used to buy it for Papa. She may have said it made a man mysterious.*

Another such flask displayed a portrait of a blonde with her chin lowered and her eyes raised. Without leaving the tub, Nadia stretched to pick it up. On inspection, its yellow contents smelt like sapwood, flowers, and cherries.

There are people who drink this in the park, Nadia reminded herself. *The cherry alcohol of the masses is her: Natasha the Blonde, not kirsch.* Even so, Nadia chose to keep the bottle close at hand, on the edge of the tub.

The water was getting high. Nadia held her breath and shut her eyes and slid beneath the film of soap, into the hot underworld where the roar and hiss of the pipes had a voice to drown all others.

What is it like to drown?

Nadia surfaced, wiped her face on a towel, and shut off the taps. They required a hard twist. Her wrists throbbed from the force and the heat.

What is it like to bleed to death?

She stole another glance at the razor and she started to cry. Silently, she held her head and let the tears fall into the blurry water.

Out in the main room, the boombox came on. The volume was adjusted up before being adjusted back down.

"Million, million, / Million, scarlet roses…"

Nadia let out a single sob, which went unheard. Then, she managed to rein in her breath, to gradually bring her heart back to its normal

walk. She lay back with just her eyes and nose and mouth above water.
   She napped.

   Through the bathwater, the sounds of a home-in-the-making faintly
reached Nadia's ears. Nastya was chopping stuff and putting a pot on
the stove. The boombox had finished describing passion and now it was
dreaming of a universe of infinite possibilities, all in a strange, liquid
accent of beats and boops and sighs. Nastya was trilling to herself and
talking to herself or—could it be?—to her unborn child, who was still
hard-pressed to develop ears on such a timeline.

   Nadia sat up again and started rubbing the cherry alcohol in her
hair and tried to make out her sister's words. *Is she practicing Georgian
phrases?*

   The apartment's front door opened and shut. Nadia wondered
whether it had more force behind it than usual or whether the water
had hampered her sense of what was loud and what was soft.

   A pair of boots made noises and then went silent. Shortly after that,
another door closed. *He's gone straight to the bedroom to get changed,*
Nadia supposed. *I hope he doesn't need a piss. Well, that's his problem.*

   A few minutes later, there was conversation in the kitchen. Giorgi's
voice was coming through quite clearly. He made observations about the
cooking and then asked whether Nadezhda had met with Ida Ivanova.

   Yes, she had.

   Had Nadezhda passed on the invitation—that Ida Ivanova and
Rosya Lekht should join Nadezha's family for dinner?

   No, she had not. Nastya recited reasons that were familiar to Nadia.
Nastya had asked Nadia to hold off on the invitation until the start of
the month because the money and the ration tickets were running ever
so slightly short.

   Why had Nastya not said something sooner?

   The answer was inaudible.

   If only she had told him, he would have taken active measures. He
could have won more at cards, if only she approved of his playing.

   Nastya lilted something that sounded slightly pointed.

   All was well, Giorgi assured her. She need not worry. The cards
were not his only magic. He had collected something else that could
easily be turned to gold.

   Straw, perhaps? Nadia wondered. *Be careful, you spinner, you dealer,
lest you should end your work by tearing yourself apart. If you were to*

grab your own leg (such a long leg), I am sure you could use it as a lever and you would come apart like a roast chicken.

Nastya was expressing some kind of doubt.

Giorgi's reassurances stopped short. "What have you done with them?"

Nastya gave a soft reply.

"Unbelievable! No, I don't believe you!" Giorgi quavered. For the first time, Nadia heard him really laugh.

"Giorgi!" Nastya cried out. The tiled wall muffled her voice but all the tones of panic were intact. Her startled shout was chased by one hollow bang and then another. "Giorgi, please, no!"

Nadia scrambled to get out of the bath. She knocked over the bottle of scent; it smashed on the floor. She threw on her dirty shirt and skirt, the nearest clothes to hand.

Bang! Bang! "No!"

Nadia eyed the straight razor in the glass dish.

Trailing water, she rushed out, down the hall, into the kitchen, to find Giorgi hauling cans of condensed milk from the cupboard and slamming them onto the counter.

"Giorgi, put those back!" Nastya hollered.

"Where are they?" he demanded as he cleared a wider and wider path to the back of the cupboard.

"I took them away," Nastya replied. She was gripping the edge of the counter as she stood beside Giorgi and glared up at him.

"Why?" he asked, without looking at her, as if he were speaking to a distant and inscrutable being.

"Because," said Nastya, "I didn't see why you needed so many bottles of wine. I never dreamt you were trading them."

"I wasn't drinking them, was I?" he snarled. "Nastya, this is waste we can't afford."

"No," Nastya corrected his interpretation. "I did have some idea of their value. I simply took them away for safekeeping." She glanced at Nadia and told her, "I'm learning what gets done for us."

"Alright, my love," said Giorgi, turning towards Nastya and holding up his hands in surrender, "just tell me where they are and I'll go get them now. Then, everything will be fine, I can offload them tonight if that's what you want."

"What I want!" Nastya half laughed.

"Nastya, please, this is not just for us. Your father is in this too."

"I see," Nastya said. "Okay, then. Anya has them for safekeeping, so what will you do, Giorgi? Will you intrude on your boss's dinner and repeat this scene with his wife? Otherwise, I suggest we drop the topic for this evening. I can get them back from her in the morning when you two men are at work."

Giorgi strode to the other end of the kitchen, sat on the stool, and crossed his arms.

Nastya pressed her advantage with a final blow: "For Christ's sake, Giorgi, you might have been more inventive than to hide them on a high shelf in my kitchen and say I shouldn't climb stools."

He lowered his voice but continued to protest. "Nastya," he said from his stool, "I only wanted us to have the means for the renovations and entertaining our guests, who are dear to us, and for other good things in life, things that you want. As for your father's part, let me explain, he seeks to relieve your mother's burden…"

"He has street dogs and street cats to feed," Nadia suggested. "Ha," she added. *Now that they've calmed down just the littlest bit, they're staring at me. "Spirit, what uncombed stuff art thou that com'st in dirty laundry to stand in yellow puddle?"*

"What have you got in your hand?" Nastya asked her sister.

"Nothing."

"You've cut yourself," Nastya insisted.

Nadia opened her hand to show that it was empty. She had dug her nails into her palm.

"You've terrified Nadia," Nastya told her husband.

"Forgive me."

"Giorgi, you must control yourself. You will be a father."

"Both of you, forgive me," he muttered. He neither looked at them nor got up from the stool. He ran a hand through his hair and then around his neck and jaw. He probably rubbed off some residue of Shipr.

A voice in Nadia's head reminded her, *Last time you held a pocket knife, Little Paw, you couldn't take a proper stab at a can of pork. Tonight, you couldn't even pick up a razor.*

Nastya inspected the cuts and said, "I'll get … some alcohol … or green stuff." She headed for the bathroom, where she discovered a broken bottle and a suffocating surfeit of perfume. "Oh, fuck," she declared.

Nadia followed and began to apologize for the mess.

"Just get me the newspaper…" Nastya rasped.

"The newspaper," said Giorgi, who had shown up behind them.

"…and the garbage bin from the kitchen and the broom and dustpan from under Nadia's bed. Stir the pot and turn down the heat."

Nadia turned towards her room.

"No, stay," Nastya told her. "Hold out your hand." Nastya skirted around the broken glass and, from the shelf, she grabbed a vial of greenest green stuff—the great balm for mankind's cuts and fishkind's fungus. With a few flicks of her sketching hand, she undid the rubber stopper, filled the eyedropper, and deposited aggressive doses of the dye into the four bloody crescents that ran the breadth of Nadia's palm. "Don't wash it. Don't touch food with it."

"I know. I know, Wolfie."

Nastya glanced at her sister's face and said, "Your eyes are red."

Nadia's instinct was to rub her face.

"Other hand!" Nastya barked.

Giorgi showed up with the newspaper and garbage bin.

"Did you stir the pot and turn down the heat?"

He did not answer. He was headed towards Nadia's bedroom.

Nastya repeated the question.

"Yes!" A broomstick clattered. Giorgi came back sighing. He hastily swept up the worst of the glass and chucked it in the bin. Nastya used the front page, with its headlines full of statistics, to wipe perfume from the dustpan.

They restructured their little cadre. Giorgi stood in the doorway and passed individual sheets of newsprint to Nadia, who sat on the edge of the tub. Nadia crumpled each sheet, ran water over it, and passed it to Nastya, who cleaned the floor.

"Talk to me," Nastya said as she picked up a slippery, perfumed shard that had evaded the broom. She dropped it into the deep bin, which smelt of vegetable peels going brown. *Clunk.* "Do you have anything more to tell me?"

Did she look at me?

"The Captain won't see the New Year," Giorgi reported. "He called us together to give us the news at the end of the day."

"Yes," said Nastya, "Anya told me at lunch."

"He is finishing out the month at work."

"Yes."

"He will go the sanatorium. Perhaps Anya will go with him."

"That's what she's trying to arrange," Nastya confirmed.

"Perhaps it would be wrong to disturb her about the wine."

"I can't imagine it making one bit of difference. Take out this garbage." The conversation died there. Nastya got up, rinsed her hands, and muttered, "Dinner."

Giorgi inspected the cleanup job, lifted a few grains of glass with his fingertips, sniffed, and then began to knot the garbage bag in the bin.

"Not that I want to meddle in official business," Nadia said, "but aren't you taking a great risk, in your position … and all for what?"

Giorgi stared down into her eyes and seemed to evaluate more than one possible answer. Then, he asked, "When the house is flooding, who stops to wipe his boots? What is the Dry Law, what is wine? Good things for Nastya matter more. I'm sure you agree, Nadezhda, just as your father does."

"Nastya herself might not agree. She might dispute the principle."

"She must always say what she thinks. I must take out the garbage." He lifted the bag and escorted it out of the flat.

That was not the battle I expected, Nadia thought. *I must call Mama tonight. I must go to her. I can do nothing here on my own terms.*

III: Orphan

1: Workbench by a Window

Nadia had suffered a loss during her first, short stay in Kiev. She had lost a hope which she had placed in the idea of sharing a home with her sister. Nadia had found herself reduced to an honorary role, "first and most important guest in this home," as Giorgi had anointed her. Children do not dream of becoming important guests in their siblings' homes. A guest (as she knew from Chekhov) is an object of civilized indulgence, a guest is not useful, a guest adds disquiet to disquiet and farce to farce, the soup gets altered by filling it out with ingredients on hand, a guest creates strange romantic combinations, a guest takes root on the cliff-edge of civilized send-offs and civilized returns. Nothing is civilized in the nature of sibling love. Siblings are fellow outcasts in an adventure of mortality.

The remainder of the summer saw Nadia as a guest in several places, where she never fully unpacked her little suitcase of clothes and books. Sometimes she was with her parents, sometimes back with Nastya and Giorgi, sometimes overnight with Rosya Lekht as an auxiliary guest by Ida's side. Anya, who began to spend weekends at the sanatorium, asked Nastya and Nadia to look in on her flat and to use it any way they wanted. Sometimes, Nadia slept there—particularly when she believed that Nastya and Giorgi had been building up to an evening of particular strife or particular romance or both. Nadia would say that she intended to stay up particularly late to read a book and listen to the radio; she could do so at Anya's place without disturbing anyone and, besides, while she was there, she would tidy up so that Anya's Monday could be a clean start, albeit in a literal sense only. Nastya seemed content with the pretence that she and Nadia shared a devotion to Anya.

Sometimes, alone, Nadia counted her money and kept an account in the back of her Lottery Commission notebook—the same one that contained her drafts of poems and letters to Gramma. People were developing a habit of putting money in Nadia's hands when she arrived or departed. Little bits came from Mama and Papa. Bigger bits came from Giorgi, who would insist on a cash bet: Nadia, he said, could not guess the number in his mind; she always guessed zero and was always right. Nastya gave and took money and generally cast confusion on the account. Anya paid Nadia a token amount—at least, when Nastya was not there to refuse it.

One evening, on impulse, Nadia abandoned Anya's place and took a bus to the library with no hope of return till morning. The library, she knew, stayed open all night. She was determined to make headway in *Great Expectations*. She kept reading until exhaustion made her head spin and her stomach hurt. Then, her cheek came to rest on the broad pages of the *Oxford English Dictionary* and she had a dream, in which she spoke to an audience about Dickens' portrayal of lawyers and convicts and workers and orphans and wards. Yuri woke her with a light shake of her shoulders. For a change, he did not make any joke, such as, "You'd sleep better underwater." Perhaps he thought the mermaid schtick had lost its shine, like seaweed laid out on a boulder in the sun, or perhaps he took the situation more seriously than their previous encounters. He admonished her for losing track of time. Surely she had people waiting for her. She should not place herself amid the after-midnight crowd. He scanned the room and, for a moment, his gaze settled on a stubble-bearded man who was leafing through books and jotting notes on loose paper. When he was not jotting anything, this man absentmindedly ran his fingers along his temples and down the corners of his eyes. One eye was surrounded by a bruise; also, he had a cut on his upper lip. He read his notes back to himself, inaudibly, and gave himself a few laughs, also inaudibly. Then, as he squinted all around at printed words, he put down his pencil and rubbed the base of his ring finger, though no ring was there. Nadia took him to be a ruined academic—unless he was only half ruined; it was hard to tell.

One hears of dissidents, Nadia reminded herself. *Does a dissident look like that?*

When the first buses started in the morning and Yuri was done his night shift, he insisted on walking Nadia to the nearby stop. A few more times, he touched her shoulder, as one might touch the handle of a mop, were it threatening to fall and spill its bucket.

At the bus stop, Yuri said something in parting and he was starting to leave when Nadia noticed another man across the street. She was sure this man had been looking at her when Yuri was looking at her and now he was leaving just as Yuri was leaving. She stepped towards him to try to make out his features in the smoggy dawn.

Yuri shouted something, grabbed her arm, and pulled her away from the curb. The bus rolled into place and its brakes made an elephantine noise. Nadia sidestepped to peek around the front of the bus. Yuri stumbled but kept his hold. The man across the street was gone from view.

"Are you here? Are you listening?" Yuri snapped at her. "Where's your head?"

"I… I thought I recognized someone." With a sensation like waking from a nightmare, Nadia realized she was shaking. "Thank you. I have to go." She freed her arm and got aboard the bus, where the driver also had words for her as she flashed her bus pass and walked by.

She got back to Anya's apartment and was able to sleep for an hour or two before Nastya phoned to ask whether she was coming for breakfast. By then, the wakeful night again seemed like a dream. *Who was there on the curb? Anyone?*

At the time, Nadia resolved to be more sensible, more sisterly, less furtive. She had begun to frighten herself with these urges to sneak away.

Visiting Rosya Lekht's place became a way to escape without having to be alone or sly or afraid. With permission, Nadia would always use Rosya's phone to call Nastya and let her know she had arrived. Nastya would say, "Good," and have her sister put Rosya on the line for a minute, for this reason or that.

Sometimes, Rosya would squint and shake her head as she listened to a question from Nastya. "Well," Rosya might say, "I don't really know how to cook that. Why do you ask?"

Rosya had dark hair with curly ends that shifted as she shook her head. When she squinted, deep crow's feet appeared beside her eyes, which were grey and busy and sometimes bloodshot. She had a complicated face that seemed to change its age in an instant yet never break focus in the course of a night's work.

Rosya's hospitality had an unconventional character. Sleep was scarcely contemplated. Snacks and cigarettes were bountifully dispensed from packs. There was no end of homemade fruit juice, which Rosya prepared in the mornings with an electric squeezer; she spiced it, bottled it, and maintained a rotation of bottles from the freezer to the fridge so that spicy, slushy juice was always available. There was never a mind like Rosya's. The clacking of the keyboard accompanied long talks on codes and history, with her audience of one or two at hand. Then, she would get up to stretch and pace and go pee out fruit juice, while Ida (working from a guidebook written by none other than Rosya Lekht) would take a turn at typing and printing and staring into the radiant depths of the colour monitor.

For a break, they would play graphical games, especially from the American section in Rosya's cabinet of diskettes. One game featured a spider attempting to escape from the floor of a cider factory, up to the attic. Along the way, it faced such threats to its life as jets of juice, guillotine blades, falling apple slices, grinding gears, and swarms of frogs, bees, and birds. Ida said it was entirely true to life.

Less whimsical versions of life were presented in simulation games. According to Rosya, America was using these games to train a new generation of managers and bureaucrats. There was a simulation of control systems in the nuclear plant at Three Mile Island. Could the player avert disaster? There was an economic simulation of an oil company, which had to pay its workers and suppliers and keep queues short at the docks and gas stations and set a price and avoid state intervention and turn a profit. There was a two-player simulation of terrorism and counter-terrorism, in which the opponents, in turn, had limited time to select their beliefs and bargaining position and actions in such scenarios as the hijacking of a plane.

There was a game about flying a space shuttle to the Kremlin and blowing up a nuclear reactor there. Rosya said it was a bestseller in the West.

There was another bestseller, all in text, about a man who went around binge-drinking and gambling and gawking at kinky women and buying sex with cash or gifts—a gift of flowers, a gift of a ring that he found in a washroom drain. His narrator used words such as "*Woah!*" and sometimes the text flashed in colours.

"Play it," said Rosya, "if you want to know stupidity up close. Anyway, I keep everything. Once a month or so, I'm obliged to write a rant to send round the world to the newspapers—my observations on the computing machinery of decadence and dystopia. I'm known not to flinch. I have a collection of Nazi punchcards, printed by an American syndicate called IBM, in a shop they opened outside the Warsaw Ghetto. Here's how it is. Our captors take a census, always a census to get the muscles moving, and it is the livelihood of scribes to punch it on paper or disk or clay, like in the days of Nebuchadnezzar II, like now—scribes to fill a storehouse as big as you like with letters as small as you like, until the roof falls in and crushes it all to dust. We have legal records of collapsed roofs in Babylon. That's how it is: the collapse of an infinite storehouse upon infinitesimal texts."

"Hmm."

Nadia expressed an interest in any readings Rosya might suggest to her. Rosya promised to give it some thought. She never suggested readings without taking a pause to study the reader.

Another game, with bright and squiggly pictures, had, as its hero, a boy with a magic pig. The lad and his ensorcelled swine wandered a fairytale forest and later a castle dungeon as they played cat-and-mouse with an evil warlock-king who needed a magic pig. The boy was always getting hungry; he could die if he didn't stop to eat an apple or somesuch. He carried one apple at a time. "Why doesn't he eat the pig?" Ida asked as Nadia translated the text for her. "That'd solve all his problems, wouldn't it? Can't you type, 'Eat pig?'"

"You know full well this one doesn't have a text parser," Nadia said. "This one is for the little kids. I can't 'eat pig'; I can't 'eat sword'; I can't 'kiss pig'; I can't 'lick mirror'."

"I mean, he could be eating magic bacon for a month," Ida supposed. "Rosya, can I pick up some bacon for us tomorrow?"

"For yourself, if you like," said Rosya, who was lying on a sofa of red leather and smoking a cigarette fast and reviewing her notes and crossing things out. She often did her thinking this way, with a clipboard propped up against her knees and a pillow in the small of her back and a floor lamp providing soft light from behind her head. She asked, "Did you test 'save' and 'restore'?"

"We did, Rosya, when you were out of the room," Ida replied. "It saves—it thinks it saves—but it can't restore."

Rosya made a mark beside something in her notes. The game with the magic pig represented a great deal to her, as it was new and elaborate and based on a Disney film, no less—so if she could get it to run perfectly on her hand-modified system, it would mean that she had caught up with the world's best while the world's best were sleeping or perhaps eating their microwave dinners. She had made great strides in graphics compatibility but disk compatibility and sound remained problematic.

Anyway, such ambitions could only be a small part of the notes. Much else was expected of Rosya Lekht, besides playing with personal computers. Always, she and her computer were short of time, no matter what they did.

Meanwhile, in the daytime, outside the smoky apartment, Ida had found a job driving a dairy truck between the City and the farms. Mostly, she carried sour cream, which was heavy, like lifting water. The radiation inspections made the delivery work even slower than it might have been and, at every chance, Ida took a nap in the truck so as to collect herself for her apprenticeship in computer programming at night.

She got asked out to a movie by a Physics student who was calibrating Geiger counters on her route. She fell asleep on their date, gave unconscious answers to his whispered questions in the theatre, and dreamt of a different middle that a film might have had.

Afterwards, as they headed out of the theatre, the young man lingered to clean his glasses under the pot lights in the hall. Ida stretched and brushed the red ceiling with her fingertips. She looked uncomfortable but he put his glasses back on to watch her. "What?" she asked him.

"I was," he began, "just wondering more about you, about what you told me during the film."

"Hmm? What did I tell you?" She looked down at him for a second and then she stopped tiptoeing. *He's not tall. I must be careful how I stand.*

He did not answer her question directly. Indeed, he might have misconstrued it as coyness. "Well, what happened to the rest of your family?" he asked.

"The rest besides me?"

"Well, the rest besides your Gramma." They looked at each other. He tried to coax a biography out of her another way. "Tell me again about your Gramma."

"Tell you again? There's nothing to tell."

If he thought this was coyness, he also thought it strange. A young man responsible for Geiger counters does not expect such coyness from a sleepy young woman responsible for truckloads of sour cream.

"Well," he gave it one last try, "you made me believe there's some mystery about her. You whispered something about Switzerland and horses and a palace, a Ruby Palace." He laughed a little. "You're a bit of a mystery yourself."

"Hmm." Ida began to walk again and he tailed her. "Sorry," she said, "my head is killing me. I must have been talking crap."

That was all the romance, for Ida, in summer 1986.

Undoubtedly, Ida's world had changed. Rosya's flat, like Nastya and Giorgi's, had an enclosed balcony. A built-in workbench ran along the broad side, under a bank of windows with casements and a transom. The bench supported a cactus, which relished the sun, and a soldering iron, which required ventilation, as well as a binocular microscope, an LED lamp, an oscilloscope, a set of screwdrivers, a kit of dental tools, a miniaturist's paintbrushes, a blue rubber mat, and other such equipment as one might put to use.

The cactus was a prickly pear and, around its clay pot, it wore an Israeli flag. There, in Haifa, Rosya had a father and brother, as well as a sister-in-law, nephew, and niece whom she had never met. Her father and Yuly's wife Minah were first cousins. Rosya was, properly, Yuly's first cousin-in-law once removed. They had met on perhaps twenty occasions. (Nadia found these details in an annotated diagram, which Ida had scrawled in her copy of Rosya's book, in the whitespace around another diagram on the evolution of operating systems.)

The windows gave an unobstructed view of the Dnieper, including a manmade beach. From a distance, the swimmers and sunbathers and sandcastle-builders seemed like the decent city-folk on Uncle Styopa's beat. Water of the Dnieper, water of the Pripyat, it all flowed by and cooled the sand and cooled the skin and washed the sweat away.

When offered the choice—where in the flat would she live?—Ida had asked for a place by the workbench, in the company of the sun and stars. Consequently, a bed was shoved up to the bench and partly underneath it, with a sheet of fireproof khaki draped overtop the blankets during work. Sometimes Ida or Rosya sat there to solder—sometimes the pair of them, Rosya guiding Ida's hand. Nadia thought her friend looked happy at those times.

Indeed, there had never been such times in the flat of Rosya Lekht.

The few nights she spent there, Nadia felt strangely at peace at the edge of the cluttered bench and cluttered Cosmos, beside her friend who seemed to have been made and broken and remade by the narrowest of probabilities, as thin even as a page or the surface of the sea, where deepest darkness meets the light.

At the end of the workweek, before midnight, Ida got a headache and succumbed to all problems, great and small. She became, again, a sinking swimmer with exhausted shoulders and brine in her eyes. Rosya added some medicinal drops to Ida's juice and told her to drink up and sleep. "You've worked hard."

One Saturday morning, Nadia got up early (climbing over Ida and leaving her asleep) and went to the kitchen to browse the bookshelves. Half the pantry was dedicated to books instead of food.

Gramma would not approve of the lack of cooking here. Indeed, Ida's weight is not progressing half so well as her training. Still, she is happy. This is a real change of luck for her at last.

Picking up a book about collective farms in Israel, Nadia lost herself in the pictures for a while. Then, when she looked up, she saw Rosya enter the kitchen in a bathrobe, finely printed with an irregular pattern of big yellow dahlias and little blue ones on a brown background. The shoulders were tight on her (and extra stitches had been added there) but the wrists flared out and ruffles burst from the neckline. Rosya got a lemon from a bowl on the counter, sliced it in half, and began grinding it into the squeezer.

"Do you read Hebrew?" Rosya asked before juicing the second half.

"No," Nadia confessed. She hesitated, unsure whether to put the book back. Meanwhile, Rosya re-engaged the motor. Raising her voice, Nadia added, "No, I would like to. I love languages."

Rosya asked her which ones she knew; Nadia said Russian, Estonian, some Belarusian from her grandmother, and Ukrainian—and of foreign languages, she was always working on English, also French, and little bits of others.

The lemon was reduced to its peel and juice. Rosya poured herself a glass and came over to the pantry to get the pepper grinder, a little bottle of vanilla, and a stick of cinnamon. She looked down at Nadia and said, "I'm told your Gramma understands Yiddish perfectly—Polish and German too."

"I didn't know that."

Rosya returned to the counter, spiced her drink, and took a sip. She seemed to consider it and then consider something else. "Do you look like her?" she asked. "I mean, did she look like you?"

"I don't know," Nadia answered as she finally slid the book back into the hole it had left. "She doesn't have any pictures from before the War."

"No and you weren't there!"

"No, I wasn't."

"My father met her, twice. First time, she's a girl crashing a wedding. My father describes her … as I think he might describe you."

"O! mercy," Nadia said. "You're going to tell me unflinchingly, aren't you, Rosya?"

Rosya smiled, in a show of all her wrinkles. "Bear in mind, my father is no great flatterer. Take me. 'Rosya has the face of a hard worker.'" She licked her lower lip and conjured what seemed a happy memory, to her. "He calls your Gramma 'a very small opera … a very small piece of opera … a sharp-voiced girl with round cheeks and a round nose'. He's not pleased with her at their first meeting. She is wicked; she's crashed Yuly and Minah's wedding."

"Crashed their wedding? You mean, showed up as a stranger?"

"Oh, no, never a stranger." Rosya kept smiling as she took another sip of peppered lemon juice. "Her sister has long been a serious rival for Yuly's love. Hearts have been broken, maybe. Your Gramma—ever the blasphemer—shows up and sips the kosher wine in revenge."

"Oh!" *Did she know that was blasphemy?* "Which sister?"

"You should know better than I."

"I don't."

"No, well, ask her. Ask Yuly. You learn nothing without asking."

"What happened the second time they met?"

"The second time, the 'very small opera' takes a pair of hand grenades and crawls along an irrigation ditch, half a kilometre in a cold autumn fog, to ambush an *Einsatzgruppen* death squad. My Papa is left facing her across a muddy pit he's been digging as his grave—he and a dozen others still alive."

Rosya added, "There's a tree and a plaque with her name in Israel for that."

"Ida would love this story."

"Yes, well, it's yours to tell now. Do ask your Gramma for her version."

"I will. Thank you." Nadia's mouth puckered and filled with spit as she watched Rosya ingest the remainder of the mixture. *What a stomach!*

Rosya bared her greyish teeth at the glass and then offered a conclusion. "You could say she's a kind of mother to kids like my brother and me, kids of survivors. You know—not that I've ever met her or any of your family—but I suppose it makes me a kind of aunt to you."

"I'm becoming an aunt, around New Year's," Nadia shared.

"Well," Rosya sighed, "if I'm an example, there's not much to it."

"The ultrasound shows it's a boy."

"Yes, I do a lot of work on ultrasound software." Rosya raised the empty glass. "Would you like one of these? I think it would work well chilled, if you're staying."

"Oh…"

The phone rang, in the main room by the computer.

"That's probably your sister," Rosya said. She put down her glass and rushed off with a swish of her robe whilst muttering, "She'll ask, do I have advice on … sex during pregnancy, probably."

Nadia lingered by the pantry to contemplate the edible contents.

Ida groaned as the phone rang a second time and half a time again. Rosya began to speak, intermittently.

Nadia looked inside some brown paper bags, from bakeries. There were mincemeat tarts, round doughnuts oozing strawberry jam, and two loaves of crunchy-crusted bread hugging chunks of almonds and cherries.

"I… No, I've never built a crib, Nastya. I suppose you'd use wood glue. Did you want to speak to your sister? She's still here."

Ida groaned once more.

Nadia shut the pantry and slowly made her way towards the phone. On her way past the fridge, she stopped to peep at the cuts of smoked meat. Like tulips, they had a smell that made her face sweat.

When Nadia entered the main room, Rosya was sitting on the edge of Ida's bed with a hand on Ida's brow. The cactus was devouring the orangey daylight as best it could, through smog. The phone's receiver was lying atop the printer. Nadia went to pick it up. "Kremlin…"

"Ha."

"You're not Nastya."

"Ha. No."

Great, he's in one of his bashful moods, when his vocabulary shrivels.
"She had to go for a pee, did she?"

"Your inference is correct."

"Ah-ha." Nadia eyed the printer and the untorn folds of paper that lay overtop and behind it. The machine had been spitting out codes even after Rosya had gone to bed. "Are you relaxing this morning, Giorgi? …relaxing with a coffee and a newspaper?"

"We were testing the crib," Giorgi reported. "We had the idea to test the crib by placing a watermelon in it."

"How did that go?"

"There is watermelon all over the floor."

"O! mercy. That must…" *…have dishonoured your woodworker-ancestors and pissed off your wife and seemed to you like a portent, which shall be told to your offspring one day.* "…be messy."

"I'll clean it up, no problem. Then, I'll go out for some wood glue. Nadezhda, before…"

There was silence for several seconds and then Nastya came on the line. "Good morning. Wake up, wake up, Little Hedgehog."

"Have you chased down the Moon, Mother Wolf, and fried it for breakfast?"

(The making of Nadia's breakfast and the telling of a breakfast story had an old significance to Nastya. Nadia was willing to participate in this kindly echo of the past.)

"I wish you and Anya were here to help us with this crib," Nastya sighed. "Listen, I have something to tell you. Papa is okay but he's had an accident at work. A box fell on his head, late yesterday. He's been in hospital overnight with a concussion but he's headed home with Mama now."

"Oh, no. Did Mama call you last night?"

"No, she didn't. She said she and Papa weren't too worried. She said he got everyone laughing about it at the hospital."

"What was in the box?"

"You should go down today and ask him."

Nadia scanned the apartment. Ida was sitting up in bed and, with tweezers, she was holding a hair from the prickly pear. She squinted at its silhouette against the orange sun. Then, she examined it under the microscope.

Rosya was bringing a tray: crunchy bread with a bowl of salt for dipping, alongside a mix of yesterday's chilled juices with wedges of fresh lemon and more sticks of cinnamon.

"Yes, sure," Nadia agreed. "I guess I can get there tonight … or else overnight. I'll have to see at the station."

Nastya assured her, "I'll tidy up Anya's place for you."

"Oh, right."

Already, Nadia was thinking of the smells of the train.

2: Scramble

Rosya took the logistics into her own hands. She told Nadia to just pack; get herself down to the station as fast as she could. Ida would go with Nadia to see which train Nadia was able to catch. Ida would come back to Rosya and Rosya would call Nastya so that Nastya could call Katya to let her know when to expect Nadia. Rosya would also call Yuly so that Yuly could tell Gramma Ninel, in case no one was updating her on the injury of her son.

Ida and Nadia, after bolting their bread and juice, scrambled from those sleepless quarters with cherry skins and almond bits in their teeth and a chill in their pulsing throats. Nadia, in particular, felt that she and her family were being given a drill, organized by a woman who possessed frightening foresight.

3: Ghost Sparrows

Down at Central Station, in the Main Hall, with a ticket in one hand and her suitcase in the other, Nadia fidgeted and paced and watched one clock and then another. Ida was sticking around with her for a few minutes at least, despite the strictest instructions to come straight back.

"You look worried," Ida said. "Come on, if anybody is immune to smacks on the head, it's sure to be your Papa."

"You are my truest comfort, Smartass." Even as she spoke, Nadia felt that the words lost their proper feeling amidst the pervasive echo of footsteps, chitchat, announcements, and escalators. She added, "Eat well, will you?"

"Sure," Ida chirped. (Ida had found a frequency that cut well through the echo.) "I mean, it's a fair fight, him and your Mama. I'd say it's where you got your sense of fairness."

"Would you? Would you say I've got one of those?"

"Hmm! If you don't, who does?"

Nadia shrugged and pivoted away from the nearest clock and stood on tiptoe to hug Ida around the neck.

"Oh, go on," Ida scoffed. She patted Nadia's back and then pushed her down to a level-footed stance.

A fluttering sound rained down from the Baroque ceiling. They gazed up to see one of the two chandeliers stirring silently.

"Ghosts," Nadia hissed. "Ghost sparrows. Where have they gone?"

"Box fell on his head," Ida muttered. She ran her fingertips across her brow and grimaced. The corners of her mouth parted.

"Headache?" Nadia asked.

"Hmm, I do … and a ghost sparrow shat on me." Verily, Ida's forehead and fingers were smeared with something like white paint, yet not white paint.

They were able to leave one another laughing.

4: Sense of Fairness

Her train left just before noon, so she got to Odessa hungry and tired at half past nine in the evening. She had not felt like eating or sleeping. As the summer went on, she felt ever more suspicious of the food in Kiev, the food at the rail stops near Kiev, the dairy from trucks such as Ida's, and certainly any mushrooms and berries one might see in the forests near Kiev. She heard rumours from Yuri, impressions from Ida, case notes from Giorgi, and history-in-the-making from Rosya. Leaves were turning red in summer. A whole herd of wild horses was found dead. The Army's conscripts had a new exercise this year: go back to the abandoned streets and apartments to shoot the pets before the pets could stray. For such a special mission, special protective gear was provided: a lead plate for one's crotch. The evacuation zone was being expanded for children and pregnant women. Giorgi volunteered again and, in the Captain's absence, he would hold command at many a sad scene. Nastya asked him to promise not to sacrifice himself as the Captain had done, not to dig in rubble or whatever else the Captain had done. She asked, if it came down to it, could he not rely on the courage of some Private instead?

He said he could make no such promise, ever, even to her. On reflection, he assured her that the risk was far less this time around. If there were a danger to men, the evacuation order would have included men. The danger in this new zone was only to children and pregnant women and babies.

Besides, Giorgi showed them, he always carried his IDII dosimeter on a string wrapped around the button of his breast pocket. The device was a little square of specially coated glass, mounted inside a metal shell that opened like a lipstick. A serial number was printed on the base to prevent any mixups. If Giorgi's cumulative dose had reached a hazardous level, the glass would be glowing now, yet, look, it was not. If they doubted their eyes, he could invite a technician to dinner some evening to demonstrate the true method of measuring the IDII's luminescence using the GO32.

"Yes," said Nastya, "I'd like that," but it never happened.

Nastya spent those days cleaning and preemptively studying the cultural-educational curriculum and being a carpenter and choking back tears, when Giorgi was away shepherding the new evacuees.

He returned with dinnertime tales. How Fenya had made the children laugh! She had narrated the evacuation as an adventure with Uncle Styopa.

"Do their pets get shot too?" Nadia asked one evening as she eyed her untouched plate of baked potatoes and sour cream. The menu had narrowed of late. Anyway, Nastya liked sour cream and potatoes, with the skins brushed in vegetable oil, the way Anya made them.

Giorgi went silent.

"Apologize," Nastya instructed, to no effect. "Apologize!" she barked as she slammed her fist down on the table. Her plate rattled. Her spoon catapulted a glob of sour cream at the window. At the age of nineteen, she knew anger in the new style and the old.

"I never said it was his fault," Nadia grumbled, *but you're quick to hear that. You know, Wolfie, he is what he is; only you insist otherwise.* "Rosya is expecting me. I should go. I'll save this for tomorrow."

As Nadia rose from the table and took her plate way, Giorgi belatedly replied, "I believe pets will continue to live there, just like the men and a great many of the women."

Around that time, Misha and Katya were headed to the hospital as they debated whether to call the kids.

The next morning, on the phone, the two sisters and Giorgi spoke about a crib and a watermelon before Nadia was dispatched.

On a train ride into the night, Nadia was seated with her own thoughts. *Ida admires my alleged sense of fairness. I don't know what, if anything, I can admire in myself.*

Nadia got to Odessa hungry and tired at half past nine in the evening, some thirty hours after a box fell on Misha's head.

5: Few True Friends

Normally, Misha would have been there to meet his daughter on the platform, outdoors behind the station. He would have stood out, even in the half-darkness between the streetlamps, as a man with springs in his knees, a man who always moves a little, albeit with nothing to do and nowhere to go. He would have looked around and nodded at people. He would have worn a shirt with two breast pockets, as symmetrical as his face: straight nose, straight jaw, straight teeth, unharmed by his boxing days. Women of all ages would have asked him for directions.

There was no one like that on the platform.

A man on a concrete bench (actually, on the base of a streetlamp) folded up his newspaper and rubbed his sunken eyes and the soft, lumpy mass of his nose, which seemed to have been smashed in some unhappy hour of his life. He got up and then he willed his short, slim, stiff legs to carry him on a path parallel to Nadia's. As they neared the station, he swerved to catch up with her in the better light under the colonnade. "Miss, hello, are you Nadia?"

She stopped. "Yes."

"My name is Avel. He asked me to meet you."

"He—Papa?"

"No—our friend."

Nadia studied the man's face, with the lights glaring down on his thin, oiled hair and his eyes surrounded by shadows (like pools of tears in old black-and-white cartoons) and his nose casting a shapeless shadow over the centre of his lips. He pulled back the sleeve of his grey jacket to check his watch—apparently a child's watch, with a cartoon rabbit and yellow chick. The rabbit was dressed as a stage magician, in top hat and tails, and he was performing a trick with handkerchiefs, to the amazement of the yellow chick. Next to the watch, the man wore a string of acrylic beads with ants of the tiniest variety entombed inside them. Every fourth and fifth ant was red, the rest black. All ants faced clockwise (from Nadia's perspective) and thus they marched forever in a circle.

"Oh, you're Avel," Nadia registered him in her mind. "You gave my sister a very beautiful can opener."

"Thank you, Miss. I was proud of that one. Yes, I thought, 'He's married a girl who can appreciate it.'"

"Some men get the girl and the can opener," Nadia remarked.

Avel did not react. He was glancing at something behind her.

Nadia looked around. By the doors stood a young man in black naval uniform. He held a sign up against his chest. The sign had her name on it.

Avel diverted his gaze. "Don't stare, Miss," he suggested. "If I were you, I wouldn't want people to link me with a name on a sign."

"Perhaps I should go see what he's about," Nadia murmured.

"Should you, Miss? You must please yourself," Avel said, "but you won't give a bad report of me if I scram, will you?"

"No, I… Well, never mind, I'd just as soon that you and I get going."

"That's the best thing, Miss. Men in uniform never get you home fast. Well, I suppose they get the nurses home fast." He took Nadia's suitcase and, despite stiff legs, he began to scurry—into the crowd, into the building, out of the crowd, out of the building. At moments, Nadia lost sight of him as she, too, put her lungs into the effort to scurry. Once they were on the front steps, Avel drew a deep breath of the tepid, humid air, which, on this side of the station, carried a bit less scent of diesel and perhaps a bit more of the sea. "Now, here's a summer night for coming home. They'll be happy to see you, Miss."

"I hope so. Everybody does seem to be waiting for me tonight. Maybe there's another girl with my name."

"Odds are."

They took the tram partway and then he walked her home. He commented on the niceness of the detached housing in the neighbourhood. Was it her mother's employer or her father's that provided such villas? Her mother's. He left her at the garden gate and said he had better not disturb the family; he knew (by reputation) how hospitable they were.

The gate greeted her hand with its familiar feel of glossy white paint cracked by salty dew and rust. The hinges creaked as Nadia entered the garden. On the path, just before the doorstep, she almost slipped on a mess of vegetable peels. Some animal had scattered them from their usual place atop the garden beds. *That would have made us a fine pair,* Nadia thought. *A box falls on Papa and I slip on the potato peels. What a help that would be to Mama!* She tarried to kick the peels out of the way.

Katya threw open the door, cried, "You're here, thank God!" and cupped her hand around the back of Nadia's head like a shepherd's crook.

Startled, Nadia gave her mother a swift but firm kiss on the cheek and then side-stepped into the narrow kitchen. All the lights were off, except for a blue flame on the burner of the gas stove. Katya went to the gate to check that it had latched properly and then she hurried back inside and shut the door and bolted it. "What's the matter?" Nadia asked. She flung off her coat and threw it over her suitcase with its sleeves inside out. "Papa?" she called.

"He's fine," Katya hissed and she flapped her hands at her daughter. "Shh, he's sleeping. Where were you, my little one? Nastya says…" (Katya bumped into Nadia as they both fumbled for the light switch.) "Nastya says you lose track of yourself sometimes and when I heard you weren't on the train…" They got the lights on. Tears were in Katya's eyes.

"I was on the train!" Nadia protested. "I've spent all day waiting for the train and sitting on the train and now I've come straight from the station."

"Then … the driver missed you. How disappointing."

"The driver, Mama?" Nadia wondered. *Has the train taken me to an alternate reality?*

"I'm sorry, my treasured one," Katya said as she turned to attend to a giant pot of soup on the stove. "I'm sorry, I wish we could have come ourselves and saved this horrible confusion and upset. Your father wanted to go but I told him he mustn't and then he wanted me to go but I told him I couldn't, so he asked, who do we know who could go? We have so few true friends in Odessa. Then, I remembered, Lieutenant Colonel Sokolov gave me his phone number—his direct line—the day I left the sanatorium and I knew he'd be back by now too. He said, if I was ever in need, I was to call him. Papa wasn't sure we should disturb him; he was already kind enough to send us an invitation to tour one of the carriers during an airshow (he knowing of Misha's interest)—but I did call him and he promised to send his driver round for you."

"Oh…"

"Perhaps he never really went," Katya speculated as she stirred the soup to break up the floating crust of fat. The fatty shards sank into the depths and she kept stirring to make sure everything got reheated evenly. "Perhaps he forgot; perhaps he told a story—that you weren't on the train; the Lieutenant Colonel believed it and repeated it to me."

"No, it's my mistake," Nadia confessed. "There was a Navy guy waiting but I sort of ignored him. I'd already met a man Giorgi sent for me."

Katya said nothing for a moment as she tasted the soup. "Giorgi should have called to tell me. He avoids talking to me now. He…" She got a bowl and spoon from the cupboard. "Nastya should have called."

"She probably lost track of herself."

"No cheek tonight," Katya chided her. "Have some soup. Have … some big chunks of chicken breast. We'll save the neck for your father. You aren't eating right in Kiev. Nastya had better be, for our grandson. Go, go sit and eat. I have to make a call."

That's a colossus you've boiled there. "Where'd you get the giant chicken, Mama?" Nadia whispered as they came through to the family room. The door to her parents' bedroom was closed. They left the main lights off but Katya switched on a lamp in the corner, plus there was light from the kitchen.

"I went to the country and strangled it," Katya replied. Nadia looked up from the dinner table and received a kiss on the forehead before Katya offered a different version. "I emptied your Papa's wallet and bought it from a farmer's wife. Her husband was in hospital for a stroke. I was hesitant because she wanted cash up front but I decided to trust her and it turned out alright, except it was a tough old bird—but alright for soup. She lost no time delivering it here this morning. We only just got home before she showed up. I guess there's still a little honesty in the world."

"Yum," Nadia breathed as she spooned soup into her parched mouth. "Black market chicken is good."

"I'd hope so," Katya said. "At least she threw in the carrots and tomatoes for free."

"Also good."

"She said the veggies were thanks for your Papa's sense of humour. 'Do you ever stop laughing?' she asked me. I have to make this call now." Katya picked up the carrot-coloured receiver and dialled a number from memory.

Nadia savoured the soup and listened as her mother's telephone voice went soft, like the chicken flesh and carrots and tomatoes and also curved slices of onions, all saturated with fresh broth.

"Hello, yes, it's me again—Katya. I'm so sorry to keep disturbing you but I wanted you to know that Nadia has come home safely. ... Yes, just an unfortunate case of crossed paths. That does seem to be our luck, doesn't it? Do thank your *aide-de-camp* for us and I apologize for the trouble and worry. Misha was most touched by your concern for us and he is so looking forward to the tour of the carrier. ... Yes. Yes, you as well."

Katya hung up and came over to the round table to sit opposite Nadia. They reached across to touch hands, Katya's right to Nadia's left. Then, abruptly, Katya stood up again and said, "You need bread ... my starving soul."

"Oh, yes, please."

Katya had gone and returned before the words were all spoken. She placed a garlic bun down on the table, tore off a morsel for herself and dipped it in Nadia's bowl, and then sat again, chewing slowly, with her eyes on her daughter. "Keep eating," Katya urged her, "and while you eat, you can think of all the stories you have to tell me."

Nadia put on a thoughtful look for a few minutes as she ate her chicken soup and bread. Then, she whispered, "I visited Ida last night. You remember I told you, Ida is in Kiev." *(That is to say, Nastya told you and I had to explain.)*

"Yes," Katya said. She touched Nadia's hand again. "You told me. Gramma helped her and now Gramma's friends are helping her. I'm sure it's the best help anyone can give, to Ida."

"I visited her and her ... host, I suppose ... Rosya."

"The Jewish woman, scientist."

"Yes. Her flat is something like a lab and a library and an arcade parlour, all rolled into one. She has all sorts of things from abroad. I was thinking she might be able to lend me books on ... just about anything."

"What a good idea," Katya agreed.

"She told me a story about Gramma—two stories, actually. Gramma crashed a wedding when she was my age and then later, in the War, she saved Rosya's father, who had been a guest at the wedding. She was very brave. She ambushed a whole squad of Nazis to rescue their prisoners. She crept up on them through fog and through muck, crawling along a wet ditch in an open field, and ... boom, boom ... two hand grenades."

Katya lowered her eyes and smiled as if to say, *I have suckled the granddaughters of a heroine.* She got up, served Nadia another half a bowl and half a roll, and said, "I have to check on Papa now."

Katya slipped into the master bedroom and shut the door. Everything was dark and silent in there. *She might be sitting at her dressing table and watching him,* Nadia supposed. *When we were little, sometimes I'd wake up to find her watching. I can remember her kneeling by the bed, I think. She had long hair and orange jammies with white-and-red ducks and red-and-white butterflies.*

While dissolving a garlicky, brothy lump that was stuck in her teeth, Nadia gazed around the lamplit room to see whether anything had changed. There was a framed sketch of the baby, as seen by Nastya during the ultrasound. There was a fuchsia cotton blanket flung across the sofa. Nadia guessed that her mother had been lying there next to the phone. There was a black ant, of the miniature variety, climbing the floral wallpaper. Nadia got up and bamboozled him until he crawled onto her fingertip. (Whichever way he turned, there was the finger, warm as a soup spoon and porous and strange.) She carried him past the stove and the pile of coats and shoes and put him out in the garden.

By the time Nadia got back to the family room, voices and light were spilling out from the bedroom door.

"No," Katya was giving an order. "No, Misha, don't get up; just open your eyes and look at me. I need to check your eyes."

"That's bright."

"Open your eyes and look at me."

"You said Nadia's here. Did your Lieutenant Sakharov find her?"

"She showed up on her own. Are you confused? Can you tell me the Lieutenant Colonel's name?"

"Sokolov, Sokolov, not Sakharov."

"Why are you getting up, Misha?"

"I want to see Nadia."

Misha staggered out the door with his wife attempting to bear his weight as she gripped his upper arm in both her hands and braced her back against the doorframe. His elbow was crushing a boob and a rib. "Misha," she grunted, "you're hurting me."

Nadia stepped forwards with outstretched arms. Misha squinted, causing a slight shift of the bloodstained gauze patch on his forehead. He opened his mouth as if to say something funny and then he collapsed in Nadia's direction.

Somehow, Nadia and Katya managed to redirect Misha's fall so that he came to rest on the sofa. There, he rolled around a little (never still), filled his lungs, and cast his eyes askance towards the curtains—towards the carrot phone, as if he reproached it for all his problems. More likely, he was trying not to look at the kitchen lights beyond his feet.

"Misha," Katya asked as an oft-ignored counsellor might ask, "should we be going back to the hospital?"

"No," he groaned, "it's too exhausting, having to entertain all those people. I give you … my private show."

Nadia sat on the sofa's arm and wiggled her father's toes and gave him a look. *You're such a kid, Papa.*

He pressed his bandage with two quivering fingers. He seemed satisfied to find it dry.

"I'll get you some soup," Katya said. On her way to the kitchen, without pausing, she touched her daughter's shoulder.

There's something Mama wants to say, Nadia inferred, *beyond the obvious expression of her love. Should I go ask her? No, not now.* Nadia turned her attention back to Misha and asked, "What was in the box?"

Misha shrugged.

"You'll talk to me, pal," Nadia growled in her impression of an American. "Don't make me flip this switch." She leaned sideways and stretched to place her finger on the light switch.

"You wouldn't," Misha whispered in a sort of whimpering laugh. "You don't have it in you. Anyway, I don't know what was in the box."

"Too bad for you." All the same, Nadia dropped the act and gave her father a shrug, imitating his.

Katya returned with a bowl of soup, containing a segment of the chicken's thick, greasy neck. "Misha, sit up to eat," she told him. He rolled into a sitting position in the middle of the soft sofa. Katya slid down onto the pillow beside him, where his head had lain. She balanced the soup bowl in her lap and broke up the neck with the spoon and studied Misha's face. "How is the pain behind your eyes?" she asked.

"What really hurts," Misha moaned with a flavour of mirth, "is the thought of the paperwork for all this."

"Shh," Katya coaxed him as she put an arm around his shoulders and tried to spoon a bit of broth and neck-fat into his mouth.

Misha had more to say. "I deserve compensation and so does this chicken's family. Nadia, find me a New York lawyer!"

"No," Nadia snickered. "You're bad enough with the police on your side. How would you be with a lawyer?"

"What disrespect, what disrespect…" Misha muttered and trailed off. Nadia came down from the sofa's arm to sit beside him and put her head on his shoulder. Meanwhile, he accepted a heaping spoonful of chicken neck from Katya. "That's very good."

"Chew. Chew," Katya urged him.

"Yes, dear, I do remember that much," said Misha, sounding for a moment like his mother, with some of the tones deadened by chicken mush (in his case) or mushy gums (in hers). "I'm just a bit shaky, not retarded."

Katya wiped some broth from Misha's lips with her knuckles. He looked vexed but he snorted and kept chewing.

"Nadia," Misha muttered. He patted her knee. "Nadia, good to have you home. Tomorrow, I … I want to show you the kittens."

"Shh," Katya cooed.

"Shh!" Misha repeated. He hugged himself and shook some more and stamped his foot hard on the embroidered rug that lay in front of the sofa. A reverberation rattled the room, enough to feel it through the surface of a second rug that hung on the wall behind their heads.

Nadia thought, as she quite often did, of Johnny lecturing her on the science of broadcasting—how the radio towers were shaking the entire Earth (and Space beyond) with encoded speeches and songs. *Can one demodulate a voice from an embroidered rug? I am exhausted and can never stop worrying and can never go back and I am beginning to hear an extra language; I don't know what it is.*

Katya got up to place the soup bowl beside the phone, on a small desk where she sometimes sewed by the light of the window facing the garden. She kept a sewing machine (her mother's) in the tall bottom drawer. Katya had sewn new curtains for her own birthday in May, not

long after the meltdown and her return from the sanatorium, using a
pool of birthday funds from Misha and Giorgi and Nastya. The drapery
was made of two rayon prints that she had stitched in vertical stripes:
pale blue waterfalls with tiny flowering vines in a pink-and-maroon
tie-dyed jungle with flowering trees. (Katya was proud to have worked
the slippery rayon without making it pucker.) The lining was cotton
filter cloth, which had been surplus to needs in the factory where Katya
worked.

She had said at the time, "I've wanted to make something like this
for twenty years," and, indeed, those rayon prints had been waiting
for her in a warehouse almost as long. None of her coworkers could
appreciate Katya's description of the curtains she had made.

Yawning, Katya switched off the lamp in the corner, parted the
curtains with her fingers, and peered out.

Nadia sat with her father in the semidarkness, beyond the arc of the
kitchen lights. By and by, Misha started to move again and the sofa's
surface shifted like a magic carpet. He was getting up.

"Papa?"

Katya shut the curtains. "Misha, what are you doing?" she asked.

"I need the toilet," he reported. He pushed away the women's hands
and shuffled at an uneven pace through the kitchen to the washroom.
As he neared his objective, he broke into a clumsy charge and slammed
the door behind him, causing Katya to falter and stop.

"Misha?" she wondered.

A vomitous moan erupted from the door and probably flew out the
ventilation hole towards the street, where it might have disturbed the
activities of cats in garden sheds or neighbours on a nocturnal smoke
break, an escape from married life in too few rooms, yet better rooms
than before—before they all came to work for the factory, which was
doing quite well for itself to be able to offer such housing as a perk to
its workers, yet, in the last analysis, it was a workplace like any other: a
pantomime, a production, a set, a script of chaotic misconstructions
using festering silences to punctuate fits of babble. Katya had her reasons
to close the curtains against a neighbourhood of coworkers.

"I'm fine," Misha gasped.

"Good!" Katya replied. She paced (as far as one could pace) and
then dumped the chicken neck and broth back into the pot. She thrust
the bowl onto a counter, sat on a stool, and held her head in her hands.

"Has he been like this the whole time?" Nadia whispered.

"On and off," said her mother. "We must keep an eye on him, my dearest. The Doctor warned us, Misha could have a relapse. He's had head injuries before, once from boxing and once from an accident in the Army."

Nadia slumped against the wall and said to the door, "We're here, Papa." Further sounds of suffering emerged, followed by further faint reassurances. She glanced back at her mother. "Mama, was there something you wanted to say to me earlier?"

"About what, my love?" Katya asked.

"I'm not sure."

"No, not a thing," Katya said. She rubbed her face and looked up to say, "Go to bed, my tired old soul. I'll have an easier time settling him once you've gone to bed. Go quietly and then I'll fetch him out of there. He's probably half asleep already."

"Alright, Mama, if you're sure."

"I'm sure. Maybe you can take him for a short walk tomorrow."

"Okay, tomorrow we'll try. I guess the cats will take him as is."

"Would the cats have married him? Go to bed."

Katya and Nadia hugged and exchanged kisses on the cheek. A short time afterwards, in her old bed in the dark, Nadia heard her parents sniping at each other as they stumbled, in stages, to their rest.

"This is your logic, to feed me more when I've just thrown up."

"Yes, Misha, this is my logic. Don't be an arse."

"Come on, Katya Kitty, you should laugh a little more. What good is anything if we can't laugh?"

"I'll try to think about that logically. Now, shh."

Nadia had opened the bedroom window for some air, as the room smelt slightly musty. This was the windward side of the house and the cinderblocks got mouldy by late summer but the breeze could be pleasant. The window sash played the part of a lethargic ghost and only a moonbeam lay in Nastya's bed. *I wonder whether her room smells of wood glue right now. Well, it couldn't be worse than Giorgi's neck soaked in sweat and Shipr. How does she feel looking at an empty crib and how does Mama feel looking at a pair of empty beds? Mama is just twice Nastya's age.*

Nadia rolled over to face the darkness of the wall.

Papa, she continued her thought, *is a loveable man and I believe*

Mama still loves him. However, however, however… I don't know. How will it be for Nastya? I ought to wish her a lifetime of happiness with Giorgi, right? I ought to feel something for my nephew-to-be whose ultrasound scan is reproduced in charcoal on the wall out there, right? He does, after all, send kicks in my direction when I am instructed to put my hand on Nastya's belly. The time is approaching when he will look at me and need to be loved by me if he is to become a skeptic, if he is to have a shield.

I will think of something else. She played the game of picturing people she had seldom met and imagining the intrigues of their lives. Overtired, she was unsure where to begin with Avel and the ants, so she passed them by. *That Marat is a curious character, with his cufflinks and camera and trip to Sweden and a face like a fair-haired jack in a deck of cards.*

6: Summer Kittens

The following morning, a Sunday, Misha was feeling "pretty much better". He began by mixing his coffee with liquid doses of a painkiller and an anti-nauseant. He asked, "Are you sure the Doctor didn't say to take these with a cocktail and caviar on toast?"

"Quite sure," Katya replied.

"Oh. I suppose we can't all have the sanatorium treatment." He gulped his coffee and gazed at Nadia down the length of the mug. He looked as if he had grown a snout, which happened to be a souvenir snout with a stylized map of places they had seen on their family vacation in Crimea.

Sniffing, Misha set down the mug and looked at an imaginary menu. "What should we order?" he asked his daughter. "The food is pretty much alright in this place but, you know, I really come to look at the waitress."

"Yes, Papa."

"Tell her I've done my best to raise you on my own."

He ended up having the chicken neck out of the soup and a slice of ham. Nadia had a stack of three miniature potato pancakes glued with redcurrant jam. Katya snatched a bite from Misha's plate and a bite from Nadia's.

"Meow! See," Misha teased, "it's just like eating with a cat. Can't you go catch something, Katya Kitty?"

She cast a heated glance back at him and he hid his mouth behind his coffee.

When Misha had finished eating, he sniffed again and said, "Come on." He was on his feet, springing around in the kitchen as he put on his jacket and checked his pockets for his cigarette case, lighter, and wallet.

"They're on the dresser," Katya said without looking at him. She was wiping grease from the stovetop.

"Nadia, come on," Misha repeated as he passed through the family room. He disappeared into the master bedroom, returned with his pockets full, and added, "The kittens are waiting. I'm allowed to go out if I'm with you."

Nadia yawned, cleared the table, and followed Misha into the kitchen, where Katya seized the dirty dishes and shooed her away from the sink. (Katya's kitchen, unlike Nastya's, was not a place for gatherings, chitchat, or assembly lines. At home, Katya worked alone.)

Misha held the door for Nadia and they stepped out into the garden, where he paused to feel his fresh bandage and stare at the scattered vegetable peels. "What's this?" he murmured. "I'd say there was a chase here last night, of one kind or another."

"You've learnt a lot from the police."

"Theory only. No real practice."

"Well, no, in your state, putting on the hat could kill you."

"Perhaps. Less talk, let's walk." Misha stepped ahead to hold the garden gate for his daughter.

On her way through, she hesitated and looked up at him to say, "I feel as if we're forgetting something."

"Yes," Misha vaguely agreed.

They searched each other's faces, as navigators might look for stars in clouded skies.

"I'll ask Mama," Nadia said. "You go ahead. Sit in the park."

"Good idea."

As Nadia re-entered the house, Katya glanced up from the dishwater and met with her daughter's questing eyes—as familiar and distant as a constellation, in the cosmos of Katya's adulthood. Katya surmised, "You need something for the cats."

"Yes."

"Well, they can have the chicken liver, unless your father wants it for his lunch. That's his decision."

"I'd say he wants the cats to have it." Nadia reached into the fridge to get a cold, squishy packet. A peek inside the layers of brown paper confirmed that it was raw liver—dark and slippery, brownish red, with a bitter, bloody smell. She quickly covered it up again and headed out with the packet in her hand.

On Nadia's way, Katya caught her arm in a soapy grip and whispered, "Do keep an eye on him, my dearest."

Nadia replied, "That's why I'm here…" *… to keep an eye on both of you.*

Katya kissed her daughter on the forehead and let her go.

Nadia went to join her father in the little park just across the intersection. He was resting with his arm over the barrel of the T-34 as he took brief glances at the sun. The morning was pretty much perfect—light scattering everywhere in the sparse, white fog.

Misha squinted and told Nadia she looked very summery. She hardly thought so. He insisted: she was getting freckles.

"Well, in that case, artists will call me *Summertime with Freckles and Raw Liver*." She waved the packet. "For the cats."

"Good."

They went to the cliff, to the stairs, and down to the boardwalk. By this time, Misha was smoking.

"Could I have one?" Nadia enquired.

Misha straightened his back and turned his head sideways to blow the smoke away from his daughter and well above her height. "No," he told her. "What kind of question is that, for my little daughter to ask?"

"Maybe I have a whole new set of questions. Maybe I have a whole slew of new reasons to question you."

"I see," said Misha. He thought, *Am I being jibed for dealing in booze? No, the funny part is, I'd say Nadia minds least of all what I do with Giorgi. We have entered the stage where it's the wives who mind.* "Okay, let's try," he conceded. "I will hear new questions—but new reasons, I forbid."

"You've called my bluff. Now I have to think of a real question."

"Take all the time you need."

After walking awhile, they came to a stretch where the boardwalk had a canopy on metal poles. To the landward side was a copse of scrubby trees and, presumably, the canopy served an all-seasons' purpose of shielding the boards from seeds, berries, leaves, and snow-laden boughs. As they approached the canopy, Misha jumped to get a look over the top.

"Not up there," he muttered. "They must be in the brush."

Under the canopy, the boardwalk ran between a pair of stone walls. One of these faced the beach, which was a good four-metre drop, and the other embraced the bare, washed-out roots at the edge of the copse. Misha peered into the little wilderness, shook his head, and then gestured for Nadia to sit with him on the beachside wall. They sat with their backs to the sun and sea.

Misha whistled in imitation of a little bird. "Let's wait and see whether they come," he proposed. "They'll smell what you've got, right enough. No need to unwrap it yet."

As they sat on the half-shaded wall, raw liver juice dripped through the packet and between Nadia's fingers, onto the stones like a sacrifice. A few early beachgoers filed past, on their way to a concrete observation platform where an open-air cafe and a row of changing rooms could be found. Misha smiled and nodded and idly bounced his fists on his knees, when he was not poking at his bandage. This time, no one stopped to ask him for directions, though a woman a little younger than he, with her hair hanging in henna-orange bangs, looked back over her shoulder. She had a twist of stifled laughter on her face.

Nadia mimed that she wanted to throw the liver at the back of the smirker's head.

"What, what?" Misha asked when the woman had gone.

Nadia shrugged.

Misha shrugged back at her.

They kept waiting. Misha let his cigarette butt drop to the beach. He watched its fall and the disappearance of its ashes into the sand.

The henna-haired woman came back in a bikini. She had freckled cleavage. *There's a target,* Nadia imagined.

"I think they're opening," Misha said, in reference to the cafe. "Do you want me to get you a drink—milkshake, coffee...?"

"No..." Nadia said. *If I'm publicly holding this liver, you're staying here beside me.*

"I might get..." Misha began, yet he stopped and fixed his eyes ahead.

Just then, a cat jumped silently out of the brush and onto the wall opposite the human delegation. She landed like a rocking horse—front legs and then back legs coming down, with a stability that seemed impossible for their slenderness and her load of milk-filled teats. A chaos of five kittens sprang onto the wall around her. Three were brindled grey-white-black-and-blonde, like their mother. Another was white with orange spots and the last, black with white abstractions.

A moment of recognition passed between the mother cat and Misha. She tilted her chin upwards and sniffed, flexing the bridge of her nose, where a dusty smear ran through the white fur. However, after this familiar overture, she got up and started pacing, placing the length of her body between her kittens and Nadia. The cat's back began to arch.

"Maybe you shouldn't look at her," Misha suggested. "Just look away and let her spend a couple of minutes looking at you."

"Alright," Nadia said. Aside, to the irked cat, she whispered, "I wasn't judging your family. I don't care how many fathers your kittens have."

"Say nothing," Misha advised.

Nadia crossed her legs and swung them over the sunny side of the wall and took in the sights of the cliffs, boardwalks, and beaches. Already, more people were emerging from the changing rooms and making their way barefoot (some of them on tiptoe) over the splintery boards, down to the strand. At this time of day, the sand was not yet hot, so the beachgoers were doing more strolling than lying down. When they stopped to talk or study the view, the women stood with their hands on their hips; the men, with their hands loose at their sides, as if they were auditioning for roles as gunslingers in the Westerns—some men in black swim briefs, some men in white, and (breaking the theme) some in colour.

Onshore, the fog had cleared almost entirely, yet it lay like rumpled bedsheets over the sleepy sea. The coast at Odessa is forgetfully calm in August, when, up North, the Gulf of Finland can foretell the autumn wind and rain. Nadia was never far from her memories of being rolled around by that cold-footed lover, the Baltic.

"Summer kittens are the lucky ones," Misha opined.

"They have a better chance," said Nadia.

"They have at least one summer," said Misha.

Once more, Nadia turned to face the young family of cats. The mother seemed less wary of her now. The little ones maintained a haywire orbit, sometimes bouncing off each other in an improvised pageant of leaps and swipes, like a mad juggler's impression of war. Nadia wondered at it: *How strange that they will spend much of their lives in solitude … especially the boys.*

"Let's see that liver," Misha said.

"Yes, Doctor," Nadia replied as she unpackaged the specimen.

The cats jumped to the beachside wall, to a spot within reach of Misha instead of Nadia. Showing her broad side again, the mother cat stepped towards the sunlit ledge and stuck her dusty nose into the ether. *Who knows,* Nadia wondered, *is she designing a cologne: liver-beach-bush-cafe-cigarettes?* The kittens ducked under and around their maternal fortress of legs and breasts. One of the brindled lookalikes got out in front and bent her head down over the ledge. The mother carefully bit the kitten's scruff in order to hoist her back.

Nadia and Misha ripped the liver in half.

The cats began, in earnest, to advance towards the meal.

"Above all," Misha said, "we need to feed the mother. Of course, if I am a kitten four weeks old, this morning I want to try my first teeth on the first liver I've ever smelt—but the rest of the day, I will want to live on milk as usual." He teased apart some sinews, gave a big hunk of liver to the mother cat, and kept talking as he ripped the rest into slithery little chunks by squeezing it hard between the knuckles of his thumb and forefinger. "However, in the spirit of socialism, let's say we give a taste of progress to everyone … and this runt here … (come on, you, come aside, they only want to hit you anyway) … he needs extra."

This puniest of the kittens was the one who was mostly black, with a white streak curving along his right eyebrow and down the side of his nose. A separate white patch covered his lips and chin. The combined effect was of a milky question mark written in his face. He had round, olive eyes in a face that was mostly round and babyish, except he was so slender in the jaw, like the old men in India.

Misha took Nadia's chunks and distributed them as well.

The round-eyed runt finished mashing and swallowing his share of the gristly liver. Then, he toddled about, squealing mutely for more, but his siblings and even his mother rebuffed him. Misha held out his slimy fingers and let the kitten suck liver juice off them.

"Should you be worried about rabies?" Nadia wondered.

"Well," Misha reasoned, "afterwards I can wash my hands at the beach."

"Do keep an eye" is the worst kind of mission. To boot, I'm probably ill suited. Nadia hesitated and then gave in and reached past Misha to let the kitten suck her fingers too. When there was no more liver juice, he seemed to accept the situation but he flopped on his side with his tummy exposed, as if he yearned to find a way to produce milk independently. Then, he rolled his neck to view Nadia on the diagonal, with his question mark askew.

"Papa," Nadia asked, "why did you ask Nastya to marry Giorgi?"

Misha, like the little cat, gave her a curious stare. He said, "My little daughter was bound to ask a question like that."

"Hmm, imagine all the other questions she's bound to ask you."

"I do, all the time. I have a hidden imagination. My teachers never knew. Even Mama and Gramma don't know, unless they are so clever it is some trick, to pretend not to know." Misha rubbed the little cat's belly and then lifted his finger in the air. A pair of fluttering paws pursued the digit. "Why did I suggest they marry?" he asked himself or perhaps the cat. "Well…"

"Well, Papa?"

"Well, I thought, what fun to be married at nineteen! Your Mama and I thought so too when we were … going on nineteen. We got married for Christmas 1967. That summer, we graduated from technical school and Nastya was born and I got conscripted. Your Mama told me I made a very dashing tank driver. She would look for me in the parades, when I popped my head out of the driver's hatch. I wasn't dashing and I couldn't drive very well. Mostly, I spent my time as a very greasy tank mechanic but she never complained, she always acted excited to see me. Well, our second year was not so fun. I was deployed to Prague in Operation Danube. I had a friend, a gunner, who shot himself. Before I got back, Grandpa Lev died in the first week of school, in front of his new class. We heard he was reciting Gorky, 'The Song of the Stormy Petrel'. He was famous for reciting it just like a flock of seabirds—very seriously, you understand, and always in the first week, to make an impression. I liked him … strange old guy. He lost his first family in the '30s. For some reason, he took an interest in my boxing. Anyway, he had a fit and died. Then, everybody was afraid of losing everybody. That winter, Nastya got sick with a recurring fever. Gramma Marusya wanted to take her to a priest and Gramma Ninel wanted to take her to a medical professor she knew in Moscow. They fought night and day. As a married couple and as Nastya's parents, we had to make a compromise, so we stopped talking to both Grammas for a month. Anyway, about Nastya marrying Giorgi, I thought, let her have fun before anything really bad happens in her life."

"Oh." Nadia touched his hand—the one that was not engaged with the cat. "You never talk about Prague," she said.

"No. No. I did one time. I tried to tell Gramma about it. I was in an accident. There was a young woman in the street at dusk. She was on a bicycle and she should have had time to steer out of the way but … I don't know, she was as bad at riding a bike as I was at driving a tank. She—Gramma—said I was no better than the men who hanged her family and she wished I had shot myself. That way, at least I wouldn't stand in the way of proper medical decisions for Nastya. She said if I was hoping for a prayer for my soul, maybe I should tell my mother-in-law. That was all at the time Nastya was sick. Gramma was very upset."

The little cat, perceiving that Misha was distracted, had begun to walk in circles, with his tail in the air and his asshole bulging from fullness. Digestion is swift in kittens.

Misha slid away from Nadia's hand and stroked the cat's body and tail, hand-over-hand, as he continued, "Some men jumped at a chance to kill. I didn't even want to drive. I just wanted to be home in bed—but that was the paradox. I knew my choice too well: do my patriotic duty, be seen doing it, or else kiss goodbye to the family life. How many times did she tell me, the last thing my father did, on his way out the door after breakfast, in front of everybody in the communal apartment and a poster of Stalin on the wall, was to kiss me on the ears and her on the neck? Well, I didn't want to be a memory of a kiss after breakfast. I just drove the tank where I was supposed to drive it and drove it as fast as I was supposed to drive it and … otherwise, where would we be? Katya would be a widow, Nastya an orphan, and you … nothing, never anything at all. I didn't want to be in Prague."

"I need your help with something," Nadia said.

She and Misha held onto each other's eyes in the half-shadows. Somehow, he looked more relieved than anyone she had ever seen.

Nadia continued, "Nastya and Giorgi, it's not perfect, you know. Nobody is perfect, I can accept that, but they act as if they expect every day of their life to be a movie—heroes and lovers—and then, when it isn't, they fight or snipe at each other over ordinary things: the money, the wine, the cigarettes, the piles of laundry, keeping company or not keeping company, when to go to sleep, when to get up, and how to spend the hours in between, the preparations for the baby, the nature of Man, the nature of money, and I'm sure over me and my habit of sarcasm. They need to make a real home and not a castle on a cliff face. Do you know, Papa? That's what I think but I'm entirely the wrong person to tell them so. I daresay Mama is the wrong person too."

"I will speak with Giorgi," Misha promised. "I will make sure he and Nastya work on these things. It's too bad he doesn't have family of his own nearby. It's better to work on these things as two families coming together."

Between Grammas, as it were? "Speaking of Giorgi's family," Nadia sighed, "do you suppose we get to meet them one day?"

"Yes, I suppose. I don't see why not," Misha replied. "We could try to lure them here for New Year's and Christmas, with the baby coming."

"Oughtn't Giorgi lure his own family?" *I mean, if his mother went to the trouble of giving birth to those boots and hat...*

"I don't really know the situation," Misha admitted. "He told me he hasn't seen much of them since ... well, since he was nineteen."

"What happened when he was nineteen?" Nadia asked.

"Didn't he say anything on those long walks of yours? He made no attempt at all to paint himself as a footloose boy in the not-so-distant past?"

Nadia went red and pivoted again to face the sea instead of her father. The cats had departed. She caught sight of them burying poop on the beach.

"No, alright," Misha said. "Well, nothing much, in the scheme of things, happened to him when he was nineteen but he did go down from the mountains to the coast and got to wear his cadet stripe in Gagra, guarding politicians and actresses when they went for a sunset jaunt under the palm trees. He got sick of that after a while. He said his best day as a cadet was when a lioness escaped from the zoo and went roaming along the boulevards. He and the old zookeeper caught up with her and shot her with a tranquilizer gun while she was taking a nap on a park bench with a belly full of seagull. Then, they had to lift this hundred-and-fifty kilo beauty onto a truck."

"Poor lioness," Nadia said. *What could be more humiliating?*

"Well, yes," Misha agreed. He slouched with one knee on the boardwalk and one elbow on the wall and his bandaged head past the ledge so that he could stare back and up at Nadia. He said, "I don't see why they couldn't lure her back with a gazelle or two. On the other hand," (he gestured at the beach or perhaps the sun or the distant ships laden with boxes to busy his hands or crush his head), "we've come a long way, dear girl. Ask Gramma how it was in Stalin's time. Probably the lioness is executed on the spot, for letting the zookeeper escape."

Nadia hooked her arm around Misha's elbow and jostled him a little as he squinted and gazed past the sand and the paw-prints, to sea. She asked him, "Will you put your wisdom in a book one day?"

"Oh, no, I leave that to you."

"There's something more," Nadia said. "I think Giorgi and one of his colleagues are having Nastya followed and photographed. I don't know why."

Misha's lips parted and his eyes moved back and forth as if he were reading. "I will speak with Giorgi," he promised again. "I will speak with him very seriously."

7: Witnesses

If her father's testament and promises stayed on Nadia's mind, then so did her mother's, which followed. *Is it fairness,* Nadia would wonder, *or simply paralysis, which makes me hear one and the other, over and over again?*

She surprised herself, though, by pressing a question on her mother, so soon after asking her father why he played the matchmaker for Nastya.

The moment Nadia chose was at the end of the day on Monday. Katya had gone to work that day and left Misha and Nadia to each other's company—two quiet walks and several quiet games of chess, no new revelations, a nap, and hours of silent reading. (Misha was reviewing his book on Naval Aviation, as well as the deck of cards from Giorgi with technical details of various planes and helicopters, in preparation for the upcoming carrier tour on Air Fleet Day.) When Katya got home in the evening, she ranted about the criminality at the factory: the theft of her thermos of chicken soup, her suspicion of a group of plotters led by the forewoman, the reappearance of the thermos but filled with dishwater instead of soup, hidden laughter.

"These Ukrainians," Katya fumed, "every last one of them would steal the flesh off her own child. That's what I told them."

Katya took over the dinner preparations that Nadia had begun. They had a soupy chicken stew in a bed of mashed potatoes. Misha took more painkillers with the meal and, when he had finished, he pleaded exhaustion and went to bed. Soon, he was snoring. Nadia persuaded her mother to go lie down in Nastya's bed. At last, after clearing the table and leaving the dishes to soak, Nadia went to sit in her own bed with a copy of *And Quiet Flows the Don*. She closed the door behind her and read to Katya for awhile—of cossacks and village gossip and a woman beaten to death for alleged witchcraft. She left a premature baby, who grew to become a hot-tempered old man who liked to fish and smoke, with a disobedient young son who liked to fish and flirt.

At the end of a chapter, Nadia put down the book and asked, "What do you and Lieutenant Colonel Sokolov do together?"

"What do we do?" Katya echoed.

"I imagined you might do lunch or museums," Nadia said. *I'd better be careful.* She licked her lips and flicked her fingers through her hair. "Do you meet up with him here in Odessa?"

"No." Katya sat up and, with a listless gaze, faced her daughter. "No, we haven't met at all since we got back. Some of the time he's away in Sevastopol or at the flight school in Stavropol."

"Or even at sea," Nadia supposed.

"Yes, he would be, sooner or later," Katya concurred.

To hell with this, I'll push it. "I just knew his friendship meant a lot to you when you were lonely at the sanatorium."

"Perhaps." Katya's hands seemed to freeze to each other in her lap and likewise she squeezed her eyes shut.

"What is it, Mama?" Nadia asked. "Talking to me can't make it any worse, surely." Nadia herself was scarcely sure of that. She heard, in her own voice, the lilt of self-persuasion, bright like alabaster, and she remembered *Crime and Punishment*, which seemed, to her, a bleak monument to confession—the giving of it (false or true), the seeking of it (false or true).

"I was so hurt," Katya whispered, "by the way they held Nastya's wedding without me. They planned it without me and they came and told me when it was all over and I was supposed to be happy. The civil witnesses were some beaten-up snitch of Giorgi's and some chit of a girl who sells Misha sandwiches and cigarettes on his lunch break. They're in Nastya's wedding photos and I'm not. They're the ones holding bouquets over her head as she climbs the Potemkin Stairs." Katya's tears and voice were properly flowing now. "I asked myself, 'What have I done to deserve this?' and then I thought how I had let you down, how I let them all take you away. Once they left me to go move into their new apartment, I decided I couldn't live with my guilt. I thought of throwing myself from the radio tower or drowning myself off the causeway or getting pills from the dispensary and waiting for nightfall to go out to the tennis court and swallow them there and lie against the net, like a fish in a fairytale granting a wish if the catcher will let me go. I was on my way to the dispensary when he stopped me and he spoke to me for the first time. He said he had seen me wandering around and was I looking for a tennis partner? I said no but he asked me to join him for lunch. For an hour and a half, I could talk of nothing but you and he listened so patiently..."

Katya eyed the stippled ceiling and bit her lip. "Well, that's all. We talked every day after that. He told me about the places he had sailed and flown and the friends of his who had died. I kept thinking of my father, the few times he spoke of his other family. That is all."

"How old is he?" Nadia wondered.

"Fiftyish?" Katya said with a shrug. Then, she drew in her breath and her eyes widened as she thought aloud, "Perhaps all my sadness is justice because I had not enough sympathy for Ida Ivanova."

"Hadn't you?"

"No. Years ago, when I heard of some of her troubles, I couldn't think about it. I regret that now. Would you ask her forgiveness for me?"

"I'm not sure she thinks there's anything to forgive. She seems to have only fond memories of you—of you and your baking, I should say."

"Then tell her I miss baking for her."

"I'll do that," Nadia promised. She folded her sleeve over her hand and went across to the other bed to wipe her mother's tears.

"Faithful soul," Katya said. "How interesting that we should both need friends, when you and I are apart."

8: Result of the Checkup

Tuesday, Misha had a checkup at the hospital. A mental and physical evaluation (involving a written quiz, an interview, a flashlight, a small hammer, a soft rubber ball, and a hallway) determined that he was fit to return to light duties on Wednesday. He seemed quite satisfied with this outcome. He said, unless he got back to his usual place fast, both his coworkers and his family would begin to find out too much about him—one in his absence, the other in his presence.

On his lunch break on Thursday, Misha went to the train platform to see his daughter off. He found her sitting on the base of a lamppost with Avel, who had come to give her a bottle of kosher wine.

"I had almost forgotten," Avel had been saying to Nadia, "he asked me for this weeks ago." He slipped it partway out of a paper bag and then slipped it back in before handing it to her.

The bottle, Nadia noticed, was the same sort of slim, dark, red-foiled model that Giorgi had brought to her parents' house before the start of the year. *I wonder whether Avel got that one for Giorgi too. I wonder whether the shape and colours are Avel's silent joke about a tall man in uniform.*

"I understand it's for a friend of yours, Miss."

"Yes, in a way," Nadia replied. "My friend is staying with a Jewish woman who is helping her start a new life in Kiev."

"Oh, a new life." Avel got out a deck of cards, depicting rustic Ukrainian folk. He showed her a magic trick: the old Queen of Spades, holding a stone, instantaneously became the young Queen of Clubs, holding a pumpkin. That was when Misha arrived.

"Avel!" Misha said. He squeezed Avel's shoulder.

Avel slowly got up and unbent his knees. He pocketed the cards, said, "Permit me," and reached up to brush his fingertips across Misha's brow. "Well," Avel concluded, "if I'm not mistaken, the bones are good. What's inside … could be just enough to get you in trouble one day…"

Misha laughed at this.

"…and not enough to get you out," Avel finished. "I'm going," he announced. "Safe journeys, Miss."

"You stay safe," Nadia replied.

"You have nice daughters," Avel told Misha in parting.

Misha nodded and watched Avel go. Then, he sat next to his daughter and patted her hand. "What's he given you there, wine?"

"For Rosya. Giorgi wanted it for Rosya. Kosher wine."

"Oh," Misha said as he fingered the yellowing region of his bare forehead, "your Ida's Rosya, I understand she's a cousin of old Yuly down the hall."

"Yes."

"Well, it's a funny picture to me," he said. "When I was a kid, I got scolded for going fishing with Yuly beyond the hours Gramma approved—and it was a serious failing of my character to accept the odd coin from him. Now she's handing off orphans to his maiden cousins."

"That's not quite how it is."

"Come on, it all has its funny side."

Nadia put the bag and bottle in her suitcase. "Ida tells me our family is a model of fairness. She also assures me you're immune to smacks on the head." Misha stopped prodding himself. "Anyway," Nadia continued, "Gramma said I could trust Yuly Lvovich. She wouldn't have said that lightly. I believe, to her, he's almost like a brother."

"Then she is humming new tunes."

"Maybe she is."

"My daughter tells me about my mother," Misha muttered.

Shall I tell you about my mother instead?

Nadia decided to shut up and sit with her suitcase in her lap. She thought of the previous night, when Misha had wanted to stay up late with her to play more chess, to even the score. "You were fighting a sick man," he told her as he poured himself a vodka. "Now I'm as fit as you." He lost all the same.

After midnight, he shook hands with the victor and went to join Katya in bed. At quarter to two, she left him sleeping and came to curl up for a quiet cry at Nadia's side. At three, Katya spoke as if she had been saving her words: "When you were born, I felt all the joys and sorrows of your life. I struggled with exhaustion. I told Misha, I couldn't have any more children after you."

Nadia stared at the train tracks—a study in parallels, a study in heat and rust. *Rosya is always talking about the future of parallel computing. I wonder whether she's any happier than Mama. Rosya does act happier—all with autumn wrinkles come early and summer eyes come late. Mama herself was a last child, last by a long shot, her father's first family a winter's tale, a sad tale, when in the end came she, frightened of herself, haunted by hungry spirits—she, a winter's dream of spring. I wonder whether, as a child, she tried to contact her dead half-siblings.*

This is morbid and gets us nowhere.

Misha said, "I wonder whether you'll have a letter from Gramma waiting for you in Kiev."

"Perhaps. Why, especially?"

"Didn't Mama say? Gramma wrote to her to ask about me and the box—and to say she was working on some prospects for your education."

"Oh."

"You don't sound too pleased."

"I am, of course. I just haven't put my head to that ... not as much as I should."

"You've had too little to do this summer," Misha said as he glanced at the approaching train. "I was a little surprised when Mama told the Young Communist League to piss off and leave you alone."

"They were probably even a little more surprised than you."

"Well, some of their parents know her."

People only think they know Mama. Nadia got up to stand eye-to-eye with the arriving passengers as they peered out their windows and gathered their luggage and made their way to the vestibules and exited onto the platform.

"You could sit," Misha told her. "They'll be a few minutes yet."

"No, no, I'm tired of sitting."

"Well," Misha agreed, "it's not the most comfortable seat." He stood up, too, and rubbed his buns. "I guess the Nation doesn't trust us with a bench."

Nadia scanned the new arrivals, who looked stifled by their train ride from early rising to hot midday. *Why can't they be trusted with a bench? Dirty joke? Scrap metal joke? Both?* She looked up at her father. She wanted to ask for his reassurance, not about the people and the nonexistent bench, but whether this week had mattered in some way. Instead, she only said, "Are you looking forward to the carrier tour?"

"Very much," Misha replied with a bounce in his knees.

9: Strokes of the Pen

She had an unsettling journey in a third-class window seat facing backwards. During the second half, at a small city called Smila, a trio got

aboard and hemmed her in, as they took the other three seats around
the narrow table. Two of them were young men—one with long, red
cheeks like a balloon and the other with sunken eyes, a wedge-shaped
jaw, and ears set high, back, and out. Their companion was a woman,
not as young. She had a moony face, big eyebrows, darkish lipstick,
longish hair, and giant tits that strained her floral-printed blouse.

The woman squinted at Nadia (or perhaps just at the evening light)
as she shoved her with a hip to make some room. The flushed man
sat opposite Nadia and breathed, "Hello, oh, going to Kiev?" as the
slimmer man locked knees with the woman. (The scanty table could
not conceal their intimacy.)

"Yes," Nadia replied. She kept her book open.

"What, what are you reading?" he wondered, wondered.

"*Emma*, an English novel," she replied.

"Oh, smart, smart girl," he said as he tapped his temple audibly with
four fingers. "I, I don't have the knack for learning, learning languages."

"Is anyone surprised?" asked the other youth.

"I wouldn't know," Nadia replied. "We're strangers, after all." She
rustled the pages of her book and underlined something with her thumbnail.

"My, my friends here made, made a plan: tonight—Kiev, tomorrow—sick for work, day after that—the weekend." He laughed. His
eyes went round when he did so. "No, no, but I am coming for a serious
purpose. I, I want to surprise my girlfriend in Kiev, to ask her to …
marry me."

"Good!" his pal sang. " 'Marry me!' You got it all out in one go."

Another rattling laugh flew from the red cheeks.

Nadia gave in and put the novel away in her satchel, by her feet.

Meanwhile, the moonlike woman showed no inclination to speak.
Maybe she's bored, heard it all a million times. No, I've got it, she's shy.

"Are they getting married too?" Nadia asked.

"They, they…?" This thought, to him, was worth a real laugh.

"We aren't getting married," said the steady-voiced one. "We only
stick together to witness the stupid things he does."

The woman took this placidly. *Maybe she's a bit simple, a docile
creature like a cow,* Nadia supposed, *or maybe it's her using him.*

"My, my girlfriend," the romantic one continued, "is studying Edu-
cational Psychology in Kiev. I, I would like your opinion on how to ask

her to … marry me."

"I don't know. I'm sixteen," Nadia tried.

"Sixteen, sixteen. At sixteen, you must have an opinion. Maybe a boyfriend has asked you or you wondered, wondered how he would ask you…"

"No…" *…and "dreaded", not "wondered", would be the word.*

"No, not asked?"

"No—but if I imagine my choice, I would prefer to be asked in a letter."

"Oh, what, what would this letter need to say?"

"That wouldn't necessarily matter much. I'd just rather it be in a letter."

"Coward," scoffed the sunken-eyed one.

"No, very, very good," the chatterer chuckled. "I can't stop laughing. I'm nervous." He untied a small canvas bag from his belt. Things inside it clacked together as he pulled at its drawstring. "Will, will you all drink a glass to my luck?"

What a fool, Nadia thought. *Oh, I suppose it's human kindness; is it? Papa would do it without hesitation. Why shouldn't I?*

They drank to this fool's luck; they drank from an unlabelled bottle, of vodka that probably had its genesis in a bathtub full of turnips.

"That's foul," Nadia coughed.

"You drank it too fast," the quiet woman advised.

Don't patronize me; it's been tried by better people.

For a while, she listened as the red-faced fool gassed about his girl-friend and his question and his nerves. She became fairly confident that these people were too absorbed in their own story to pose any threat to her, so she was able to watch as she might watch a movie. She accepted a second glass and the lopsided chitchat started to seem quite funny.

As they approached another stop, a small city called Bila Tserkva, the woman leaned across the table. She whispered to her boyfriend, "Give me some money. I want to buy something here." He shrugged and shelled out enough for sausage rolls and perhaps a refill of moonshine. "More," she told him.

"More for what?"

"Surprise for you," she whispered. "A friend of mine says she found something nice here, something her boyfriend liked."

Shrugging, he let her take his money clip. "Big mystery."

She widened her eyes at him, got up, kissed him, and somewhat pressed herself into his hands. Then, suddenly, she walked away and went to the end of the car to wait at the door. His eyes followed her. She did not look back.

The other guy eyed the steel ribs of the ceiling. He had half-formed phrases on his lips. Perhaps he was reciting his proposal.

Should I change seats? Nadia wondered. She stayed. She preferred to remain forgotten in her corner, if she could. Outside the window, the world was getting dark. She shut her eyes and found a memory waiting for her there. Rosya had mentioned this place, Bila Tserkva, as the site of a massacre in August 1941, just a month before the very same murderers arrived at Babi Yar. At Bila Tserkva, some of the Fascists hesitated near the end, when they still had ninety captives: infants and small children, wailing in a locked room, where they had begun to starve and eat the paint off the walls. The bothered soldiers lodged a complaint via their army chaplains and then waited for a Field Marshal's command, whereupon, in the end, the "technical procedure" went ahead: the soldiers dug a pit; the little ones were loaded onto tractors and driven to this grave; and the local collaborators, who had, just days earlier, received new uniforms and the title of Ukrainian Auxiliary Police—they being, in all eyes, dispensable souls—they were the ones to fire the bullets and they quaked as they did it and sometimes shot a child four or five times before death. Their handlers, the more experienced German executioners, recorded how poorly the Ukrainians had done.

Thereafter, at Babi Yar, the killers operated together with no complaints—much alcohol but no complaints.

The train doors opened and the car became more full. Night-shift workers were headed into Kiev. As it happened, Yuri came aboard. *I guess he lives out here, in the City's blind spot, not fully a Kievite.* He did not notice Nadia, nor did she notice him until he was already past. *Should I call after him? If I did, he'd see me here with this pair and what's left of the vodka and he'd have reason enough to tell me I'm drowning my soul.* This glimpse of him—of his square rims, wavy greyness, and troubled drudgery—this glimpse made her feel ashamed. *Look twice at me. Here's how I am, here's how anyone can see me, as soon as I'm away from my family, as soon as I've made my pleas and sympathized with theirs.*

A few minutes later, the doors shut and the lads started to bicker.

The woman with the cash, the dough, the cabbage, the what-have-you-there—she had not returned.

Her soulmate pined for her: "Bitch! What the fuck?"

The effervescent one sputtered, "I, I guess we'll never know what her friend's boyfriend liked." With his laughter, he sprayed spittle onto Nadia, who was just waking from a catnap.

His pal showed him the predicament in a different light: "This affects you too, piss-hole. You've lost a civil witness there, not to mention the money I was going to throw at you."

"Oh, oh." The putative groom looked to Nadia and asked, "Will, will you witness my wedding?"

"No," Nadia said. *Forty to one, neither will you.*

"Are, are you sure? Have, have another…"

The pal said, "Above all, he needs you to talk to the bride."

"No," Nadia told them, "I can't go with you. My brother-in-law will be waiting for me at the station in Kiev."

"He, he looks out for you," the balloon-faced one remarked.

"He's a cop," she stated.

Thereafter, they did not press the invitation.

When they arrived in Kiev, Nadia lingered until the two guys had gone and then she ambushed Yuri on his way out. "Hello," she said.

He showed faint surprise. "Well, what are you doing here?"

She told him about visiting her parents in Odessa.

"Good," he said.

"Do you live a ways out, Bila Tserkva, maybe?"

"Yes, my mother is out there too. I look after her."

"Good."

"We're blocking the aisle." He nudged her shoulder blade to get her to go ahead of him. "Keep the flow going," he muttered. "That's one thing I know."

They got to the door and stepped down to the platform. Nadia spotted Giorgi further along. He was questioning the two guys. He had found the mostly empty bottle in its pitiful hiding place—the bag tied to the belt.

"That's my brother-in-law, over there," Nadia confided in Yuri.

"Which one?"

"The tall one, the detective."

"Where…?"

"Over there, see?"

"Where...?"

Oh, I'm being teased. She rolled her eyes at Yuri.

"Mermaid," he said, "I have to go."

"Right. This weekend, do you have day shifts?"

"Yes."

"I'll probably see you."

He nodded, said, "Bye," and walked away.

Giorgi jabbed a finger downwards at the suspect. Nadia saw it as a pen threatening a balloon. Then, in the next frame of this cartoon, Giorgi became merciful, he upended the bottle to pour the contraband into the cracks of the concrete (*"Good riddance to such poison! Never make it again!"*), and he dismissed them with a sweep of his hand. They scurried away down a stairway. Soon after, this stairway produced an echo of a stutter of a laugh.

Giorgi stuck his finger in the bottle, tasted it, grimaced, and gave the bottle to a nearby granny to recycle.

Nadia strolled over to the Lieutenant and saluted him. She put on a preposterous grin like a staged photo of a small yet victorious woman in wartime.

"Nadezhda," he said. "Ha. At ease." He stooped to try to take her suitcase. "You are a welcome sight in Kiev, always joyful."

She held onto her case and its precious cache of toilet paper. "I need a washroom," she informed him.

They agreed to reconvene in the Main Hall. By the time she got there, she was feeling a few new kinds of remorse about the moonshine. She had done her best to straighten her sweaty hair.

"Are you fatigued after such a warm day on the train?" he enquired.

"I am," she replied. *I deny everything. When I left, the toilet was like a mountain spring; the walls, like untouched glaciers.*

"I listened to the weather reports," Giorgi explained.

"Man predicts Nature," Nadia reflected, "whilst Supernature strikes by surprise."

"You must remind me," Giorgi said, "which dissident is that?"

"Me—just something in my head." *Is he making a joke—that he knows I'm forever his dissident sister-in-law?*

They proceeded to the underground parking, where Giorgi had left the cop car in a reserved space next to a pillar. The pillar and wall were covered in graffiti, in black paint on a background of white: twin thunderbolts, swastikas, "Heil Hitler", "Love Your Own Race", "Cops=Yids", "Cook with Gas", "14/88", "Glory to Ukraine", and more. Perhaps only a single coat of white had been used; the viewer could discern (if only just) one or two earlier layers, including a rainbow peace sign, "Long Live Butterflies", "Atoms Cannot Be Peaceful", and "Gorbachev—Murderer of Afghan Children".

"I made notes on these," Giorgi said.

Without further comment, he unlocked the passenger door, held it for Nadia, and closed her in. She stared ahead at the windshield and the black words. She could hear the car's boot open and close. Moments later, Giorgi ducked into the driver's side, started the engine, and told her, "You have something sloshing around in your case."

"Oh…" …*you dickhead…* "…did you break the bottle?"

"No, impossible," Giorgi deduced. "I heard it slosh. A broken bottle cannot slosh."

"Right, you have me there." *You're itching to step up to Captain.* "Well, it's the kosher wine you ordered from Avel," Nadia said.

She did not have Giorgi's full attention; he was performing contortions to do a proper shoulder check as he pulled out past the pillar.

"He hadn't forgotten about it," she strung him along, "but it took him some time to track down a rabbi who'd bless it just for women and police."

While turning, he glanced sideways to read her face.

The driver-side mirror touched the pillar. With a sound like a wheezing cat, the glass smashed and the steel arm twisted back on itself.

Giorgi bared his teeth. He pulled the car away from the post, got out, and slammed the door. At this point, the mirror fell to the ground. He picked it up and banged it against the pillar to knock out the last of the glass.

Clutching her stomach, Nadia shook with silent laughter. *Think of what Nastya would have you do.* She held her breath and managed to control herself (a little) as Giorgi got back in the car. *Remember, he does have a temper.* He chucked the mirror's broken shell in the back seat. She pinched her nose and started to cry. He studied her expression.

"Nadezhda…" Giorgi began. He lingered on the cusp of offering her a suggestion, which turned out to be, "…let's deliver that wine tonight."

"What?" she squeaked.

"Your friends stay up late, don't they?"

"Yes…"

"Then why not surprise them?" He grabbed the gear shift and drove to the exit at a decisive pace. "Don't be upset about the mirror."

"Okay, I won't." *I ought to say something more sympathetic.* "Will you get in trouble for dinging the car, you being off duty?"

"No, it's insignificant," Giorgi assured her. "Besides, Nadia, I am never off duty. I am always … 'going through the snake hole,' we say in Georgian. I'm the man who will volunteer for anything."

…or else you're just a snake in a hole.

"Of course," Giorgi continued, "we've made you into the perpetual volunteer in your own way. Go to Gramma, go to Nastya, go to Anya, go to Ida, go to Misha and Katya. I believe there is something in you of your Gramma, the medic, and like her, you go about it quietly."

Nadia wanted to say something about Gramma and the hand grenades but she weighed her words and missed the opportunity.

"You have an inherited desire," Giorgi continued, "to live as others do not live, like the characters of literature. When you read to us in their voices, it makes me realize, we cannot keep you to ourselves forever."

They were coming onto Victory Avenue, which had taken this name the previous year, for the fortieth anniversary of Gramma's arrival in Berlin. Nastya had mentioned the highway's renaming in one of her spiels about the improvements to Kiev.

The empty mirror had fallen on the floor and it was bumping around as Giorgi passed other cars. Nadia imagined the sloshing, sacred wine. Likewise, she imagined Motherland in the gaslight of the Eternal Flame. *I'm exhausted. I'm sick of it all. If I puke, shall I do it on him?*

Giorgi had a suggestion: "Perhaps, in a year or two, you could find a volunteer post that would let you travel, meet new people."

Perchance to build bridges, of the literal kind, in Mongolia.

"Gorbachev is big on friendship," Giorgi said. "Maybe he'll make new programmes for young people to travel. You speak English, you'd make us look good, you could go to … India. When I was a kid, I was fascinated by India."

Presumably by the erotic art.

They were passing the Hero City Obelisk, with its portrait of Lenin under a victory medal, and (opposite it) the Circus building, like a cake with wings. "Stop here," Nadia said. "I'll check whether they need a travelling clown…" *…or two. Ida would come. We could help the lions escape.*

"Ha."

"I'm falling asleep," Nadia admitted. "I'm probably acting silly."

"Yes, sleep. I'll drive."

"You're in a hurry…"

"…to get there and back to Nastya."

"Oh."

Soon, everything vanished into a numb, oblivious sleep without dreams. When Nadia awoke, they were parked in view of Rosya's building. Giorgi had rolled down his window. He was having a quick smoke. He held the shell of the mirror in one hand as an astray and, in his lap, he had one of his notebooks open.

What has he written, that he contemplates now?

Giorgi butted out his cigarette and dumped it, with the ashes, out the window. "Shall we make our visit?" he asked.

"I suppose we shall," Nadia replied in a bleary voice.

Giorgi bookmarked his page with a scrap of slim, orange ribbon. He shut the notebook, buried it deep in the pocket of his baggy trousers (beside his cards and other things), and returned the broken mirror to the back seat. "I might keep it around," he muttered.

They got out of the car and went to the boot to fetch the wine—slowly now, like little children killing time on a strange occasion, perhaps playing with nested dolls while older siblings fastidiously dressed themselves for an evening at the ballet. Giorgi opened the hatch; Nadia opened the suitcase; she passed him the bottle in the paper bag; he pulled off the bag, shrugged, and passed it back to her; she put this empty sleeve in her case and snapped down the latches; he shut the hatch and fiddled with the lock once more.

They approached Rosya's building, which stood on a grassy embankment with a winding path, potted flowers, and a bower of X-shaped arches built from steel beams, vaguely reminiscent of the anti-tank barriers in the history books, yet wired up with mercury vapour lamps that seemed to turn skin green. By this light, Giorgi scrutinized the wine bottle's label. "Did Avel say it's good?" he asked.

A lone cicada was clacking. The air had a hint of deep, wet sandpits, brushing against the smog and chrysanthemums.

"He didn't feel the need to say," Nadia replied. Peering out of the light, she looked back towards the river, with its parkways and rectangular fountains and linear beaches stretching towards construction zones where more of the sandy soil lay upturned. "Giorgi, what do you think of the neighbourhood?"

"Oh," Giorgi breathed, "Nastya tells me it will be very fashionable. Did you know, most of this district is new within the last ten years?"

"Yeah."

Between black clouds, the moonlight fell on the white, concrete building like a flashlight on toy blocks, arranged in an L shape and stacked higher towards the corner, like a double stairway to nowhere. The place had a doorkeeper named Oleg, who recognized Nadia as they approached the windowed foyer. He was a silent, square, bald man, with a range of expression to match his plain grey uniform. Rosya somehow knew that Oleg had a growing boy, a collector of comic books. Sometimes, she got the import/export agents to slip a few into a box of computer stuff and so she supplied the boy. As of summer 1986, he was the only kid in Kiev who was getting newly released, square-bound, glossy fantasies of dark and star-spangled vengeance, replete with carnage, super-cars, mutants, mafiosos, masked vigilantes, and English exclamations of "son of a bitch", which, mercifully, his mother could not read. For the boy's sake, Rosya had managed to put off the task of vilifying his hero in the press.

Oleg let them in and gave Giorgi a stare as Giorgi passed him the peaked cap. (To be fair, Oleg gave the same stare to Nadia. Other times, she had thought he gave a different stare to Ida. *Perhaps I am wrong. Perhaps I am no connoisseur of stares.*) He told them to get on the elevator; he would call up to Rosya. They walked past him and past more potted plants and also past a two-headed bust of Marx and Lenin.

Here we are again in an elevator—you and I and grease and Shipr. I believe the grease is top grade here but you and I and Shipr have not changed.

"You never said your friend had a doorman," whispered Giorgi.

He never whispers and now he whispers in an elevator. Well, who knows, maybe Oleg listens to the elevator. She glanced up at Giorgi and shrugged and said, "You never asked."

They ascended to one of the high floors in the centre block. *Ding,* went the elevator in a top-grade tone.

They knocked on Rosya's outer door, which had a square-and-diamond pattern, like a quilt, stamped into its steel sheath. They heard the muffled opening of the inner door.

A pair of deadbolts turned and Rosya answered the gate. She had on a long, linen dress with large pockets, a lot of buttons, and rolled-up sleeves. Quite possibly she had been wearing it at the office that day. Her face bore a calm, hospitable look, without much exercise of her wrinkles. Nadia had the feeling they had come at a bad time.

"Hello, such a surprise," Rosya was saying.

One hand behind his back, Giorgi bowed.

Rosya grinned and decided to josh him. "What, is Elizabeth II standing behind me? Come on."

"What if she were, what if she were?" Giorgi asked the world. "Dear lady, it is you I have come tonight to meet, you who are so dear to our Nadia. I could not wait another day," he said as he made the bottle leap from behind his back into his open hand, "to bring you this token of friendship and appreciation, from Nastya and myself, with our thanks for your plentiful good advice."

"That is kind," said Rosya, using both hands to receive the wine bottle like another person's baby or an unsought, puzzling award. "I can see … how you and Nastya are alike, giving such thought to the little things. Alright, Giorgi, come in and see my home. Nadia, nice to have you back. Your Papa…?"

"Much better, thanks."

"Good."

They stepped across the threshold, into the openness of the living room or lab. Giorgi scanned it from side to side.

Where's Ida? Nadia worried.

To orient the detective, Rosya said, "We just throw our coats over the radiator," and she gestured to the hot water unit nearest the entrance. "That's the bathroom and my bedroom over there," she said as she indicated two doors on the right wall, "and the closet and the kitchen over there" (to the left). "There's Ida's bed and the workbench … the computer table … my sofa … the other sofa. Sit—or feel free to browse the shelves. Everything you see has a purpose; that's not to say it's all purpose-built." The tour was complete.

Giorgi followed Rosya as she moved some boxes of equipment and switched on extra floor lamps.

Ida stepped out of the bathroom. A cloud of bath-steam came with her, to blend into the general haze of the apartment. She had on her jeans and half-buttoned plaid shirt, like the day she visited Mother Motherland. She was also wearing a new article: a slender crown, handmade from a set of capacitors. She had used the good stuff: glass-encapsulated silver mica with thick aluminum contacts. She had soldered the legs in series to form a shining band beneath those jutting, glassy pillows of greenish blue (pale as if the sea had tumbled them since she was born), each one a slightly different hue due to manufacturing variances.

"Hmm, hello," Ida said with a cursory look at the other people. "I was just trying on this..." (she pointed to her crown) "...enneadecagon."

"Nineteen-sided shape," Rosya explained.

"To adorn a many-sided young lady," Giorgi elocuted.

"I just finished it this evening," Ida stated. She went to sit on her bed and gaze out over the Dnieper and do up one more button.

She's not usually so numb anymore. What happened while I was away? Nadia imagined Ida spending many hours forging this crown, only to wear it in the tub with her eyes focused on infinity.

"Ida, this is Giorgi," Rosya told her. "I don't believe you've met."

"Hmm?" Ida twisted around to get another look at him. "Oh, Giorgi, sorry," she said. "I know you. Nastya showed you to us, in her drawings. I was thinking you'd know me too for some reason."

"By your voice on the phone," Giorgi suggested.

"Hmm." Ida turned halfway towards the window so that she could glance between it and the company inside. They were all reflected in the pane of glass as if they were spirits who had risen from the river and flown to the enclosed balcony for a look.

"Of course," Giorgi continued, "we knew you were staying here. Nastya and I knew so, from Nadia. We wanted, albeit belatedly, to welcome you to Ukraine and to celebrate your definite good fortune and ours, with this emblem of tradition," (he gestured to the wine bottle in Rosya's arms), "for you and your distinguished host."

"Hmm. Man, thanks."

Nadia, who was standing by a corner of the guest sofa, bit her upper lip and ran her fingernails along the stitches in the leather with a scratching sound. She cast an upward glance Ida's way but got no notice or, at least, no reaction.

"Well," Rosya suggested, "Giorgi and Nadia had better sit and share one drink with us before they get back to Nastya. Come, Ida, you'll sit on my sofa."

This was a rare offer. Rosya's sofa was a place of sanctuary, accommodated to Rosya's bad back and Rosya's deepest thoughts.

Giorgi and Nadia took the guest sofa. Rosya placed the bottle on a box halfway between the two sofas, went to get juice glasses from the kitchen, and then came back to pour and hand out drinks.

Everyone waited.

Rosya sank down to join Ida on the master sofa.

"How's your back?" Ida asked Rosya.

"Bad."

"How's your back?" Nadia asked Ida.

"Hmm, you know. How about your Papa's head?"

"Still there."

Rosya parted her lips. She seemed to be considering a toast, yet she paused to brush a strand of wet hair away from Ida's face and tuck it under the crown of capacitors. Ida did not react.

Giorgi proposed, "To our lovely ladies!"

Rosya lilted at him, "No, you're using that one wrong!"

"Am I? I see three!"

She shook her head. "Whatever you think you see, Giorgi, that toast is for a group of men to make to their wives."

"I never knew, I never knew. Imagine all the other toasts this little Georgian must have mangled. Ha. Then, how does one…?"

Ida offered her thoughts: "Men don't do well outnumbered."

"Oh," said Giorgi, "listen, this outnumbered man wants to keep the peace. Let's drink to … to peace. Ha."

They drank to peace. The wine was rather sweet, rather raisiny. Nadia expected it would do no good for her sickness nor her drowsiness. On a whim, she recited Lermontov's short poem, "The Sail", the easiest one to memorize in school, and it ended, " 'As if in tempests there were peace!' "

"Bravo!" said Giorgi.

Nadia reminded the audience, "Lermontov loved Georgia. He said Georgians were natural, honest people." *He never praised Shipr, as far as I know.*

" 'Blue haze'," Ida echoed from the first line. (She interrupted something Giorgi had wanted to say. He began to look perplexed.)

"The colour of that is nice," Rosya noted as she held her glass to the lamplight: "something like tea and strawberry jam. Now, I would mix that with fresh plum juice and possibly green apple."

"Really, would you?" Giorgi enquired.

"I would," Rosya reiterated. "We'll have to get some on the weekend."

"The weekend," Ida murmured.

Giorgi took up the new theme, "The weekend!" They drank to the weekend.

"Homer described the sea as 'wine-faced' or 'wine-eyed'," Nadia said.

"Hmm."

They drank to some kind of sea.

"Well, to youth," Rosya proposed, "and all possibilities."

They drank to youth and all possibilities, except that Ida did not speak the words. With that, they emptied their glasses.

Rosya re-corked the bottle. "Giorgi, three of us here have work tomorrow and you still need to reunite two sisters before the night is done."

"True," said Giorgi as he crouched forwards to place his glass on the box, "but..." (he slid his ass and baggy trousers back onto the sofa) "...forgive me."

Did he just fart?

Giorgi continued his apology: "Before I go, I regret to trouble you with one or two queries of an official nature."

"Not tonight," Rosya said. "Look, I'll gladly see you at my office in the morning to help with whatever case you have."

"My queries are for the younger lady."

The three women voiced their reactions at once.

"Surely not," Rosya said.

Nadia half remembered a phrase of Gramma Marusya's or a picture that had frightened her as a child, something about the Devil sitting on a sleepy person's chest. "Giorgi," she requested, "couldn't you take me home?"

"Hmm?" asked Ida, who had been pinching the crown on her head to check whether the solder joints were firm.

Rosya sat back down by Ida and reiterated, "Surely nothing to do with Ida is so urgent that you'd keep her from her rest tonight. She's been driving all day. She'll be driving all day tomorrow."

"Maybe," Nadia tried, "I should call Nastya to see how she is."

"No," Giorgi answered Rosya, "only, one of our junior officers is checking up on migrants this week and this officer, she is rather eager. She studies the files to a point of zeal, she goes prodding around at workplaces, she talks, she talks, ah! … and I found she has Ida's case on her desk for tomorrow. Okay, ladies, I simply suggest the following: we cover the roster of foolish questions tonight; I go home and type it up straight away; and, in the morning, I tell the junior officer it's closed. Now, will you let me handle it this way?"

"That is up to Ida, of course," Rosya said. "Whoever handles her case, she has nothing to fear. Her migration papers are in order. I helped her with the process myself, a few weeks ago, when she decided to stay and take work here."

"Well, Ida Ivanova," Giorgi coaxed her, "what do you say?"

Ida looked to Nadia.

Nadia, reluctantly and not altogether soberly, gave her friend the smallest of nods. *Him tonight or Fenya tomorrow… Damn him, he has to be chosen!*

"Sure, man, ask. We'll make it a game." Ida's eyes flashed wide in the lamplight and then she rubbed them hard enough to make squishing sounds.

"Ha." Giorgi pulled out his notebook and opened it to the book-marked page. The orange ribbon slid to the floor. "Oh," he said, like a little boy viewing his mistake as a discovery. He bent to pick it up.

Nadia was sure she had seen the ribbon somewhere before. She had the disorienting sense that she was forgetting something important, something that could be anything, perhaps even something to do with this ribbon. Giorgi set the ribbon on the sofa and Nadia took it for examination.

Ida watched Nadia pull and curl the ribbon as Giorgi began to ask questions. He started with Ida's work. What was her schedule? What were her routes? She answered easily enough. She offered descriptions of some of the landmarks that helped her get from one depressing field to another as she drove hundreds of kilometres in a day.

"Then," she rambled, "eight kilometres after the overpass, I usually go down the side road and eat my lunch in the old cemetery. There's a big arch where the plaster is all chipped and the stones are weathered, maybe sixty, seventy years, so it has good handholds. I try to exercise at lunch, like we should, so I climb the arch and sit on top while I eat. If you stand up, you can see all the way back to the overpass, to the train tracks, but I never see anyone visit the cemetery. As far as I can tell, there aren't even any tramps in the area."

"You are…" (Giorgi said as his pen twitched and danced) "…wise to be so vigilant of vagabonds. Does anyone go with you?"

"No, I go alone."

"Does anyone ever hitch a ride?"

"No. I go alone."

"I myself like a companion when I'm driving," Giorgi said.

"Hmm, I don't. I guess we're different."

"Now," Giorgi continued as he flipped the page, "I understand you make deliveries from farms to urban markets."

"Yes, dairy."

"Mostly sour cream," Nadia added. She was making progress in the analysis of the ribbon. At some time or other, it had been knotted, leaving creases.

"Right," Ida elaborated, "it's a dairy truck for processed dairy. I make the pickup wherever the dairy is processed. That could be right on the farm or it could be in a little farming town nearby."

"Do you…" (Giorgi sucked a question out of the hazy air) "…deliver anything from city to farm … or from one farm to another farm?"

"No," Ida said, "it's a dairy truck. I drive a dairy truck." She attempted to mime *a dairy truck* but gave up and began to cast a forlorn and anxious look at the corner of the ceiling.

The ribbon smelt of rosewater. *Yes, of course, he bought a bouquet of seven roses, wrapped in paper, tied in this—roses from a subway station granny, roses behind his back for Nastya. Now, she or he has cut the ribbon into bookmarks.*

"Excuse me," Rosya interjected, "you said you needed to ask standard questions for a migration check-in."

"Yes," Giorgi stated, "I am asking about Ida's job."

"Well, sometime soon," Rosya pushed, "can we cover her living arrangements and be done with it?"

"Yes. Yes, I know it is late. I am coming to that."

"Ida lives here," Rosya summarized. "That's her bed. You saw her on it earlier. We are all, as it happens, intruding in Ida's room but that's because it may be the best room in Kiev."

"Ida," Giorgi asked her, "is this where you live, this room?"

"Yes, this room."

"And you sleep in that bed over there?"

"Sleep there. Eat there. Do my projects. … Sure, man, it's my bed."

"Show me any other space that is yours. Where do you keep your clothes?"

Beneath the linen dress, Rosya drew in her breath, hard.

Ida sprang up, went to the closet by the kitchen, and opened the sliding door to show a wardrobe that was, clearly enough, for Ida's work, Ida's leisure, Ida's body, not Rosya's.

Giorgi followed her, glanced from one end of the closet to the other, said, "Thank you for obliging the question," glanced into the kitchen too, and then returned to Nadia's side, on the guest sofa.

Ida shut the closet and rejoined Rosya, who gave her a slight nod. The lower half of Rosya's face had wrinkled in a grimace as she clenched her jaw.

Giorgi wrote something and turned to another new page. "Does any other person also sleep in this bed?"

"Hmm, just Nadia, when she's here."

"No, no," Giorgi corrected her. "I will … put 'no one'."

"Oh, honestly!" Rosya huffed. "This is absurd."

"Forgive me," said Giorgi, "but such embarrassing questions have become a social necessity, since, these days, with so many migrants in Kiev, there are certain elements who would exploit the housing shortage by creating shared accommodations on an illicit basis, even in violation of the sanitary norm."

As a mental exercise, Nadia translated this into plain language. *We have too many drifters, paying rent on the black market, living too close, and possibly fucking each other.*

"Well, as you can see," Rosya said, "we are compliant with the requirements. Ida and I have more than twelve square metres each, we have separate rooms, and even if you dispute the definition of this room as Ida's room, it doesn't matter. Ida and I are both women, so we could legally share one room."

"Your understanding of the regulations is perfect," Giorgi agreed.

"Yes and I used a tape measure," Rosya said, "and Ida lives here as my flatmate, on a permanent basis. She is my friend."

"Thank you," Giorgi purred, "I shall ensure it is expressed thus in the file."

Rosya got up and went to the radiator by the door to pick up Giorgi's coat. "If you don't get home," she said, "Nastya will have your nuts off."

Giorgi ignored this remark and asked, "Ida, are you not married?"

"I am not married."

"Have you never been married?"

"Never been married."

"Have you turned down many hundreds of offers of marriage?"

"Enough to not be married."

"Ha." Giorgi flipped the page in his notebook and continued, "Ida, do you have any children?"

"No."

Standing over Giorgi with his coat in hand, Rosya tilted her head and told him, "I would have imagined your files were more complete."

Giorgi shook his pen, which had run dry. He also shook his head and said, "Dear lady, the practices in this country are so far from scientific, you might never imagine the failures we see, when it comes to haphazard records." Rosya opened her mouth to offer a comment, yet Giorgi continued, "I once met a famous magician—a mindreader, well known in Gagra—who put the wrong date on a form and so he obtained an invalid permit for his street performance and, albeit unwittingly, induced an audience to join him in an illegal gathering."

Nadia asked, "Did you get him to teach you his tricks?"

"Ha. True wit. Yes." Giorgi looked down at the fresh page and drew swirlies to prime the pen as he said, "Now, Ida, are you married?"

"Never married."

"Do you...? Oh, excuse me, no, no children."

After another minute of this, Nadia found herself unable to follow the words, no matter how repetitious. She felt as if she were surrounded by cubist representations that ought to have been the people she knew. She scarcely detected the moment when it stopped and Giorgi, closing his notebook, stood up to take hold of her elbow and take his coat and suggest they go.

Go where? Nadia wondered.

"Look," Rosya said to Giorgi, "Nadia is exhausted. One glass has finished her and Nastya ... might finish you if you take her home like that. Let her stay."

"If Nadezhda wishes," said Giorgi, releasing her elbow.

She looked at him and nodded.

"Well," Giorgi muttered, "I should phone Nastya to let her know not to expect her sister tonight." He went for the phone by the printer.

"One moment," Rosya said. She butted ahead of him to tear off a printout and put it in a drawer. "Protocol, you understand. Please, use the phone."

Giorgi made his call. Nastya's tone, like a steam train on a mountainside, was audible to all. He did his best to tell a story about one errand turning into another and then Nadia deciding to stay with Rosya Lekht "... and Rosya's friend and roommate Ida, of course."

Nadia supposed her sister said, *"Maybe you should stay too and at least let me sleep half a night."*

"No, I am coming straight home now. No, just a few notes to type, hardly any work at all but ... to clear my mind, my love. You know I need to type things up to clear my mind." He listened to a short riposte. "Ha." He listened to a longer instruction. "Rosya is..."

"Nastya, goodnight!" Rosya lilted from the sofa. "I'm headed to bed!"

"Yes," said Giorgi, "and Nadia is asleep already." This happened to be true, at least for a moment.

As Nadia opened her eyes, she saw that Ida had gone back to the window. The capacitor-crown now encircled the pot of the prickly pear and Ida was pulling at her hair to break the snarls and squeeze out the damp. Rosya went over to hold Ida's shoulder and say, "I'll bring you a brush and hairdryer."

"Hmm, okay."

Rosya went to her bedroom. As she opened the door, Giorgi stretched the phone cord a little and craned his neck to try to see inside. She shut it behind her. Soon, she came back and passed the instruments of grooming to Ida.

Giorgi said something loving and hung up the phone. He announced, "Ladies, now I will leave you. Everything is fine, rest assured. You may... You may drink a carefree toast in the morning, with the wine that looks like tea and strawberry jam. Ha." He hesitated—unfolding and refolding his coat.

"Have you lost something?" Rosya asked.

"No, everything is perfectly in its place and you and your radiator have warmed me and this coat but ... may I, dear lady," Giorgi enquired, "stop to avail myself...?" He pointed to the bathroom.

"Oh, I ... had rather you didn't. Piles of laundry," Rosya told him. "Oleg, downstairs, can show you the men's room."

"Ah, then, I shall go to Oleg." He lingered barely an instant, in which he eyed Rosya's bedroom door. "Ladies, I bid you goodnight."

He was dispatched with a faint chorus of parting phrases, followed by the *clack, clack* of the twin deadbolts. Ida switched on the hairdryer, just on low but enough to distance herself further from all conversation.

As Roysa finished shutting the doors, she made an expression as if blowing smoke and she began to look at the places Giorgi had been. "He didn't leave anything, did he?" she asked.

"Oleg has his cap," Nadia mumbled.

"Right," Rosya breathed. She went to the phone, picked up the receiver, and attacked the rotary dial with a series of stabs and twists. "Oleg," she said. "Yes. Do you have the Lieutenant's hat? Make sure he gets it back. So that you know, he was a real prick about Ida living here." She hung up abruptly and turned to face Nadia and briefly showed her teeth before coming to put an arm around Nadia's shoulders. "Nadia," she asked, "what was all that? Why did he come?"

Nadia replied with a stunned, sleepy look and a shake of her head. "I'm sorry. I'm sorry, I don't know."

Rosya was still waiting for an answer.

"Oh, it's possible," Nadia supposed, "he was looking for a way to log some time, to say he was working tonight." Even she felt that this explanation lacked something. *Would he really...? Let's say he goes into the station in the morning and reports, "Bandits vandalized the car last night while I was out saving the Nation." "Giorgi, how did you save the Nation?" "Thinking of duty, I left my pregnant wife in bed and went to triple-check the personal details of dairy-driver Ivanova from Estonia." "Giorgi, that is exemplary: decentralization will lead to acceleration!" Well, it's not his favourite kind of tale; it has no lionesses or magicians or ladies of luck, no nudes at a picnic, foreign mafiosi, children in a radioactive forest, dinner guests.*

"I see," was all Rosya had to say. "Okay, Nadia, you'd better bed down with Ida. I'm shutting it off. I'll just go do some thinking in my room."

Rosya checked that all her computer equipment was off and then she unplugged it from the mains. The apartment, she believed, could be susceptible to power surges and lightning strikes, even on a night that seemed fine. If everyone worried about the machines as much as Rosya did, it might have been a normal summer, with a reactor making a boring hum a hundred kilometres away.

Ida switched off the hairdryer and ran the brush all over her scalp, in time to hand these tools back to Rosya as Rosya came to inspect the workbench. "I hope you sleep," Ida said.

"You too," Rosya replied. "Do you want to take something?"

"No."

"You handled it well, this evening."

"Hmm."

Rosya touched Ida's shoulder and then left for bed. Nadia went to the washroom (where there were, indeed, piles of laundry) and then she came to sit, queasily, beside Ida in the window. They could see various paths and ornamental features by the green light of mercury vapour lamps on various slopes outside. No one was around, except for one cop car heading towards the highway.

"The driving itself is not so bad," Ida said.

"No?"

"No, I … am even quite good at getting from 'A' to 'B'."

Nadia waited. Would Ida say more? Apparently not. *Enough about "A" and "B".* "Mama says, she misses baking for you."

"Hmm. Those were good times." Ida felt the bones of her face and said, "I want to sleep now. You lie on the window side." Nadia did and Ida went to turn off the last of the floor lamps.

They lay in the dark and Nadia, at least, felt time slip away, as if watch hands were moving across the insides of her eyelids, as if ants were rolling the world around and around. She felt hot and sick and confused.

"Hmm, just remembered," Ida said. Nadia could feel Ida's breath suddenly closer. Ida was reaching over her, for something on the workbench.

"Remembered what?" Nadia hissed.

Ida flipped on the LED lamp beside the microscope. "This," she said. Nadia squinted into the clinical, prickling brightness as Ida tilted the base of the microscope and pulled an envelope from underneath. "Your Gramma sent me a letter for you, inside a letter for me."

"Oh, right. She told my Mama she'd written." Nadia took it in hand and she rolled onto her back to study the envelope: the arthritic scrawl, the stamps, the bulge. A lot had gone into this one. "I didn't know she'd sent it to you."

"Neither did I, till I opened mine ... hmm, was it yesterday?" Ida stared down at Nadia and mimed, *Open it; open it!* in the air around the envelope. "Go on, I think it's good news for you."

"I've become wary of news somehow."

"Hmm, not when it's from your Gramma?" Ida asked. Nadia shrugged and continued to demur at the mimed suggestion. Ida made fun of her: "Miss Cat's nine lives are all still with her."

"Oh, fine, Smartass!" Nadia shot back. "I will open my letter..." (she huddled against the workbench and began to rip the envelope) "...but you'll be lucky if I show it to you, you calling me a coward!"

"Soft life you've had, Little Paw. Soft life." Ida lay back and dangled her fingertips to the floor. She whispered, "What's to be afraid?"

Nadia was reading the letter and the enclosed bundle of papers silently to herself.

Ida had shut her eyes. "You have a rare chance," she paraphrased (for the outer letter had given her the gist), "if you want and if you try ... if you play it cool ... a rare chance at getting an elite education in Moscow."

Nadia found herself confronted with a one-year plan to accelerate her to the end of high school and then get her into Moscow State University Named After M. V. Lomonosov. The 18th-century school and its namesake represented the Russian Enlightenment, the Language of Literature and of the People, the Science of Progress and of the Cosmos. Here, the Nation had educated such writers as Turgenev and Chekhov, as well as such statesmen as Suslov (called an ideologue, a kingmaker, a Pope of the hardliners) and Gorbachev (called a lot of things, yet difficult to pin down).

Ida sat up again and loomed over Nadia and mimed, *A rare chance!* as likewise she breathed in her ear, "A rare chance!"

"Oh, quit it!" Nadia hissed. She shuffled the profiles of various academics who had agreed to meet her to assess her potential. "This is so like Gramma." *"She goes about it quietly,"* indeed.

"Hmm?"

"I mean…" *(What do I mean?)* "…she must have been writing letters all summer (at least!) to make a thing like this happen. She must have called in every favour she had. She must have conned them all into believing I inherited her smarts and her convictions—me, the resurrection of her in her youth, a prodigy, a hero. One hell of an act, I'll have to give to … Academician Kiselyov here and Academician Popova and … this one. … Oh, frig, look at the Library; I'd live there." She studied a brochure about the famous Moscow University Library, shaped like a half-open hinge or a leather-spined book, with a round tower at the corner. "Two million foreign books, they say." Nadia peered more closely at the people in the pictures and began to wonder what role she would possibly play in this crowd of cherry-picked youths who smiled unusually, as if confident in their future and their good looks, as if they could banish suffering anytime with a flash of insight in the auditorium or a flash of genitals in the coed dorm. "Who do you think goes to an elite university?"

"Not me, Little Paw. The only way I'd get into any university is as a case study. I made Rosya admit it, nobody educates the crazies."

With sadness, Nadia looked over her shoulder, into Ida's eyes.

"Oh, don't give me looks. You have your chance to do something, which is a step up from … doing shit all. Your Gramma said, she'd like me to be the first to congratulate you. That's not a bad compliment, is it? Understand me, Little Paw, I'm happy for you."

"I'm not sure I am."

"Hmm, you do suffer for your fairness."

That's not why I suffer.

"Here," Ida said as she reached towards the workbench again, "maybe you need the enneadecagon."

"Maybe that's what's been missing," Nadia agreed. She allowed herself to be crowned while looking at reflections, hers and Ida's, in the window. Ida seemed to settle her attention on the coronation scene for several seconds but then her gaze drifted far away, towards the river, perhaps towards other lands.

Nadia folded the papers and returned them, in the envelope, to the safe place under the microscope stand.

"I'll tell you a story from my travels, a story of the fields," Ida whispered as she switched off the LED lamp and extinguished the reflections. "This is a strange story of life and death. Even the lambs look worried. They look twice worried, I should say. I'm referring to two-headed lambs who are now being born near the Exclusion Zone..."

10: Travel Plans

"Ida, why not plan a vacation?" Rosya proposed at breakfast. She had served Ida and Nadia each an experimental breakfast sandwich made of toast, honey, chocolate ice cream, strawberry mush, and an over-pour of hot tea with lemon. This kind of sandwich was served in a bowl with a spoon.

Through aching teeth, Ida cited a fact: "You don't take vacations."

"I know I don't," Rosya said, "but you could."

Ida contemplated the possibility. She had taken back the crown during the night and it shifted as she flexed her brow. "You mean ... on my own?"

"Why not?"

Ida stirred her sandwich and whispered, "What's to be afraid?" Then, aloud, she asked, "Do people on vacations...? Do they sleep with strangers?"

Rosya, on her sofa, snickered and coughed on the smoke of her cigarette. She dropped a few embers, which seemed bright in the grey, early light, and she flicked them away from her clipboard. "I believe it's been known to happen," she replied.

Nadia minded her own sandwich. *Please, you two, let me keep my clean memories of a family vacation in Crimea.*

"Hmm?" Ida wondered. (Nadia, sitting next to her on the bed, could see Ida's eyes narrow slightly.) Ida tried again to get the facts: "Rosya—or Nadia, you've been on vacation—I mean, what kind of rooms do people have on vacation?"

"Oh." Rosya amended her answer entirely: "Ida, I am sorry, it's a perfectly rational question. People on vacation may pay for a private room."

"Hmm." Ida considered this as she watched Nadia slurp a spoonful of sandwich. "Hmm-hmm. I've ... never been on my own—not in a place overnight."

"I have," Nadia offered, "at Anya's apartment."

"What Anya?" Ida asked.

Nadia retold the story of Anya, the Captain, their childlessness, his mortality, and Nastya's volunteerism in their black-market childcare scheme.

"Hmm, that Anya." With a slow, mechanically perfect gesture, Ida swept her spoon towards the bowl's far edge, raised it (a flying basin of breakfast liquid), and sipped the chocolatey mixture from it sideways, perhaps in imitation of something she had seen in a movie about a justly doomed aristocrat. "Okay, Little Paw, since you have the experience in vacationing and taking over a place for the night..."

"...and getting kicked till I bruise..." Nadia added around a mouthful of chocolate, "...and having to translate American smut..."

"...you may plan my vacation for me," Ida concluded. "Don't kid yourself. No one can stop you from translating anything. You do it to show off."

"Just for that—for your lack of linguistic appreciation—I'll send you on vacation to a mime colony."

"I'd like that. Thank you."

"Time to go to work," said Rosya, bringing to a close this initial planning session for a fantasy vacation in the unspecified future.

The three women stuck together as far as the transit station. Ida took a bus whose marquee read, "To nowhere". This meant it was going to the depot, which happened to house dairy trucks as well as buses.

Nadia and Rosya shared part of a subway trip. Side-by-side, they sat in motion. Rosya announced her intention to say little: "I'll let you read. You look as if you've got a headache."

Nadia nodded and gulped. "A bit. I don't need anything for it."

"No, well," Rosya said with her gaze fixed on the ceiling, "you are your Gramma's charge. I understand she's done well for you—or more than well."

"Ida told you about Gramma's letter."

"Certainly."

"So, do you have any advice for me?"

"A bit, if you want it," Rosya replied.

"Yes, please."

"My general advice is, don't screw up."

Nadia tried to absorb this (and to gauge it) as the subway system her rocked discomfortingly. "Anything else?" she wondered.

"You are finite. You aren't forever. All of this is dust." Rosya was lighting a cigarette.

I'm not sure this is helping. "Well," Nadia pressed for a different answer, "what advice do you generally give Ida?"

Now, Rosya did look at Nadia, as if to confront an impertinent question. "My advice for Ida is much the same. Why should it be different? I do tell Ida to let me help her—but you, Nadia, don't need my help. You don't lack for people to help you—to soften the consequences of your errors. Learners make errors; learners struggle to fix errors, to fix anything broken; life presents an excess of difficult material to learn and, to boot, an excess of broken shit. I'm finite too."

True, fair, but you do have a lot of cigarettes.

The lights flickered. Nadia felt a strange shock inside her aching head, as if a wire had been yanked.

When Nadia arrived at Nastya and Giorgi's apartment, she found no one in. She let herself in with a spare key, took off her shoes in front of the doll faces, put her suitcase in her closet-room, and went to the kitchen to look for a note on the counter. The facts were there on yellow paper.

"Anya to sanatorium, emergency. Minding children all day. Might take them out. Use up fish paste for lunch. Love." The words were accompanied by a drawing of a pregnant wolf jogging on her hind legs.

Nadia spent the day reviewing the documents and writing to Gramma and placing calls to secretaries at Moscow State University Named After M. V. Lomonosov to enquire as to when Academician Kiselyov and Academician Popova and Academician The-Other-One might be back from vacation and available to interview her as per the generous offer in the letter of such-and-such date, to discuss her prospects for the following year.

She learnt that her question might be answerable next week. This forecast seemed almost encouraging, on a fine Friday in summer.

Near the end of one call, someone buzzed the apartment twice. By the time Nadia got off the phone and checked the intercom, no one was there.

That's odd, she thought. *Two buzzes are not an accident. Stop this; stop thinking like a detective. Two buzzes are of no astronomical signifi-*

cance.

Already, it was past three o'clock and she had not had lunch, so she dropped the case of the buzzing intercom and went to deal with the case of the fish paste. She spread it on a toasted rump of rye and served herself this open sandwich with a bottle of fizzy lemonade. *This fish paste tastes of apples and onions and brine—all left to soak a day. Ida would be disgusted. Papa would banter. Anyway, this is a lonely end to a creature that swam in the sea.*

Whether it was the leftover paste or the sum of her intake over the past twenty-four hours, Nadia soon felt queasy again and she lay down in the sunny alcove to sleep it off. She wondered where Ida had taken her daily break. She wondered how the cats were keeping, in meat and milk. She wondered about life in residence, life in Moscow, especially in the winter. Even at an elite university, she imagined, the dorms would be something like the communal apartments of old, except that the residents would be selected from the most naïve and impractical segment of society. Their shared fairytale might unfold around a crowded table with a wobbly leg, tottering beneath a load of marked-up books and uncleared plates. There would be a centrally controlled radiator that got hot as a stove's insides or cold as an ice-swimmer's balls.

Who, there, would bake and sew and tend the sick, on a night before final papers or exams? *Ida is not wrong: soft life I've had, compared to some.*

11: Adoption

The weekend—the weekend to which one drank toasts with raisin wine—saw the unexpected arrival of new life.

On Sunday after lunch, Misha showed up at the door with a wooden crate that made him look like a farmer—perhaps like his father, if his father had stayed on a quiet farm (an Estonianly quiet farm at that) and lived to experience the creeping onset of middle age. Misha had taped a piece of cardboard overtop the crate as a lid. Between the horizontal slats, a pair of round, olive eyes was peeping at the world; a mouth like a pink pair of pliers was squealing; a black-and-white leg was sticking out and spilling sand.

Nastya gave a startled cry of "Papa!"

"Where can I open this?" Misha said by way of greeting. He had slipped past Nastya and was looking down the left and right forks of the hallway. "He's busting to get out. Poor little guy, he's been trying to bury his crap for an hour."

Nadia (from her closet-room) and Giorgi (from his alcove, via the main room) came out in time to hear and smell this fact.

"Shoes, Papa," Nastya said.

"Can't," Misha told her, "not unless... Giorgi, would you...? Nadia, would you...?"

Nadia tossed a book back on her bed and grabbed the crate as Misha lowered it to her level. "Little Man, it's you—my liver-loving friend!" she crowed.

He punched the cardboard but found it too well taped.

"You've met?" Nastya asked.

"He's one of the ones from the beach," Nadia told her.

"Perhaps to the..." Giorgi began.

"Take him to the kitchen," Nastya concluded. She held her belly and looked at everyone as if, for a moment, she believed they had all planned this as a surprise. "Papa, what's all this? You never let us take a cat home!"

"Come on," Misha grunted, perhaps at the laces of his sports shoes. They were a high-ankled pair, white with blue stripes and dirty-white rubber soles, almost like boots, for all seasons. "Mama never let you," he corrected Nastya.

"This isn't like petals on a breeze," Nadia noted. The kitten chased his tail and destabilized his environment. Again, clumps of shitty sand spilt over the rim of a plastic tray that Misha had set in the bottom of the crate.

"Come," said Giorgi. He tried to reel his sister-in-law towards the kitchen.

"Tugging my elbow doesn't help," Nadia complained.

"Forgive me."

"These two," Nastya told her father, "are always squalling these days. What does it matter, I suppose, if you bring me a fourth baby, with fur?"

"My heel is stuck," Misha grunted. He jerked at it and almost fell off the stool.

Nastya braced herself against the wall and gripped the shoe between her knees. "Pull," she told him.

When Misha was free, he hurried to the kitchen, almost slipped on a piece of torn cardboard, and found Nadia sheltering the kitten between her neck and her shirt collar as Giorgi studied the ceiling.

Remembering to protect his wife's kitchen and family, Giorgi bent to pick up the cardboard, lay it atop the stinking sand, and nudge the crate into a corner. "Papa," he asked, "by what inspiration did you bring us this…?"

"…cat," Nadia helped him. "Kitty."

"Ha. Yes, this 'kitty'. Ha."

"Oh, he's here to watch you all," Misha said.

Nadia nudged the cat to make him jump from her shoulder to her father's. "What happened to his family?" she asked.

Misha covered the kitten's ears and face with his hand. "Caught, maybe. I found him alone, terrified, hiding under the boardwalk." He lifted his hand and twirled his finger and pointed to each person to make the kitten look. "Watch … her and her and him. You watch them."

Nastya snorted. "Do we need watching?"

"Well, dear children," Misha told them (and, with his eyes, he included Giorgi among the children), "it's the way of the world that we all need spies. Giorgi, you must know the concept—and Nastya, you rat on everyone to Mama."

"I do not!" Nastya gasped.

"No?" Misha asked. He nudged the kitten's paw to prevent a downward step, venturing towards the hairiness below Misha's neckline.

Nastya glared at her father and drew in her breath and her lower lip.

"No?" he repeated. "Oh, then I'm wrong. I can see how much it upsets you when I'm wrong. Anyway, I had hoped to use Nadia as my spy but I suspect her of being inwardly divided—like Dostoevsky's philosophising murderers, whom she always enjoys—so instead I've brought this fellow," (he plucked the cat off his shoulder and dangled him in the air to force him to dance), "and he, as you'll see, has no qualms about anything. When he looks at you, you can all remember that I'm looking too. When he scratches, remember, I can scratch." He set the little cat down and running. Then, he let out a laugh. "The looks on your faces—I should be on the stage!"

"Ha. Ha!" Giorgi boomed. "Misha, let me get you a drink."

"Sure. Surprise me … with some ridiculous cocktail they drink in Gagra," Misha said as he wandered off after the cat. The pair of them ended up on the sofa in the alcove, where they had a good tumble until the cat leapt away to investigate the papers, pens, and typewriter on the coffee table.

Silent glances were being exchanged in the kitchen as cardboard and clumps were thrown away and hands were washed with scented soap. Nadia was doing her best to look just as baffled by Misha's speech as the others were.

"Make Papa a soda with condensed milk and a raw egg," Nastya told Giorgi, "and a get dish of condensed milk for the cat." Then, she followed her father and beckoned for Nadia to come along.

Misha had begun to type out a joke in which all the wives of all the Premiers chanced to meet on a night train to Tomsk. He chortled as the cat bit off chunks of the moving page. Misha was a rapid typist, with a fighter's hands and a clerk's experience.

"I guess it's just as well he eats it," he told his daughters. "I write like a camel walking backwards; I can't see where I'm going."

Nadia pointed to the page and said, "I like Mrs. Stalin's line."

"Do you?"

"Yes." She read it aloud in a soft, despairing voice: " 'The children's cat is missing. I have gone from town to town—now, to Tomsk—in the vain hope that I can find some record of her execution.' "

Nastya muttered, "I'll get myself a chair."

Nadia kissed Misha on the brow and suggested, "Mrs. Gorbachev is wearing a fur coat that the press have photographed in England; she's shopping for a plain coat to wear at home; and in Tomsk she hopes to find the start of the queue. Nastya, I'll get your chair."

Misha kept typing.

Nastya rolled her eyes and relinquished the dining chair that she had been dragging from the table. She let Nadia hoist it into the al-cove—over the sofa, over Misha's head, over the amazed kitten on the coffee table—to place it by the window.

"Sorry, Love," Misha said, "want the sofa?"

"No, I need back support. Nadia, where's my pillow?"

"I saw it under the table," Nadia said as she went crawling to fetch it.

"Where is Giorgi?"

They heard the toilet flush.

This crowd has got him worried. Since the evening at Rosya's place, he tries to plan ahead. Who knows what could have happened to that cop car? The historic outcome hinged on Oleg's cooperation.

"Well," Misha remarked, "maybe he wanted to sit down too. We'll have to send Nadia for my drink, after she gets…"

"…the imperial pillow," said Nadia, emerging from the table's underworld with dust on her palms—dust and little bits of old potato skin and sour cream. *Nastya's picky fingers aren't reaching the far corners these days. This is nothing, though; she may have worse to come. She's never cleaned up one of Cherny's pukes from a stack of kindling after Cherny returned from the hunt.*

Nastya took the pillow, squeezed past the sofa, and seated herself uncomfortably, with her elbows pointed apart and her hands on her knees. She sat facing her father, who was not facing her.

"Where is that guy?" Misha was asking. He did not mean Giorgi. The kitten had momentarily lost everyone's attention and, consequently, disappeared.

Nadia went down again, this time to look under the sofa from behind.

Giorgi could be heard whipping up Misha's drink in the kitchen.

Nastya just sat and began to smile.

"Where is he?" Misha wondered again. He was looking under the sofa from the front. He and Nadia could see one of each other's eyes.

"Shall I tell you?" Nastya asked.

Nadia pushed herself to her feet and noted, *Enter Giorgi with an egg soda in a beer mug and condensed milk in a saucer.* He stopped, balanced the saucer atop the beer mug, and took her elbow in case she was dizzy. *Damn him.*

Misha was crawling between the coffee table and Nastya's feet.

"Papa," Giorgi offered, "here is a youthful sort of refreshment for a…"

"Where is the little shit-maker?" Misha wanted to know. "I give up."

"Giorgi," said Nastya, "look how timid our new arrival is. He needs a hero." She pointed to the bookcase, to the kitten, whose round eyes only just rose above a stack of documents on radiation safety.

"Gotcha!" Misha said. He wiggled his fingers sorcerously, all along the edge of the stack. The kitten jumped atop the papers, making them slide. He steadied himself and then began to chew an index finger.

" 'Miiishaaa,' " Nadia said in kitten tones, " 'where's my snack?' "

"Go on, Giorgi," Nastya whispered. She reached out to touch his wrist as he stood on guard. "Go on, give him the milk."

Giorgi attempted to pass the saucer to Misha.

"Good—no," Misha said, "Giorgi, you put it there. We'll just move this… rocket-lamp-thing." He nudged the acrylic lamp aside and patted the bare space on the shelf. "You put it there so he knows it's from you."

"Just think of him as a lion," Nadia suggested. (She added a bit of a roar to the word "lion".) She freed her elbow and leaned on the top of the sofa to watch this show. "Hey, Brother. Feed the lion."

"Black-maned lions," Giorgi informed them as he stepped over his father-in-law, "are the ladies' men of the East African savannah. They are known to attract more lionesses than their blond-maned counterparts."

"Son, if you say so," Misha chuckled. He rolled onto his side and raised his eyebrows at Nastya, who did the same in reply.

Giorgi set down the saucer and watched from on high as the cat snuck out from his paper shelter to lap the sweetened milk. One's mind travelled to a watering hole in the smouldering heart of Africa. "Dark-maned lions," Giorgi continued, "do have more difficulty lounging in the sun. They absorb the heat around their necks. This causes them to perspire to a dangerous degree. They must drink often or else dehydrate."

They douse themselves in extra Shipr. They play a better game. Dark-maned lions are rare-good sports. They never cheat at cards.

The kitten soon cleaned the saucer and licked the corners of his little mouth. His gums were an angry red. He studied his surroundings and then began to chew the metal nose of the rocket.

"Oh," Giorgi fretted, "it was a gift, meant as an honour…"

"Oh, let him," Misha insisted. "I'll tell you something she has right—Gramma has right; I was thinking about it. We're better than the decorations. We're better than medals and statues, plaques and prizes, wreaths and flowers, and all this tat—or if we aren't, then cats are. Dogs are. Horses are. Kids are. Giorgi, remember I told you that. You'll understand when you're a father."

This, Nadia told herself, *is a funny sort of lecture, delivered by a man lying on the floor in a corner. I do love that man.*

"I sincerely hope so," Giorgi said. "Papa, let me ask you in earnest, how can I…?"

"He's bleeding!" Nastya wailed. "He's broken a tooth!"

The kitten spilt red drool as he eyed his fallen premolar.

"He'll get more," Misha scoffed. "Baby teeth are made for breaking. That's the time to learn to fight." He swiped at the air near the kitten.

The kitten swiped back and accidentally rattled the rocket lamp. He scrambled up to another shelf, ran behind a row of cultural-educational textbooks and, in doing so, flashed an ominously full asshole.

"We have to name him!" Nastya said. She punctuated this important realization by clapping her hands, twice, on her knees.

"Rocket," Nadia suggested.

"People will think of wristwatches," Nastya said, in reference to the Rocket brand.

"Cosmos!" Giorgi dubbed him.

"People will think of pencils," Nastya said, in reference to the Cosmos brand.

"Cats play with pencils," Misha rebutted.

"Cosmos is a good name," Nadia conceded.

"Okay. Cosmos," Nastya agreed.

"Now," said Giorgi, "I have named the Cosmos. Ha." He picked up the lamp in his free hand and said, "When I was a kid, I dreamt of being a cosmonaut—perhaps even an ambassador to alien civilizations."

"Oh," Misha wondered, "is that drink for me?" He sat up, with his knees against his chest to save space, and he took the mug.

Giorgi was lost in thought. He ran his thumb over the toothmarks in the soft metal.

"Nastya always wanted to marry a cosmonaut," Nadia teased.

"Did I?" Nastya asked. She continued to watch the bookshelves.

"Didn't you?"

"You must be thinking of Ida," Nastya replied.

Giorgi put down the lamp and stated, "Ida Ivanova never married."

Nastya and Nadia would have left it at that.

Misha sipped his egg soda and formulated a subtle question. "Giorgi, why do you say she 'never' married?"

"I say it as a matter of record."

"I'm sure you do but why say 'never'? The poor girl must only be nineteen. Plenty of people go a different way after nineteen, if they can."

Giorgi touched his lips for a moment and stared, as if through the bookcase. Then, he said, "I ask myself whether she is not older. She herself could not know, so it would be an absurdity to put it to her as a point of doubt. However, Misha, you are correct inasmuch as the records say nineteen."

"Okay," Misha groaned as he pushed himself to his feet. He tapped the books but got no reply. "Cosmos, let's go play something else."

" 'Miiishaaa,' " Nadia mewed at him, " 'give it a rest. I wanna hide.' "

"Wise words," her father said. "Being an aunt will suit you." He started to shuffle out of the alcove like a crab, with one arm twisting every which-way to keep his drink aloft. He stopped, looked at Nastya, felt her belly for a moment, and then moved on, saying, "If you're lucky, he'll be just like me."

"Sure. Unbreakable," Nastya said. She reached up to touch the remnants of the scab on her father's forehead. "Yes, let's hope so."

For those few minutes, a crowded alcove had made a set of the six of them: Nadia and Nastya and the foetal boy and Misha and Giorgi and Cosmos. *These are all children—Papa too. They will fight and try—as they did fight, did try, are fighting still, and are ever trying—to patch a happy ending on a dubious beginning, to make a quilt from rags. There will be bunches more children from such a bunch of children. They will chance it. Animals, in general, know the wager of life, yet it is the prerogative of mankind (progressive or no) to make the wager in full view of history.*

Nadia would remember those few minutes as a time when the wager seemed a relatively cheerful proposition.

At the same time, though, she wondered what had happened to the quilt that she and Gramma had given to Ida. She had not seen it in a while—or had she seen it in the closet with Ida's clothes? *That would make sense. She hardly needs a quilt in summer, to keep her warm while she's soldering.*

She wondered how Mama was faring—whether, in her time alone and not with any cat, she was in her kitchen or out in the garden or at her sewing machine or on the phone to Sokolov or, most likely, in a queue—*all while I stand here and find humour in the follies of my fellow children.*

She was excited about the prospect of raising a cat. She was trying to put off the inevitable thought of going it alone in Moscow. *How can*

I say 'alone'? Gramma has known solitude—not I. What I have, close or distant, is a living family—three and soon-to-be four generations, four already if we count Cosmos.

Papa stayed for dinner and took the night train back to Odessa. Before he left, he made an outing to the playground to exchange soiled sand for fresh sand—or, at least, sand somewhat freshened by last week's rain. "What I had in mind," he explained, "was that you could change sand at the beach. Of course, I suppose the river doesn't clean sand as well as the sea."

Giorgi agreed as to the problem: "No, without the salt and the tide…"

"Well," Misha continued, "in a few months, he'll be safe to roam on his own and he can learn where it's acceptable to dig. There'll be lots of snow. He probably won't stray far. I hear you can freeze your nose off in Kiev." He kissed his daughters' noses and gave a corollary: "We should do New Year's and Christmas in Odessa—perhaps, Giorgi, with your parents, too. Okay. Time for me to go back to Mama."

When Misha left, Cosmos was still hiding at the back of the bookshelf. *Perhaps he's setting up a radio transmitter, camouflaged as a ball of dust.* That would be the only practical way for Cosmos to send his observations to Misha, since these two would be parted by Time and Space, in measures so vast to a kitten.

12: Joy and Bitter Accident

Cosmos loved heights. He loved to look down on the world. He loved it when Nadia held him overhead and slowly danced in circles to the songs of Alla Pugacheva. He loved it when Nastya got up on the high stool to place him in the cupboard with the decorative plates. He especially loved his final cupboard-visit ever, when he discovered that he loved to watch plates fall and shatter, like colourful meteors wreaking havoc on a planet below. He loved to ride around the apartment on Giorgi's shoulder. He loved the smell of Shipr, even if it made him sneeze, and he had to be restrained from chewing Giorgi's shaven throat. Whomsoever or whatsoever the kitten loved, he loved with a boundless passion.

Giorgi came to expect the daily new discovery of feline bite marks on his pens, his bookmarks, and even the leatherette covers of his notebooks. During the nights of typing, he took breaks to deal cards in a flashy style,

for the sole purpose of letting Cosmos catch them in midair. Giorgi
left his boots lying flat on the floor so that Cosmos could explore them
like tunnels. Giorgi placed his cap upside-down in the bookcase so that
Cosmos could use it as a bed. Giorgi borrowed one of Nastya's rayon
bras, which was not fitting her these days, and he put it in the cap as
a silky blanket. Giorgi had play-fights with the kitten, endured many
little bites and scratches, and let the kitten pin him to the floor.

Nadia began to ask herself whether Giorgi might, in a certain light,
become an adequate family man. *Did Nastya foresee such scenes? Did
Papa?*

This happiness was brief, like an airshow, and it ended when Nastya
had her next check-up at the hospital. Giorgi went with her. The
physician's assistant made a remark about the cat scratches on Giorgi's
hand. Hearing this, the doctor weighed in forcefully, with much to say
about the foetus's susceptibility to feline-borne parasites and disease.
Nastya was initially skeptical of these warnings. (They were not the first
warnings she had heard in her months as a married woman.) However,
she began to falter when, to her surprise, Giorgi broke down in a stream
of silent tears. He sat on the edge of an examination table and kept
running his scratched hand over his eyes and into his hair as if to hide it
there.

The couple went home in fear. Giorgi entered the apartment ahead
of Nastya and, as he uttered confusing advisories and apologies, he
moved the box and kitten into Nadia's room and shut them in. All
the while, Nadia was lying on her bed and attempting to translate a
passage from *Great Expectations* as a showpiece of her linguistic abilities.
She was on her umpteenth version of the line, "I sometimes have sick
fancies." On the side, she was also drafting a point-form self-eulogy.
She received Cosmos and cuddled him in her armpit. He purred and
sneezed and was oblivious to his new predicament, while she began to
grasp its gravity only when Nastya came into the hall to shout the details
of her appointment through the door.

Nadia was to keep the kitten company until they decided what to
do.

Nadia suggested in reply, "Should you call Yuly and have him put
Gramma on the line so you can ask her about it?" *I believe I've just
given reasonable advice. Dare I put on paper that people come to me for
"reasoned and fair advice"?*

On the other side of the door, Nastya went silent for several seconds. "Are you there?" Nadia asked.

"No. No, it would get back to Papa," Nastya surmised. "He'd be hurt and he'd feel I'd ratted on him to his mother."

Stalemate. That's fairness, alright.

"My love," said Giorgi, "such a problem must be pondered over a pot of tea. When I was a boy, I played with my grandmother's old-fashioned tea set and she would say, the reason we have tea growing in our foothills is that Chinese men lost their way in the mist. Come now. Nadia, please stay with Cosmos."

His voice sounds extra thick. On top of that, he's thinking of childhood again. Giorgi is becoming a desperate sentimentalist.

"Ow!" Nadia protested as the kitten went for a mouthful of armpit hair. She pulled him out of her sleeve, tucked him under the covers, and bamboozled him into chasing her fingers and chewing them through the blanket, as if the floral pattern had become carnivorous. Later, she would discover that he lost another of his milk teeth under there.

After a while, Nadia slipped away. Cosmos stayed, settling near the foot of the bed as a small lump.

Shutting her door behind her, Nadia came out to the kitchen and then the main room and finally the alcove, where she found Nastya and Giorgi sitting on the sofa in silence. They were holding hands. Nastya was being swallowed by the soft cushions, yet she seemed not to care. On the coffee table, steam was rising from a pair of daisy-patterned teacups and a matching teapot. Giorgi was still wearing his boots.

"Oh, it's heartbreaking," Nastya sighed. "He's such a joy to me."

"Then again, my love," Giorgi reasoned, "perhaps a friend of ours—perhaps Anya Vladimirovna—is more in need of such an amenity—such a diversion—as this handsome and playful young animal. Who better than Anya to nurture a growing cat?"

Gramma? Nadia asked in her head.

Giorgi kept praising Anya and the cat and the joyful life they could share. "With him there, kids would love her flat even more!"

"At Anya's," Nastya supposed, "I could go see him most days. Nadia would be looking after him for now and probably we could have him back after the baby is born."

"Yes," Giorgi agreed. "Yes, Nadia can take him there tonight. He can be a surprise for Anya when she gets back."

Such was the safety plan. After all, they could re-house a kitten at will, yet they could not, for love of the world, move a melted reactor to the Moon.

Nadia packed her papers and books and wrote a list for Nastya and Giorgi about phone calls that might come from Moscow. For each possible caller, she drafted a personalized message of thanks, as well as a set of positive responses to every likely query or request. She wrote an effusive explanation of her absence: she had left her usual workspace (her home library, near her phone) to give practical help to a friend whose husband, a police Captain, was suffering from grave injuries sustained in the line of duty. *(Say nothing of radiation. My environment is conducive to perfect health. Say I am always doing such things. As much as I would have liked to spend this summer in a volunteer project with the Young Communist League, I am a girl with a deeply traditional sense of my duty in the home. One hopes that my university experience will round off my bookishness and bring me out of my shelter.)*

Giorgi dropped her and Cosmos at Anya's place.

For days ahead, there would be much to rearrange: words on a page, sand in a box, food in a kitchen, dust in corners. Nadia and Cosmos shared a deep capacity to continue their activities in any surroundings, at any hour, whether under a blanket or under the sun. Sometimes, when she closed her eyes for a think or a nap, she imagined herself sitting on a remote beach with books and cats and dunes and pines; sometimes Ida, sometimes Johnny too. The cats, of course, were naked; sometimes not just the cats. Sometimes the wind seemed talkative—like one's memory of a childhood companion, who would be Nastya—and sometimes it seemed as if a baby were crying in the trees.

Who knew that Anya was allergic to cats? One night, she arrived home unannounced—already in tears—to find her apartment contaminated, from bath to bed, with short, black hairs.

Nevermore did Nadia stay at Anya's place.

Having received a phone call from Anya, Giorgi went to pick up his disgraced sister-in-law at the curb. She was sitting there, in the darkness under a broken streetlamp, beside the boxed, squealing kitten. With one hand, she held her cheek; with the other, she scratched at the slats of the crate, beneath the folds of her sweater, which she had draped all around it to keep him warm. "I know. I know," she was telling him. "I know. Me too."

As the headlights of the cop car approached, she let go of her cheek and shielded her eyes. The cheek hurt, where Anya had hit her, and Nadia suspected it was starting to swell. *A fine lot of explaining I'll have to do with Academician Popova.*

Giorgi was folding and unfolding himself to get out of the car. Now, he was sizing up the scene for an instant. *Does he see my face? Does he hear Cosmos?*

"Nadia, come," Giorgi said as he hurried to hang his coat on her shoulders. (Most of it fell to the sidewalk.) "Come. None of this is your fault," he assured her. "Tomorrow, Anya will bitterly regret her stupidity. Sergei will tell her she is a fool, at a time like this, to drive away her friends—and to hurl words of abuse at such a clever and handsome, innocent young animal…"

"Let's not talk about it now," Nadia suggested. She lifted the crate and carried Cosmos to the car. Giorgi held the back door and she put the little passenger in where the crooks would go. She whispered some words of reassurance and then she got in front as Giorgi held that door too.

"I am of half a mind," Giorgi continued as he settled into the driver's seat, "to issue her a warning for the uncivilized disturbance she has created in this building tonight. There were calls—do you realize, there were calls?—and I had to assure the station, assure them twice, I could go handle it alone, whatever this riot was. She knows how seriously we must take disturbances these days." He was gearing up madly as he pulled away from the curb. "A single spark can turn to a firestorm, which is all the extremists need…"

"Shh, shh!" Nadia pleaded with him. "You're distressing Cosmos!"

She was looking over her shoulder at the wailing cat when Giorgi slammed on the brakes. Her swollen cheek collided with the headrest.

"Ah!" she gasped.

Giorgi shouted something in Georgian.

Thud. The car rocked. Sand shifted. The kitten flopped down. Nadia felt a spasm in her neck. She caught a glimpse of a garbage bin as it spun from the force of the car hitting it. A man (who must have been either stealing the bin or rummaging in it) fell over in the street. Giorgi threw open his door to shout something again and the man just got up and ran.

"Ah!" Nadia repeated.

Letting the tramp go, Giorgi shook himself and made a new attempt to take in his surroundings. He observed, "Nadezhda, your cheek…"

"Is Cosmos okay?" she asked.

The kitten started squealing again, over and over at an irregular pitch and interval, like some mysterious signal on the shortwaves.

Giorgi got out again and opened the back door. He ripped off the cardboard cover of the crate and brushed away the sand that had spattered Cosmos. The kitten pounced on Giorgi's hand to grab and kick it with all four paws and bite it with a mouthful of loose teeth. "He is fine!" Giorgi yelped. "Take him! Hold him! He requires your tenderness to calm him and…"

"I … don't want to turn around," Nadia said. "My neck hurts."

"I'm bringing him to you." Giorgi was soon in the driver's seat again. "Here, take him in your lap and cover him with your sweater." He extracted the kitten from his bleeding hand and left him squirming under Nadia's supervision. Then, Giorgi went to move the bin out of the road. He returned and started bleeding on the gear shift and the steering wheel. The car went into motion again.

Nadia patted the kitten and, for the moment, he settled. *He's come through this better than I have.* She wanted to puke from the pain.

"Nadezhda," asked Giorgi, "do you want to go to a hospital?"

I wonder whether he's ever taken someone like Ida to a hospital, against her will. "No," Nadia said. "Please, can you take me to the train station? I want to take him to Gramma. I want to go back to Gramma."

"Tonight?"

"Yes. Please."

"No, do not hurt us so. No, to see you leave in the night, when you are injured and bewildered—no, we could not forgive ourselves!" Giorgi protested.

"I want to go."

"Tonight, I am taking you to Rosya Lekht and Ida Ivanova."

"They do too much for me." *I sound like Gramma.*

"We all do what we can," said Giorgi. "We are part of a society."

Is that what you were shouting at the tramp?

Giorgi continued, "When I left, Nastya was going to phone Rosya so that she will know to expect us."

"Alright," said Nadia, who perhaps had only a bit more choice in the matter than Cosmos did. "Alright, for tonight."

Giorgi went silent, as on their previous drive to Rosya's place. For a minute, Nadia wondered whether he had an agenda in returning there. She dismissed the idea as too neat, under the circumstances.

Cosmos wriggled. He pushed his head and torso between two buttons of her sweater but then he somewhat settled again. Tense and alert, he moved his neck in oblique arcs; he was looking up and backwards and sideways, out one window and another and another. *You're taunting me with your gymnastics,* Nadia thought as she stroked his chin. *A wonder-kid like you will train for the Olympics and forget about me, whilst I strain myself to convince Academician Kiselyov that I can hold my head upright to read a book.*

Of her few car rides, none had ever felt so long.

When they arrived, Giorgi wanted to make a new cover for the crate. The trunk contained everything he needed and more. He had a roll of good tape, a pair of scissors, and a hand mirror of Nastya's. (These items were intended for an automotive repair job that he had not yet completed.) He also had a burlap bag from a grocery trip. He cut the burlap to size, taped it down on three edges, slid Cosmos under the fourth edge, and taped that as well.

"You will be able to free him," Giorgi instructed Nadia, "by tearing away the tape on just one side. I have left this long flap to make it easier and I will put the tape and scissors in your bag."

"Oh, right."

Giorgi carried Cosmos, as well as Nadia's satchel. She clutched her suitcase against her gut.

They climbed the hill. On the way, Nadia puked under the bower. The puke glistened in the greenish light.

Oleg spotted them and came to hold the door. As these guests entered, he tapped Giorgi's shoulder and said, "You cannot go up. Only she can go up."

"I must carry these for the young lady," Giorgi explained. "Nadezhda has injured her neck and on no account..."

"You cannot go up," Oleg repeated as he displayed the flat of his palm. "At this hour, it is improper."

"I am here as a detective..."

"You are here as a driver. You cannot go up."

"Then, will you carry these up?"

"I can carry her things to the elevator," Oleg stated. "I cannot go up."

"Why can't you?"

"I am here as a doorkeeper and the hour is exactly the same."

Without moving her neck, Nadia cast her eyes upwards towards Giorgi's face. She reckoned he was searching for an article of law that might make this whole nocturne explicable if he were to end it by arresting Oleg or perhaps smearing a handful of sandy shit across Oleg's hairless scalp.

Finding no such article, Giorgi said, "Yes, forgive me. Nadia, take care of Cosmos. Take care of yourself. Why not set him down when you're in the elevator?"

"Good thought," Nadia grunted.

"I am ... headed back to Nastya," Giorgi breathed. "She will call in the morning. We will ... sort out whatever is next."

"Goodnight," said Nadia.

"Goodnight," said Giorgi.

"Goodnight, Comrade Lieutenant," Oleg chimed in.

Giorgi brushed past Oleg, set the crate and satchel down on the desk, stuck his fingers between the slats to say goodbye to Cosmos, adjusted his cap, clutched his bitten hand, and then stalked out.

Oleg, true to his word, helped to move the luggage as far as the elevator and no farther. Nadia rode up as Cosmos squealed to her from the floor.

"I know," she moaned. "I know." *On top of everything else, he probably hates the smell of grease.*

Ding. They had arrived.

Painfully, slowly, Nadia shouldered her satchel, stacked the crate atop her suitcase, and lugged everything to the apartment. She struggled to ring the doorbell with her elbow.

Ida, in her pyjamas, opened the double-layered doors and said, "Hi. I got Nastya's call."

"Hi," Nadia groaned. She stepped inside and knelt on the floor to unload all her cargo. The burlap had a wet wrinkle in it where Cosmos was attempting to chew his way through.

"Who hit you?" Ida asked as she locked the doors.

"Anya. Anya and a later a headrest. Car accident."

"Hmm. Funny, isn't it, how driving safely is a menial job? I guess Giorgi is a bad driver and Anya is a bitch."

"These days, she's not herself," Nadia murmured.

"No? Who is she?"

"I'm not sure we can solve that riddle tonight." Nadia tore off the tape on one edge. She watched (exhaustedly, sweatily) as Cosmos propelled himself into the open room. She gestured feebly to the scattered sand and to a turd-end, which had fallen to the floor behind the cat. "Sorry for the mess."

"I've seen shit on floors before," Ida stated.

Cosmos was jogging around the apartment. He had never seen anything like this maze of boxes, wires, and machines. He was anxious to explore.

Rosya was nowhere in sight.

"My neck is killing me," Nadia told Ida. "The accident gave me a hell of a jolt. Giorgi nearly creamed a homeless guy."

"I guess he wasn't 'vigilant of vagabonds,'" Ida cracked.

"Ah! Stop, stop, don't make me laugh," Nadia pleaded. She held her breath for a second before adding in a historian's tone, "He was distracted and unlucky. His mind was on his feelings for Cosmos."

Ida stared down at her friend with a look that said, *You've let your fairness become absurd.* Ida asked, "His feelings for ... the whole Cosmos?"

"No, the kitten. He named him Cosmos."

"Hmm! Hmm, Cosmos." Ida watched the kitten, who was now doing an orbit around the computer desk as he sought the best spot to jump up. "What, because he's black with a little light?"

"No, because Giorgi wanted to be a cosmonaut."

"Hmm, Nastya's dream man." Ida flexed her shoulders and quickly added, "Stay still." She placed her hands on either side of Nadia's neck, from behind—barely a brush at first but then a brace just firm enough to dampen any painful motion.

She means to stake me like an apple tree.

Ida said, "Get up slowly. Let's get you lying down." Perfectly and in no hurry, she relocated Nadia to the bed, had her sit, and eased her onto her back.

The kitten, having a concept of a bed as a social place, jumped up to see what was going on.

Nadia told Ida, "You could be a surgeon, you've got such steady hands."

"Hmm. Stay still. I'll be right back." Ida went to the kitchen. Nadia could hear her opening a drawer.

"Which knife will you use to operate?" Nadia asked.

"Stay still!" Ida called back. The drawer shut and then the fridge opened and shut. Ida returned with a set of towels twisted around ice. Slowly, again, she raised Nadia's neck and began to arrange icy towels around it.

As Ida moved above the sickbed, Nadia had a sensation like looking down the wrong end of a pair of binoculars. The kitten, too, was watching Ida's every move.

All this, Nadia thought, *just to get me settled for the night. Meanwhile, that tramp may be bleeding inside, for all I know.*

Ida knelt near the foot of the bed and stroked the kitten's neck. "This," she whispered to him, "is how we handle necks. Hmm."

"Where's Rosya?" Nadia asked.

"Hmm, on a date. I guess it's a date."

"Why, what's the story?"

"She and a professor in Khabarovsk are sending teletype to each other on the computer. They have a pair of university computers that are wired to each other by the phone lines. He even sent her a picture of himself."

"Khabarovsk, that's…?"

"…north of Vladivostok, eight hundred kilometres. He books time on the computer first thing in the morning to write to her."

"Oh, right."

"A lot of the time it breaks down—the system, not the … you know…"

"…mutual feeling?" Nadia suggested.

"You got it, Little Paw. There's a look of 'mutual feeling' in her cheeks, when she comes home from these late-night communications."

Nadia contemplated this gossip as she stared at the stippled ceiling, where the lamplight stroked each ridge and left a shadow on the far side. The snowy mountains of Kolyma look like that, from a vantage point high above the clouds. From on high, neither gold nor bones can be seen.

Ida was repeating the lesson for the little cat: "Yes, this is how we handle good people's necks. Now, bad people's necks—Nadia's Gramma might know how to handle those. Hmm."

"Truest comfort," Nadia muttered.

Ida got to her feet and said, "You should have something for the pain." She disappeared into Rosya's bedroom and came back holding a medicine bottle with a dropper cap. She set it on the coffee table and then crossed to the kitchen to fetch a glass of plum-and-apple juice, which was not at all to Ida's taste, so she was happy to get rid of it.

Cosmos raised his chin in Ida's direction as she returned.

Ida prepared the mixture by lamplight and watched each drop dissolve, like an animation of a water spirit fading to nothing in a muddy river. Meanwhile, Nadia was explaining how the kitten had made his way from the boardwalk in Odessa to his first, second, and now third apartment in Kiev.

"Hmm," said Ida. "Nastya wanted something else, more than her stray." She handed the glass to Nadia.

"Well … in a sense," Nadia said. She tried to drink the painkiller but its bitterness made her gag on the first sip.

Ida offered, "I could drizzle it on a wedge of lemon and you could suck it."

"Torturer," Nadia rasped. She held her nose and downed the liquid.

"Better," said Ida as she took back the glass. For a moment, she stared out the window at a line of streetlamps down by the river. Then, she turned around to go set the glass on the coffee table.

Cosmos stepped onto the workbench. He began to eye the prickly pear and its surroundings: the soil, the pot, the flag, the capacitor-crown. He arrived at the idea that he might soothe his gums by chewing the crown.

"Ah!" Nadia cried out as her muscles reacted to this sight. "Stop him!"

"You there—don't suck solder," Ida told the kitten. She hooked her hand around his chest and frogmarched him away from the hazard. Having failed to dance away from her grasp, he gaped at her angrily as she set him down. "Don't give me looks. What do I call you, little Devil, hmm? Cosmos, hmm?" The name did not seem full enough to Ida. "I'd rather you were Tentser. You can be Tentser II of the Cosmos."

"Far better," Nadia agreed. "I'm sure Yuly and Gramma would both like you to have a cat."

"They might. I don't know what Rosya would say."

"You can talk her round to it."

"I've invaded Rosya's life," Ida said flatly. She whisked her hand away as Tentser II of the Cosmos attempted to bite her.

"He's hungry," Nadia said.

"Shall I be your serf, Little Father?" Ida asked the cat. She bent down to nuzzle his face and kiss his eyes. He seemed to take kindly to this. "Okay."

Once more, Ida left for the kitchen.

Nadia wiggled her toes to try to keep the cat occupied. She could feel the ice melting around her neck.

"We don't really cook," Ida was saying, "and we don't buy canned stuff." She rolled all the pantry shelves—out, in, out… She rummaged in the fridge and cupboards and pan drawer. Twenty minutes later, she returned to the main room with a steaming, fatty-smelling bun in a bowl. "Somebody gave me a bunch of these at a factory on my route, so I was defrosting this one to pack for my lunch in the morning. They have a filling of ground meat and sour cream and stuff—still a work in progress, this recipe. The assistant chef gave me her latest because I shared a smoke with her when she was out having a cry."

"How's her work shaping up, then?" Nadia asked.

"Hmm, you know." Ida set the bowl down on the bed and she hustled Tentser/Cosmos towards the piping-hot contents. He inhaled, took one step back, lunged, bit into the pastry shell, tore away a morsel, shook it, and formed a sufficiently high opinion of the assistant's work to start gorging himself on it.

" 'Iiidaaa,' " Nadia mewed, " 'nice of you to give me your lunch.' "

"Hmm, sure," Ida murmured. "Be glad for inconsistency, in rolls and human beings."

"And cats," Nadia added. She stared at the ceiling and listened to the mashing sounds. "He'd suit you," she said.

Ida was still pondering inconsistencies. "Nastya said Giorgi chickened out at the little elevator."

"At the Mother Motherland, right."

"How'd he plan to fly in a space capsule?" Ida shook her head and then looked at Tentser II. "Are you serious about wanting me to take him?"

"Why not?"

"Hmm, I might not be the best one for him through all his living days."

"Look, it's up to you. I had planned to take him to Gramma tomorrow."

"Let me think about it," Ida said. The conversation halted there. Ida began tidying up. The empty bowl, the sand, the shit, the box—all went away. The box ended up in Ida's closet, which she left open for access. She was just putting the broom and dustpan back there, when the lock began to turn in the outer door. Ida went to adjust the items on the coffee table. She picked up a Rubik's cube, sat down on Rosya's sofa, and busied her hands with the cube.

Rosya came in. She was wearing cherry-coloured lipstick and a triangular shawl of sky blue. Beneath it, she seemed to be dressed for work as usual.

Ida asked, "Were you able to transmit a photo?"

"Yes."

"Hello," said Nadia.

"Hello," Rosya replied. She headed for her bedroom as she started to unwrap the shawl. After spending a minute in there, she came back with a question on her face.

"Right here," said Ida, dipping her chin towards the coffee table and the medicine bottle. "Nadia needed something. Giorgi smashed her neck." She continued to fiddle with the cube.

"What?" Rosya wondered.

"Car accident," said Nadia. "Don't make so much of it. Giorgi was distracted and upset."

"Well, poor Giorgi," Rosya muttered. She picked up the bottle and juice glass and went to the kitchen. "Oh, hello!" she said to someone there. She called back to the main room, "Which of you has been repopulating the Earth?"

"Say little," Ida whispered. She set down the cube.

Rosya continued, "A baby animal has crawled out from behind the fridge." She followed him as he jogged back into the main room. "I saw him and I half expected he'd be leading a parade of baby animals. 'Let's conquer the virgin blue.' "

"Hmm?" Ida wondered at the phrase.

"Oh, it was a slogan in the early '60s," Rosya said, "when we wanted the ducks and rabbits to breed faster and the corn to grow at the Arctic Circle. There's a poster in my head of a swarm of ducklings parading out of an egg and carrying blue banners." She laughed, with many wrinkles, and repeated, " 'Let's conquer the virgin blue!' "

"Hmm." Ida did not find this slogan funny.

Tentser II jumped up onto the computer desk, slid on a printout, and bumped his nose against the printer.

"He's cute but what exactly," Rosya asked, "did you two have in mind? He is … one of your adventures, is he?"

"He's Nastya's," Ida said, "but she thinks a cat would be bad for her baby."

"Oh, does that mean Giorgi doesn't want him?"

"No…" Nadia began.

"Probably," said Ida. "I want to name him Tentser. Would that be alright?"

"Yes, well," Rosya said, "Yuly might like that, coming from you, Ida." She looked all around (for the cat had vanished) and she rolled the medicine bottle between her fingers. "Were you meaning to keep him?"

"If it's a problem," Ida said, "he can go to Nadia's Gramma."

"No," said Rosya, still rolling the bottle, "if you want to look after a kitten, I don't see why it should be a problem. I believe cats aren't much work once they're grown." She returned to the kitchen. She could be heard mixing herself a drink from the contents of the fridge.

"How is your head tonight?" Ida asked.

"Bad."

"How about your back?" Ida followed up.

"Bad. Those chairs at the university…" When Rosya returned, Ida put down the Rubik's cube and yielded the master sofa. "Thank you, Ida. Nadia, I hope you haven't sustained any permanent damage. I'm not a believer that pain does any good for strengthening body or soul."

"No?" Nadia wondered. *Cigarettes and lemons, yes, but pain, no?*

Ida was pacing and swinging her arms and perhaps looking for the cat and perhaps wondering (with a certain sense of boredom) whether she was getting enough sleep to safely drive a truck.

"No," Rosya reiterated, "but of course … I forget what I was going to say." She lay back and sipped her drink and stared down the length of her sofa at the powered-off computer and the wet-haired, injured guest and the reflections that always haunted the window as long as the lights were on.

Please, Nadia wanted to say, *now that I have drunk the waters of the Lethe, when may I have darkness instead of the sight of this stippled ceiling?* Instead, she asked, "How did your back get to be so bad?"

"Mine?" Rosya asked.

"Yes."

"Skiing. My father thought I should ski, in a former Age."

"Why?"

"I suppose an athlete should be a hard worker."

"Okay," Nadia agreed, "all things being fair, a winner has to work for it." She continued to stare at the stipples and to contemplate icy mountain ranges where a skier might fly, a convict might dig. "Then, what happened to your back?"

"I landed upside down in the Carpathians, at New Year's, in my first year of grad school. I was three months in hospital and lost my place in the programme."

Ida had walked into her closet. "Hmm. I see you've pissed in your sand and gone to sit in my underpants."

No one remarked on these observations.

"Mind you," Rosya added, "people in my family have been going to the Carpathians for generations and it's almost always death for us. I had great uncles on both sides of Brusilov's Breakthrough in 1916."

Should I ask about Brusilov's Breakthrough or more about her back? "That must have been a bitter disappointment," Nadia said.

"You've studied Brusilov's Breakthrough," Rosya surmised.

"I meant the setback in your education."

"Yes, Nadia, but it could have been worse. I could have been written off entirely. As it was, I got my breakthrough in the Space Programme instead."

"That must…"

"That reminds me," Rosya said, "Ida, I wanted to tell you something." She took her last sip of medicine as she waited for Ida to emerge.

Ida wandered back into the space between the sofas and her bed.

Rosya continued, "An old colleague of mine, a friend, he has a cottage he isn't using these days."

"Hmm," Ida murmured, "you should go, take somebody your age for company."

Rosya put down her empty glass and said, "I meant to give that advice to you. You and Nadia and the cat could go for a weekend. Nadia, how about it?"

Nadia flexed her cheek to feel the hurt of the swelling. She wondered, "What if your friend is allergic to cats?"

"He's not allergic to cats," Rosya assured her.

"How do you know?"

"His kids had a cat. I know the family."

"…had a cat," Ida echoed. While contemplating this historical footnote, she dug an ice cube out of a sopping towel and began to rub it across Nadia's cheek, as if to paint a cold stream of tears.

Nadia squinted at Ida's backlit face. *Tired blue eyes.* Ida was looking back at her but (Nadia supposed) more in the way one might look at a roadmap.

Rosya added, "The cat lived at the cottage. The girl told me fairytales about him and the boy drew pictures, very realistic."

"Hmm."

Rosya gave her final reflection on the matter: "I suppose he was anybody's cat, anybody who was around. Cottages are like that—not my thing but I'd say you've earned a try of your own."

"Hmm."

My thoughts too, Nadia told herself as she studied Ida's eyes.

Soon after that, Rosya picked up her medicine bottle, got another glass of juice, and went to bed. Ida swapped the ice for a bundle of hot laundry. Tentser/Cosmos curled up by Nadia's neck and purred like a small motor until he and she were both asleep.

Ida went out with a set of keys that she kept hidden in her closet: keys to utility rooms, keys to back exits, keys to the roof.

IV: Jynx in the Tree

1: Arrival

They were running out of weekends in summer and it was already settled (inasmuch as Gramma had arranged it) that Nadia would be going back North to finish high school.

Ida took charge of planning the trip to the cottage. Rosya's friend owned a car and liked to drive it to the real boondocks, so his cottage was not an easy place to reach by train or bus. Ida decided to get there by dairy truck.

The real coup was to pull it off with a kind of honesty. Ida finagled a swap of routes so that she would do a delivery to a nearby town on Friday afternoon, a pickup from a nearby farm on Monday morning, and an off-record stop at the cottage in between. A collaborator at the truck depot would record that the vehicle was getting sanitized that weekend. Indeed, Ida would let the truck air out at the cottage.

Nadia and Tentser/Cosmos would ride with Ida as she made her rounds on the Friday and the Monday. Nadia (though unfit to lift sour cream) could comfort the kitten.

"How's your neck?" Ida called as she jumped down from the cab of the dairy truck with her arms spread wide. This was early Friday morning, at the delivery entrance of Rosya's place. Having left the whole building asleep (save Oleg), Ida had already gone to the depot and was backtracking to pick up Nadia, Tentser, and the luggage.

"Much improved," Nadia replied as she stirred from her seat on a mound of surplus concrete, which had been excreted at the edge of the drive during construction.

By Nadia's side, Tentser was watching the world from his newest accommodations: a wicker picnic basket, wide and tall, with leather straps and brass buckles to secure its top. Ribbons were threaded through the gaps in the wicker and knotted at both ends so that the cat and his governess could play tug-o'-war forever. At the bottom was a deep nest of crumpled brown bags and tissue paper, all smelling of bakeries.

The rest of the payload was also arrayed on or around the slopes of the concrete dump.

Ida pulled open the loading doors at the back of the lorry. A mass of refrigerated air slumped out to greet her. "You don't mind cold sleeping bags, do you?" she asked as she lifted them up and chucked them on the floor.

"No, it'll be a bonus," Nadia predicted. "Nastya called to tell us the forecast. We're in for a scorching weekend."

Ida kept jumping on and off the truck to load stuff.

Nadia added, "She sends her love and says thank you for looking after Cosmos."

"Hmm-hmm."

Soon, they were off and rolling, by highway and by bridge, into the wakening hinterland. Tentser rode on Nadia's lap, with the basket open and his eyes and ears sticking above the rampart. He quivered when Ida gave the order to roll down the windows two centimetres.

"We're out of the smog," Ida said, "from now till Monday evening. I've resolved to clean my lungs."

Nadia took this announcement to be metaphorical. Only later, when they stopped at a desolate War memorial and got out straws to drink their thermoses of chocolate-ice-cream-mint-tea, did Nadia discover the fact: Ida had no cigarettes, not on her person, not in her truck, not even in an unassembled form.

"No cigs," Ida summarized. "I quit."

"When?"

"Before you woke up."

The memorial had a T-34. Tentser, in his basket, perched atop the commander's cupola. Nadia and Ida reclined on the upper glacis. With each sip, they worked at banishing the second wave of sleepiness that comes after an early start. Meanwhile, they availed themselves of the vantage point, for the tank was on a ridge at a kilometre's distance from the highway. As the plaque told them, a brave delaying action had taken place here in 1941.

Ida dug into one of the many pockets of her work clothes and took out a boxy, clay-coloured plastic microswitch. She held it between her thumb and forefinger and began to twitch to make it click.

"This helps me," Ida explained.

"With what?"

"Not smoking."

"You have nothing to smoke."

"Still, it helps me."

Once they had slurped the last of their drinks, Ida put away the microswitch, Nadia retrieved Tentser, and they got back in the truck.

"You're about to see your first dairy run," Ida promised.

They had several pickups and deliveries to do before lunchtime. As they progressed, Nadia studied a map and tussled with Tentser to keep him from biting holes in it.

At the farms and factories, people knew Ida. They asked to see Tentser. They looked at Nadia and surmised, "She's the one who gave him to you," or suchlike. They wanted to hear the news and gossip from other places on the route. A leathery-faced woman (who was sun-weathered rather than ancient) gave Ida a carton of eggs, in thanks for an occasion when Ida had driven the woman to visit her son at a reformatory a hundred kilometres away.

"How is he?" Ida asked.

The woman's small eyes flashed. "He's out of there," she warbled, "and on his way to Kabul. 'A place opened up,' he says."

Ida clasped the woman's hand and, in one motion, they parted ways.

Nadia remarked to Ida about the decoration of the eggs. The woman had drawn hippie flowers on them with markers.

With noon approaching, Ida got a pair of sunglasses out of the glove compartment. They had squarish frames that looked huge on her face beneath her kerchief. The reflections ranged from silver-blue to yellow.

They delivered dairy for lunch to an airbase-cum-radar-station. The sentries dawdled a bit—pacing around the truck with their automatic rifles at their sides, checking papers, making Ida lower her sunglasses, scanning everything with a Geiger counter—but in the end, it was their soup's sour cream.

From the movies, Nadia had a vague idea that in America, a similar base might be receiving Coca-Cola to wash down hamburgers.

Once they left that place, Nadia reported, "The map says it's a children's camp."

"Obviously," Ida said.

They covered a great distance in the afternoon. The dairy truck hummed across Ukraine like a hybrid of a mammal and a bee. As much as Nadia relished this image, she refrained from sharing it. She did not wish to imply even the remotest similarity between Ida's new work and the pollination of apple trees.

They stopped for a late lunch in the courtyard of a boarded-up distillery, which (in its history as a building) had also been a fortress, a military academy, a nursing school, a hospital, and a prison. The distillery's steel gates had been scrapped, so the dairy truck faced no obstacle (except uneven pavement over the cobblestones) as it crossed the bridge over the dried-up moat. They got out, sat on empty casks beside a ruined wall, and ate butter tarts and sour cream as they watched a flock of sparrows flit back and forth between the turret roofs and the cherry-laden shrubs in the surrounding steppeland. Tentser was allowed to get out of his basket to eat and watch, provided that he stay within arm's reach of Nadia. His jaw quivered at the unreachable birds.

Within the courtyard grew an old pear tree, which had re-sprouted from its roots. A remnant of the original trunk stood upright in its saplesss, splintered afterlife. The newer incarnation bent towards the sunny breach in the wall, so an extremity of its canopy hung over the barrels and visitors. A wryneck flew in and out of a hollow in the dead trunk and she poked her beak into ant-holes in the ever-teeming wood. Whenever Tentser ogled her, the bird hissed and swung her neck, almost in full circles, like a snake.

Ida said, "That's a witch's tree. If you chop down a tree like that, you die and it comes back. If you graft to its branches, your children die."

"Shh, Tentser and I won't sleep tonight."

"You and Tentser love my bedtime stories." Ida got up on her barrel to inspect a lonely piece of russety fruit. She felt its skin, pinched it, and then jumped down without having picked it. "Come on," she said, "let's go."

They saw, in their travels: the swift progress of convoys across the steppes; the inertia of water in gas station toilets.

Near the end of the workday, on a road that meandered along the banks of a slow, wide tributary, they came to the remote town whose dairy requirements had afforded the pretext for their journey. The chief distinctions of this locality were a glass factory and a supermarket. The latter was a showpiece, a favoured architect's pet project, a promise of the future, out of all proportion to its surroundings, yet notably having a glass facade. As they drove up to it, they could see the queues stretching through its emptiness.

After rounding the corner to the building's concrete backside, Ida slowed the dairy truck to a crawl. "Loading Bay 4B … 4B … 4B," she muttered to herself as she scanned the unnumbered gates.

Nadia buckled down Tentser's hatch in anticipation of a stop.

"Let's ask those guys," Ida said as she came to a halt and rolled down her window.

By the wall, two men were arguing about sausages—sausages in concept, as opposed to sausages at hand, since there were none of the latter (and this was the crux). One man had his back to the wall and the other was almost barrelling into him with furious gestures.

"How can you be out?" the gesticulator demanded of the gesticulee. "You got the delivery this morning, I heard so from the driver himself, you have the quota posted in the store, so unless we had a population explosion at lunchtime, unless we are in the movies and it all comes and goes in an hour—out of Mama, off to work, to a hero's grave—unless time is running in reverse, unless the pigs came to get the meat back, surely there is at least enough sausage for dinner!"

"I can't explain to you…" the trapped man protested.

"Can't explain? You've stolen it!"

"…if you're of no mind to understand."

"You couldn't settle for half; you've stolen the lot!"

"Go home."

This cold rebuff was answered by a shove. "Who got it all?"

"Do you want the police…?"

Ida interrupted the argument by steadily and continuously leaning on the horn. Tentser panicked and began to throw himself against the wicker. Nadia struggled to keep the hamper from flying off her lap. The men by the wall were similarly alarmed. Relenting for a moment, Ida bellowed, as if to the deaf, "I've got dairy for Loading Bay 4B," and she finished by giving them one more honk (a quick one) to show that she could.

The pushy guy was first to recover. He asked whether Ida had any eggs.

"No," she replied, "it's a dairy truck."

He sucked his teeth and left around the corner of the building.

The other guy got organized to receive the load. Despite the summery conditions of the Friday afternoon—and perhaps because his integrity had lately been questioned—he decided to have everything done by the book. The delivery took an extra long time because the cold room already had a large stock of sour cream and Ida had to help move the old stuff to put the new stuff at the back.

When all was done and they were on the way to the cottage colony (just another 50 kilometres) and Tentser was attempting to bury an odourous crap in the bakery papers, Nadia asked, "Do you have many days like that?"

"Like what?" Ida asked. Her fingers and jaw had been shivering, if only a little, but she reset them to their right state.

"I don't know, it's quite a jumble of distressed beings and heavy cream."

"Oh. Work is."

There, on the side roads, winter had often been a lingering guest; work crews had not. The conversation in the truck, like the asphalt beneath it, crumbled a bit each time a wheel hit a bump. Ida (being aware that her two passengers shared a predisposition to dyspepsia) went down to first gear and did her best to steer around the potholes. At last, the truck snaked off onto a country lane of dirt and grass, which (in the dry weather) was less bad than broken pavement.

Ida muttered directions that she had memorized. Nadia consulted the map that she had marked. Tentser sniffed the unfamiliar backwoods air.

After taking one fork and then another, they were in the real woods and then the colony. They had their noses tickled by the scents of the dense gardens, weeds, and trees that filled the gaps between the cottages. Branches scuffed against the roof of the dairy truck and leaves poked through its window slits as it made slow progress past one eclectic bolthole after another. One cottage could be bare, weathered planks; the next, cinderblocks painted mint green; and the neighbour after that, whitewashed bricks adorned with murals of cartoon animals. The fences could be miniature pickets in the American style or corrugated iron to block all eyes or stacks of tyres crafted into palm trees and still more cartoon animals.

"Rosya says," Ida recalled, "it's an old-fashioned place with frilly woodwork and a black corrugated iron fence and wind chimes like spaceships made of forks and spoons on a flagpole out front."

"Very traditional," Nadia said. She closed Tentser in the hamper and rolled down her window all the way to listen for the wind chimes.

" 'No apple tree is immune to worms,' " Ida said in proverb. They drove over a patch where the road was mushy with rotten crabapples. Most likely, rodents had plucked them prematurely from the tree.

"I can hear them," Nadia said.

"The worms?" Ida wondered waveringly. *The rodents?*

"The wind chimes."

"The wind chimes."

Ida eased off the gas almost entirely as the truck approached a curve in the lane. Then, with a final lurch, they rolled round the bend.

A mournful peal from Tentser mingled with the jingling of the chimes.

"There's our place," Nadia said. The cottage's second storey had ornate eaves like a wedding cake, on a bent roof like a Tatar's helmet clad in iron strips. This eminence, this skyward flourish, peeped over the fence and around the neighbours' trees. A flagless flagpole jutted from the fence at an angle and dangled its spacefaring cutlery over the lane.

Had mankind not crossed the steppes and the stratosphere, Nadia supposed, *no such cottage would have ever been conceived.*

Slowly, carefully, Ida parked near the chimes. "Sit tight," she instructed. She got out, climbed onto the hood of the truck, and reached overhead to untie a key from its place amidst the chimes. Then, she leapt down and went to the black fence to unlock its gates.

"That was Rosya's idea," Ida said as she got back in the truck with the key in the palm of her hand.

"She's been playing the games," Nadia deduced.

"Hmm, long time."

Ida took the dairy truck into the yard and sighed as she put it to rest for the weekend. At last, they had arrived. They rolled up their windows and opened the doors, to be greeted by the scent of compost and pumpkin pulp.

Nadia shuffled onto the sideboard, placed Tentser back on the seat, jumped down to the ground, and reached up to retrieve Tentser.

Ida observed this drill as she was circling the vehicle to check for tyre punctures. "Tentser," she instructed, "share your growth spurt with Nadia."

" 'Iiidaaa,' " Nadia mewed, " 'no fair; I need my growth spurt more.' "

Ida wiggled the windshield wipers, frowned, and glanced at the fence. "I guess no one will steal them here."

"I won't if Tentser won't," Nadia promised.

Ida went to lock the gates.

Nadia took Tentser to the porch, where she sat on the steps and let him leap out of the hamper, into her arms. From a common vantage point, she and he took stock of the yard in the dappled evening light that filtered through the trees. An array of five compost boxes stretched along the fence and, behind each box, a white number was painted on the fence: 1989, 1990, 1986, 1987, 1988. *Someone is composting for the long term. Mama would envy this other gardener, yet look how the fruits lie on the ground.* Well-fertilized tomatoes, pumpkins, cucumbers, and squash had grown on this patch all summer, only to be eaten on the vine in these last days. Some of the bitemarks were still seeping juice through cracks in the sun-shrivelled flesh. Fumes of sweet, fermenting pulp escaped from holes in the pumpkins. A mulch of pallid pumpkin flakes had drifted across the yard like early snow.

Tentser sneezed.

"Every sneeze in *The Odyssey* is an omen," Nadia told the cat as she held him to her chest and rubbed his belly.

He bent his neck back to stare lovingly into her eyes.

"Look at you..."

"Don't meet his gaze," Ida warned as she climbed the steps. She wiggled her fingers at Tentser to distract him. He threw a punch in Ida's direction, missed, and then continued to give Nadia a loving yet smug look.

"Look, his question mark has faded, his streak..."

"Hmm-hmm." Ida knelt and reached through the rails of the porch to get another key that was stuck to the back of a rain barrel with a magnet.

"...above his eye. There's just the peak over his nose now. What am I saying? You're even more handsome this way. Tomorrow," Nadia promised the cat, "we'll clean up the garden for you."

"We'll find a phone box," Ida muttered, "and call Nastya."

"Why," Nadia laughed, "so she can send Giorgi to help? …have him live out his days as Tentser's gardener?"

Tentser took offence at this laughter, his pupils went round, and Nadia barely pulled back in time to avoid having her nose bitten. She did get a hard smack to her cheek, to add a scratch to the fading bruise.

"Ow!" she yelped.

"I told you," Ida said as the door yielded to her. "Get him inside."

"Bad boy!" Nadia hissed.

Flustered, Tentser submitted to a higher grade of hug as Nadia gripped him by all fours and hustled him across the threshold.

"Who'd wanna be a cat out prowling all hours?" Ida said as she shut the door behind them. "Only a cat, is who."

They were in a vestibule, with the inner door shut as well, and this little room smelt of musty newspapers, which were stacked against one wall. Opposite the newspapers was a standing coat rack.

Tentser leapt from Nadia's arms to a branch of the coat rack and he perched there awkwardly, eyeing the ceiling.

"I've never seen him do that before," Nadia said.

"He's still new to the job," Ida said. "Come on, let's have an explore. I feel like cooking, fill this place with the smell of something good."

"Yeah, it's fusty or something," Nadia agreed.

"Something ripe too," Ida noted as she opened the inner door and stepped into a hallway. "Probably the last person left some apples out, Antonovkas maybe, they always smell. We'll get rid of those and no problem."

Two doors, left and right, presented themselves to a newcomer. A little further along, this hallway was crossed by another in a four-way junction, with a window nook straight ahead. Cloudy window-light and a chair's long shadow stretched diagonally across the floorboards.

Nadia already thought, *There's more than one layer of nostalgia here.*

Ida opened the door on the left. There was the kitchen, squarely arranged with full-height cabinets and cluttered shelves and a dry-sink and a whitewashed brick stove and a firewood rack, all around a table of thick maple planks, suitable for chopping pumpkins.

Ida declared, "First try, found the kitchen. Lucky, right?"

"Right," Nadia agreed.

Behind them, the coat rack wobbled as Tentser jumped down. He skirted around Nadia's and Ida's legs and entered the kitchen.

"Go on, then," Ida told Nadia. "One woman and a cat are enough for this kitchen. Go see the rest with a poet's eyes."

"Okay. You are lovely sometimes."

"Hmm."

The hallway's end, at the far side of the cottage, had a narrow sitting area with an ornate wooden chair by an arched window. On the sill, on a doily, sat a chunk of meteoric rock, pitted like a weathered piece of bone. An asymmetric arrangement of panes framed a view of a rangy rose garden. Crossing the junction, Nadia approached the window and found that one small pane, in the upper right, could open on a hinge; the rest were fixed in place. The glass was slightly wavy and denser near the bottom, as if, in old age, it were regressing towards its native sea. An autographed photo of Gagarin hung on the eastern wall, where the evening sun crossed the cosmonaut's face in distorted ripples of orange. Beside him, a kerosine lamp and little mirror hung from another hook. This alcove reminded Nadia of the chancel of a church—a faint memory of a childhood outing with Gramma Marusya and Nastya. Had Mama been there as well? Nadia recalled with an unsettling sense of certainty that Mama had been both there and not there. Perhaps two or more occasions had collided and fused in the dreamspace of early memory.

At that time, Nadia reflected, *I was as near to being a baby as I am now to being a university graduate.*

She turned around. There was a fracas in the kitchen.

"Stay back!" Ida belted out.

"What's wrong?" Nadia called in reply.

A pan went *bang* like a bomb.

Tentser came skidding down the hall in pursuit of a terror-stricken mouse—a tiny fugitive weighed down by a pair of ears and a tail.

"Protect Tentser!" Ida commanded, without leaving the kitchen. She dealt a second, third, and fourth thunderous blow of the pan.

From the hall ceiling, dust cascaded onto the zigzagging kitten and mouse. Nadia knocked the meteorite to the floor, grabbed the lace doily, threw it over the mouse, balled it up with the creature squirming inside, and chucked it out the hinged pane. Then, she sheepishly faced Tentser, who was staring wide-eyed and breathing through his mouth. He was either vexed by the dust or astounded at Nadia's incompetence as a huntress. She knelt to dust him off and check him for wounds.

The doors of the kitchen cupboards were clacking and clucking.

After a pause, the pan clattered to the floor and Ida let out a ragged sigh.

"He's okay!" Nadia reported as she wrestled the cat into a protective hug. This last clang of the pan had startled him. "Are you okay?" she asked.

"They went at him five to one!" Ida gasped as she staggered into the hall. She ran a skinny hand across her dusty brow. Then, with a wavy motion, she pointed a dusty finger towards the kitchen. "Don't go in," she warned. "You don't want to go in. You don't want to see, Little Paw, it's blood and mouse crap everywhere. Those buggers were living in the cupboard. I knew something stank."

"Okay. Shh," Nadia breathed into Tentser's ear.

Ida continued, "One of them: dead in a pile of shit already, maggots crawling out. The rest: moved house to the next cupboard over. Buggers."

"I'd better put Tentser back in the truck," Nadia said.

"He doesn't want to go back in the truck," Ida asserted. *Where did you get that idea?* She crossed the hall, threw open the door opposite the kitchen, and raced in to surprise anything living there. "Plants," she muttered. "I wonder who does the watering."

Nadia heard pottery and furniture being dragged hither and thither. She did her best to distract Tentser by madly stroking his face and kissing his eyes. *I'm going to assume he didn't blink in direct contact with the prey.*

Presently, Ida returned to the hall to report, "That sunroom is fine. Plenty for him to smell that isn't mouse shit. Put him in there."

"Okay." Before the cat could stop purring, Nadia airlifted him across the threshold and shut him in with the varied flowers—hanging, climbing, or standing—spilling perfume and secrets in the southerly evening shade. There was even a baby-dwarf lemon tree, blooming in its befuddlement about the season.

Ida shuffled to block the kitchen door. She pulled it shut as Nadia looked that way.

"Will you sit down?" asked Nadia, opening her palm towards the nook. "Please, if we aren't going back to the truck, I'd like to just sit still."

"I don't mind getting our stuff from the truck," Ida replied. "You sit."

"No. Sit with me..." *...and hush, lest we rouse more mammalian* *souls or dislodge a rafter.*

Ida folded her hands behind her back and dawdled down the hall. Coming to the junction, she leaned forwards to peer left and right.

Nadia cleared her throat as she lingered behind Ida in the dusty hall.

Ida hopped across the junction and settled into the chair with her back straight and her hands on her knees.

Nadia followed and squatted in the corner between the window and Gagarin. She put the meteorite back on the sill. Then, without getting up, she patted Ida's knee and asked, "You okay there?"

"Hmm-hmm!"

"Okay. What are you doing?"

"Sitting still."

"Right." Nadia hesitated before adding, "I will too." She sat on the floor, hugged her knees, and flexed her feet under the chair. After a moment, she requested an estimate: "How old do you reckon this place is?"

Ida puffed out her lips and guessed, "Older than anyone! Older than Tentser."

"The pumpkins are older than Tentser."

"But are they as sweet?" Ida wondered. "Sweet boy."

"Now, that window," Nadia rambled, "looks like something from Tsarist times. Sit at the window and wait for your messenger—or be the messenger, bringing a love letter one day, a challenge to a duel the next."

After an appropriate pause for the window's social history, Ida said, "Let me know when you're better or when you need the chair."

"I'm fine," Nadia said. *I'm almost certain I don't hear anything in this wall.*

"Let's go explore the rest," Ida suggested.

"No," Nadia said.

"No?" Ida asked.

Nadia shook her head. The nook became even quieter after that. Nadia could hear Ida's breathing—deep, forceful, conscious. Ida was staring through her.

"Look," Nadia said at last, "we could take the truck anywhere."

"Sure," Ida said, "Saturday night, early Sunday, we could be in Finland, if I stay awake and the men on duty stay asleep, all the millions of them, and the women on duty, kids on duty too. If they'd sleep, we could exit and go try our luck in another world."

"That's not quite what I meant."

"Didn't you? Well, I could drop you in Moscow on the way."

"That's hurtful."

"Not meant to be, Little Paw."

If you say so—but I know you and love you and, right now, I don't like the sound of your breathing. Nadia picked at a splinter in a floorboard. After too long a pause, she sighed and said, "I only meant, we don't have to stay in this particular mouse shit. We could go camping in a park or a ruin. We could crash with your friends on a farm."

"They have problems."

"We could go back to Rosya."

"She has problems too."

"But you—better than some—you do your share wherever you are."

Ida was adamant. "We are not going back. You can forget it. I am not driving back on these cow-shit roads tonight, not in the morning either. I am not showing up at Rosya's door saying I couldn't spend one weekend away because there were mice. I am not dropping you at the station, not with Giorgi and not with the frigging cologne-drinkers, to bum a ticket and go tell your Gramma we couldn't hack it with a kitten and mice in fairytale land. I already sent her a letter saying I had this all planned."

Ida shut up and hung her head. Her eyes went kiting away from Nadia, away from herself and the present, and seemed to settle in a blameful stare at Gagarin, who answered her, as he answered everybody, with his laddish grin. *I came from humble parents—carpenter, dairy maid; I was a child and a saboteur in the War; I became a steel-worker and the first man in Space; my comrades and I liked the mountain lakes, the cliffy seacoasts, the booze, the speedboats, the girls in uniform; it was fun; one time I jumped off a balcony; I aced the psychological evaluations and excelled in math; I blushed when I told dirty jokes; later, testing fighter jets, I crashed and died. How is that for 34 years of life?*

Nadia was unsure whether her friend might scream or laugh or cry.

"We'll stay," Nadia whispered.

Ida nodded.

Nadia added, "I'm sure it's going to be an unforgettable weekend."

Ida did laugh a little at that. "Yeah," she coughed. "We have our memories—not a full set, maybe, but some."

"The schoolbooks," Nadia mentioned, "said Gagarin had perfect recall."

"I'd forgotten that," Ida said.

Nadia shrugged. "Maybe he didn't really."

Ida repeated her earlier suggestion: "Let's go explore the rest."

"Alright."

Ida stood, picked up the chair, and asked Nadia whether she could see anything on the underside.

Kneeling forwards and squinting, Nadia discerned a maker's mark along with the date 1905 and a scratched-out double eagle replaced by a star. She relayed her findings and finished by saying, "This chair saw the beginning and end of the Revolutionary years. I guess it's seen a lot of ends."

"Shit," Ida said. "I was hoping to find another key." She put the chair down, wandered into the western corridor, and fruitlessly jiggled a doorknob. "Rosya said her friend's bedroom would be off limits."

With her hand on the window sill, Nadia pushed herself to her feet and, as she waited for a bout of dizziness to pass, she took a last look at Gagarin through a nebula of phantom stars. *I could disassemble your frame, Yuri, and ransack it for secrets, but I shall not.*

By the time Nadia rounded the corner, Ida was squatting, peering through the keyhole, and giving a report: "He's got a big bed with a stars-and-planets blankie and an even bigger blackboard with equations."

"Come on!" Nadia scoffed.

"Look for yourself, Little Paw."

"No, we're his guests."

Ida backed away from the bedroom door and continued down the passage to find a stairway sprouting off it at the end. Nadia followed her friend up to a landing, where a small, lozenge-shaped window cast light on a door. The door had the distinction of being painted a warmthless shade of pink, like a rose dying in early frost. Around the frame, chips of the lead paint had flaked away and half of them lay with the underside facing up, to show dark splinters or a previous coat of yellowed white. This door was not locked but it was sticky, so Nadia took a turn at it and, to her satisfaction, got it to budge with a kick. Beyond the threshold, they found a large attic, a storey and a half high at its centre. The whole space—a greater volume than the living areas below—was empty except for a stepladder with its top amidst the cobwebs and the crossbeams.

"Everything but the rope," Ida muttered.

Nadia stayed silent. The air was stifling, with an unnatural scent of heat trapped by wood, like being buried alive.

They wandered briefly in the emptiness. Through a gabled window trimmed in more pink, they had a view of the dairy truck, the pumpkins, the compost bins, the fence, and a single-storey cottage across the lane. The neighbour-man was scraping gunk off a barbecue grill on his back deck while the wife attempted to round up the kids for an end-of-day exercise in picking vegetables.

For the moment, Nadia was not in a frame of mind to study this diorama. "Let's go back down," she suggested.

On the way out, Ida stood on tiptoe to feel along the top of the door frame. She found nothing but dust and desiccated exoskeletons: a spider and a wasp.

Back on the ground floor, the final branch of the hallway was lined with deep shelves. Some of these held rows and stacks of books, arranged like rustic masonry: books behind books atop books between books. Another pair of shelves was completely bare, yet beside it stood a stepping stool, suggesting a possible use as a bunk bed for two children or two petite women. Other shelves were repositories for batteries, board games, and suchlike: the stuff of ebbing time.

Nadia scanned the block letters of the book titles. Science fiction novels and nostalgic stories of frontier life in Kazakhstan chaffed against histories of the Space Programme and of Mesopotamia, as well as discourses on optical-mechanical engineering, gardening in Ukraine, and parenting in the '60s. She picked up a parenting book and checked the blurb in case it was something an aunt should know:

"How to inspire children to get engaged in practical science, to read books, how to teach them to understand, appreciate, and create beauty? How to educate schoolchildren to be industrious, selfless in their devotion to the Motherland, the ideas of communism, how to raise them as collectivists, honest, modest, cultured people, how not to miss the ultimate goal behind the daily private tasks of upbringing?"

How to inspire the nephew-foetus? How to educate a mote to be a new and better man? How not to miss the stop at Moscow? She set it down.

The last part of the hall hooked towards a back entrance, which gave close access to the rose garden, an outhouse, and a sauna. The outhouse had, thankfully, been slaked with lime and ashes since its last use. The sauna was well stocked with rocks and logs for its heater, as well as a rack of felt hats and mitts, a case of Hungarian brandy (in various flavours), a pot of honey for coating oneself, and bundles of wilted birch boughs for flagellation.

Nadia possessed a certain degree of book-learning about saunas, as authors were wont to write of them. Papa was of the opinion that the Sauna's mystic traditions were all innocent enough. Mama disagreed and had imprinted on her daughters an aversion of such places, in favour of the Palaces of Culture. One evening, when Nastya had stayed late at her painting class to mop the spattered floor and clean all the brushes down to the roots, she had first met Johnny, who was leaving the amateur radio room with an armload of equipment. He explained to her that he often took things home for overnight repairs, to cover up for the inadvertent damage done by younger boys and girls. Nastya had said he was kind to do so; she herself had a younger sister who was ashamed to make mistakes.

Was she struggling, then, this younger sister?

On the contrary, this younger sister excelled in her studies. She had a gold medal (which would later disappear, her own carelessness, Johnny would never steal from a friend, how could Ida ask that and make Little Hedgehog believe such an evil thing? The medal soon afterwards reappeared.)

Johnny would sometimes break plans and go off without the girls for a weekend or a month of weekends. Johnny would return and say his head was clearer because he had spent time at a sauna—or else he would return, say nothing of his absence, but give little gifts and lessons.

"You sleeping here, then?" Ida asked. She was more than ready to leave the sauna after a glance around.

Nadia got up from the bed of planks where she had flopped out for a moment's reverie. "Sorry," she muttered. "Got dizzy."

Having explored the place, they agreed to face their most pressing problems as guests there.

The first problem was to sanitize the kitchen. They located a shovel, a sack of lime, and a watering can in a lean-to by the fence. Nadia carried the sack and can. Ida operated the shovel. The carcasses and the bulk of the shit got buried deep inside the tannic stew of rotting leaves and vines in the 1988 compost box. Then, scoops of lime were spread liberally over the affected areas of the kitchen floor and cabinet. Ida put on her sunglasses. An application of water brought the lime to a boil and achieved sterilization, albeit at the cost of melting the cabinet's paint and the antique patina of the floorboards, to leave the wood as white as it had been in the sawmill when it flew through the hands of a different generation, risking eyes and fingertips just the same.

"There," Ida said, chokingly, as she left the kitchen and shut the door.

Nadia patted Ida's back.

Ida asked, "Do you think it's fit for use now, when the fumes die down?"

"Honestly, no."

"Neither do I. I can cook in the sauna."

"That might be for the best."

They were not immediately hungry. Having scorched away Death and Pestilence in their plainest manifestations, having established that meal preparations would be feasible, they decided where to rest their heads.

"I'll camp in Tentser's jungle," Ida said. The sunroom was certainly the finest part of the cottage, if a bit flowery for Nadia's nose. The heavens, if one looked up from the floor, were a combination of the original French-imitation plasterwork (feathers and blossoming vines) and a geranium-shadowed view of the stars above the corrugated iron fence. One could almost imagine oneself in the tropics, with scorpions instead of mice, and debauched French painters wanting to portray one and one's cat in lunatic colours.

"All the same," Ida asked, "would you be happier with the books—or in the truck?"

"No," Nadia said, "it's good to be with you and Tentser."

Ida and Nadia brought in some necessities, including the chilled sleeping bags and a box of unused newspapers for Tentser. The three of them shared a bedtime snack of raisin buns from Rosya's favourite bakery. Then—exhausted, rattled, aching, and breathing strange air—they crashed in paradise.

2: Day of the Party

All day long on Saturday, the sun felt warm like a bed. Tentser woke everyone early, to get ahead of this sleepy weather.

Nadia hollered as the kitten tugged at her throat with his teeth.

Ida, who had been poked in the eye, was already up and getting breakfast. Unseen by Nadia, the sauna's smokestack was puffing. Ida emerged from her sweltering, makeshift kitchen, came in the back entrance of the cottage, and wandered back into the sunroom with two forks and a large plate of golden-orange pancakes covered in orange caviar.

The salmon caviar had been a "splendid weekend" gift from Giorgi. He had obtained this can (and likely others) from an unspecified source (likely Avel) and, to personalize it, he had tied one of his scraps of orange ribbon around it in a bow. *The man is like a seabird blown inland,* Nadia had thought.

Tentser went running to Ida as soon as she re-entered the room. He opened his jaw wide, like a wrench, and let out a plaintive wail.

"Whaaat?" Ida asked him. "Has Nadia has been torturing you?"

" 'Iiidaaa,' " Nadia interpreted, " 'Giorgi sent that caviar for me.' "

"Lieutenant Giorgi Licheli," Ida breathed. "Raisin wine, typed reports, kittens, caviar…" She set the plate down on the floorboards and handed one fork to Nadia. "Here's my riddle. Why couldn't the fish eggs stay in the fish?"

"Why?" Nadia asked as she forked out a kitten-sized bite of pancake and caviar for Tentser to munch off the floorboards.

"Regulations. The sanitary norm. There in the fish, they had less than twelve square metres each … so they got relocated to the can."

"…so they got relocated to the can. Good one." Nadia took a bite of the pancakes, which had a sweet and unexpectedly rich vegetable flavour, to go with the briny beads. She asked, "What's in the batter?"

"Fresh pumpkin," Ida replied.

Nadia quietly gagged. "From the garden?" she mumbled.

"From the garden. The rodents missed one."

"You got the step up on them … again," Nadia said. She swallowed.

Ida reminded her, "The sauna is clean. I used a different frying pan than…"

"I'm sure you did." Nadia smiled, waved her fork jauntily and went for another bite. "Mama would approve—a fine creation from leftovers."

"Thank you." Ida served another bite to Tentser. Then, she herself began to eat.

After breakfast, they went out to the yard to rinse the plate and forks under the rain barrel's tap and to put the remaining caviar back with the dairy. They returned the sleeping bags, too. Ida let the engine run for a bit to revitalize the refrigerator. She and Nadia stood by the truck as it shook and rattled, adding a rhythm to the dawn chorus of frogs and birds.

Tentser was standing upright in one of the sunroom windows.

Ida attempted to combine a frog and a bird in one sound. "That's a winged frog," she explained.

"The neighbours will love us," Nadia said.

Ida stopped her imitations and got out her microswitch instead. Punctuating the syllables with clicks, she asked, "What do you want to do today?"

"Sprout wings like your frogs—and learn their language, as you've done."

"Go swimming?" Ida suggested.

"Sure, swimming. Gardening. Working on my translation."

Ida nodded. She was familiar with the effort to translate *Great Expectations* and its supposed implications for Nadia's future.

Someone knocked at the iron gates. Nadia cringed. Ida killed the engine.

The knocking continued in a beat that sounded like a march. For a moment, the wind chimes chimed without wind.

Pocketing her microswitch and removing her keys from the truck, Ida went to open the gates. Nadia followed and, across the threshold, in abrupt silence, they met the gaze of an owlish man with large eyebrows and little hair. He was wearing a nondescript grey suit and red tie, which seemed odd attire for knocking at cottage gates in the vegetable-picking hour of the morning.

"No," he said, "you are not Pyotr."

"And you are…?" Ida asked.

He blinked at her. "I am Chessmaster at the camp down the lane."

"Comrade Chessmaster, good morning," Nadia said.

He nodded and began to explain the opening move of his day. "On my morning walk, I check to see that everything is fine at Pyotr's. This leaves him free to come and go according to his disposition and the dictates of his responsibilities. If I find him in, we may pleasantly pass half an hour in conversation over tea. If I find him out…"

"Where is the kettle?" Ida asked.

"The kettle," Comrade Chessmaster replied without hesitation, "is near the back entrance, behind a book on metallurgy, where Pyotr can easily fetch it for the sauna if he chooses." He recaptured the initiative by asking, "Have you had the privilege of taking breakfast in Pyotr's sunroom?"

"Yes, actually," Nadia replied.

"Have you taken the liberty of putting fresh lemon in your tea?"

"No, I'm not sure we should…"

"…and it's only just bloomed," Ida pointed out.

"I know," Comrade Chessmaster countered, "but you could have visited before, many times for all I know. I do not question Pyotr on his guests."

"We've just been this once," Nadia said.

He nodded excessively. "Pyotr's lemon tree," he said, "was one of my seedlings. I gave it to him when he was in mourning. As you know, yellow is the colour of mourning."

"Yes, of course," Nadia agreed. *Yellow flowers, yes, but whatever.*

"I water it and all the plants when Pyotr is away."

Ida surmised, "You stack the newspapers on your way to water the plants."

"Yes, the news is of no importance to me, it cannot sway a game of Chess, but to an engineer such as Pyotr, politics are fateful, so you, too, should water the plants and keep good order."

"We won't let the standard slide," Nadia promised.

After another nod, Comrade Chessmaster said, "I must be going. Come down at eight o'clock, if you wish to join the morning's matches. I assume that at least one of you plays chess."

"We both do," Ida replied.

Nadia thanked him for the information and the invitation. Then, Comrade Chessmaster left in the direction of the river.

They shut the gate and went to sit on the porch. Without the truck idling, they could hear other cottage-goers showering and breakfasting at various distances from Pyotr's place, this pumpkin patch, this cosmic crossroads.

"I never knew yellow was the colour of mourning," Ida confessed.

"Yellow flowers," Nadia stated, "mean somebody is dead or your boyfriend is dumping you."

"Wild. Where do you get this stuff?" Ida asked.

"Nastya got a library book on it when Gramma Marusya died. Mama was in bed crying and Nastya took me out to pick flowers."

"Where was your Papa?"

Nadia had to think about this. "Trying to get ahold of his mother."

"Where was she?"

"Moscow. We went to a meadow and picked rapeseed to send off Gramma Marusya and red poppies to greet Gramma Ninel. Nastya said that was the thing to do."

"Only two kinds of flowers?"

"I picked cornflowers for Mama."

"Hmm."

"Nastya kept some of the petals in a diary. For a few years, she showed them to me sometimes to help me remember."

After a brief pause, Ida got up and turned to the door. "Let's get changed and go to the river," she suggested.

"Okay," Nadia agreed. She was a bit relieved that Ida felt no need to fight in the chess round after all.

They got their swimsuits from their bags in the sunroom. Ida also had two old robes of Rosya's; one of these was for Nadia.

Nadia went to the attic to change and, before coming back, she took a minute to peep at the cottage across the lane. This one was clad in emerald-green boards with rust-red trim and it had a high, wooden fence, painted likewise. Beyond the back deck and gardens, the yard sank and then rose more steeply to meet the remnants of a forest or perhaps a long-neglected park. To Nadia, this hodgepodge cottage colony had a whiff of green bones—a village that died.

"Ready when you are!" Ida called.

They left Tentser closed in the sunroom, where he was busy pawing and sniffing a fallen lemon blossom. Periodically, he leapt back from it in surprise.

Meanwhile, they stepped out in overlarge floral robes, which seemed out-of-place for want of bright umbrellas. They strolled down the lane in the tracks of Comrade Chessmaster. They paused when they came to the unmistakable site of his teachings.

The chess camp was a two-storey, L-shaped, brick building, painted in alternating blocks of black and white, with murals of swanlike horses and knobby men. A hard-packed dirt courtyard was set up with chairs and chess tables around a pair of sizeable oaks, whitewashed around the base of the trunks. Away from the trees, a long-handled, blue pump stuck up out of the ground and it had a horse's eyes and forelock painted on it in red, above the spout. A hose ran from the spout to feed a pressure tank on the roof of the building.

"Fanciest place in town," Nadia remarked.

"Yeah, it's all for the kids, except when it isn't," Ida said.

The camp-goers, ages nine to fifteen, began to file out of the building for the too-familiar ceremony of raising the flag. They had wet hair from the communal showers, the collars of their uniforms were wet from the drippings, and, to Nadia, it was strange to remember a recent time when she had endured the same lack of privacy. *Now I harbour complaints wherever I am. Ida begins to wonder whether I mind her presence at night. How we change.*

One of the youths was selected to do the honours with the flag. Another was selected to work the pump. This was the only chance to replenish the tank between shower-time and breakfast.

Ida whispered to Nadia, "Your sister does love you."

Nadia gave her friend a confused look.

"Don't you remember," Ida asked, "how she volunteered for an extra year of this crap, as Youth Leader?"

"Yes."

"That was to watch your back."

"Oh, Sister," Nadia sighed without quite knowing why.

"Let's move," Ida said.

Past the camp, the lane gradually petered out in a spongy field near the river. Grass filled the space between the ruts and then one rut continued on its own as a walking trail, through a willow thicket, to a rickety fishing pier surrounded by lily pads. A trio of rowboats sat on the shore, where they pinned down a bed of brown leaves from the previous fall.

They went a little ways upstream and found a spot where a granite boulder stuck out into deeper water. They laid their robes like tapestries on the rock and set about diving and climbing. The stone's gritty crust grated against their skin but at least they avoided wading through the slimy shallows.

After a while, Ida stopped to get her microswitch from the pocket of her robe and she sat, making clicks and studying the clouds. Nadia sat too. She had been gathering pebbles from the riverbed and now she made them jump like little frogs across the surface. They sank far short of the middle. Out there, a man in a rowboat had come to fish.

By and by, Ida asked, "Do you think that fisherman is watching us?"

"Oh, I don't know."

"What about the kids in the trees?"

Nadia looked around. "What kids?"

"They left—or maybe they just hid themselves better."

"Oh."

Ida got up and loudly announced, "Those gardens won't weed themselves."

The fisherman looked their way.

"Weirdos," Ida whispered to herself as Nadia followed her away.

They walked back past the pier. One of the rowboats was gone, leaving a silhouette in the rotting leaves.

They walked back past the chess camp. The morning's matches were just concluding; the timers had run down; the laggards and the blunderers had lost; pieces were being returned to starting positions; notation sheets were being gathered and taken indoors; lunch awaited.

Comrade Chessmaster was lingering in the yard, with one hand on an oak trunk and another over his mouth as he watched his pupils departing. He spotted Nadia and Ida and lowered his hand to gesture questioningly at them.

Nadia thought, *He's mocking us for being no-shows.* "Comrade Chessmaster," she said, "how was your morning?"

He nodded. "More or less, they are coming into their stride. Come back at one o'clock, if you wish to test them then."

"Do you enjoy it?" Ida asked.

Comrade Chessmaster nodded again and said, "Yes."

Ida attempted to shake river water out of her ear.

"Shall I tell you something you might not know," Comrade Chessmaster asked, "something about Turbanov's victory in 1956?"

"Hmm?" Ida wondered.

Taking this as an affirmative, Comrade Chessmaster confided in them, "Turbanov owes that victory to me."

"Oh!" Nadia said.

Ida interpreted: "You lost to him on purpose."

"No!"

Ida tried again: "You lost to him just because."

"Turbanov won," Comrade Chessmaster explained with a click of his tongue, "because I fought Voskresensky to a stalemate."

"Who came in second?" Ida wondered.

"Voskresensky came in second," Comrade Chessmaster replied, as if amazed by her incomprehension. "He fell short of Turbanov by half a point. This is what I have been telling you."

"Still, third place isn't bad," Ida offered.

"Why do you mention third place?" Comrade Chessmaster asked. "Do you have some particular interest in Kim's career?"

Nadia interjected, "Tell us about your match with Voskresensky."

Ida excused herself: "I need the ladies' room." She scampered into the building and left Nadia listening to a detailed account of the extraordinary circumstances surrounding the match. That was the year Comrade Chessmaster started growing lemons. He secured himself a place in an expedition to Istanbul, not out of any great admiration for the chess players who frequented that peninsular capital, but rather because he coveted the seeds of such peculiar Turkish lemons as the Interdonato with its pointy nose, a shape that fascinated him; later, he would see its likeness in the Soyuz capsule. At any rate, whilst extracting seeds of a lemon in the courtyard of an Istanbul hotel, he chanced to discover Voskresensky's aversion to the sour fruit. The mere sight of its sliced flesh made the man slobber and slur his words. All the more humiliating was this debility because Voskresensky was dining with a ravishing Turkish beauty, a competitor, whom he had brazenly shown on his arm all week long. Therefore, a few months afterwards, when facing Voskresensky in a more prestigious event in a more reasonable location, Comrade Chessmaster wore an enamel lapel pin depicting a lemon.

Ida strolled back out and interrupted the tale with a question: "What kind of lemon would you grow in a pot if you wanted a good juicer?"

"What else," asked Comrade Chessmaster, "would you wish of this tree?"

"Hmm, high tolerance of air pollution."

Before Comrade Chessmaster could furnish any recommendation, a boy came racing out of the building. He had serious news. Some of the chess notation sheets had gone missing from the table in the lobby. He named the pairings of contestants who had vanished from history in this way.

Ida applied pressure to her microswitch in a single, slow click. Nadia glanced at her. Comrade Chessmaster picked up on this eye movement.

"Weren't they scrap?" Ida asked. "Weren't those games already over?"

Nobody answered.

"Hmm, sorry. They were right outside the ladies' room."

"Nevermind, 'Hmm, sorry,'" snapped Comrade Chessmaster. He walked over to the nearest table and, in the shadows of the oak leaves, he began to replay the table's last game, jotting down each move as he went. "The damage you can do is limited. I remember every move in every game I see and every game I read, which is to say, every game worth playing. If I go to a fallout shelter when Reagan hits the button, we can rebuild Chess at least."

Ida was twisting her eyebrows skeptically as she pointed at one of the pieces he had moved. He faltered, picked it up, and then forcefully put it back in the very same square. All the while, he kept talking.

"The only real damage lies in the disrespect you pay to Chess. You deprive others, whom you might infect with your scorn, you deprive them of a great treasure passed down from mind to mind and civilization to civilization. These children learn (the ones who are able), they learn of life through Chess. Practically everything worth learning in life has its double in Chess: strategy, craft, memory, reason, order, rebirth, victory, loss…"

"Stalemate," Ida suggested.

He flinched but continued, "Of course, Chess is also the allegory we know so well, of war won through sacrifice."

Nadia spoke the words that had been coalescing in her mind: "Practically everything in life is more important than chess." She pulled her courage into her chest to whisper the corollary: "Practically anything is better than war."

"Some boys these days," Comrade Chessmaster remarked, "do turn to pacifism to get a girl—a pretty one, mind you. Where does a pacifist get that?" He touched his cheek where hers was bruised and scratched.

"He's immature," Ida concluded. "Let's leave him to talk to his toys."

They did so.

A few minutes later, as they re-entered the cottage yard, Nadia leaned against the hot fence and began to snicker. Ida, however, voiced an earnest reflection: "A man like that would never suit Rosya."

"What?" Nadia asked. "How could you imagine her with him?"

"Not him, a man like him. I just hope she's found someone with more common ground than lemons and games."

"I'd think Rosya wants someone more alive."

"Well," Ida hesitated, "her interests do span the millennia. There's always the risk of her latching onto something that's wrong for her."

"Like skiing in the Carpathians?"

"Like that," Ida agreed. She added more ominously, "Like the other thing."

"Sex?" Nadia asked.

"No, Little Paw, the other thing in the Carpathians."

"Brusilov's Breakthrough?"

"That. As far as I understand, it did no good for anyone."

"No, you're right." *Two great uncles of Rosya Lekht died fighting for two empires that collapsed in the following two years.* Nadia nodded and stared. *At this point, Nastya would cry but if I did so now, I doubt it would be for the right reasons.*

"Let's get you out of the sun," Ida suggested.

"Okay." Nadia peeled herself off the fence. The back of her robe and swimsuit were drying out already.

They went to the sunroom and found Tentser stretched in a sunbeam. His slender chest heaved like waves over black sand. He shifted to display himself perfectly as a feline anatomical diagram in kittenish miniature. He bent his head back to make room for a cavernous yawn; his tongue waved independently in space; his eyes almost brushed the floor.

"Can't you sleep?" Ida asked him.

" 'Iiidaaa,' " Nadia complained on the kitten's behalf, " 'I'm bored. When can I go out to play?' "

"Hmm, come on, then," Ida consented. "You can help in the garden. You have more experience moving dirt than Nadia does."

As they gathered their knockabout clothes, Nadia felt obliged to describe the veggie garden that she had helped Mama plant in Odessa.

"Hmm-hmm!"

I suppose I shall content myself with that. Nadia returned to the attic to don her gardening attire: a rayon headband made by Mama from leftovers of the curtains; and a pair of Nastya's old pyjamas from unmarried life. Nadia looked out the window again. The neighbour-man was down on his knees; he had a toddler on his shoulders; the man was picking up spilt coals and placing them in a wheelbarrow. The bigger children were inspecting the wheelbarrow and the coals and one of the toddler's legs. They moved the leg like a pump handle and seemed satisfied with its condition.

Ida stepped out into the pumpkin-strewn yard with Tentser in her arms. She hoisted him up, nuzzled the pads of his hind feet, and set him on the roof of the dairy truck. He looked down at her for a moment and perhaps even listened to something she was saying, until he spotted Nadia in the attic window. Then, he began to emit squeals in her direction. These were muted by the glass.

He's not afraid of heights, Nadia reflected, *but rather of high-up things. Does such a phobia have a name?*

Ida, too, noticed Nadia, beckoned to her, and made a face in imitation of Tentser's.

Coming down, Nadia mimed.

From the other yard, the toddler gave her a worried look.

Does he think I'm a spook coming to get him? I'll do something mundane to dispel such a notion. Nadia balled up her wet clothes, pretended to clean the window, and then left.

As the sun got hotter and hotter, Ida and Nadia took time to clear the pumpkin patch and prune the rose bushes. They left the pumpkin seeds and rose hips to dry in the sun. Everything else—pulp, stalks, brambles, leaves—went into various stages of compost according to Ida's judgment.

Tentser watched the doings and exploits of a pair of squirrels who ran atop the fence. They appeared to be lovers, angry at the world or at least at the gardeners, but the particulars of squirrel ecology might not have been clear to Tentser. He bared his wobbly teeth at them and made chittering noises.

At last, calling their labours enough, Nadia and Ida washed the worst of the dirt and mush and prickles from the crevasses of their hands. They conked out on the steps. After a breather, they told each other two things in perfect agreement: first, that they had done an honest job; second, that Comrade Chessmaster would surely take credit for it.

"His revenge…" Nadia sighed.

"Do you want another swim?" Ida asked.

"Maybe."

"You do stink," Ida added.

"Right."

"The river might or might not help."

"Let's swim regardless," Nadia puffed. "This is the century of action."

"You're wise when you're sweaty. That's why people want you around."

"Lucky me."

They collected Tentser from his conference with the squirrels. He had become spooked. Perhaps he sensed in the manic rodents a portent of summer's end, an end to the kitten-age, so (with slight protests) he surrendered himself to the dual-maternal care of Ida-Nadia. They conveyed him to the sunroom and closed him in there with the last of the orange caviar from Giorgi-Avel.

They sorted their packs to take with them this time. Perhaps it was the century of over-preparedness too.

Soon, having changed from gardening clothes back into swimsuits and robes, Nadia and Ida found themselves stopping in the lane, as if to be softly questioned by the wind chimes.

"I don't want to go past the chess camp again," Nadia confessed, "and I don't want to go back to that diving spot where people were looking at us."

"You think they were?" Ida asked.

Nadia shrugged.

Ida admitted, "I don't know what to do here—in general."

"Let's think," Nadia suggested. "Maybe something will come to us."

"Hmm. … Hmm."

They lingered beneath the wind chimes.

Across the lane, the neighbour-woman opened the high, narrow gate and came out with an embroidered rug resting in the crook of her arm. Flowering vines were the design. She nodded at the new visitors and unfurled the rug and began to beat it against the emerald boards of her fence.

"I don't know…" Ida began to repeat.

"Going for another swim?" the woman asked. Having sprung this piece of familiarity on them, she added, "The children saw you earlier. They play at being spies."

"Going for another swim," Ida echoed.

"Yes," Nadia affirmed.

The woman informed them, "You can take a shortcut across our yard. That way, you don't have to meet so many people."

Ida vaguely nodded as she imagined the route and its sparse population.

"Thanks," Nadia accepted, "much appreciated."

"Sometimes," the woman said as if hinting at a shared secret, "we just want a quiet walk, don't we?"

Somewhere behind the fence, the neighbour-man and the neighbour-kids yodelled at each other.

"My Kazimir wants dozens of children," said the woman with a laugh that seemed more retiring than the wind chimes.

"O! mercy," Nadia said.

The woman laughed some more and beat the rug some more and soon found herself short of breath. She leaned against the fence and placidly puffed, "Don't worry."

Nadia crossed the lane to support this stranger's elbow and to look at her more closely, in an involuntary surge of curiosity. *She's not showing (at least, not in that pinafore-apron-summer-dress) but perhaps she is pregnant. On the other hand, perhaps, Nadezhda, you are holding the elbow of an ill woman, an ailing mother of many, a dear lady in need of magic tea that flows only from the pots of mountain springs. O! mercy. The spirit of Giorgi has followed me here.*

Ida approached, not quite so close, to shoulder the rug and offer the advice, "You could find your dozens any day of the week."

Kazimir's wife squinted and wondered, "How do you mean?"

"Go to an orphanage."

"What a thoughtful girl you are."

"Hmm, now where's this rug go?"

"Take it through," said the woman, recovering more of her breath, "and spread it on the deck, out back. Our guests will be sitting there this evening—the ones who want to be nearest to Kazimir and his barbecue."

Ida went ahead, while Nadia lingered at the woman's elbow to assist awkwardly in a side-by-side traversal of the narrow gate.

"I get these dizzy turns," the woman confided in Nadia.

"I see."

"You're both thoughtful girls."

"Oh…"

Coming round to the back deck, they found Ida sitting cross-legged on the rug and Kazimir (a sturdy, if full-bellied, man of middle age) pensively setting up a barbecue. At his side, he had a bin of meat and ice and another bin of fuel. The children were lurking around the corner of a shed. They had a slate and coloured chalk and were discussing a plan amongst themselves.

"Well, Ida," Kazimir was saying as he tested the barbecue's legs and filled its man-sized tray with coals, "I worry for the kids, if we are to continue another generation down this path set by Stalin and Hitler because, Ida, the lies have not stopped. Today…"

Ida's eyebrows had gone slanty and she was clicking her microswitch in a rapid rhythm: four and a break, four and a break.

"Kazimir," said his wife, "you have everything out too early."

"I have to practice," he told her.

"Then practice what you'll say."

"I have to think who's coming," Kazimir prompted himself.

His wife (accompanied by Nadia) climbed the steps, reached into her apron pocket, and presented him with a typewritten piece of paper. "I made you a list," she said, with a hint of feminine swagger.

"So many people!" Kazimir observed at a glance, without taking the list into his own hands. "I hope nobody leaves hungry."

His wife put away the paper and rolled her eyes. "Kazimir," she simpered, "we have enough sausages to feed the district!"

"You hear?" Kazimir asked Ida and Nadia. "Stick around and fill yourselves up! Do you want something to drink while…" He picked up a space-age water pistol and, into the barbecue coals, he fired a dozen shots of a fluid that smelt suspiciously like Shipr.

"Best not before swimming," Nadia reasoned.

Kazimir lit a roll of newspaper and prepared to throw it on the coals.

"On your way back…" Kazimir's wife began to propose. Then, her eyes followed her children, who had shouted that they were going down the lane to play. "Why are you taking the hose?" she asked. Rather than answer her, they hurried onwards, so she deemed it necessary to go supervise this play, lest it cause water depletion and undue damage to the neighbourhood.

Well, I'm done holding elbows.

Kazimir looked a little disappointed that he had lost his regular audience for the blast-off. Nonetheless, he tossed the burning newspaper in time to save his fingertips. As the flashfire cast its reflection in his bugged-out eyes, he drew in his belly, threw back his hands, and let out a showy moan of awe.

"Pooh," he whistled in the next breath, "better let that die down some."

Dense, white smoke engulfed the deck area and everyone stepped away for a breather. Kazimir got the sudden idea that the girls wanted a tour of his yard. He began with the water system: the trough alongside the fence near the gate; the pair of winches to raise or lower the trough to adjust the water pressure; the hoses for the shower and the sprinklers. His wife grew tulips, as well as other flowers whose names escaped him, and potatoes, onions, tomatoes, and peas. He proceeded to show off the mud pit that he had recently made for the kids. There, he had felled several big oaks with his chainsaw. Their leaves, in the fall, had always made the yard smell and the roof rot. Now, with enough sanding and varnish, their stumps made beautiful seats, especially the double stump where he and his wife liked to cuddle and watch the kids. The rest of the wood, they were burning in the evenings. Their fire pit was a star-shaped arrangement of cinder blocks, between the flowerbeds and the veggie garden. Last, he pointed them to a shortcut to the river, past the mud pit and over the hill and through the woods, where, he said, a piece of the fence had washed out in a mudslide. He meant to replace it one day with a rustic stone wall and an arch where the children could charge tolls like cossack highwaymen. For now, he could go no further; his post was at the barbecue.

"Odd pair of girls," he told his wife when she got back.

She agreed, "Something about them…"

"Still, they're Pyotr's guests," he stated (and he churned this banality with such intensity that it could have been TV news), "and I told them to stop by anytime, to fill themselves up."

His wife said, "The blond one certainly needs it."

Meanwhile, Ida and Nadia had trodden over the ant-eaten remains of a fencepost and gone in search of a more secluded swimming spot than before. They stopped in sight of an eyot with a sandy shore where the roots of berry bushes lay exposed. A narrow channel, with a surface like hammered bronze, separated this island from its admirers.

"We could swim there," Nadia suggested.

A distant, clouded look crossed Ida's face.

"…or keep walking," Nadia said.

"Sure, Little Paw," Ida said, "we can swim there."

They left their robes and packs in the fork of an old cherry tree, which no longer did much with its summers. The few cherries it bore, the birds had already eaten, yet it ventured to be elegant in its inwardness of gnarls and ovate leaves.

Ida placed her microswitch between her back teeth. Then, she and Nadia waded into the silty channel. The current fluttered slimily around their toes and, as they paddled into deeper water, they found it fast enough to force them to work on a diagonal against it. Aching a bit in shoulder, neck, or jaw, they arrived at the slim beach on the eyot.

Nadia stretched out on the sand, belly-down, her chin resting on her crossed arms, and she stared into the root system of the island. Ants had somehow colonized it—or had ants been there before it was an island?

Ida wiped the microswitch on some ferns. Then, she sat with her toes past the waterline and she looked up and down the river while making a few experimental clicks, covering the range from shallow to deep.

"Microswitch okay?" Nadia asked.

"Tastes a little greasy," Ida replied, "but yeah, no problem."

"Good."

The sun began to prickle them beneath the skin and it made Ida see afterimages of the ripples on the water.

Nadia picked through the sand for bits of glass and pottery. She rolled onto her side to excavate a trench, yet it yielded little and flooded fast. She got up to extend her search—first into the roots, where bigger pieces could get caught, and then back out into shallow water. She imagined people who might appreciate this piece or that and, for some reason, Yuri kept coming to mind.

They had another swim and another breather.

After a while, Ida said, "Cherry trees don't usually live long."

"How long is not long?"

"Hmm, twenty years. They can live to be a hundred or more but something usually kills them long before that."

"Longer than cats, still."

"Hmm." Ida continued, "I read a manual about cherry-growing after you left. I was hoping to get away from cider apples. Then, it all fell apart."

"That's sad."

"Well, we're here now," Ida said, "on this island plugging up this river."

"That's one problem oceans don't have," said Nadia. "We should go to sea."

"No, you should go to Moscow."

Nadia did not answer. She held in a sigh, gleaned another treasure from a waterlogged snarl of roots at the very end of the beach, and asked, "Would you like a bottleneck as a ring?"

"Possibly," Ida replied. She sprang up and walked over to have a look at the pale blue band that might have once been the lip of a fizzy-lemonade bottle. "That does suit me," she agreed. "I'll wear it on my pinkie, there." She studied the ring and both sides of her own left hand, as well as the gradually fading scars of her wrist. Then, she clasped the microswitch for a few clicks.

"Swim back?" Nadia proposed.

"Sure, Little Paw."

After they reached the shore, they shook a few ants and aphids from their robes, wrapped themselves up, and sat in the tree fork. A slight breeze moved the finer branches overhead. They played at catching the leafy shadows in their open palms. From time to time, Ida used her longer reach to steal shadows from Nadia.

"I wish I had a camera," Nadia said.

"Rosya asked whether I needed one," Ida mentioned, "but I said no."

"You do need one. You have a kitten."

"He's lived with an artist already. I'm other things to him."

"You're other things to many people."

"Hmm."

"... and no one else makes crowns of capacitors."

"That may be true."

Nadia brushed an ant off her hip. "Tentser is waiting," she said.

Ida hissed in Nadia's ear, "He is waiting!"

Nadia lowered herself to the ground and Ida leapt down beside her.

"Goodbye, tree," Nadia said.

Ida shook hands with one of its branches.

To end the outing, they walked back the way they had come. By and by, they passed over the rotten fencepost and over-hill towards the amphitheatrical back yard, where Kazimir was burning pork.

The children were running around naked at the edge of the woods. Ida and Nadia walked past them, came down the hill, and circled around the mud pit, which was fast turning crusty in the sun.

"Word has spread!" Kazimir called from his post.

Ida and Nadia stared up at him. They had not the slightest idea what he meant, yet he continued to speak from his podium in the white smoke.

"You really got up his nose! I thought he'd never be angrier than he was with me when I was sawing trees! 'Noisy, noisy, can't play chess!' " Kazimir did his wacky impression of Comrade Chessmaster. He jumped up and down, making his deck creak underfoot. The children saw him and laughed.

Kazimir's wife came out of the cottage to give him an opened beer. She smiled at him and rubbed his bare belly as he imbibed.

Kazimir raised his half-empty bottle in the visitors' direction and reminded them to come fill themselves up anytime.

"Kazimir," his wife simpered, "we should be offering them food."

"Oh," Nadia protested, "we're too hot for barbecue food right now."

"I have an apple cake that's cooled off," said the wife. She took the now-empty bottle and flitted inside (inside the cottage, not the bottle).

"We're always feeding people!" Kazimir explained.

Ida looked green, as much as one could with a sunburn. The thought of cold apple cake was enough to bring acid to her throat, almost to her nose.

One of the children began to shriek and flail, as if blanketed in flames. A bee or a wasp had stung, the others called out in alarm. Kazimir vaulted down from the deck, ran through the gardens and up the hill, and started to slice the buzzing air with his barbecue spatula.

"Save yourself," Nadia whispered to Ida. "I'll stay for the cake."

Ida squeezed Nadia's hand and left.

Kazimir's wife strolled back onto the deck, squinted at the scene of pandemonium on the hill, and beckoned to Nadia, *Come up for cake and lemonade.* Visibly, the cake had come out not-quite-right—as if a confectioner's pet phoenix had pooped clots of cinnamon over a mound of apple slices in a nest of gooey batter before self-immolating at too low a heat. The lemonade was gritty, being supersaturated with sugar.

Nadia mentioned that Ida had had to leave.

"Does your friend have stomach problems?" asked the wife.

Nadia gestured noncommittally as she chewed.

"A lot of people do, when they come to us from the City."

The wounded child came to the deck to tell a tale about the sting and beg for a piece of cake.

"You've had yours," said his mother, "and the rest is for our guests." She touched Nadia's hair. "You must take the last piece back to your friend."

That's the hand that strokes Kazimir, Nadia thought as she continued to force-feed herself.

On the barbecue, the sausages began to explode. Kazimir, with another child on his shoulders, ran back to his post.

All the children were laughing again, except the one who had been stung and had been refused the cake. For him, Nadia got some of Yuly's sovereign green dye from her bag and she applied it to the tip of his nose, where he said the pain was. Then, she made her excuses and left with as much cake as remained.

"A very odd girl has given you a very green nose," the boy's mother said.

Across the lane, behind the corrugated fence, Nadia scraped the cake into the 1989 compost box, buried it with a pitchfork, and rinsed the plates and forks with a watering can. When she dunked the watering can in the rain barrel, a giant bubble burst to the surface.

She left the borrowed kitchenware on the porch and carried the watering can indoors, through to the sunroom. There, she found Ida pacing and shivering a bit in the shoulders, despite the day's heat being held captive by the windows. Ida had changed into her jeans and her black-and-white flannel shirt, perhaps to match her stripes to Tentser's abstractions. She was looking in and around every flowerpot. Tentser was doing the same.

Ida noticed the watering can and said, "Good thinking, we'll need that." She pointed to a translucent, foamy stain on the floor, where half-chewn spiderwort leaves were stuck to the petrified wood. Ida's other hand was clasped around a damp clump that she had just dug away from the base of the lemon tree. Behind her, a geranium lay in ruins; its hanging basket had been ripped from the antique plasterwork. She summarized, "He's been busy."

"Right," Nadia muttered. "Tentser, how'd you like to see the highest part of the house?" She scooped up the young cat in a big-sisterly embrace. He gyrated, punched her throat, clambered to her shoulder, and nibbled on a sweaty lock of hair beside her ear. "Yeah, you're going to the attic," she told him. "You can continue exploring your passions there."

After Nadia carried him upstairs and into the bent pyramid that was the attic, Tentser leapt from her shoulder to the top of the stepladder. There, he immersed himself in the task of listening to the roof.

Nadia shut him in and went back to supply Ida with newspapers and a broom and a small wheelbarrow to cart the debris out to the 1987 compost box. They grumbled to each other and started to laugh and then Nadia groaned about her stomach. "You have to eat, though," Nadia adjured Ida. "You'd be dishonouring my sacrifice if you didn't. You and Tentser need something."

Ida got a couple of eggs and a jar of sour cream out of the dairy truck and made creamy scrambled eggs for herself and the cat.

They spent a lazy couple of hours in the attic. They tried to open the window and failed. They told each other it was just as well, for an open window could be an invitation to anything that had not yet infiltrated the cottage. They brought their chilled sleeping bags up from the truck.

"You aren't cold?" Nadia asked as Ida continued to shiver.

"Cold?" Ida wondered with a shake of her head.

"No, ignore me."

They rested. Nadia tried to edit her excerpt of *Great Expectations*, while Ida clicked her microswitch and whistled a repertoire of invented birdcalls to make Tentser's ears prick.

"How's the microswitch working?" Nadia asked.

"You know."

"Choosing a longer life is no bad thing," Nadia said.

"Hmm. I'm just choosing about pocket money. Cat can't eat

cigarettes."

"I suppose you'll be surrounded by Rosya's smoke anyway."

"Hmm." Ida left the attic for a minute and came back with a shawl of Rosya's wrapped around her neck. She sat and sniffed it.

At dusk, as the smoke of the barbecue started to dissipate, Nadia and Ida strolled down to the river once more (this time, past the silent chess camp) and they sat on a pair of tree stumps. They viewed the cattails, the rippling currents where the water was deep, and a ramshackle boathouse on the far bank. These were details, disappearing into the mirrored blue sky, stained by darkening clouds, and fringed in red around the forested horizon.

They listened to the cicadas. Now and again, Ida rubbed her thigh to make the microswitch click inside her pocket. The air began to cool off, yet it was calm and it was heavy with the smell of muck and reeds. Ida tucked her jeans into her socks, pulled her sleeves down to her palms, and raised Rosya's sheer shawl from her shoulders to drape it over her crown like a veil.

Nadia swatted mosquitoes and hugged her own bare knees.

After a while, they decamped back to the cottage. As they came in earshot of the wind chimes, Ida said, "I've decided I'd like to go back North before 1990."

"Why 1990?"

"There'll be a total eclipse in the North. I've decided to see the eclipse." Ida clicked the microswitch a number of times, at a steady interval. "I've read that in a total eclipse, for as much as four hundred and fifty seconds, the day goes as dark as night and all the birds just stop."

"Stop?"

"Hmm. The word I read was 'stop'. I guess they shut up and stand still or go to roost. Wouldn't it be extraordinary if they all stopped in the sky?"

"Extraordinary."

"They'd be like things you see in frozen ponds, after the snow melts, things that fell in, except they fell into the sky."

When they reached the cottage, they brought the half-dried pump-kin seeds and rose hips inside and laid them out on newsprint in the sunroom, in the former place of a geranium's shadow. They put their shoes and socks in the vestibule and creaked barefoot up the soft, aged steps to the attic.

The attic door was becoming sticky as the evening damp set in. They took turns hurling their modest weight against it as Tentser stuck his forepaw underneath to swat their toes. At last, the door budged, the cat leapt back, and they trudged into an atmosphere of musty heat.

"Now the window…" Nadia muttered.

Tentser rubbed Ida's legs and led her towards the base of a pitted beam. A collection of dead ants lay around it. Ida followed the beam and noted that it ran over the ladder.

Nadia was swearing. Finally, the swollen window budged with a honk like a goose. She knelt by it and sighed as she felt a slight breeze on her mosquito-bitten, sweaty skin. She started to scratch but then realized she had cracked a fingernail, so she chewed off the weakened part and flicked it out the window.

Tentser jumped up onto the sill, stretched his forelegs, stuck his ass high in the air, sharpened his claws on the splintery wood, and then sat there. His tail began to twitch as he stared with gilded eyes of kittenhood at the darkening patchwork of cottage country. Scattered lights and voices and odours flitted in the vast domain of his senses. Candles and kerosene lamps lit some of the other cottages' windows. Flashlights, in the hands of drinkers, wobbled along the paths. Campfires were getting hotter.

"They're burning sausages again," Nadia said about the neighbours. "They've switched to an open fire."

"What are they burning…?" asked Ida, who had lain down and shut her eyes. She murmured a clarification: "…besides sausages?"

"Smells like oak."

The neighbours and guests were chitchatting about the goodness of fire and smoke. They were reminiscing about the finest smoky fires of the past and debating how to make an even finer smoky fire in the present. Someone had gathered a sheaf of herbs or perhaps just grass; they were debating its identity. They were also debating whether to dunk it in the rainwater trough so that it would smoulder.

Nadia announced the news: "They've thrown on some wet weeds—maybe dill. Plenty of smoke. … Now they're bringing out heads of garlic."

"Hmm, keep the mosquitoes down."

"They've decided to break out the cloves, not burn the heads whole."

"Hmm-hmm, things will never be the same."

"I know," Nadia agreed. "We're watching a future generation of leaders out here. We're practically learning to be leaders ourselves."

"Are you hungry?" Ida asked.

"Maybe. You?"

"I don't know. If we're not sleeping," Ida suggested, "let's at least go inhale some of the smoke."

"Okay. I'll close Tentser in."

The young cat tensed and he glared at her with giant pupils as she pulled him away from this newfound world. She set him down on the floorboards and prodded him with her foot to keep him at bay while she lowered the window. She left just a sliver open but he jumped back up and put his nose down to the sill to sniff as much of the smoky free-for-all as he could.

"We'll be right out there," Nadia told him. "You'll be able to see us from here and what's more, we'll be able to see you. If you're a good cat, we might bring you back something meaty and strange."

"Don't negotiate with him," Ida said. She was on her feet. She was checking the contents of her pockets. The microswitch had gone a bit sticky so she blew on it, explosively, to dislodge any grit. Its clicks seemed to satisfy her after that. She returned it to its place and got out her truck keys. "Let's go see what we can take to a fire."

Nadia followed Ida to the stairs and asked, "Shall I just leave the door open for him?"

Ida paused and then shook her head. "No." She trotted down the stairs and eyed her army pack in the vestibule. "I'd better take it." She stuffed one of the newspapers in it. "We can wrap some food for Tentser—or just hide it and chuck it."

"You're really looking forward to this," Nadia remarked, as she grabbed a dress from her pack and threw it on over her swimsuit.

"Hmm. Be a realist, Little Paw."

They picked up the borrowed pie-plate from the porch and went to search the dairy truck for any slow-burning morsels that Rosya may have sent. They settled on a bag of tangerines. "You could throw the peels in the fire," Ida asserted.

"You could grill the tangerines whole," Nadia suggested.

"Wouldn't they explode?" Ida asked. She answered herself, "You'd cut them in half."

They crossed the lane and found the green gate off the latch. They entered and decided to shut it behind them.

"Too many things around," Nadia said, "to be taking chances."

"Too many things," Ida agreed.

The front yard was empty. Out back, the crowd was clapping as Kazimir's voice rose in a series of exclamations about Ukraine.

Ida gripped Nadia's wrist and whispered, "Let's not rush in while he's speaking. I have a feeling he might work me into his speech."

"You're right," Nadia breathed. "Then they might turn on us and pelt us with apples."

"You laugh, Little Paw, but I've had a premonition."

"Well, let's drift on the margins and eavesdrop," Nadia proposed as a compromise. Tugging Ida with her, she crept along the less conspicuous route, between the cottage and the shed. The children were someplace else.

"I want to tell you something," Kazimir was saying, "and I want you to listen seriously. Today, my wife and I met a thoughtful girl who asked, 'Why are there so many orphans in our Nation and what is to become of them? Who shall care for all these lost children of Ukraine?' I stood before her and I saw, reflected in her clear eyes, the wrongs being heaped upon yet another young generation by those who would have us continue down this path set by Stalin and Hitler. A life is still held cheap and the lies go on and on while…"

Kazimir's children were howling like wolves in the woods.

Kazimir's wife, who was mingling with the crowd and accepting whispered praise for her husband, suddenly looked around with a frown. She might have wanted to run to the woods. On the other hand, she had promised Kazimir that she would rotate the sausages over the fire pit every couple of minutes. Someone had to do it while he spoke—and if it meant that she could not yet change out of her apron-dress, so be it.

"Our mothers and grandmothers," Kazimir boomed, "whispered to us of famine, when they could find the words at all. All her life…"

His wife eyed the baying woods, the spitting grill, the hushed garden, and the creaking deck. She had told Kazimir previously that she had misgivings about any gruesome subject of oration at a late-evening cookout for families.

Ida prompted Nadia: "Are you catching everything?" (Kazimir had switched to the Ukrainian language for the biography of his mother.)

Nadia tried translate but then lost focus.

A number of guest-children, in series, scurried back from the woods. They complained to their parents of the host-children's relentless ululations. Kazimir's wife intervened, went to retrieve her pups, and led them around towards the front of the cottage, straight past Nadia and Ida.

At least they're wearing clothes now, Nadia observed.

"Hello," they all said to each other. "Hello…"

The child with the stung nose wanted to give Nadia an update on his health but his mother hurried him along: "You all need a nap. Scoot. You can come back out in half an hour—if you're good!"

By the time Kazimir's family had filed through the cottage's front door, he had finished his back-deck oration. He descended briskly to his fire pit to check the state of the sausages; they had missed a rotation already.

The most eager of the guests were piling extra bundles of oak twigs atop the vigorous fire. The sticks let off slender trails of smoke and then, too soon, the flames spiralled around them, grew, and sent feelers towards the meat.

"Shall we take over the tangerines?" Nadia asked.

"He's got the grill too low to the fire," Ida muttered her critique, "and they're over-kindling it all to hell. Let's go."

"Perhaps you could stay and advise him."

"Oh, I don't know."

"Couldn't you get them to produce something edible—for Tentser's sake?"

"Fine," Ida said. "Just give me a minute to think of a plan."

"Wow them with grilled tangerines," Nadia suggested, "and then take over."

Ida shook her head. "Nothing is that simple, Little Paw. We don't know anything about grilled tangerines."

"No, but it sounds impressive!"

"Could backfire. I'll lead with advice on making smoke."

"Alright, go!"

They had tarried too long. The chance to enter the spotlight was no longer Ida's.

Cries of "O!" erupted around the fire pit. Kazimir's wife had sailed out of the cottage in a red dress with white polka dots. She hefted a red boombox onto the rail of the deck, switched on a cassette of rhythm and blues, and, from her place on the rug in the lamplight, she was twirling her skirt and rolling her neck and making eyes at her husband. Well-wishers jostled Kazimir's shoulders to get him moving in her direction. Kazimir climbed the steps. They touched; they jived. Despite clutter, noise, smoke, and sweat, they jived. Kazimir grabbed her waist and raised her in the air.

Ida whispered, "Now he's gonna chuck her on the grill."

At the same time, a camera was clacking. The photographer, who had maneuvered away from the crowd, rushed to kneel in the grass in front of Nadia and Ida as he turned his wide-angle lens on everyone but them. "Woman flying, lit from below", the caption might be.

Ida looked tempted to kick him in the head. She and Nadia exchanged a glance, for they had recognized Marat and his light brown suit.

"You'll stain your knees," Nadia warned him.

Marat sprang forwards for a few shots, his body braced against the deck-rail. Then, he stepped back to answer, "That will be a problem for Monday."

"I should go…" Ida murmured.

"No…" Nadia protested.

"…go wait by the fire," Ida insisted, "and maybe talk heart-to-heart with those freaked-out kids. If anybody wants me, I'll be with the kids."

"Okay," said Nadia, in a state of nonplus about Ida's newfound interest in the kids. "I'll catch you up." *I guess I'll stick around with Marat.*

Ida swung her bag of tangerines as she walked away.

Marat seemed to ignore her. He juggled lenses into and out of his hip pockets as he continued to play his role in the dance.

When the song was done and the deck had been yielded to other romantic couples, Kazimir's wife came over, offered her cheek for Marat to kiss, and asked him whether the lighting had been alright on Kazimir.

"Yes," Marat replied, "and I was sure to get your pearl buttons in focus."

"Marat…!" she simpered.

"These buttons," Marat told Nadia, "have been in three generations of wedding dresses."

The hostess protested, "Now you're trying to embarrass me!"

"Not at all, I'm simply pointing out to Nadia how meticulously you plan an end-of-summer party."

The woman patted Nadia's hand and said, "I trust you to talk sense to this man." With that, she set sail afresh on the tides of garden-guests.

Marat snapped a few shots here and there. He ended on the wide-angle lens again. "Let's finish this colour roll while we have any light at all. 'Talk sense,' " he muttered.

Nadia lowered her head and ran a hand through her river-tangled hair.

"I haven't had time," Marat continued, "to do a proper clean of my lenses since I arrived. Would you think me rude if I disappear?"

"Can I come too," Nadia asked, "and watch you clean your lenses?"

"If it wouldn't bore you," he said.

"If it wouldn't annoy you," she countered.

"No, it wouldn't," he answered. He stepped back towards the fence and decided to go behind the shed, where the children maintained a rendezvous point, complete with coloured chalk, slates, crate-furniture, and a kerosine lamp. Nadia followed and he asked her, "Do you smoke?"

"Occasionally."

Marat dug a cigarette case and lighter out of the inside breast pocket of his jacket. Nadia placed a hand on the case, *May I see?* and he relinquished it. She sat on a crate, he lit the lamp, and she ran her thumb over the detailed scene etched into the front of the case. A tall ship (a frigate) was listing on a choppy sea, whose waves merged into the endless hair of a woman floating neck-deep in the foreground. Her big eyes and eyelashes looked like sunbursts over a comparatively small and sternly angled nose and mouth. A Hero City of Kiev medal was stamped into a corner of the sky. Clearly, the medal had been there first, before somebody engraved the woman, ship, and sea.

"Who's she?" Nadia asked.

Marat replied, "The fantasy of one of my shipmates, in the Navy. I assure you, this is far from a realistic picture of life in the belly of a submarine."

"Too bad, it's beautiful."

"According to rumour," Marat related, "you are addicted to English literature. A couple of things must be said. The English make eloquent lunatics. The English are not objective about the sea."

Nadia took out a cigarette, made a face like the one on the case, and handed it back to him. He gave her a light and she smoked in silence.

Marat sat on a neighbouring crate, set down the cigarette case, unslung his camera, and began to inspect the purple and yellow reflections of the lamplight in the lens. He detached the lens and checked the back element too. "There's a mark," he said and showed it to Nadia.

She nodded in acknowledgement of the pinpoint imperfection: an opaque blue-grey dot with a barely visible tail.

"What did that, we may never know," Marat said. He looked around, as if to seek an answer anyway, and he found a small tin of toffees on the shed's rear window sill. He dumped the toffees (in their black-and-yellow paper wrappers) onto another crate, checked that the tin was not sticky inside, set it down, and tapped it twice with his fingernail. "Ashes, please."

"Anything to oblige," Nadia exhaled. *Why am I here?*

"These rear coatings are delicate," Marat said. He got out a soft, white square of cloth, touched it to the ashes, rubbed it against itself, and then made two light, circular swipes across the surface of the glass. He inspected the result and then did the same for an even finer mark on the front element. "There."

Nadia's gaze drifted towards the lane. One of the eaves of Tentser's attic, with its antique woodwork, was visible over the fences.

Marat reattached his wide-angle lens and then emptied his hip pockets; he still had his standard and telephoto lenses to inspect.

"What did you do on the submarine?" Nadia asked.

"Polished the periscopes."

"Oh, right. That must have kept you busy."

"Yes."

"Did you do any spy missions?"

"Yes. I infiltrated Oxford."

"Come again?"

"I snuck ashore in Canada, in a port called Halifax, and went to a movie theatre called the Oxford."

"You must have got a medal for that."

Marat changed the topic: "I understand you're staying at the old place."

"Over there? Yes."

"How do you like it?" he asked.

"Oh, it's like something from a fairytale," Nadia said. She blew smoke out her nose and added, "Certainly it has creatures living in it."

Marat sighed, "So Fenya tells me. She's the one who checks up on Papa, beyond his workdays at the Arsenal."

Nadia unwrapped this statement and found something that surprised her. "Your Papa is Rosya's friend."

"Yes and your friend is Rosya's apprentice. I discovered the connection only yesterday. I had planned to visit Papa down here but then Fenya filled me in on his movements and various other people's."

"Yet you came."

"I had promised Kazimir and Svetlana that I would come and photograph their party. They always have a bed to spare for a guest."

"Oh, I'm sorry we put you out."

"You haven't; it does me no harm to change my plans. Serendipity is a photographer's friend. Perhaps it is your friend as well."

Nadia gave him a look that said, *I shall consider your sagacious riddles later.* She asked, "How do you know Kazimir?"

"Through Svetlana," Marat replied. "Sveta was always here in the summers. Her grandparents had this place. They were somebody's personal staff. Then, they got retired here for loyal service to that somebody."

"Then, you and she and Fenya were children together."

"Well, we're five years apart, each way. Sveta was nineteen when I was fourteen when Fenya was nine. That summer, she brought Kazimir with her and I took some photos for them. I had never witnessed such a courtship and it seemed too good to let the chance slip by. Fenya became horribly jealous."

Marat simply ended his story there.

And? Nadia asked with her eyes.

Marat provided an epilogue: "Sveta and Kazimir still ask me to take photos and I still oblige. At least it shows Fenya that I'm not at her sole command. Kazimir has aged, though; he stumbles through his stunts with more and more talk, more and more fat."

Nadia suggested, "Perhaps one can smile and safely tune him out—if one isn't a pig or a tree."

"Kazimir cannot be ignored," Marat warned. "He is the rising power in the Plumbers and Steamfitters Association of Revolutionary Ukraine. He has become an outspoken critic of Gorbachev and the Party, since, in the end, it falls to members of the Association to face the water problems in the aftermath of every great disaster. Plenty of contaminated firefighting water and coolant water was sloshing around Pripyat and (let us not forget) the Kiev city reservoir is just downstream. Kazimir can tell you all this if you dare to ask. Anyway, be aware, his popularity is considerable. There are those who see him as the future leader of an independent Ukraine."

There must have been times in Marat's childhood, Nadia imagined, *when his mother was unsure whether he was being sarcastic.*

"Excuse me," said Marat with a slight wave of his camera and its polished lens. He had photos to take. This gathering could be historic.

Ida, having made her offerings to the hosts and having voiced what advice she could, slipped away from the crowd to find Nadia behind the shed. "What did he want?" Ida asked.

Nadia shrugged. "To talk."

Ida glared and tried another question entirely. "Missy—wife of Kazimir—what's her name?"

"Svetlana."

"She seems to think we're dear friends of Marat. As it so happens, it's his bloody Papa lending us the cottage." Ida eyed the cigarette.

"Marat told me. He didn't know till today."

"Didn't he?" Ida shot back. "What, nobody knows fuck all in a family?" Her voice seemed to scrape something deep and hollow.

"Don't snap at me," Nadia said. "Have the fucking cigarette if you want it."

Ida announced, "I'm going for a walk." She swerved out of Nadia's sight in an instant and hurried onwards—around the shed, around flowerbeds, past the mud pit, past shrubs, and over the wooded hillock. Children roared at her in a play ambush; she roared back and the kids squealed and laughed.

Nadia stayed in her hiding place, butted out the cigarette in the toffee tin, and wept silently, perhaps for a long time. She rubbed her arms and the hairs stood on end.

At the front of the shed, a man coughed. Nadia wiped her eyes and sauntered out to find Marat there. He was cradling his camera at his waist as he faced in the direction of the lane.

Marat was looking up. Tentser was looking down. Clouds of dew were creeping upwards, above the fence-line, to the pointy-arched tops of the sunroom windows and over the little lozenge-window at the head of the stairs, yet the one clear window was where Tentser sat. The Moon lit his eyes and the dew.

"You've seen our kitten," Nadia noted.

Marat nodded. He swapped his lens for the longest one, from his most stretched pocket. After taking a couple of photos, he said, "We've had a cat in that window before—when we kept it up as a proper family cottage."

"Then, I'm pleased to revive a tradition."

He nodded again and glanced at her. The heat of the fire, now wafting across the yard, had started to make his cheeks flush and he was getting sweaty under the eyes. "What do you call him?" he asked.

"Tentser."

He reached into a pocket. "Where did you get that name?"

"Ida chose it. A long time ago, Rosya's cousin had a little girl with a cat named Tentser."

Marat got out his cleaning cloth again. He unfolded it and, by the light of a lamp over the shed door, he slowly, lightly wiped his camera's eyepiece, which was fouled by a streak of sweat.

Why doesn't he say something?

When Marat was done, he put the cloth away and said, "This would be the cousin who was oppressed, in Stalin's time."

"Yes. You must know Rosya well."

"Not really. I do have childhood memories of her visits to our flat in Kiev. They had a certain structure. Before dinner, she would listen to Fenya and me; at dinner, she would compliment our mother; and after dinner, until late, she would get into deep debates with our father. One evening, he was reminiscing about his old boss, Korolev—about Korolev's frailties and insecurities, which, in my father's view, had cost us our chance at the Moon. Rosya, of course, had never met Korolev but she was aware that he had once been a prisoner in Kolyma and she described to my father how Korolev would have suffered, as her cousin had suffered and so many others had suffered. She spoke of daily shootings, beatings, impossible work quotas, and such hunger and cold that it destroyed a man piece by piece—his teeth and memories falling out of his head one by one. That, I remember her saying. I remember also the mention of a wife and little girl who became lost forever."

"And a cat whom the little girl loved."

"That, Rosya did not mention. I certainly would have committed that to memory as well."

"I see." Indeed, Nadia did see that even as Marat spoke, he was mostly looking at Tentser/Cosmos. *Still, I got him to say something.*

Bang-clang-clang-plop!

Nadia and Marat jumped as somebody dumped an armload of firewood into the rainwater trough. Marat raised an arm as if to shield his head but instead he banged his elbow on the corrugated iron eaves of the shed. Many eyes fell on him and Nadia. Several people burst out laughing.

Marat whispered something ("Fuckwits," if Nadia was not mistaken). He left her side and went to inspect another reflection of the Moon, in the water around the logs. He took a photo but he told the party, "There's no sense soaking those in water. A few minutes in water won't do anything at all except make them steam. If you want to soak them, add some beer for flavour."

The others began to debate this wisdom amongst themselves.

Marat came back to Nadia and told her, "That's all there is to being a manager."

"Oh, right," Nadia said. "I don't know much about managers. I guess Ida would."

"She's cooking your dinner," Marat said. He led the way.

Nadia followed Marat away from the shed, into the garden, to see that Ida had started a breakaway campfire on the hardened soil of the children's mud pit. The kids had evacuated their muddy toys—the tanks and trucks and cars, the clowns and circus animals and goblins and witches—to regroup them as an audience further up the slope. Some kids were sitting with the toys and guarding them against a prankster who had threatened to cut off the clowns' and witches' hair for kindling. Other kids were bringing Ida anything they could purloin from the main campfire's supplies. Ida, having smelt too much burnt sausage already, was stacking bricks to raise a grill high above the flames.

"Ida, are you sure you don't want witch hair?" the prankster called to her.

"Never!" she called back. "That would be cannibalism!"

"Ida is a witch!"

"Hmm! I never eat other witches. Now, as for children...!"

Shrieking and laughing, the kids ran uphill and dispersed into the dark woods. A minute later, they would come back, like birds to roost.

"I'll leave you two," Marat said to Nadia. "I want to go find something."

"Find what?" Nadia asked. She saw that he was rewinding his film. She guessed he had been shooting while the kids were screaming.

Marat changed his film. The exposed roll went inside one breast of his jacket and a fresh roll came out of the other. At last, he said, "I remember cherry trees growing wild along the river. If we're smoking sausages, we'd do much better to mix fruit wood with the oak." Without further explanation, he left for the gate just as Ida looked their way.

What twist of management is this? Nadia wondered.

From the pit, Ida stared. From the window, so did Tentser. Marat, however, looked at neither anymore.

Nadia took it all in, wished for something to numb a headache, and began to take a slow walk towards her friend.

"Sorry," said Nadia when she reached Ida's fireside.

"Hmm, okay," Ida told her. "I may need you to sacrifice yourself again."

"How so?"

"Distract these monsters if they really turn on me."

"The kids?"

"The kids."

"Oh, right. I guess I can do that."

"I know you can. Now," Ida finished, "I need to concentrate."

Nadia went amongst the kids. Chatty or quiet, they all seemed unfazed by her presence, even as she paced around them and looked over their shoulders at the props of their play. *Nastya would be better at this.*

A bunch of the girls had set up a kiosk on a flat-topped rock in the woods. For lighting, they had hung flashlights from branches. They were selling words scratched on birch bark: "Harvest", "Meeting", "Afghan", and so forth. They also stocked sticky, green pinecones to pique the senses. They did a brisk trade with the passersby who fled from Ida or went back to see her again. Payment was taken in pebbles or wood chips.

When the prankster came, the storekeepers informed him that his money was counterfeit; they would report him. He responded by grabbing all the pine cones and making a dash. Nadia wrestled him to the ground and tickled him until he surrendered in a flood of tearful laughter.

Sound travelled strangely to and from that wooded hill. The river played tricks; so did the planet, perhaps.

At one point, Nadia thought she heard Japanese voices.

Later, dogs started barking. A man cursed. That was just down the lane.

"I'll be back," Nadia told the kids.

The prankster jibed that Nadia had to go see her boyfriend.

Nadia ambled to the tall gate in the tall fence of emerald-green boards and rust-red topknots. She opened it and gazed along the gentle curve of the twin ruts. Moonlight and the lights of lanterns on fences and the upper-storey lights of the biggest cottages completed the patchy impression of a road.

Marat was coming down the path with his camera slung round to his back and his arms laden with cherry wood from a tree that had never been pruned. Green suckers balanced atop his armload of black-barked branches. He twisted and scurried to evade the dogs' attentions; they leapt at the wealth of sticks. At last, he slipped inside the tall, emerald-green and rust-red gate, which Nadia held for him. She chucked a loose bit of wood to the dogs and then shut them out and pulled the latch string.

"You found your cherry boughs," Nadia noted, with a slight smile, as she began to follow Marat along the fence, to the trough.

"I did." Marat dumped his load in the beer-laced rainwater and then he squatted beside Nadia. He knitted his fingers and rubbed his thumbs together, one over the other, over the other. He glanced at her and glanced towards the lane. He looked perturbed.

What? she asked him silently. *Do you know something I don't know, some secret of life and death? Was I wrong to give cherry wood to the dogs?*

He replied, "I found a tramp camped there, under the cherry trees, just a little ways upstream. I spoke with him to say it was a pretty spot."

I gather you'll speak freely with anyone. "And?" she asked.

"He asked about you and your friend. He said he saw you earlier."

"Oh," Nadia murmured. "We didn't see him. I didn't see him." She looked around for Ida. Ida had stepped away from her fire to rub her eyes and to pace amid the shrubs and swing her arms.

"Then, he wasn't bothering you," Marat concluded. "You have no objection if I invite him to join us—he being one's fellow man."

"None, when you put it that way."

"Good." Marat stood up, started to go, and added, "You can put the cherry cuttings on Ida's fire when you think they've had a good soak."

"Okay."

He returned to the gate, opened it a crack to check for dogs, and then made his way back out into the deepening night.

Once more, Nadia went up the hill. She managed to get a moment alone with Ida by telling a trio of kids to stop following Ida; stop being copycats; Ida could swing her arms on her own; go turn the skewers; it was important.

"Did you see anyone," Nadia whispered, "when we were swimming at the island?"

Ida shook her head and yawned.

"What about afterwards, when we were sitting in the cherry tree?"

Ida shrugged. "Nobody. I get tired of looking."

"Marat says he's met a tramp by the river who might have been watching."

"Marat is so good," Ida sighed, "to care for a serf-girl's modesty."

Nadia made a sound of protest under her breath.

Ida cut her off: "I don't want a fight, Little Paw. I don't want to fight with anybody. Maybe a tramp looked at us. I don't know. There's no point fretting now."

"I'm not but Marat wants to bring him…"

"Little bandits," Ida griped softly about her helpers. "No stoking the fire! Remember, I told you, we're smoking them slowly, slooowly, sloooooowly…" She brushed Nadia's shoulder on her way to reassert control.

Other children called Nadia deeper into the woods. She helped them conduct a search for the source of counterfeit pebbles until Marat returned.

When he came, he came alone. He found that his cherry-wood had been taken from the trough. He loitered (with an air of managerial oversight) in the vicinity of Ida and the sweet, rich smoke.

Nadia came down to meet him. By the mirky firelight, her look of curiosity took on a leery edge. *Well, then?* was the question on her face.

Marat reported on his mission: "He says he might come later, if it's quiet."

"Hmm, we all make our choices," Ida said to the fire.

To Nadia, the prospect of meeting this tramp began to seem less real. She went on a tangent and asked, "Do you have any photos of your travels?"

"Yes, Sveta asked me to bring some." Marat processed something for a moment and then declared, "I wouldn't mind sitting for a few minutes to show them to you and her. I believe she's inside."

"Go on, Little Paw," Ida permitted it. "She is the hostess and you've barely said hello to her."

Here we go again, for a sacrifice should be made twice—the second time, to an anthem of derision. "Of course," Nadia answered Marat. "Thank you, it's a nice idea."

Nadia followed Marat up to the deck, indoors to the kitchen (where flies were licking meaty plates and beating at the windows), and through to the living room or study. They found Svetlana in an armchair in the corner. She lifted her head out of a doze, guessed Marat's intention, and pointed to her writing desk. "Your album..." She also noticed Nadia. "Oh, you can show her as well."

"Don't get up," Marat insisted. He took cushions from a sofa, heaped them near Sveta's chair, and set the album on her footstool. Marat and Nadia sat on the cushions, Sveta leaned forwards, and they all began to hand around photos in this lopsided triangle.

There were Cubans in fedoras, chinos, and shirts unbuttoned to the chest. Those were the men, of course. The women favoured colourful, modest dresses. The cars were attired likewise; they were shining, unspoilt beauties, until a lack of parts left them sitting on cinderblocks by the curb. Marat had done a summer exchange in Havana in his student days. He had worked as a statistician doing something related to sugar exports and this post saw him ensconced in a Spanish-colonial office building overlooking the port, when he was not off in the hills, sweating his eyes out as he watched sugar cane being loaded onto ox carts. Marat's boss at the sugar statistics office was a black man, a professorial type, who made a humorous point of sending his best-dressed worker to the fields.

"How interesting," said Svetlana. She asked, had Marat danced any salsa? He had not, as such. They moved on to the next section.

There were Syrians in suits or turtlenecks or robes, living in concrete city blocks or mud-brick desert towns. Marat's boat had been based in that country, on and off. A young woman in a beret and camouflage uniform featured in several scenes. Consistently, she bore a clenched grin and a slight squint—perhaps force of habit from standing watch in the sun. *Breathe the air, scan the air, breathe the air, scan the air...*

"Who is she?" Svetlana asked.

"A local counterpart," Marat replied.

When it was Nadia's turn for a close look, she checked the backs of these photos and found the caption, "A local counterpart". *That will teach me: look at the damn picture, not the words.* She noticed, in a head-and-shoulders shot, that the woman-soldier wore a pendant: a heavily eroded silver coin with a woman's face and a drilled hole to fit the chain. She questioned Marat about it.

"Yes, it was a good-luck charm of hers, a 3rd-century piece: Queen Zenobia, who won independence from the Romans. This Lieutenant, her grandfather had worked in archeological digs for the French." He showed pictures of sandstone columns and sandstone arches, bones of an empire, sand built upon sand, only to be worn away by sand.

"You meet interesting people," Nadia said.

"I find something of interest to me, not that it's automatic. If I let myself get bored, I would have succumbed to madness and vice long ago."

Nadia wondered whether his interest was, in part, the heft of the warrior-lady's boobs. She kept that question to herself but she did ask Marat whether his time in Syria had inspired his moustache. He said it had.

Sveta was still looking at ruined temples. She said something about the power of rulers in those ancient times and the veneration of temporary things.

"Do you think so?" Marat asked. "The premiers and presidents and submarine captains of today wield power that the pharaohs and caesars never did. All that we know could be gone upon entry of a code, upon turn of a key."

"Yes. My God. You and Kazimir should speak of such things," Sveta sighed. "Marat, can you show us something joyful?"

They moved on to the Swedes, who had the eyes of insomniacs, every last one. Nude statues were everywhere and shopping malls were full of clothes. Little girls carried colourful leather purses and wore lace-up blouses, button-up vests, jeans (indigo blue or apple red), and high heels. A roomful of writers and artists sat at computers to design photo-illustrated books and glossy magazines. The printing press was controlled by computers too.

Here was a set of vignettes in a pair of lives. A young, unmarried couple (engineers at the camera factory) legally shared a flat. They left their flat one morning, went to buy a car, had no money for the car, promised to pay for the car later, and—that very morning—drove away with the car. They drove around the countryside, bought food, drink, and petrol with further I-owe-yous, and stopped for a picnic near a medieval church on a hill. All the while, they got Marat to photograph their car-day, free of charge.

"What happened when they didn't pay?" Nadia asked.

Marat and Sveta stared at Nadia. *What kind of upbringing have you had?* "They did pay," Marat said. "They still are making payments on the car."

"Oh. Excuse me. Of course."

The nude models, of whom Fenya had spoken, were absent from this album. Nadia kept quiet about them too. *If I asked, "Did you shoot any nudies?" or "Did you meet any gays?" you might just let Sveta stare me down again.* "Other places?" she asked.

Cuba, Syria, and Sweden were the selection that Marat had brought. He wished to spare them the horrors (so he said) of the high seas.

Nadia remarked, "Giorgi would be envious of your adventures."

Svetlana sleepily pondered this unfamiliar name.

"Truth be told," said Marat, "he must see a lot, depending which way he looks."

"Marat," Sveta sighed, "whom are you mocking now?"

"Why should I be mocking anyone? I'm not. Nevermind what I say. I am not a man of words. I am just a man watching a civilization."

"Does Fenya see a lot?" Nadia asked.

Marat straightened a stack of his photos and parted his lips.

"You are thoughtful," Sveta told Nadia, "to come with Marat to see me. Your friend and all the children must be missing you already."

There's a hint for the ages. "Yes. Nice to see you and this place and the picture show." Nadia got up and gradually (but not too gradually) walked the trail of pleasantries to her exit.

At least I didn't get slapped or called an ugly pacifist. I'm becoming a more and more welcome guest by the day. She waved to Tentser as she walked back to the mud pit.

Ida had ordered the children to bring potatoes and build a pyramid. This was, in part, a stratagem to distract them from their questions about the timeline. As hours passed and the rising smoke made ponderous progress through the meat, Ida periodically grabbed a few potatoes with the tongs and buried them in the embers. After twenty minutes, she would get them out, split them, and tell the children to go snack on them with salt and a drink of tomato juice. Marat emerged from the cottage to place these rations on the deck rail for the kids.

Such measures, along with the children's own ability to organize themselves in play, did succeed in quieting the unrest for a time. Later, Nadia intervened in the play to keep it from turning to bickering. She told pieces of stories and let the kids flesh out various roles.

Ultimately, nothing could reconcile the equations to the expectations. The children grew tired. They were watching the fires through their eyelids, turning the black night red. They became disillusioned with Ida's slow approach to smoking meat. They returned to the main fire, attempted to catch up with the adult ramblings, ate burnt sausages, got sick to their stomachs, and had to go to the outhouses and to bed. Their parents departed with them.

By this time, Svetlana was back in general circulation, as was Marat. He bade goodnight to some of his acquaintances and took his last chance to shoot them. They would come out as grainy figures in the faint, smouldering light of their cooking fire. The hosts pressed upon him the idea that he should take a couple of beers to the odd, thoughtful girls who had distracted the kids.

Nadia was just helping a father who had come back to locate a favourite toy.

Marat—with three bottles and a bottle opener in his hands and his camera hanging from his neck and his pockets full of lenses and film—looked haggard as he walked up to Ida for a first attempt at a proper conversation. "You must be thirsty," he said. "Look what that lot drink and it can't be said they're oiling their brains."

"Hmm."

"You have thinking eyes," Marat said as she accepted an opened beer.

She also grabbed the bottle cap from him, pocketed it, drank half a bottleneck of beer, and eyed Marat and the fire alternately.

"How is Rosya?" Marat asked.

"Hmm, you know," Ida sighed. "She has me for a roommate, by choice." She drained the rest of the bottleneck and blew air through her lips with a rattling sound.

"You were the kids' favourite tonight."

"Novelty," Ida said. "Look how it lasts."

Marat took a sip and frowned. He philosophized, "Surely some young people do form attachments for a lifetime. Nadia, surely, is very attached."

"She has an education to get; it's not where I am," Ida said, "but she is a good friend but I don't see why any of this worries you."

Marat glanced about and lowered his voice. "You were my sister's case for a time, I don't know why, but it seems to have gone by the wayside. She is, thankfully, building a reputation for cases that amount to nothing and I have done my bit to help her do just that, while building a fine portfolio (if I do say so) of people misjudged by our civilization."

"That's an artful apology," Ida muttered.

"Now," Marat continued, "I needn't follow you and you needn't follow me but it's quite nice to share a beer. Here comes your friend."

"Found Funtik the Piglet," Nadia announced. "Bedtime is saved."

Marat passed her a beer.

Nadia thanked him and took a couple of gulps as if it were water, though she found it a bit bitter for her taste. She was more accustomed to the non-alcoholic stuff sold by street vendors, with its breakfasty taste of bread and sweets.

Ida took two more bottle caps from Marat.

Nadia and Marat discussed his photography for a short time, while Ida turned the sausages and the three of them finished their beers.

Marat then licked his thin moustache and wiped it dry with his knuckles. He said, "I should go tell our friend that everybody is clearing out."

"Maybe he just wants to sleep," Ida supposed.

"He seemed wide awake," Marat replied, "but we'll see." Shifting the weight of his gear, he turned and took the shortcut through the woods.

After that, the mud pit was almost silent. Only a few sounds drifted down, only briefly. Kazimir made funny voices, perhaps specific imitations, and the children laughed, albeit in a hollow, weary timbre.

Somewhere, an animal gave a strange bark, with an undertone like a wobbling sheet of metal.

Svetlana stepped out onto the deck, looked around without a word, and then went back inside to turn off all the lamps.

The bark came several times again, without answer—and then, no transmission.

The Moon had climbed into the clouds, as if it were a shattered traveller who ended the day in a dormitory bunk, with the covers pulled overhead. The treetops were dark. Tentser's window was dark. Everywhere, the lights were extinct, except for the embers in the mud pit and the stars in the rifts between the clouds.

One and then the other shall die, Nadia supposed. The heat in the pit was tapering off. Her arms and legs—first insect-bitten and then touched by microscopic, drifting ashes—now were getting chilly in the breeze. She whispered, "Marat has been ages."

"Hmm, maybe the tramp cut him up and stole his camera."

Nadia shivered and eyed the trees.

With her stick, Ida struck a charred oak log and it spat a column of sparks. The firelight flitted across her face. "Maybe," she breathed, "it's the tramp Giorgi ran over. Maybe he was stunned; he stumbled around Kiev and fell into the river like Rasputin and drowned and washed up here and he's been waiting for you…"

"He's not the only one waiting!" Nadia snapped. "Tentser will be crying his head off! Aren't those sausages ready yet?"

"Be patient, Little Paw. This slowness is a gift." Ida darted towards the rekindled fire to get a closer look at her creations. Then, just as quickly, she withdrew. "The skin is going to be perfect—bright and crinkly like the best-wrapped present."

Here again, she's remembering the works of Mama—Mama on special occasions for Mama's daughters. Did Ida make some heroic effort to guard these memories against electrocution? Ida must be the most grateful child Mama never had.

Weary-minded and sore, Nadia got up, rubbed her butt and neck, and went to stand on a big stump behind Ida. She peered over Ida's shoulder, into the whitish smoke around the grill. Nadia snickered, "Your hair smells like smoked meat."

"Be serious, Little Paw. These are sacred rites."

Nadia stepped back, sighed, and exchanged glances with the toys on the slope. "We should have brought blankets," she said.

"Hmm, check in my pack," Ida told her, "at the bottom."

Nadia picked up the army pack and took it over to the double tree stump. She sat astride one stump and the pack sat opposite her. She dug past the newspapers and other bits of daily life and found, in the depths, the quilt of colourful birds and flowers. *They fell in there and froze.*

Just as Nadia was about to say something to Ida, a man stepped out of the woods and picked his way down the slope—cautiously, as if he expected a mudslide or an ambush by treacherous toys. "What've you been doing lately?" he asked. "*Qu'avez-vous fait ces derniers temps?*"

Ida said nothing and did not look his way. She made herself busy with her work's conclusion. With tongs in hand, she was selecting sausages, un-skewering them, and laying them out mechanically on all the newspapers that Nadia had unpacked.

Hugging the quilt, Nadia stood and leaned into the darkness in a kind of unintentional bow. "Johnny?" she asked.

He came into the firelight. For all that he was grinning, he looked awful. He had grown a small beard of matted curls, which matched the now-broken edges of his front teeth. His lower eyelids sagged, making the shape of his eyes seem like a stranger's, and he stared as if this encounter (and every encounter) were the stuff of science fiction.

"Then…" Johnny began again, hesitantly (for he was still not one for chitchat), "…what've you been doing lately?"

"Answering questions," Ida said, "questions about…" She trailed off. She was kneeling on the ground and digging the final batch of potatoes out of the ashes to wrap with the sausages.

"Questions about…?" Johnny echoed.

"Hmm, about whatever. Questions about marriage. Questions about dairy trucks."

Johnny looked troubled, puzzled, and amused. His mouth was slightly open. He quit looking at Ida's backside and instead looked into Nadia's face. His lips began moving silently.

"Johnny, ah … Johnny," Nadia repeated his name ever so softly, "why don't you come sit down?" She moved Ida's pack to the ground and spread the quilt of birds and flowers across the double stump as an invitation.

He gave a twitch of a shrug as he unshouldered his own pack—an army pack just like Ida's and several million others. To the ground it went, beside Ida's. As Nadia sat on one of the stump's heads, he sat on the other like an image in a trick mirror. He assumed a bizarrely formal posture, with his shoulders back and his hands on his knees. He nodded at Nadia and nodded at Ida's backside.

"Do we get to eat?" Nadia asked Ida.

"Hmm… Have this one." Ida passed a packet and a fork to Nadia. Then, she did the same for Johnny, for whom she finally spared a glance. "Have this one."

He beamed, opened the packet, and began to shovel in mouthfuls that he chewed off-centre. The fork was the kind with a big, fluted, plastic handle, which he gripped as intently as a small child or an arthritis-sufferer might do. "Good food," he panted over the piping-hot meal.

Nadia savoured smaller bites, in spite of herself, as she watched the mashing motions of Johnny's scabby mouth. "This tastes like magic pig," Nadia joked. She supposed that a magic pig, in its last act, might well turn one's mouth into a cauldron of porky smoke in which elusive cherries danced.

Johnny smelt like river water. His hair had a crust of dampness. *Poor, poor fool, you bathed just before you came to see us.*

Ida herself was not in any hurry to eat. She had begun to transfer some of the abundant food to her pack. She looked around and asked, "Am I keeping one out for Marat?"

Johnny mumbled, "He said he'd watch my camp for me."

"Photograph it, too," Ida supposed.

"He liked the spot. I chose it *pour des raisons artistiques*. Good reception."

"What kind of antenna are you using?" Nadia asked.

"Random wire all around the cherry trees, a good six metres up. They're big."

"What kind of receiver?"

"Military thing. Nothing like it. Fucking heavy. I've carried it a long way."

"I'd like to hear it," Nadia said.

"Are you still doing any shortwave listening?"

"No."

"I am," Ida said. "There's a big radio room in my building. Nobody is ever there except, I guess, to change the reels." She mimed, *They spin and spin.*

"Ah, interesting," Johnny breathed.

Ida finished packing her bag and left it where it was, beside Johnny's. She kept one bundle of food for herself and went back to the big stump.

"What else," Johnny asked, "is in your building?"

Ida shrugged and mashed a bit of sausage into her potato and said, "My roommate has a computer."

Johnny stopped shovelling. He took a minute to swallow and to clear his throat as he prepared to speak in earnest: "Ida, you must be doing alright."

"Hmm."

Johnny shifted his tongue and swallowed again. "That Marat, I like him."

"Then I hope he likes you," Ida said in her flattest of pancake-flat tones.

Johnny ate the rest of his meal. Then, he pressed a clean bit of newspaper against his lips like a napkin or a pad of gauze. He crumpled it up, threw it on the cinders, and watched it shrivel, burn, and vanish.

"Johnny, how did you get here?" Nadia came out and asked.

"I walked," Johnny answered. "I've been walking since spring."

"Alone?"

"Not if you believe the American preachers on my radio. They say I never walk alone."

Having relayed this scrap of intelligence, Johnny changed the subject and asked about Nastya. He listened to a report from Nadia about the Lieutenant, the foetus, and the orange-coloured kitchen. He wanted to know what distinguishing hobbies Nastya's husband might have.

"He plays cards," Nadia told him. "He recently discovered a love of cats."

Johnny waited and then, realizing there was no more, looked away into the night. "Come see me in the morning," he requested.

"Are you going?" Nadia asked.

"Yes. Marat says he can bring me some chemicals and show me how to process film in my tent."

"Go to Marat, then," Ida said.

"See you in the morning," Johnny concluded. Nadia reassured him that it would be so. With unsettled expectations, he returned the way he had come.

Ida kicked dirt into the ashes.

"Marat has made a friend of him," Nadia observed.

Ida replied, "Marat may get a surprise."

"What do you mean?" asked Nadia as she gathered the quilt around herself.

"Hmm, ignore me, Little Paw. I'm just … out of … everything, for a while now." Ida picked up the remaining backpack and yawned without a sound.

" 'Mornings are wiser than evenings,' " Nadia advised. She was remembering the fairytale of Vasilisa the Beautiful, who, in her darkest hours, always received such comforting words from her magic doll, a keepsake of a dying mother's love.

"Thanks," Ida replied. "Does the doll need a little more to eat?"

"No, we're good to go. The doll says it's time to sleep."

Via the gate and the dark lane, they returned to their cottage. Ida cajoled the lock. Once inside, they went straight up to the attic. Tentser was not to be found; a mad search ensued; the cat must have spirited himself out the crack of the window; no, no, it was fine; he was in Nadia's sleeping bag.

"Okay," Ida sighed. "You just crawl in with him. I'll get him his meat."

Ida sank down to her sleeping bag and dumped the army pack in front of her. Then, Nadia could see by starlight that Ida was spreading the contents all around. Ida continued to do so for an oddly long time.

"Something wrong?" Nadia asked.

"What the fuck is this?" Ida whispered to herself.

"What's what?" Nadia hissed back.

"This isn't mine," Ida said. For a moment, her voice carried a hint of childlike alarm. "This is…"

Nadia scrambled out of her own sleeping bag and came over. She, too, was surprised to see the collection: desert camouflage clothes, a can of stewed meat, a roll of foreign money, two rolls of toilet paper, a pack of condoms, binoculars, a portable radio, an instant camera, a stack of photos bound by a slim rubber band, an ammunition clip, a handgun, a bayonet.

"Don't touch anything," Nadia warned.

Ida snatched the stack of photos.

"What are you doing?" asked Nadia, who had not looked closely at the pictures. Rather, she had found the weapons disconcerting.

"Going to burn these," Ida said. She was at the attic door. As the door was swollen, she gave the knob a yank, only to have it come off in her hand.

"What's in them?" Nadia wanted to know. She came up to Ida's side and angled for a look at the photos but Ida whipped them into the air, out of Nadia's reach. The edge of the stack brushed a low beam, the jolt caused the frail elastic to burst, and, with a flutter like panicked birds, the pictures scattered across the floorboards. Tentser shot out of Nadia's sleeping bag to attack the black-and-white squares of instant film.

Ida gave up and said, "Have a good look." However, she did kneel by the kitten to put an end to his play-hunting. "Don't eat emulsion. I'm going to get our meat back, as soon as I get out of this room."

Nadia gathered the photos and went to inspect them by the window. They were still partly sorted, having landed in clusters. She found several images of elaborate antennae, strung between trees or even between cliff faces in desolate landscapes, such as alpine lakes and dried-up canyons. These had been at the top of the stack. A greater number of images featured young men in their swimming briefs or army shorts. Some-times, with the army shorts, they wore their boonie hats too. Often, these lads were caught up in roughhousing or horseplay, if they had not simply stopped to pose for a hug or pose with a fishing rod or pose with a machine gun or somesuch. Then, one young man in particular posed naked for a series of shots by window-light in some dusty, con-crete shelter with wire mesh instead of window panes. He had a rather lovely face, slightly trapezoidal, with dimples, dark hair, light eyes and a hauntingly forgiving expression. His dimples were flanked by fluffy bits of facial hair that could almost be called a moustache and beard. Finally, at the bottom of the stack, the photographer had kept a few pictures of Ida, circa 1983—Ida lying shirtless in a field and staring upside-down at the camera, Ida squashing a tick between her thumb and forefinger, Ida grinning and showing off a bronze ring and floral crown that were clearly meant for a bride.

Ida now held the bayonet. She was attempting to force the latch.

"Did you and Johnny get married?" Nadia asked.

"No," Ida replied as she worked the knife between the door and the frame. "We booked an appointment at the wedding palace but we didn't go. The Nation will always remember that we wasted its time." The latch gave way to the blade. All mechanisms fell to the floor as Ida pried open the door. "Now," she said, "pack it all up. One way or another, I plan to get rid of all that tonight and get Tentser his supper."

Bewildered, Nadia began to repack Johnny's portable property. Rather than handle the gun and ammunition clip directly, she wrapped her hand in the quilt, to ward off detectives.

Ida resettled Tentser in a corner, with three matching bottle caps as his playthings. As she and Nadia left, Ida pulled the swollen door shut by way of the hole where the knob had been.

3: Departure

At some point, Nadia lost track of the bayonet. She would later remember that she saw Ida put it in its black rubber scabbard. After that, it was simply part of the night.

Similarly, the photographs became flakes of soot, rising from the sauna's stovepipe.

They ran into Marat in the lane. He was creeping out the gate at Svetlana and Kazimir's place, where he had deposited his black-and-white film processing materials after his endeavour to revolutionize Johnny's artistic technique. He mentioned this right away. He still had his camera around his neck and now an army pack slung on his back. He held a flashlight, which he was careful to point at the ground in order to share the illumination rather than blind anyone.

"How are you two getting on?" Ida asked Marat. She added, "He says he likes you but I know he's a handful."

Marat nodded. "He's anxious," he said. "He discovered that you and he swapped backpacks and everything else flew from his mind."

"Hmm?"

"He seemed too embarrassed about it," Marat went on, "so I'm on this one last mission for him."

"Man, thanks," Ida said as she took her pack off Marat's hands. She pried open one edge of the flap and sniffed inside. "Hmm, yeah. Nadia, have you got…?"

"I, I, I do have…" Nadia faltered.

"Great," said Ida, "let's walk it back to Johnny."

"As you wish," said Marat. He gestured with the flashlight, *I'll lead the way,* and in an awkward triangle they proceeded through the gate, past the darkened cottage, along the garden paths, and onwards.

The scent of smoked meat followed them everywhere.

As they passed the hilltop where the kids had played, they heard the wind cresting in the top branches of the pines.

"…stakeout…" Ida muttered.

Marat, who had already started down the slope towards the broken fence, faltered and scanned the eroded path with his flashlight. "What?" he asked.

"I was just thinking," said Ida, "about the little Kazimirovs doing ambushes and stakeouts. They'd be sheltered here while they wait."

"They would," Nadia agreed.

Ida added, "This must be a good windbreak for the garden too. I guess it must be sunny on that other slope since Kazimir cut down the oaks." She asked Marat, "Do you know whether that stuff about his Mama is true?"

Marat hesitated before answering. "Strictly speaking, I don't know. One does not find it much in albums or diaries, much less museums, yet every family in Ukraine has its stories of famine."

"Hmm."

The rest of the walk passed without chitchat, except between the river and the restless trees. Nadia imagined their conversation.

The river asks, "Do you remember the longboats sailing to Byzantium? Some of your siblings may have been masts."

"No, no, no, we are young," say the trees. "Somewhere an oak might remember, if it has not been put to the chainsaw for the stink it made in the fall these last thousand years."

Nadia's shoe snagged something and she felt a series of weights fall nearby with a *clink-clink-clunk.*

Marat sighed, "He could have left off his alarm." He pulled up a string that had been staked into the earth with a bit of wire. On the other end, a bunch of bottles had been balanced on a log. He tossed the apparatus off the path.

Within earshot, amidst a colony of cherry trees, a light came on in a tent and Johnny stumbled out with a bottle in hand. His boots were loose. His ankle gave way and he sat on a tyre wrapped in a lattice of antenna wire. (Wherever he went, he set up such pieces of all-weather furniture, of his own design.) "Marat," he hissed, "did you get it?"

Marat flicked off his flashlight and they entered Johnny's camp.

"Ida, Nadia," Johnny said as he set down the bottle, pulled up his boots, and straightened his back. Nadia noted that he was drinking the same beer as the hosts had served at the party. He flashed a brief grin, with rough teeth, and he gestured to another piece of furniture—a two-wheeled cart with steel-clad sides, where swooshy letters spelt, "Forward to Victory!"; it looked as if it had escaped from a small-town war museum.

"Johnny, Johnny," Ida said. "You haven't been yourself tonight. Where would you be without your stuff?" She coaxed Nadia, "Give Johnny his stuff."

Nadia held out the pack to Johnny as if it were a bomb that only he knew how to defuse. He answered with a look that said he knew nothing of the kind.

"Drop it in the tent," Johnny told her, "by the radio. Try the radio. You'll like it."

"Okay."

The steel-clad receiver sat in the tent like a fat king under a canopy. *If that had fallen on Papa's head, it would have been fatal.* Overhead, a system of cords and hooks and clips supported a couple of battery-powered pocket lanterns and a small collection of black-and-white prints—presumably recent ones, including cherry trees and the Kiev subway system. The floor was padded with cardboard sheets. Wire baskets, of the kind used for dairy deliveries, held bottles and firewood and rolled-up clothes. A bedroll and mosquito net occupied the back part of the tent, next to the radio.

Outside, Marat was making chitchat about the week ahead at the Arsenal Factory. Ida asked him something about computerization of lens design.

"At Hasselblad…"

"…but here? Are you doing it here?"

"Not in any haste."

The conversation shifted to something Johnny wanted to know.

Nadia took a minute to study the many knobs and toggle switches. She concluded aloud, "I'd want to read the manual for this one—or see its master tune it." She jumped in surprise to find that Ida had crept into the tent behind her. "You're as sneaky as Gramma, sometimes."

"Hmm. Did you check all these photos?"

"Sort of. Nothing worrisome."

Johnny ducked into the tent and Marat also stuck his head past the flap.

"Yeah," said Ida, "you've got your stuff, got freedom on two legs…"

Johnny elbowed his way between Ida and Nadia. He moved his pack from one spot to another, placed his mostly empty beer bottle in a rack, and then flopped out on his bedroll.

Ida continued, "…got your brain in one piece…"

Marat squinted, rubbed phantom shapes from his overworked eyes, and said, "I'll leave you all. I want to head out early in the morning, so let's wish each other well. Johnny, stay safe."

"Marat," said Johnny. He did not qualify this acknowledgement in any way.

Nadia attempted to craft an original wish for Marat. She said, "I hope you always sail above water from now on. You'll see more that way."

Marat nodded. "I hope you find what you want in your studies."

Ida told him, "Go get some sleep. Drive safely."

"Tell Rosya," Marat said, "I should like to take you two to dinner."

"Hmm-hmm."

When Marat left, Johnny switched on his radio. An instant later, a voice-like trill came through, albeit too faintly to reveal its language or even gender. A sound like crashing waves kept covering it up. Johnny attempted to fine-tune it without much success. Meanwhile, he wondered, "Who's Rosya?"

"My roommate," said Ida, "and friend." She looked to Nadia and said, "Let's get back."

"Will you still come see me in the morning?" asked Johnny as he stared at the diodes of the radio.

"No," said Ida.

Johnny looked at Nadia, who did not answer. He lay back, shut off the radio, and muttered, "Okay. Enough said."

"Come on," Ida told Nadia.

"Johnny, take care of yourself," Nadia said.

"You bet," he replied.

Ida pulled back the tent flap and nudged Nadia out. Silently, they trudged away. Nadia looked towards the river, as she wondered whether they were near the eyot. Anyway, she could not see it in the darkness. She reached to squeeze Ida's hand and felt the weathered glass ring there.

Now, Nadia thought, *it's the last day of August. Somehow it feels like the last summer on Earth. My mind is already a year ahead, packing itself up for the mud and snow and giant libraries of Moscow, as if nothing else can happen, as if the nephew-foetus cannot be born, as if the kitten cannot become a prowling tom, as if I will never again love the person beside me. There are thickets of books in my mind. There are wrynecks and Geiger counters, speaking to the mute and masked masses of mankind.*

"Ida!" Johnny called.

Ida and Nadia turned around. Johnny was holding the tent flap and staring up at Ida or the constellations or something as he squatted there, in his little bubble of battery-powered light, on the edge of night.

"Hmm, what?" Ida asked.

Johnny's other hand was being shy; he held it in the small of his back. Then, with a sharp breath as if he were preparing for a dive into depths unknown, he showed his hand and stuck the handgun's barrel in his mouth.

Nadia shouted. As if possessed, she shouted words with no plan, words with no heralding voice in her mind. She found herself skidding to her knees to plead the case of Johnny before the judge of Johnny, all while fearing to touch him lest he explode.

Ida strode towards them and barked, "No! Not to me! Do I deserve this? Am I supposed to mourn your brains splattered on your rubbers and dollars and radio? One look and they'll lock me up. Hand it over. Hand it over!"

Sobbing, Johnny spat out the gun and surrendered it to Ida. "I..." he blubbered. "I love you."

"You don't!" she screamed in his face.

He gasped a little more and squeezed Nadia's hand and then managed to bring his tears under control. "No," he said to Ida. "No, I'm sorry."

Marat came running. His camera and neck strap swung and twisted like a seasick pendulum and chain. He came close enough that he might speak softly and be heard. "What's the matter?" he wondered. Then, he backed away a couple of steps as Ida half-turned with a swing of her arm.

"Johnny wanted to shoot himself," Nadia replied, "with that gun."

Johnny gave faint confirmation: "I guess I did." He released his grip on Nadia's hand and wiped his eyes on his sleeve.

Marat reached out as if to shake hands with Ida. "May I have that?" he asked.

"Not now," said Ida softly. She held the gun off to her side.

"Alright," said Marat. Perhaps unconsciously, he echoed Ida's tone.

Johnny gestured hazily at Ida and the gun. "Take it away," he said. "Take…" He looked back into the tent, even as Nadia tried to restrain him in a kind of hug, in which gravity gave her the role of an anchor.

"Johnny," Nadia whispered, "Ida doesn't need anything."

Ida echoed, "…doesn't need anything."

"Ida, please," Marat said, "come with me and talk with me. A change of company could do everybody good. When we've talked, I suggest you can decide what to do with that weapon: shoot me or throw it in the river—or both."

"Hmm, okay."

"Nadia," asked Marat, "are you fine here with Johnny?"

"Yes?" *Philosophically, yes. I'm not chicken and I'm not one to change my colours.*

"We're fine," Johnny said. He settled down. Nadia let go of him.

"Indeed," said Marat. He made a managerial sort of hand gesture and began to walk away. Ida followed a couple of paces behind and soon they disappeared, somewhere along the shadowy path between woods and river.

Nadia brushed dirt from her skinned knees. Johnny offered her a quarter-full bottle of beer to empty over the scrapes.

Such gallantry.

"Want to come back in the tent?" Johnny asked. "More radio?"

"No. I'd rather sit under the cherry trees," Nadia said, "and look at the Moon and clouds."

"Binoculars?"

"No." *We'd find no swimmers now, I hope.*

After a last glance inside his tent, Johnny left his treasures and devices there and followed Nadia along the path of his feed line to the antenna-bearing trees. He and she sat amongst the roots and put their backs against a fat, gnarled trunk and faced the silver traces of the current.

We can just sit here like cats, saying nothing. I've never heard of a suicide in a group of sitting cats, so perhaps they are a good example to us.

"I'm sick of running," Johnny muttered at last.

Nadia told him, "You'd have an easier time of it without a communications receiver and a hundred metres of wire."

Johnny wheezed. "No," he said, "it helps me bear it. One good thing about the nights is the reception."

"You can thank the ionosphere for that."

"I build it these shrines." Johnny gestured at the wire in the trees.

"Yes," said Nadia, "I'm perhaps the greatest admirer of your work..." *...or else the sorriest scholar of your life.*

A drizzling wind was rising off the river.

Johnny's mouth twisted. For a second, a funny question took shape on his lips before he gave it breath: "Do you feel, like in a nightmare, that all our suffering is a form of mockery?"

Nadia hugged her knees, crossed her feet, rocked slightly, and watched Johnny as she might watch a horrifying reel of documentary footage—the sinking of a ship, with all souls racing to scale the prow. *Now play it in reverse, play all History in reverse, and the ships spout out of the sea, Gagarin descends in his rocket, Gramma stuffs horses back in the womb, the prisoners seam up the scarred mountains with gold, and early Man jumps into the trees to return the fruit to the bough.* She replied, "Yes, I suppose I do."

The rain flew in their eyes, harder now, and made the canopy of cherry leaves sound like beating wings.

"Tut, tut, it looks like cats and dogs are pissing down." This was his best impression of English chitchat. He stuck out his tongue to catch some drops, though his beard was doing so already.

She said, "Tell me about the suffering."

Johnny licked his cracked lips. "I'll tell you about the mockery," he offered instead. "I was sent to Afghanistan and it didn't improve me. I stole money from some crooks and deserted the Army."

This news was like swallowing ice. Still, Nadia repeated, "Tell me."

Johnny considered it. "When I was walking, I imagined telling someone but I didn't think you."

"Then imagine I'm whoever—Ida or whoever."

"I meant to stop troubling Ida."

"I remember when you troubled to stop her from drowning."

Johnny ignored this offer of righteousness—or whatever kind of offer it was. "Every army," he said, "has crooks and some of the crooks in one army meet some of the crooks in another. An American guy, Special Forces, complimented my English, said I talked like the BBC World. He was the man with the endless cash." Johnny snotted as the copious rain entered his nose. "I want to find a place to smoke," he coughed.

"Let's wait for them to get back," Nadia said, "and we'll head for the cottage."

"I won't leave my radio."

"No, alright, let's gather the antenna." *When asked, I'll give this whole conversation as an example of my good counsel.*

Johnny went from tree to tree, using the knots and crotches as footholds, and with his head and hands amidst the high branches, he disentangled the wire bit by bit to chuck it down to Nadia. He told her to get a pocket lamp from his tent and she held it for him as if to sweep the sky for bombers. The downpour stung his cheeks. He began to rush and swore at anything, possibly at the trees, which did not even have cussable anatomy.

On one of the sobbing gusts of wind, another sound rose to the surface, a sound like a hammer on metal—and then a second one like it.

Nadia's hand jerked and, by this fault of hers, the beam of light struck Johnny's eyes, he tried to shield himself, and, on the rain-slick footing, he lost his balance and fell from the cherry tree like a shot bird. At the climax of his plunge, his foot got tangled in the antenna wire and, for a split-second, he was hanged upside down, spinning, until a scaffold branch broke and he twisted to land sideways on a rock. The branch crashed down on top of him.

"Johnny!" Nadia shouted as she knelt over a splintered mess that smelt of cherries. She searched the pile by flashlight to check whether it contained all Johnny's parts, including his soul.

He began to moan, "Ah, ah!" and then reproached her: "Stop blinding me!"

"Sorry, I'm sorry!" She set the pocket lamp on the ground and helped him shift the branch off his arm.

Johnny sucked air through his ragged teeth with an unintended whistle.

"What was that bang?" Nadia asked.

"Not a gun," Johnny groaned.

"Oh." Nadia picked up the light and scanned the river. She found nothing but a shifting impression of dangerous water.

"Put it out," Johnny whispered.

She did. *Stupid Nadia,* she told herself. *I'd make a poor soldier indeed.*

They listened for a minute, in darkness and in wet. The hammering sound came no more.

"Something blew over," Johnny supposed. He changed the topic. "My ankle is bad."

"Sit up for me," Nadia said.

Johnny rolled upright and whimpered as he held both hands to his side, where he had fallen. He eyed his ankle tearfully as he attempted to flex it.

"Do you want the boot off?" Nadia asked. Already, it had twisted and come loose in his fall.

"No." Johnny pulled the boot back into place. The effort stoked the pain in his arm, side, and ankle and sent a hot spasm into his heart, even as the rain pelted his face.

"You've done one better than Ivan Ilyich," Nadia remarked.

"Gerasim, hold my legs up," Johnny whispered with a hint of an agonized laugh. He added, "Don't really. Help me to my tent."

Nadia struggled to find a good way to prop up a man who might have cracked a rib on one side and an arm and ankle on the other. She settled on the idea of leaning into the good ribs, sticking her head in his armpit, and holding his back and stomach as they shuffled along. Like this, they managed to reach the tent and duck inside. The rain seemed even louder there.

Nadia flicked on the pocket lanterns—an illusory comfort.

"I'm still not leaving this radio," Johnny asserted as he sank beside it and spread his hand atop it. He rested one hip on the cardboard floor and looked up in an oddly classical pose, like a martyr.

Am I cruel to wonder whether part of this suffering is play-acting?

Nadia knelt by the tent flap and reeled in the antenna with sharp tugs that snapped the remaining twigs in its grasp.

Another flashlight beam bobbed into sight and it began to scan the moving wire. Marat's voice filtered past the rain: "...and now a cat's favourite game."

Suddenly, Ida stuck her head inside the tent flap. Her hair was flat from the rain and her eyes looked wild. After a second, she asked Johnny, "Did Nadia beat you up?"

Johnny replied, "She made me fall from a tree."

"Clever of her."

Nadia explained the accident and insisted that they take Johnny to the cottage.

By this time, Marat was listening too. He was squatting behind Ida and wiping his nose and moustache and checking that his lens caps were tight. He was first to agree, Johnny had to be moved to shelter.

"Marat," Johnny interjected into this conversation about himself, "can you carry my radio?"

"I should consider it an honour."

"Nadia," Johnny continued, "you take the antenna." (She was already coiling the wire—one of her jobs of old.)

"Hmm," said Ida, "so I get to carry the Prince."

Nadia took the backpack full of meat and Marat took the one with the money. There would be no more confusion of the two.

They decided to take the long route back. Johnny said he could bear the pain.

Nadia, having one free hand, was restored to the post of torchbearer. She looked out for the wharf and rowboats. The rain pattered miserably on the lily pads. The willow branches flailed in the wind.

After they left the riverside, the swampy field flooded Marat's, Ida's, and Nadia's shoes. Marat was bogging down under the radio's weight.

At the chess camp, Comrade Chessmaster was working the pump. *Perhaps,* Nadia imagined, *he goes out for a nighttime walk and then he showers. Perhaps he has baby lemon trees in need of constant nursing.*

Seeing the oncoming horde, Comrade Chessmaster stepped into deeper shadows behind a low, gnarled oak branch. Nadia strobed her light at his peering eyes and he fled inside his castle.

"Do you need help?" Johnny called after the stranger. "These people only want to help! … Who was that?" he asked as Ida hustled him along.

"A local figure," Marat replied from the rear of the procession. He added abruptly, "Do you have an 'Off' switch like your radio?"

Johnny sucked his lips and seemed to take this admonishment to heart.

They trudged up the lane, between fences and fences that funnelled the wind into a gale at their backs. One moment, it made them feel weightless; the next, it nearly flung them face-down like cards from a dealer's hand. As they reached Pyotr's gate, the flashlight revealed the dismal sight of the wind chimes, in two broken strands, lying silent and bent in a mud-puddle.

The black fence wobbled, thumped, and chattered in the storm. Here and there, it bore bright gouges where the chimes had struck on their descent to Earth.

"Shit," said Marat as he mourned the loss of a knickknack so dear to his father. "Mama made that for him."

Nadia offered comfort: "Maybe you can fix it."

Ida slung Johnny's good arm over the flagpole and let him slump against the fence. He eyed her profile as she worked to unlock the gate. Nadia pointed the pocket lamp at the lock and it cast some light back on Ida's face while leaving the rest of her silhouetted, from Johnny's perspective.

A part of him reckoned he had lost a good thing. On the other hand, a lot had happened, he was pretty much done counting the losses, and he believed that in a few centuries, everyone else might be done too.

Nadia doubted whether Marat had heard her, so she leaned back and repeated her message upwind of his ear: "Maybe you can fix it." Still, he did not reply.

They got past the gate. Runoff from the compost boxes had stirred up the smell of pumpkin again. Nadia also detected a whiff of diesel fuel but she put this out of mind for the time being.

Once they were all inside, Marat set down the radio atop the stack of newspapers and he heaved a ragged sigh. Nadia unshouldered the roll of antenna wire to go with it.

Ida was already helping Johnny onwards to the chair. Before sitting, he braced himself against the wall, got out his lighter, and lit the kerosine lamp for a view of Gagarin's grin.

"Ida," Johnny asked as he gripped the window sill and hopped backwards into a sitting position, "do you want a smoke?"

"…want a smoke?" Ida echoed. She wiped rain from her face.

Tentser began to howl. Ida left Johnny and went upstairs.

Johnny gazed down the hall at Nadia and shrugged.

Nadia tapped Marat, who was standing limp-armed like a doll. "Look after him, okay?" she said. "Ida and I need a minute."

He nodded.

She ducked into the sunroom to gather dry clothes and then took these and the food bag up to the attic. Soon, she and Ida and Tentser were reunited in the relative privacy behind the closed (but knobless) pink door. Ida had brought a lamp from the stairwell and hung it from a hook on a beam. Farther overhead, the rain fell on the roof's iron shingles with a rhythmic rattle like a train. Tentser wanted to show them his bottle caps. Tragically, they had become wedged in awkward cracks where the floorboards did not quite meet the angled beams. The hands retrieved the bottle caps and served him sausage and potato on a bed of newspaper. Though he spat out bits of newspaper, he did his utmost to wolf the sausage and potato. As he ate, Ida curled up in a corner near him and rested her head on a beam. Nadia sat cross-legged, with her toes towards Tentser on one side and Ida on the other.

"You got rid of the gun?" Nadia asked.

"Hmm, it went blub," Ida said. Her eyes were shut.

"What about the knife?"

"Knife?" Ida murmured.

Nadia decided, for the moment, to let it be. "You should eat too," she insisted. "You're not eating enough for somebody who doesn't really sleep."

Ida opened her eyes partway, leaned across the floor, and, with out-stretched fingers, picked some sausage and potato from the untouched end of Tentser's meal. She leaned back, shut her eyes again, slowly munched, and nodded. "Alright," she said.

Nadia put dry clothes in Ida's lap and said, "Get changed."

Ida nodded again and waited for Nadia to retreat to the far corner. They both changed. Afterwards, Ida dragged her sleeping bag to her corner and stuffed her bundle of wet clothes underneath it as a pillow. She lay on her back.

Nadia came over again and patted the cat and also patted Ida's hair.

Ida whispered something inaudible. She squeezed her eyelids tight, gave a sigh between clenched teeth, and stuck her hand under her collar to rub her shoulder and armpit. A little louder, she whispered, "What the hell do we do?"

These words, Nadia took note, *should be the title of a manifesto for our times.*

"Give me any ideas you've got," Ida insisted.

"You and I can get him to Odessa," Nadia proposed. "Papa and Avel might know how to use his money to smuggle him out on a ship."

"Avel—Giorgi's snitch? The raisin wine guy?"

"Yeah."

"Fuck. That's desperate."

"That's all I've got."

"Yeah, it's … bound to be better than any plan of Johnny's. Can your Papa keep himself well out of the picture?"

"I guess he mostly does."

"Well, don't mention him to Marat."

"Right."

They heard footsteps on the stairs and a whisper at the door.

Ida rolled over and squinted at the knob hole. "Come on in," she said, "it's open."

Marat pushed the door wide, stepped inside, and silently studied the damage as he pushed it shut again. "Am I interrupting?" he asked.

"Not at all," Nadia replied.

"We were just saying," Ida added, "how quiet it is on these country nights."

Marat said, as if in agreement, "Johnny has gone into in a reverie. He told me he wants only to listen to the rain on a proper roof and windows."

"Hmm."

"Bring him up," Nadia suggested. "Tell him it sounds even better up here."

"I will." Marat lingered. He eyed Tentser and Tentser's meal.

"There's enough for you," Ida told him. "I mean, there's more in my bag." She pointed and sneezed.

Tentser jumped and hissed. Nadia picked him up.

Ida rubbed her nose on the back of her hand and finished her speech on the food: "The cherry wood did add."

"How fortunate," said Marat, "to have cherry trees." He came over and, in passing, stooped to scratch the kitten's neck. "Tentser, very pleasant," he said. He nodded at Nadia as she restrained the squirming feline, who was enraptured by the novelty of a camera swinging on a strap. Marat moved along, took off his jacket and camera, and set them against a diagonal brace. He lifted the flap of Ida's backpack, picked a meal, and began to unfold it where he stood.

Ida watched as Marat paced around the attic and ate. He stopped to study the ladder. He set the newspaper, meat, and potato on one of its steps.

"Aren't you going to finish?" Ida asked.

"I am," said Marat, "after I help Johnny up the stairs. To appreciate anything fully, one should leave halfway through and return."

I should be interested to know how this maxim applies to births.

Once more, Ida seemed to doze.

Nadia suggested, "Tell Johnny you're taking his radio to the world's biggest attic to string the antenna. He might make the stairs on his own."

"You know," said Marat, "it seemed bigger when we were children. I had blackout curtains on the window and I hung photos from these beams to dry. Fenya redecorated after I went away to university."

Ida kicked Nadia in the back and said, "Rosya and I won't redecorate."

"No. Good."

"Your sister will for the baby."

"Yes."

"You can write to let me know whether your Gramma has redecorated but I'd guess no; Yuly neither."

"No."

Marat nodded at them and left.

Ida adjusted the bundle of clothes under her sleeping bag and she curled up to stare at the door. Defiantly sticky, it still managed to cling to its frame. "A lot of doors I've seen," she said.

"A lot you've gone through," Nadia observed.

"Hmm." Ida squeezed her eyes shut and held back a yawn, which brought tears. She whispered a plan. "If I can get a couple hours' sleep, I can drive. We can be in Odessa by lunchtime, maybe send Johnny to this Avel and go see what your Mama is cooking. She and I can catch up and you can go for a walk with your Papa and ask his help. We can stay for dinner and the night and then early, early Monday morning, we come back this way and do the dairy run. Monday night, we're in Kiev when Johnny is hopping a ship. We tell everybody we decided to pay your parents a surprise visit before you go back North. True story.

"Besides," Ida finished, "it means Tentser can see your Papa."

"Makes sense…" Nadia agreed …*inasmuch as nightmares and secrets do make sense…* "…but I have no idea how to find Avel."

This unexpected blank in the geography made Ida pause. She concluded, "Johnny will have to wait somewhere and your Papa will send Avel to him."

"The Potemkin Stairs," Nadia suggested. As soon as she spoke, she suspected her psyche of sleepwalking. She was placing Avel at the Stairs only because he had been there in Nastya and Giorgi's wedding photos. *Why not reuse the scene where our troubles start afresh? If worse comes to worse, we can re-enlist the sandwich-and-cigarette girl from Papa's work: be one more body once more.*

"Sure," Ida hesitated, "only…"

"Only…?"

"Aren't they the giant stairs in the musical…"

"Silent movie, *Battleship Potemkin*."

"…where the soldiers shoot everybody…"

"Right."

"…and the baby carriage rolls down, down, down…?"

"Right."

"Hmm, only…"

"Yes?"

"Well, I was thinking…"

"Yes?"

"What if Johnny can't make it up and down the stairs?"

"There's an escalator next to them."

"Okay. They must have added that after the film."

"Maybe fifty years after."

Ida frowned at the roof. The chronology of cinema had fallen apart for her. She said, "At the boarding school, they made out it was new."

Something went *thump* on the attic stairs.

"Careful!" Johnny snapped.

Marat said something haughtily apologetic.

Ida asked, "The *Musketeers*, it was new?"

"Of recent vintage, when the four of us saw it."

"Hmm, okay."

Nadia added, "Nastya warned me off it when it first came out. Too sexy."

"I liked the Spanish lady," Ida said, "when she prayed to Mary and sang that song about her dagger. I prayed to Mary a bunch after that but it wasn't the same without a dagger."

" 'The truth is a sharp knife,' " Nadia quoted.

"Hmm," said Ida as Johnny stumbled through the door. He gazed all around the room and then he hobbled to the ladder to rest a knee on a step.

"That's Marat's food there," Nadia mentioned.

Johnny glanced at it and shrugged his one good shoulder. "Who's that?" he asked about a hidden creature who was rustling newspapers in a basket.

Nadia described the origins of Tentser/Cosmos.

"He gets around," Johnny noted. The cat peeped above the rim of the basket. "I like his story. Marat? Marat?"

Marat, bent like an overbearing bough, rose up from the stairway and lugged the radio across the threshold of the attic. The hundred metres of rolled-up antenna wire hung from the crook of his arm. Nadia was on hand to shove the door shut behind him.

Tentser had already scurried halfway across the attic by the time the exit was decisively denied to him. Suddenly, he converted his escape attempt into a leap and a scramble, which took him to the top of the ladder. Johnny reached up to pat him but got a scratch across the knuckles in reply.

"*Tsst.* Tough kid," Johnny said.

A pair of long, metal objects clinked in Marat's pocket as he trudged towards the ladder. He set down the radio, dropped the antenna coil atop it, and considered his labours done. Johnny ignored the offerings at his feet, for he was busy wiggling his bleeding fingers at the cat. "You did that," Johnny told the kitten. "You! You'd do it again but I've got your number now."

Marat sighed. He picked up his food and, in the process, almost got a scratch of his own. Then, he went to sit beside the beam where he had left his jacket. From his trouser pocket, he drew a knife and fork, which he set on either side of his dinner, on the newspaper. From his jacket, he dug out his lenses, lined them up, and began to clean. Occasionally, he stopped for a bite; in between bites, he licked his moustache.

Nadia watched and wondered, *Should I say something about the mice?*

Ida lay inert, on her back, with her hands folded across her breasts as if in prayer.

Tentser earned another scolding: "Bandit!"

"Ida's sleeping," Nadia whispered to Johnny. "Stay there." She padded across the floorboards to retrieve Yuly's sovereign green stuff from her pack. Coming back to Johnny, she took hold of his hand. He had been sucking his knuckles. He looked down at the floor. She applied the drops.

"Don't get a taste for nursing," Johnny warned her. "You might get addicted."

"Shh. Be quiet and I'll string you an antenna."

Johnny went silent and indicated with a wag of his scruffy chin and his weary eyes, *Go on, then, get it up.*

Treading lightly, Nadia made the rounds of the attic and wrapped the wire in squarish spirals around the crossbeams. They were low enough that even she could easily flick the wire's end overtop and pull it tight from below. This was slow going, though. *I hope we all give Ida time to sleep, perchance to dream.* Marat had time to second-guess his cleaning job and start over. Johnny continued to lean on the ladder and stare Tentser in the eyes.

When Nadia was done hanging the antenna, she followed Johnny's directions on connecting it to the appropriate terminal post on the radio. Then, she flipped a switch to invite other sounds to join the beat of the rain.

A woman's voice, in Japanese, jumped from the radio with a breathy sort of empathy for mankind and the cherry trees. At least, that was Nadia's best guess as to her theme. No one in the attic knew a word of Japanese.

"I had it tuned to NHK World," Johnny said, "but you can change it to whatever you want."

Nadia slowly rolled the dials, like wheels of some cosmic chariot, and the peoples of the world faded in and out. So did the squeaking and warbling of strange machines that existed to speak to each other in code. Music, from classical to electro, filled some of the other pigeon holes in the vast and mostly vacant system. She stopped to listen to a song that was (the host said) from his favourite new album of the week. A choral track in an African language wove its way around saxophones and an offbeat, wistful lead in American English: "People say she's crazy, / She got diamonds on the soles of her shoes. / Well, that's one way to lose these / Walking blues..."

Johnny closed his eyes and bowed his head before Tentser, who tentatively pressed his paw against the back of Johnny's skull but then decided to remain atop the ladder instead.

Nadia went to sit between Ida's feet and Marat's lenses. She, too, shut her eyes and listened to the music programme.

The host said it was controversial that the singer had gone to South Africa to record the album. Marat added some remarks of his own about Apartheid and the exploitation of Man by Man.

"Yes..." Nadia agreed as she fell asleep.

"How long can it last?" Marat may or may not have asked. "Can this civilization of ours go on another millennium, another two or even four, building its space stations the way that Egypt built the Pyramids, as our numbers grow to the tens of billions and we bend, we break the bones of Man, bones of Earth, bones of the Cosmos, Atom, Genome towards we-know-not what end?"

"No..." Nadia asserted. "They'll build..."

Ida was kicking her when she awoke. Marat had gathered his clean lenses and gone over to photograph Johnny and Tentser. The kitten was on Johnny's shoulder. The tormented yet perpetually amused young man seemed to have become fused to the ladder, as if he heard a joke just before an omnipotent bastard turned him to a pillar of salt.

"I'm going to check the truck," Ida told Nadia.

"I'll come with you," Nadia said.

"No, get yourself ready. Get your map book and memorize the way. I might need help. I've never actually driven at night."

"Right."

"I'm going to check the truck's fridge," Ida announced for all to hear.

Tentser jumped to the floor, meowed, waved his tail this way and that, and pranced towards the door.

"While Ida does that," Marat suggested to Nadia, "let's you and I get Johnny lying down in the corner."

Before vacating the spot in question, Ida grabbed the wet bundle from under her sleeping bag. "These can go out," she muttered. "Johnny doesn't need my clothes."

Johnny shrugged as he continued to lean on the ladder. His gaze followed Ida's backside as she walked past.

"Not now," Ida whispered to Tentser. She lifted him away from the door and plopped him back on the window sill.

Johnny told Marat, "I'm used to being on my feet..."

Marat finished, "...or foot as the case may be. Come." He was done with Johnny as a model and wanted to grant him rest.

Ida left without another word or glance for anyone.

Marat and Nadia escorted the limping nomad of the airwaves to his repose.

Johnny lay on his good side, peering towards the eaves. He discovered Tentser's bottle caps and began to nudge them slowly, lightly, back and forth. The crinkly edges made scraping sounds, like fingernails. The cat came prancing back.

Marat returned to the radio and knelt by it to gaze into its face. The music had faded to almost nothing—sleepy waves of slightly melodic static. He seemed puzzled by the array of knobs and switches for various filters. With his eyes, he beckoned to Nadia, *Come enlighten me, would you?*

Nadia came over to kneel alongside him. *We must look like a pair of Persian figures in a storybook.* Bowing towards the box of wonders, she worked the controls and managed to cut off some of the higher-frequency noise, leaving a slightly clearer but jug-bellied tune.

"You'll move him tonight, will you?" Marat whispered.

Nadia nodded.

"That's for the best," Marat agreed. "Put him as far as you can from my sister and your brother-in-law and don't tell me where. He's better off if nobody can follow him."

Who sees much, trusts little, Nadia supposed.

"Nadia," Johnny asked as he and the cat moved the three bottle caps, "do you know the rules of this game?"

Now this one, does he see much? Does he see little? She came over to survey the ever-morphing triangle. "Well, I know enough to see you're losing," she informed Johnny. "Your every move is a joke. Next to him, you're a monkey."

Johnny palmed one of the bottle caps and raised his fist elusively high in the air. Tentser stared up at it as if at the Moon, if the Moon had green spots.

"That's cheating," Nadia ruled.

"Baa, baa!" Johnny bleated at her. "Baa!"

Tentser's pupils went wide.

I wonder how Nastya's baby will compare to these two.

Johnny put his hands behind his back, then showed Tentser his empty palms, and finally made the bottle cap appear from behind the cat's ear. He rolled it between his fingers, rotating it like a Greek shield with a patterned rim to dazzle the adversary. Then, in a flurry, the cap clattered to the floor and Johnny withdrew his hand just in time to avoid another scratch.

"I have some reading to do," Nadia said. She sat near the players but on the opposite side of a beam, with her back to them, as she dug out her map book from her pack.

Marat had gone to the window to look down into the yard. Ida, with a flashlight, was walking around the truck in an outward spiral. She knelt, touched the earth, and smelt her hand.

Nadia glanced between her map and Marat. His face gave no clue as to whether Ida might be napping in the dairy truck or preparing to fly it to the Moon.

"Shit," Marat whispered as he edged away from the window. "Sveta is watching."

"Did she see you?" Nadia hissed.

"I'm sure she did. She had one of her perturbed looks."

"Any chance she saw Johnny?"

Johnny glanced up from his corner, yet he stroked Tentser's neck and continued to shuffle Tentser's bottle caps.

"Not from her angle," Marat replied. He chanced another peek. "Now she's out with an umbrella. She's coming."

May she blow away in the lane! Nadia thought, almost in prayer.

"I'll head her off," said Marat. He was on his way out the splintered door. On the stairs, his shoes clattered with a workaday sound: *I'm late, I'm late....*

Johnny remarked, "He'd wear himself out on the road." He lay back and looked for leaks in the roof and studied the structure of the crossbeams, like ribs of the Cosmos. Perhaps he imagined ways to design new antennae. "What I always liked about you," he told Nadia as she sweated and studied the roadmap, "is how you're waiting to be what you'll be. Chasing things makes people bad. You pass the time very well, by reading and listening and making jokes."

How flattering. That's what I'll propose to do at uni—or in a camp, with the engineers of Chernobyl. She looked over her shoulder at Johnny.

From his quilted jacket, Johnny dug out a block of something wrapped in waxed paper and foil. At first, Nadia mistook the contents for crumbling chunks of chocolate. Then, Johnny mushed a bit of it between his fingers as if it were a sugary dough. With his other hand, he got out a black cigarette case that bore a medal for long service in the KGB. He adroitly unpacked the case. He spread the sandy, sticky stuff on paper, mixed it with flakes of tobacco, rolled it tight, and licked the final edge to seal it.

"What are you doing?" Nadia asked. She put down her map book and stood up to face her old friend.

"Oh," Johnny muttered as he gestured vaguely at Nadia with the joint, "I'm smoking this now. The Afghans have been doing it since there were Afghans—a bit like … I don't know, rugs. Did you know, they have kids making rugs and it's like kids drawing pictures, they draw whatever gets into their heads, so they have kids putting Kalashnikovs and hand grenades and helicopters and personnel carriers and opium poppies on rugs and they do the bombers like birds with little beaks. Some guys buy those rugs for souvenirs and maybe they even feel good about it because it's giving money to the kids. I mean … giving money, it's hardly better, it's probably money the guy stole in the first place and it's not as if he'll be around to stop whoever skins the kid."

"Johnny," Nadia endeavoured to reason with him, "don't." She tried to hold his hand, tried to take the joint from him, but he just turned away.

"Can't think of one reason why not," he said.

Tentser was circling the people and rubbing the beams.

Let's start small. Nadia picked stray grains from the floor and said, "You don't know whether it'll hurt the kitten. He's tiny."

Johnny looked over one shoulder at Nadia, looked over the other at Tentser, and hugged himself for a moment as he chewed his lips.

What's this? He's cold, he's wrecked, he's laughing at me? What?

"Have it your way," Johnny sighed. He stood up and started walking along the back wall, as far as possible from the window. He stepped over the ends of the diagonal braces as he went. "I'll have a smoke on the stairs," he said.

Nadia restrained Tentser from following. She scooped him up and

balanced him on her shoulder as she dug into her pack for pencils and
her Lottery Commission notebook. She spent a few minutes charting
routes and tabulating distances, speeds, and times. On and off, she did
this with her eyes closed; she was perhaps more exhausted than she had
ever been. She imagined the potholes that would be unavoidable in the
dark. By and by, she set aside her task, returned Tentser to his ladder-top,
and went to join Johnny on the landing.

As she pulled the door to its sticking place, she coughed on the
smoke that curled upwards from the light of the joint to the light of
the lamp. The smell was dizzy, candied, floral, spacey, like sucking fresh
plums while pouring diesel. Nothing in her memory came close—not
Shipr, not Bulgarian tobacco, not all the bouquets and sweat on May
Day.

Johnny was sitting on the top step. He looked askance at Nadia and
said, "Nastya wouldn't approve."

"No? Of what?" Nadia stepped around Johnny and plopped herself
down two steps below him, where the air was slightly less heady. She
stared up at him and past him, at the lozenge window, which seemed
big compared to his head.

"Of you being here with me," said Johnny. "Of me breaking her
policeman's laws. Of Ida and Tentser not being the Virgin and Child."

"That's unfair, isn't it?"

"He scratched me for no reason."

Nadia sighed and rubbed her forehead. *Enough clowning around.*
"Johnny," she said, "I don't know what happened with you and Ida and
Nastya. Nobody ever told me and it's not as if you're telling me now. I
don't know whether Ida has half forgotten it, on a better day. A lot has
happened in Ida's life. Ida and Nastya do speak to each other. Nastya
gave Ida Tentser…" …*in a manner of speaking…*

"Well, I didn't know that," Johnny huffed. "I didn't get the tele-
gram."

"…and you might also consider," Nadia said, "Nastya wasn't the
one who got Ida pregnant."

"Oh, stop. Your family are fools. Now you want to be told? The
whole thing was an injustice, beginning to end. I never got anyone
pregnant. Ida got raped by some man—raped by some man more than
once, I suspect. I've seen it in Afghanistan. Some men, they don't just
go on a rampage and leave, they want a captive. Ida, a born captive…

That's the shared guilty secret, you know, is captivity, never mind a rampage, can't foresee every rampage, but we damn well all built this dungeon. We all sweep a corner of it or at least sit by a broom and say we're on break. 'Let me find a little wallpaper,' we say, 'and my part could be a palace—if not a palace, a modern facility—and we'll all be okay if I cook for my guests over the holidays.'"

Nadia tried and failed to think of any words while Johnny snubbed out his joint.

He continued, "To be fair, about Ida, let me say, I managed to make matters worse. I told her, she and I could get married and have the kid. My reasons were selfish (utterly selfish) and Ida figured me out, so that idea was short-lived. Nastya drew several wrong conclusions and, I guess, cried to Mama and Papa. You got your share of the fallout, all part of growing up. The End. What are your plans for the holidays?"

"Whatever has happened to us, I don't agree it's the end."

"Afghanistan is."

Nadia asked, "Where are you right now?" Johnny did not respond. She put it to him: " '*Why this is hell, nor am I out of it.*' "

"Yes."

Nadia reached up to put a hand on his shoulder. He pulled away, grabbed his jacket from the bannister, and got up to leave.

"What, just like that?" Nadia demanded more.

Johnny planted his feet and, with full force, swung his jacket against the walls and bannister, over and over. Buttons flew off. Nadia ducked and covered her head. Johnny flung the heap of synthetic fabric on the step next to her and then he went at the rail with his fists. He grimaced and finally sat back down, atop the jacket, with his beaten hands in his armpits.

Nadia touched his shoulder again. He saw that she was trembling a little and he supposed that he had frightened her a great deal but that she was doing her best to hide it out of kindness.

She put her other hand on his knee and said, "I don't think you're 'utterly selfish'."

"You should," he told her. "An Afghan man, a contact, got killed because I was careless. He got killed for having sex with me. He got killed because, me being clever, I have an instant camera and I take pictures."

Nadia moved her hand from his knee to his elbow and, as if automatically, she said, "No one is clever in love, Johnny." She added, "Cruelty sneaks up on lovers."

"Cruelty has no end," Johnny said. "So say the faithful, the believers in eternal Hell. They took pictures when they beheaded him. Somehow, pictures can go back and forth and I daresay copies go to the KGB and CIA and all. There'll be a share of the fallout for me; only, someone must be biding his time and I don't mean Allah, He's an impatient fucker."

Downstairs, the front door banged shut, perhaps in a release of human energy, perhaps in a gust of wind.

"Now, Ida's coming," Nadia said. "Listen to her and we'll get you past today, anyway."

"Sure," Johnny replied. "Yes."

I do hope it's Ida, not Sveta or Fenya or the daughters of Nyx, coming to cut the night's end.

Floorboards creaked and then Ida started upstairs two steps at a time. She stopped halfway, sniffed her hands, and then stared disgustedly at the two figures in the lamplit haze. *You've degraded the memory of smoking.*

"What's wrong with your hands?" Nadia asked.

"Nothing," said Ida. She flexed them. "There's a thief out tonight and I hope he got a mouthful of diesel while he was at it."

Johnny took his hands out of his armpits for a self-inspection. They were scratched, green-spotted, and starting to swell. Even so, it was with renewed curiosity that he asked, "Truck got siphoned?"

"Truck got siphoned. Maybe it was Comrade Chessmaster."

"Comrade who?" asked Johnny.

"The 'local figure'," Nadia told him. "Maybe it wasn't," she added. *What about the kids with the hose? No, this is absurd.* "Whoever it was, it's bad luck."

"Well," said Ida, "he left enough luck in the tank to get us out of here. We'll stop when we see a station."

Johnny said, "Takes ages to siphon a truck dry."

"Where's Marat?" Nadia asked.

"He went with Sveta," Ida said. "She wasn't leaving without him. She said all his prowling was confusing the children."

"Well," said Nadia, "it's time to go. We'll never confuse these cottagers again."

"Hmm."

"I usually leave in the dark," Johnny mentioned.

"Just for this time," said Ida, "you're leaving in the dark with us."

Johnny got up and propped himself against the bannister that had lately borne his beating. He hobbled up a step, peered out the little window towards some star, and declared, "I'll go wherever you say, *insha'Allah*."

4: **Non-honeymoon**

On the rough, dark roads to Odessa, Nadia thought of her people. *Nastya will be listening to the weather of all Ukraine. She will have taken the boombox to bed, in place of Tentser and Giorgi, for the Lieutenant will be typing one last report while he eyes the rocket lamp where the kitten's bite marks lie. The nephew-foetus will be beating an encoded message on his mother's inner walls. Rosya will be rereading a printout of the evening's messages from the professor in Khabarovsk. Gramma will be shaking off the nightmares by disinfecting Cherny's wounds and writing to her old friend, the archivist, who is to put me up for the night when I go for my interviews in Moscow. Yuly, if he has nightmares, will wake from them alone. He has had neither a cat nor a personal letter for forty-five years. He could call his sleepless cousin-by-marriage but he will not, not at this hour. Papa will be snoring. Mama will be restless. Yuri will be cleaning the library.*

Ida and I, we are driving with a cat, who can see in the dark, though we can't. Behind us, we are moving a fugitive in a refrigerator.

Tentser is not pleased with this ride, yet for Johnny it must be worse.

Johnny and Ida are going to Odessa for the first time—a non-honeymoon that we all have prepared for them.

I am gathering nightmares of my own, to relive on Moscow nights, if I ever make it to such a paradise as the university dorm.

Maybe Johnny is right. Chasing things—hunting things—is hardly the best way to discover the best in mankind, the best in the animals, the best in ourselves and the Cosmos.

Ida had confiscated Johnny's cigarette case for the duration of the drive. "You can't smoke back there," she had told him. The case, with the KGB long-service medal, was rattling somewhere under Nadia's seat.

I hope Johnny stays bundled up and doesn't breathe too fast.

At dawn, they stopped by a cornfield. They opened the rear of the truck to replenish its oxygen. Johnny was looking a bit flushed but he assured them it was nothing compared to wearing a chemical protection suit in the desert.

They nibbled on cold sausage and sour cream. After eating, Tentser hesitantly dug a hole in the wet, sandy roadside.

"You don't have to bury it," Ida told him. "They'll be spraying shit all over here when the harvest's done."

Tentser buried it anyway. He felt compelled.

Nadia kept watch over the kitten. She walked behind him as he gadded over to a fencepost to sharpen his claws on the splintering wood.

Ida stared across the field at an imaginary procession of workers and machines, stretching into the mists and mazes of past and future mornings. As of August 31, already, most of the crop had been harvested in its green youth for silage. The dream of corn-fed cattle filling the steppes was an oldie, as dear as men in Space, yet the Khrushchev faithful, unlike Nastya, had been heedless of the weather forecasts at most destinations. Now, no one much trusted this ex-American corn, so, where it was sown at all, it tended to get an early execution date instead of growing sweet for the human mouth.

Johnny circled the truck and hopped up on the sideboard to peer in the windows. "Where's my cigarette case?" he asked.

"Somewhere in that cornfield," Ida replied. "I threw it pretty far."

"What?" He climbed atop the truck to survey the field. (His limbs seemed almost fully better or almost fully numb.)

"She's winding you up," Nadia said. She picked up Tentser, hugged him with one arm, and brushed the dirt off his dangling paws as she returned to the truck. The cat purred and craned his neck to give Johnny a smug look.

"Maybe you could get off the roof," Ida said, "to not be such a target. Give him one smoke—regular—and then we're moving on."

Johnny shivered but complied. He gave Ida a repetition of, "One smoke, regular, moving on!" as he came down, marched towards her, and saluted.

"Boots," Ida said.

"Laces," Johnny shot back, in a game of word association.

"Kitten shit."

"Chem suit."

"Hero."

"Worker."

"Sour cream."

"Kitten shit!" Johnny finished. (To repeat oneself was to concede.)

Nadia came over to present a cigarette that she had hastily rolled. Tentser was howling in his basket in the truck.

"Go on, you fool," Ida scoffed, "smoke up and wipe your boots."

5: Strange Wreckage

The mist burnt off and the roads got better. The landscape seemed to set itself right, a spark of sanity was awake, and Ida and Nadia watched for a gas station. A dairy truck fuelling in daytime should stir no curiosity.

Tentser, after forty-eight hours of overstimulation, finally ran out of adrenaline and conked out in his basket as the search for gas went on.

Nadia had been waiting for a quiet moment of daylight. She steadied her breath and asked, "Do you think Johnny has killed many people?"

"Hmm, not as many as your Gramma…" Ida replied.

…and yet more than Papa, Nadia reminded herself. *Will he take pity on Johnny? Will he take pity on Ida and me, more than Gramma did on him?*

"…but your Gramma," Ida continued, "is a different field of berries. We should be near…"

"…Voznesensk." Nadia had navigated them to a small city that she knew as a rail stop between Kiev and Odessa. This route was not quite the shortest but, she had reasoned, it offered safer opportunities for oxygen breaks and it put them in reach of alternative transport in case the dairy truck or its back passenger could no longer endure.

Some 44,000 souls now lived in Voznesensk because, in Catherine the Great's reign, it had seemed a good place to put a cavalry barracks and a bridge, downstream of the granite-faced rapids in the Southern Bug. For a time, it had been a growing trading post, the kind of place one might seek a second chance after a misfortune elsewhere. Despite the cavalry, many Jews had settled there, becoming a quarter of the population, leaving families who survived one thing and another, until they all died at the hands of the Fascists. Nowadays, the city had a leather factory, a furniture factory, a crane factory, and, of course, a gas station.

The gas station had been undergoing upgrades, even an architectural rebirth—really something to see, if only these dairy truckers had come one day sooner.

As they drove past the low-rise apartments and walled factory yards, along a flat, empty boulevard towards the gas station, they saw what looked like a pair of giant, steel udders upturned in the wreckage of a collapsed crane. The dairy truck pulled into the lot and stopped short of the tangle.

Through her windshield, Ida stared at the dented junk as if at the dried-up seabeds of Mars. "What happened here?" she murmured.

"What is it?" Nadia asked.

"That, Little Paw," said Ida, "is one of the fancy gas stations. They have one in Kiev. Those go up on an arch and they look like flying saucers with tentacles you pull down to fill your tank."

"Oh, right." *Perhaps it is not important right now to mention...* "They look like teats on a pump."

"Hmm. Sometimes I call the truck Baby Calf."

Baby lost Mama, Nadia thought.

Ida rolled down her window to speak with a lone man in overalls who was clearly mourning the loss. He kept holding his thighs and rocking mirthlessly and then running his hand over his head. He was bald down the middle, like Gorbachev, but without the birthmark.

"How about it?" Ida asked.

The man groaned and threw up his hands.

"What relation?" Ida tried again.

"We made the crane," he sighed, "made it down the street, and now I have to answer to the ones in Kiev who sent us these..." He gestured to the extraterrestrial boobs.

Ida's curiosity was not sated. "What did happen to the crane?"

"You know, they're not earthquake-proof!" the bald man snapped.

"Hmm?"

"Last night's earthquake happened to the crane," the man stated. He frowned. "What route do you drive?"

Ask too many questions, Nadia thought, *and you get one back.*

"We're not driving a route," Ida replied. "We're delivering this truck."

"Oh."

Nadia chimed in, "My buddy and I take shifts. Long haul."

Ida glanced at Nadia as if to say, *You're trying too hard, Little Paw.*

"Oh," the man repeated. "The old pumps over there still work but just… If you're going West or South, you may find things worse." He seemed to sink back into his own dilemma after that.

"Maybe no one from Kiev will find out," Ida offered hopefully.

Come on, Ida, enough chitchat, let's go!

"Too late," said the mourner. "There were two Kiev detectives down here an hour ago, checking the trains."

6: Last Dispatch

The next and final oxygen stop was in a patch of daisies and purple loosestrife, in a gap in the windbreak beside a potato field. They were just an hour away from Nadia's parents' house in Odessa.

Ida took Tentser for a tumble in the wildflowers. "You let Johnny out," she told Nadia.

Back there, Nadia found that Johnny had wrapped antenna wire all around the racks of the refrigerator. As fresh air rushed in, he shut off his radio and uncovered his face. He had been wearing the swim towels from the girls' luggage as a headdress and veil.

"Last night," Johnny reported as he wobbled to the threshold, "Romania had the earthquake of the decade. People felt it in Kiev."

"Hear that?" Nadia asked Ida.

"Hmm."

"What else did you pick up?" Nadia wondered.

"There's some cop chatter between here and Kiev," Johnny said. "I didn't catch much of it—crap reception, different lingo. Got a smoke for me?" he asked as he hopped down from the truck. "Hang on," he added. He traipsed off through the wildflowers, past Ida, and went behind the windbreak for a piss.

Ida stared at the sky and covered Tentser's eyes.

On Johnny's way back, Tentser took a swipe at his bootlaces.

Nadia asked, "Any details at all…?"

"What?" Johnny asked as he shook his foot free of the cat.

"…from the police radio?"

"Just one thing," Johnny said as he accepted his ration of one cigarette. "They're looking for a guy named Avel."

7: Devourers of All

On the outskirts of Odessa, Johnny got back his freedom and his cigarette case, if such things could be called his.

Nadia had given Ida directions to a deserted park, where sometimes Misha had gone with his daughters and sometimes he had gone alone. This wasteland was no place for a kitten, so Nadia left Tentser in the basket in the truck.

They had stopped at a place where the rutty track circled back on itself, in a clearing at the base of a hill. The slopes were covered in yellow grass and thorny, red runners, spreading from a thicket on the crest. A few young maple trees competed with the red vines.

Johnny puked in the grass and then sat on a rock to study a map that Nadia had drawn for him. He was to walk (or else hobble) to the Potemkin Stairs.

Nadia promised that the radio would be safe and that Johnny would be reunited with it soon.

Ida was checking the tyres.

Hearing voices, a pack of street dogs loped over the crest of the hill. They stood on the slope impassively and eyed the travellers and truck. There were eight dogs in all—four of each sex, easily distinguishable by either a dangling penis or a pincushion of teats. These animals were, like Coleridge's ancient Mariner, "long, and lank, and brown, / As is the ribbed sea-sand."

Johnny slowly stood up. His injured ankle wobbled beneath him, just enough to be noticeable.

Two of the pack broke away and began to circle wide.

Ida stepped back onto the sideboard.

"Who likes smoked meat?" Nadia called. "Hey?" She clapped her hands over her head and walked towards the rear of the truck. "Hey?" she repeated as she hopped up into the refrigerator and stamped her feet. *Ukraine may make a cossack of me yet.*

The dogs began to scatter and swerve and make feints backwards and forwards. Someone let out a beggarly yelp that she had learnt somewhere.

"Hey? Go get it! Go get it!" Nadia sang from her balcony.

The pack scrambled to chase flying hunks of meat and potato. If fragments of saturated newsprint clung to the food, the mutts (unlike Tentser) were unconcerned. All of it went the same way. *Behold the mortal kin of Anubis, the Dog Who Swallows Millions. Behold the last judge of Egypt and his young cousin, the first wet-nurse of Rome.*

Johnny, with his pack on his shoulders, came over to Nadia for a last request. He said, "Give me one of those and I'll go."

"A talisman for your journey," Nadia said as she handed him the last of the fire-cooked meals. He accepted it with both hands. She reassured him, "We'll see you in a few hours or Papa or Papa's friend will…" *…if all goes well.*

The omega male trampled the grass, found Johnny's puke, and ate it.

Ida was back in the driver's seat. She honked the horn three times to further disperse the dogs and, perhaps, to summon Nadia.

"I'll be at the Stairs," Johnny said.

8: Eggs and Laundry

Ida was worried. "We don't have much for your Mama. Why'd you throw all that good food to the dogs?"

"Instinct…" Nadia replied *…and the sight of Johnny's puke. The smoking of the meat may have been perfect, yet the keeping of it was not.*

"Well, at least we have the eggs," Ida said. "She can use those for baking. She can probably trade half of them for butter and sugar."

"Probably," Nadia agreed. She pointed past the windshield. "Our park. Our tank. Our house. Our garden."

"Don't boast, Little Paw," Ida told her, "and don't point."

"Right, okay."

"Hmm, you do have it nice, though," Ida admitted as she slowed the truck to a duck-dawdle. "I mean, it's cozy, a little house, little playground. This'd be a nice place for a kid."

"Yeah, we came to it a bit late but yeah. Mama and Papa tried hard here…" *…to provide what might be called a decent finish, a decent end to growing up.*

"Maybe it won't be too late for your nephew," Ida supposed. "Maybe he'll have nice, long visits here."

"Maybe you're right," Nadia said. "I guess that'll be up to Nastya."

"Hmm." Ida coaxed the dairy truck around the corner and parked it in front of the garden gate. Afterwards, she groaned and squeezed her eyes shut.

"We made it," Nadia said.

"Just. Okay, okay," Ida murmured. She adjusted her rear view mirror for a look at herself. She patted her pale cheeks, pulled her hair tight into a bun, put on her sunglasses, checked the reflections from various angles, stuck out her tongue at herself, and took the sunglasses off again.

Tentser, who had gone silent on the last leg of the journey, began to mew a plaintive mew. *Let me out, let me out.*

"Yes, we're here," Nadia reiterated. She opened the truck door and stared at her erstwhile home from an unfamiliar height. *This must be how the place looked to Giorgi.*

Ida got out and balanced with one foot on the sideboard and a knee on the hood as she reached to remove both windshield wipers.

Nadia unlatched the garden gate as Ida locked up the truck. Together, the girls and cat came up the path, in the noon light, in an atmosphere of fresh thyme; some of its sprigs had just been picked for lunch.

Katya flung open the door. Misha was just behind her with his hand on her shoulder.

"What's wrong?" Katya asked. "Why are you here?"

"Nothing's wrong. I was missing you," said Nadia, "so Ida said we should come."

"She's lying," Ida interjected. "I was missing you, so Nadia said we should come."

"Oh, oh," Katya faltered, "come in, you two ... three?"

Misha said, "I guess the little guy in the basket was missing me."

"He was," said Nadia.

"Misha, how's your head?" Ida asked.

"Ah, in one piece," Misha replied as he circled the kitchen to make way for everybody. "How's...?"

"My head's okay too. Soup smells great."

"Misha..." Katya attempted to rally him. "Misha, do something with..." She pointed to the basket in Nadia's hands.

"Cosmos, long time..." Misha greeted the kitten.

"Tentser," Ida corrected him. "He's Tentser now. Katya, what's in...?"

"Onion, thyme, baby carrots," Katya listed as she went to tend her latest soup, "vegetable stock, cheese pancakes..."

"...leftover cheese pancakes," Misha said, "from an eggless and sugarless..."

"...from the breakfast you didn't stay to finish."

Look at this match that Grandpa Lev made. He took an interest in sparring indeed.

Nadia handed the basket over to Misha, who asked Katya, "He can go in the girls' room, can he? I'll make sure he..."

"Take in the girls' luggage too," Katya instructed. "Will he damage the luggage? Are you staying? Are you staying?"

"I hope so," said Ida.

Tentser clawed at the wicker and squealed as Misha carried him away.

"What is it?" Misha asked. "Are you finding it all too different from your towers in Kiev? Oh, oh, you've got your claw stuck..."

Nadia slipped away to the toilet.

"Dearest, are you alright?" Katya asked through the door.

"Fine!"

Ida began to explain, "...ate some apple cake that didn't agree...," but, just as fast, she made an exit. "Truck's locked. I'm coming."

Through the ventilation pipe, Nadia could hear sombre tones of disagreement over ways to park and unload a truck. Here were two people who had definite and particular views on matters of transportation.

For a few seconds, toiletries on the sink and shelves jittered like wind-up toys. Through glass and porcelain, the aftershock made itself heard.

Poor Johnny, thought Nadia, *he might not make it to the rendezvous at all if his courage and digestion fail.*

When Nadia returned to the kitchen, she saw two windshield wipers on top of the fridge. Mama was whispering to herself and stirring the bubbling pot. The front door was wide open. Papa and Ida were in the street, collecting Nadia's dirty laundry, which had spilt from an overstuffed suitcase.

"Oh..." Nadia groaned.

Katya became alert to the situation. "Go set the table," she told her daughter. "Go."

"I should..."

"Go. Make tea." Katya grabbed the laundry basket from a corner near the wet room and she marched out into the street.

"There's a couple of towels in there," Misha said. He picked them up from the refrigerator floor and held them up as if they were unstretched canvases that he hoped to appraise. "Whose boot prints...?"

"Give them here," Katya ordered. "Ida, just repack Nadia's books and put the rest in the basket. There's a good girl."

Nadia went back and forth between the kitchen and family room with a clatter of spoons and a clinking of tea glasses. *All the while, Johnny walks. He was probably walking when that orderly, what's-his-name, Andrei, served tea to Ida and me.* Nadia and Ida crossed paths around the dining table.

"Don't worry, Little Paw, your books were well padded." Ida carried the suitcase into the sisters' bedroom. She lingered there, behind a closed door. "No—not to eat!" she told Tentser.

Presently, everyone but Tentser reconvened in the kitchen. Mama made final additions to the soup's seasoning. Nadia made the tea. Ida sorted the colours from the whites. Misha brought in more luggage and shut the door. "This quilt," he said, "does it go...?"

"...on Ida's bed," Nadia said.

"Nastya's bed, then," Misha said. He delivered it and came back with Tentser on his shoulder. The cat leapt across the kitchen and ran into the wet room to hide behind the washer-dryer. Misha fingered a hind-paw scratch on his neck but did not complain of that. He said, "If you need anything else from the truck, I'll get it later. There was some wire and electronic equipment under the quilt."

"That's for Rosya," Ida said.

"Then you won't need me to bring that in?"

"Nah, leave it."

"Good, it was fucking heavy."

"Was it?" Katya asked. She turned off the burner, moved the soup pot to check for spills underneath, and then moved it back.

"Yes, it was," Misha answered. He rested against the refrigerator and, with lowered eyes, watched Nadia make tea. "You should always fold your clothes when you pack," he whispered to her. "Really, it'd save time..."

"Misha," Katya said, "it all just goes in the wash."

"She'll be expected to show up crisply ironed," Misha pressed his point, "on the morning she's interviewed at Lomonosov University."

"Yes, Papa."

Ida mouthed, *Yes, Papa.* Misha stared at her. She announced, "I'll lock my truck," and then slipped past.

Katya put the lid on the pot, turned around to face Nadia, and said, "I haven't hugged you yet." She made up for it, in force.

Ida came back inside, with something long wrapped in newspaper. Katya let go of her daughter and said, "Ida, I haven't hugged you either."

Ida half-turned to cuddle against Katya on one side and to protect the hidden object on the other. "For you," whispered Ida.

"What?" Katya gasped as the newspaper slid and fell away from the Great Unknown—an egg carton. "Dreams come true!" She gave Ida a final pat on the shoulder and took hold of the carton to show it to Misha. "Well, Misha?" she asked.

"Well… Ida is very thoughtful," Misha replied, "very thoughtful, Ida." He stooped to pick up the newspaper. He set it atop the fridge with the wipers.

"I mean," Katya said, "our future isn't all powdered eggs. You said we could only look forward to powdered eggs, no better than when we were kids."

Misha squinted at his wife. "Didn't you say that?"

"No, Misha, you did. Oh, Ida, you drew flowers on them! You must come see my curtains." The eggs ended up on display on the counter, while Katya led a quiet Ida into the family room.

Misha stayed in the kitchen and stroked Nadia's cheek with the back of his hand as she checked on the steeping tea. He lingered over the fading bruise and recent scratch but let them pass without remark. "You've picked a good day to bring eggs," he told her, "and some lively company."

"Why?"

"Oh, Mama's been a bit lonely. Her aviator is coming to dinner but we were resigned to the prospect of being a boring couple of hosts with a boring menu."

"Never," Nadia said.

"Well," Misha sighed, "you haven't been here when you weren't here. Mama and I can just about manage to show off Nastya's sketches without Nastya but when it comes to your literary recitals…"

"I see the difficulty."

Curious murmurs came from the family room. Nadia half suspected Ida of indulging in animal mimicry.

Misha supposed, "Maybe, in general, we need more guests."

"What sort of guests?"

"Oh, feline are best," Misha opined. He gazed in the direction of the family room and bedrooms and said, "Come with me after lunch. There's someone I want you to meet."

9: Sunday of Aftershocks

Contrary to Nadia's understanding, her father did not intend to take her to meet a cat. Rather, he needed her to speak English to a man.

Misha told Katya he was taking Nadia downtown to see which ships were in harbour. Katya insisted that Nadia take a shower and change before she left the house. There were some old clothes of Nastya's that might fit her.

"Stay away from anything unstable," Katya warned. "Stay away from the Mother-in-Law Bridge."

This local name evoked the wagging, swaying Jeanne Labourbe Bridge, a pedestrian overpass that linked the posh districts on two ridges, overlooking the dockside warehouses below. Like a rocking horse, the steel bridge stood on a cartoonishly slender tetrad of splayed legs. Between these ran a brick-paved span, 130 metres long and nine storeys high, above a boulevard with a good deal of truck traffic. Breezy, diesely, and never at rest, it had a reputation as a place for larkers and neurotics. Come with two friends, jump on it, and feel it wobble. Come alone, jump off it, and never feel again.

Misha visited the Bridge most days, either on his lunch break or after work. He was undeterred by tremors or auguries. Once he and Nadia left the house, he wasted no time in asking, "You're not afraid to take the Mother-in-Law Bridge, are you?"

"No but…" *…I have worse fears and…* "…can we take the Potemkin Stairs?" (The Stairs and then the docks were a short walk from the Bridge.)

"Yes, if you want," Misha replied. "Maybe we'll see some newly-weds."

Nadia rolled up the long sleeves of her borrowed dress—a grey-and-black paisley covering that Nastya had worn to church. *I wish I had cigarettes hidden up here, in honour of my sister's wily side. After meals, she would offer to light one for Papa and, if his case was full, she would palm one while I asked odd questions.*

There was time for a few odd questions as they walked across the park to a bus stop and waited there. No one much was around, on a Sunday of aftershocks, when the steps down to the boardwalk had caved.

Nadia asked, "When did you last see Avel?"

"When?" Misha echoed. "A couple of days ago. Friday, after work."

"How did he seem?"

"He didn't 'seem' anything."

"Oh."

Misha began to smoke. He rubbed the seagull on his cigarette case and then sighed and put it away. "He was headed to Kiev. He said Giorgi's Captain had died and he wanted to attend the funeral."

"Oh, so sudden."

"Well, they buried him quick, if that's what you mean."

"I suppose it is."

"Nastya called yesterday once it was over. She said Giorgi was shaken by it. He had trouble reading his piece."

"Oh." Nadia imagined him typing up multiple eulogy drafts on Friday night, after she and Ida had buried the mice. "How was Nastya?"

"Well, she said Avel cheered her up—sat with her and told the baby's fortune while Giorgi did his ushering and pallbearing. Apparently, our grandson will do well in life if only they name him Daniil."

"The equipment you saw in the truck, it's a radio."

"Okay. And?"

"We were fiddling with it and we got a police channel. We heard there are police from Kiev looking for Avel at train stations."

"Must have forgotten his hat," Misha joked, yet, all of a sudden, he looked as if the sun could not warm him.

A bus pulled up and they got aboard. There was no one else but the driver. Nadia and Misha sat at the back (she by the window) and, as they rode the route, Misha whispered to her about the person he wanted her to meet.

After seeing Avel on Friday, Misha happened to have an abundance of caviar and he went looking for ways to trade it. Mama had already said that Lieutenant Colonel Sokolov was allergic to caviar and became ill at the sight or smell of it. As a child in the Siege of Sevastopol, he had lived on a cache of the stuff and, more recently, when the doctors diagnosed him with anemia, they had prescribed it to him in kilograms, only to discover that the roe had betrayed him.

Anyway, Misha had not meant to talk about Sokolov. The caviar and Misha found interesting company over a case of vodka, a cage of chickens, a sack of sugar, a box of bras, and a tournament of speed chess. There was an American sailor watching. He barely spoke a word, had not even come to play, but as a lark he had run away from his boring handler; such was this man's thirst for a taste of the real thing. This impulse of his was a curse on everybody because the handler and a policeman caught up with him and the cop broke up the game. Others fled but Misha took pity on the foolish foreigner and stayed to negotiate with the cop, whom he knew to be an old drinking buddy of Giorgi's. Sadly, the handler drove a hard bargain for the loss of his virgin principles. All goods were forfeit, yet all souls were free, and (from a peep at the cop's notebook) Misha got the sailor's name, rank, and ship: Gawain Price, Chief Mate of the tramp freighter *Lady Blue Light*. Misha was sure of the man's gratitude, if they could meet again and if Misha had the benefit of a biased interpreter to boost him.

"He could bring a dessert to dinner," Nadia said, "and chat about the sea with our guest of honour."

"That crossed my mind," Misha admitted, "but no."

"No, well, no." *The last time you welcomed a new kind of man at Mama's table, he picked up all the cards and shuffled. By scheme or by blunder, he shuffled us all and shuffled his way into Nastya's bed and then into Chernobyl and out. Well, all this shuffling turned out to be Ida's luck, up to a point. Anyway, if Giorgi and his wine and cop car and roses can work a metamorphosis in months, perhaps I should take hope and believe that a new, new man, with a freighter, might rearrange Johnny's life in a day.*

"Will you help me?" Misha asked. "You aren't ashamed of my ways?"

"I never have been…" *…and now is no time to start.*

Misha nodded and bounced his fists on his knees. The bus thumped over a crack. "Good," he whispered. "You know, a Chief Mate is a good man to know. He oversees the cargo and the rounds. A Captain is too busy to see for himself, what with reports to hear and orders to hand down."

"Maybe I should be a Chief Mate."

"Maybe you should." Misha corrected himself, "No. You should be a leading lady. Mama tells me that Lomonosov has a famous Students' Theatre."

"Yes." *Let us have a recital.* "I believe Gramma's friend, the archivist, studied Fine and Performing Arts there."

"Don't let that discourage you."

Through the grimy window, Nadia stared at the sunlit sea. She tried to picture the life of this woman who, as a favour, had kept Grandpa Pasha's file open since Stalin's time. Nadia mentioned, "I'm to stay overnight with her, when I go for my interviews."

Misha said, "I met her when I was a kid. I always thought she knew for a fact that my Papa was dead."

"Oh."

"Yeah, some friend."

"Papa," Nadia asked in a low whisper, "would you blame me, if I took a very great risk to help a friend—a friend on the wrong side of everything?"

Misha turned her chin to see that she was holding back tears. "What?" he asked. "What, is this about Ida?"

Nadia shook her head.

Misha inferred, "You're exhausted, everything seems worse."

"No, everything really is bad."

"Then no need to think you'll find the right side of anything. I daresay my Papa didn't but he did love Gramma and you and I are here."

"He's not."

"No, he isn't, but we're different people in different times."

"He went to war and you went to war…"

"I wouldn't say 'war' in my case."

"…and now my friend has been to war and his way out has been no way out at all. War isn't about coming home and home, for some people, isn't about much at all."

"Shh, now. You can tell me more when we walk."

10: Confession

Looking down the Potemkin Stairs, one could see only landings; looking up, only steps.

Johnny was sitting on one of the granite blocks at the edge of the steps, with only his head and neck visible to his descending rescuers. A maple tree, just beginning to turn rusty, cast its shadow over him.

A seagull might have seen everything more clearly. Nadia and Misha approached, exchanged a few words with him, and moved along. He soon followed and, after reaching the bottom, he strolled parallel to a concrete wall. On the other side, birds perched on the railway masts and cargo cranes. Johnny came to a place where the barrier wall was interrupted by a red brick warehouse. A high-up window had been removed for masonry repairs. A ladder lay on the sidewalk. He set it up and climbed in.

Misha was waiting to catch Johnny as he lowered himself from the window ledge, into the dank warehouse. The ceiling dripped, with a faint echo that scurried from place to place. There were steel shelves, crates, bits of garbage, and workbenches for packing and unpacking stuff and typing out forms. At the far end was a gate out to the dockyard.

Nadia found a stack of chairs, got one for Johnny, helped him get his boots off, and suggested he put his swollen ankles up on a bench.

Misha, like a believer, spoke of a plan for Johnny.

Johnny listened and pensively scratched beneath his socks. He handed over the bag of money that was requisite to the plan, yet something, apart from the present predicament, sat ill with him. "Misha," he interrupted, "I want to confess, I once stole from you."

"What did you steal?"

"A measuring tape."

Misha spread his hands like bookends on an empty shelf. He asked, "Did it do you much good?"

"Not in the long run."

"No," Misha said, "so sit tight here and don't steal anymore. You don't have the patience to fake the forms and ledgers."

Johnny nodded.

"Come now," Misha told his daughter, "it's your part."

11: Translation Work

The freighters, in so many bright and dirtied colours, dallied and bustled in the presence of the great cranes.

"I'll show my ruby brooch," Misha said, "and you speak English." (He meant to show his employee ID badge to the *Lady Blue Light*'s watchmen.)

Their request to board, to meet the Chief Mate, met with confusion, followed by whispers between shipmates.

"There's some bookkeeper and his daughter want to see Pricey."

"That's a new one."

After a short wait, they gained admittance to the deck and then to halls that smelt of brine and blistering paint.

The steel hath bubbles, as the water has, / And these are of them.

At a cabin door, they were received by a stocky man with a short, bristly, orangey-brown beard, brown hair, and searching, brown eyes. He was perhaps forty. "Alright," he told the crewman who had escorted the visitors. "I've met him. He's no trouble. Alright."

The crewman left.

The stocky man continued to speak across the threshold. "Well, you got me outta deep shit the other night," he said to Misha.

Misha crossed his arms and clapped his hands on his elbows and nodded.

Nadia was doing a final rehearsal in her head.

"Here," said Price, moving his fingers in his trouser pocket with a faint *chink-chink*, "I want you to have something." He fished out a lapel pin. "This is … the flag of my home province, Nova Scotia, in Canada…"

(Misha fondled the freshly affixed flag.)

"…and I'm pretty sure I have one that's a lobster for…"

"Mr. Price, I am very pleased to meet you," Nadia said.

"Oh, it's Wayne, dear, hello." He gave up on finding the lobster pin and instead lightly shook her hand.

"Gawain?"

"No, 'Wayne' is better."

"Wean."

"Yeah, that's it. What's your name, dear?"

"Nadezhda Mikhailovna. Nadia is better."

"Right. That's easy. Nadia."

"Yes."

Price glanced down the corridor, one way and then the other. His right eye moved to farther extremes than its partner did.

"I am learning English," Nadia told him.

"Are you, now?"

"Yes. I read and translate English books. Charles Dickens."

"I shouldn't wonder. I mean, you're smart people, right down to the gambling chess maniacs."

Nadia nodded and nodded as she strained to process this man's speech. *This Nova Scotia,* she supposed, *must be something like the marshes of Kent.*

"Well..." Price hummed.

Now is the time to chitchat for dear life. "Please, where is your city?"

"I'm not from the City. I'm from a fishing village called Terence Bay ... but that's quite near a city called Halifax."

"Halifax!"

"You've heard of it?" Price asked.

"Yes."

"Have you really?"

"Yes. Halifax," Nadia stated, "is a city for sailors and travellers, a cultural city like Odessa. Halifax has the Oxford Theatre." *I sound like a half-wit's encyclopedia.*

Price nodded and smiled, which only made Nadia more nervous. "Well, dear, Nadia, dear," he said, "you must've studied your atlas pretty well. That or you have a sailor friend."

She denied it: "No..."

"No? Let me guess again. You have a friend who makes art films. I'm sure I saw a poster for a Russian film at the Oxford. Your friend's in export."

"Yes," Nadia faltered. She decided to sew something of this cloth. "I have an artist friend. Life is very hard for him here."

"Oh," said Price, "why's that, now?"

"He is..." (Nadia glanced at her father and wondered how much of this he was getting) "...homosexual."

"I see." Price looked at Misha too. Misha was smiling and nodding. Price gave Misha a nod, which made Price's right eye float up and down.

Nadia continued, "He is in great trouble. He will go to prison. Prison here..."

Price sighed under his breath and both his eyes wandered. "Jesus, I do pick 'em," he whispered to himself.

Nadia went mute as she struggled to parse the words. Misha sensed that the moment was ripe—or rotten. He risked it and showed the cash.

"His films do well, then," Price sort of sang as he pushed Misha's hand back in the bag. "I won't ask whether I'd have seen them."

Confused, Misha looked to Nadia.

"No," Nadia told her father. "I am sorry," she said to Price, "for taking your time." She took hold of Misha's wrist to lead him away.

"Hold on, there, Nadia, Misha, just..." Price put his own hand into the mix. "Look, come back later. On the middle watch—between twelve at night and four in the morning—I might be able to help out, if all signs point to a quiet night. We head out at first light, so it's tonight or never, to get him on this ship."

Nadia translated this for Misha. Then, she wanted to know, "What does it mean, 'if all signs point to a quiet night'?"

"I mean, I'd be happiest," Price said, "if everybody with a badge or a gun, on land or on sea, was busy someplace else, away from my ship."

Nadia shrugged and eyed the ceiling and asked, "How is it possible?"

"You tell me."

She translated for Misha, who nodded and gave a thumbs-up.

"Okay," Nadia told Price.

"Right. Well, bring your friend later and bring that bag and we'll see."

"Then," Nadia insisted, "you will take him to Halifax."

"I might. I'll ship him where I can, if I can. No films, you hear me?"

12: Final Doubts

Johnny was somewhat alarmed to hear of his filmmaking career. Misha, too, was surprised at his daughter's degree of guile and its success thus far.

"Well," Misha remarked, "we're losing Charlie Chaplain to America."

"Losing, sure," Johnny said. "They buy men dead or alive." He turned away and rested his brow against a steel shelving unit. Nadia pictured him in the dusty shelter in Afghanistan with the other young man, the one with the merciful eyes and fluffy pre-beard, the one who got beheaded.

"Maybe," said Nadia, "Canada is different." *On the other hand, Doctor Anton Igorevich Yahontov stocks brochures for visiting Canadians.*

Johnny had his own doubts. "I've heard Canadians on the radio. They're just the earnest version, like East Germans."

"All the better," Misha maintained. "You can sell your life story to a bunch of earnest people and get interviewed on earnest radio and imagine Nadia tuning in, far away, so she knows you're okay."

Johnny went quiet. He refused to respond to any further coaxing from either Misha or Nadia. At last, Misha came out and asked, "Well, are you going or aren't you?"

"I can't make up my mind," Johnny mumbled.

"You can't stay here," Misha told him.

"I can't go," Johnny said, "if I don't say a proper goodbye to Ida."

13: Need of a Good Worker

At a payphone, Nadia stood watch while Misha told a tale to Katya.

"Nadia's on her way. I'm at work. I wanted to check in on a big shipment and try to get things moving. Grain. From Canada. People have to eat."

Nadia imagined her mother's words or feelings. *"People who have to eat should consider people who have to cook."*

"Katya," Misha blurted, "one more thing: can you spare Ida? I need a good worker here. Well, we have a truck that's stalled and Ida might be able to jumpstart it. No, we have to move this truck, it can't stay where it is. No, well, it's a long time since I was a mechanic."

He finished with love and promises.

"I feel guilty," Nadia confessed, "leaving this to you and Ida."

"Don't. I would feel better," Misha said, "if you kept Mama company."

14: Tragedy Before Dinner

When Nadia arrived back, her parents' street was getting dark. Although there were streetlamps at the little park with the seesaw and the T-34, the bulbs were smashed, perhaps by natural disaster or by a tramp trying to sleep.

The dairy truck was gone.

Katya was peeling potatoes when her daughter came through the door. "I was beginning to think," said Katya, "I'd be having dinner alone."

"Sorry, Mama," Nadia murmured. *Now I shall tell an abject lie.* "Papa is really trying hard to stay in the good books at work."

"Well," said Katya as she dug out a stubborn eye, "I wouldn't know about that. I'm an honest worker and the factory provides this house, doesn't it, but am I in anyone's good books? I suppose one woman on the line had to be just competent. Anyway, I've been thinking, I should apply to go on a course in quality inspection. I just need someone to help me knock on the right door."

"What's for dinner?" Nadia asked.

"Meatballs and mashed potatoes," said Katya, "good and filling and hot."

"Yum. Can I help?"

"No, go take a look at the shelves. See whether there's anything you want for school or anything Gramma would like. Ida already chose some things for herself. She says she likes to pack the night before work."

"Oh, right," Nadia said as she moved into the family room and began a dawdling survey of the shelves. *To respect a place is to treat it like a library.*

"Quite the traveller, Ida has become. She's driven all over Ukraine. She says she dreams of one day finding her cousins in Switzerland. That part, to me, sounded like a fairytale but all the same, she's as bright as ever when you get her on the right thing. Doesn't she know a lot about computers!"

"She does."

"There's talk of getting one in the factory and Ida had a list of questions she imagined I could ask the management! 'Well, Katya,' she says, 'if you're going into quality control, it'll be a valuable tool to you, to track and analyze the data.'"

Nadia smiled to herself, though she never felt more afraid. *By my sweat alone, a machine could tell I'm part of a conspiracy.* She touched the spine of *Crime and Punishment* but left it where it was.

She settled on a photo-illustrated copy of *The Cherry Orchard*, which Mama had bought for her on their visit to the place where it was written: Chekhov's White Cottage in Yalta, his "hot Siberia", where he lived with his mother and sister while he was dying of tuberculosis. The disease had not so much troubled him in the cold Siberia, on his solo journey to Sakhalin Island, yet what a difference a few years make.

She took the play to her suitcase in her bedroom. The door was closed despite the apparent emptiness of the room. Ida's stuff was all gone. Nadia frowned. *What was this door proposing to do? Prevent the spread of the damp? Guard the privacy of characters in books in luggage?* She shut it anyway on her way out.

She returned to the kitchen to find her mother cracking a decorated egg into a mixing bowl of ground beef and rice.

"Where's Tentser?" Nadia asked.

"I had to close him in your room again," Katya said. "First he wanted to get in the dryer and then the refrigerator and then on top of the stove and then he kept sticking his paws in my sewing machine, and finally he went under your covers. I hope he doesn't suffocate but it seemed like his least foolhardy idea. He's like having a baby who can run and jump and bite."

"He's the darling of Kiev," Nadia asserted.

"Well, well," said Katya, "it's good of him to come back to see us." She began to roll meatballs in her palms. "Of course, I will be a good hostess to him, as I am to everyone who crosses the doorstep to my kitchen. I can't fathom the abominable behaviour of that disgusting woman in Kiev, the one Giorgi thought would take him and take you too, I suppose, as if you didn't have a family, as if you didn't have a future but to play housemaid to some defective, allergic bitch of a wife to a moribund cop. Nastya told me what that woman did."

Nadia rubbed her cheek. "You can't blame Giorgi for that."

"And the car crash?" Katya asked. She was building concentric rings of meatballs as she placed them one-by-one in an oiled pan.

"Well, not a crash…"

"I'm very proud," Katya went on, "of the way you've prepared yourself for the highest academic opportunities. That's your doing. I'm very proud and tonight I just want to share my pride in you with my very dear and distinguished friend, who's been longing to meet you since the hour he and I first spoke. I had hoped your Papa would be here too but there you go."

"If it could be helped," Nadia said, "I know he'd rather be home now."

"Well," Katya sighed, "with the cat here, I suppose I believe you. Give a man what he wants and he'll be home early every night."

"Mama!" Nadia groaned.

Katya shrugged and looked at the ceiling. "…truly wants…" she qualified the maxim. "Tomato juice," she whispered to herself, "sour cream…" (She got these staples from the fridge, placed them on the counter, and popped out to the garden. Nadia watched through the open door as her mother dashed to the target in the darkened garden and then back into the light.) "…red pepper. I have been saving you." Katya grabbed an onion and head of garlic from her pantry. "Here is all anyone needs for an excellent meatball sauce."

"When's he coming?"

"Should be anytime now." Katya tilted her head as she chopped. "He was supposed to get off duty an hour ago. Why don't you find some music on the radio? He likes classical. Only, make it very, very soft. I can't get the factory out of my head these last few nights."

Nadia wandered back into the family room and gently turned the black dial (the volume) on the little white radio, with its three buttons for three channels and its muffled voice behind plastic bars. (Reception here was poor compared to an apartment building with a shared antenna on the roof, yet such were the oddities of living in a private house granted by a factory.) Classical music was monopolizing the air. *Surely, it is the balm for an earthquake and all manner of ills. Marat might draw a comparison to Nero's singing.*

Between lengthy descriptions of two pieces of music, an announcer gave a terse update on the earthquake. All necessary help had reached the people who needed it. All others should remain alert amid ongoing aftershocks but stay put unless otherwise indicated.

Katya entered the family room as Prokofiev's *Dance of the Knights* was beginning to play. She gave an inventory: "Potatoes boiling, meatballs frying, sauce starting to simmer."

Nadia turned off the radio. "A bit much," she said.

"What is?" asked Katya as she sat on the sofa and began to undo the bun in her hair.

"Tragic ballet with meatballs," Nadia replied. She went to sit with Mama. "Your cooking and your company should be enough."

"Oh-ho, at the first sign they're not," Katya instructed, "you're to interrupt my chatter. You'll be far more interesting to him, my nightingale, than hearing me sing my litanies for the umpteenth time."

"I disagree," Nadia said, "but I shall try not to disappoint you."

"Tosh." Katya fanned out the ends of her hair. "How…?"

The lampshades trembled, causing oscillations in the globes of light on the ceiling. The phone rattled, one of its feet slipped off the edge of the sewing table, and it plummeted to the floor with a ring, which signified nothing.

Katya sighed and went over to pick it up. "This floor," she complained, "isn't level at the best of the times. Maybe I should have been an airline stewardess. Can you picture me, my treasure, dodging up and down the aisle with a smile and fetching and comforting while all hell is breaking loose?"

"Like in *Air Crew*, when the cabin is depressurizing?"

"Yes, yes, like your crazy movies." Katya knelt, tugged the hem of her dress out from under her knees, and cradled the carrot-orange phone in her lap as she untangled its coils. She reminisced about the family's moviegoing days. "When you were little, seeing those with you was as if your Papa and I were kids for the first time too. We never had that kind…" She shrugged and stood.

An instant after Katya restored the phone to its place, it rang. She picked it up immediately and answered graciously, "Yes, hello?"

Nadia could tell that the voice on the other end was Nastya's.

"Oh, it's you!" Mama laughed. "Hi, dear."

She cries for my calls and laughs for Nastya's. Well, I'll take the tears.

"No, no, no, we haven't slid into the sea. No. No, were you…? Your dishes! Giorgi says what?" (She stopped laughing.) "Oh, oh, those poor people. No…" (she pulled back the curtain to peep out the window) "…everything is fine here. He was good to think of us. Nadia and Ida are with us. Yes, why not?"

Nastya began to testify. Nadia and Ida had told Nastya and Rosya…

Katya interrupted, "Well, one way or another, they're with us." She reverted to laughter. "He is too. Tell Giorgi. Tell him the desperate hoodlum is sheltering with us."

Nadia's heart clenched, until she realized that her mother was referring to the kitten.

"Yes, sorry, dear, I'm expecting another call. We love you. Go back to bed. Baby needs you to sleep. Goodnight." Katya hung up. She looked at Nadia and reported, "These aftershocks really are deadly, even if they seem small. Apartment buildings are collapsing in Kishinev, maybe other places too." She returned to the sofa and clasped her hands close to her face, with her thumbnails pressing into her lower lip. "There must be hundreds of souls trapped in the rubble. Army and Police are being dispatched from Odessa. That's what Giorgi heard. Even an Intourist Hotel was damaged; Nastya heard that on the boombox, on Voice of America." Katya got up. "I just have to turn down the meatballs."

"What next?" Nadia whispered as she followed her mother into the kitchen. *Right now, Johnny is in a brick warehouse, with horrible reception, but he has probably asked for his radio. He's had a smoke while Papa and Ida bring it from the dairy truck. Now, he is catching the barest fragments of chatter as he wonders whether the cops and soldiers are coming out tonight to fry his meatballs. Well, for now, they have other worries—but he's still stuck ashore.*

"Next," said Katya, "is dinner with our guest. No matter what, no matter if there's a war on…"

…and there is, Nadia thought.

"…we do our best for our guest," Katya instructed. With a clatter, she grabbed a spoon from a drawer and took the smallest taste of the simmering sauce from the frying pan. She dolloped in more sour cream, stirred, and said, "Perhaps, my sweet one, you could shower before he gets here." She put the lid on the pan, pushed her fingertips along her daughter's scalp, and sniffed. "Wash your hair well. Does Ida smoke?"

"No, Mama." *Ida quit and now I only smoke with men behind sheds and in stairways, men who have camera lenses to clean or vivid horrors to chase.* She added, "Ida and I were making smoked meat."

Katya frowned. "You aren't hanging around at sauna parties?"

"No, Mama."

"Go wash your hair," Katya reiterated.

"Alright, Mama." Nadia pulled her mother's head down to kiss her cheek. Then, it was time to leave Katya's kitchen to Katya.

"Your clothes are in the dryer."

"Thanks, Mama," Nadia replied as she shut herself in the narrow room with the washer-dryer, toilet, sink, and shower. She saw herself in the mirror—ringed eyes and the yellow-bruised, claw-slashed cheek that Comrade Chessmaster had mocked. *Mama, Mama's friend, let's dine by candlelight.* She also saw a column of ants—sparse, yet no doubt on a mission. They were marching to and from the vent hole. *I'll pretend I didn't see you. I'm not keen to squish you, nor to admit I let you go.*

She set aside her dirty clothes, turned on the shower, and attempted to banish smoke with steam. She wanted to find oblivion in the automatic actions of washing her exhausted body. However, on and off, she caught herself picturing a place of execution—a soundproofed closet with a drain.

There was no music, no radio playing under this roof now. Katya preferred to cook in silence.

More water, hotter water. Johnny escapes to a land of tropical storms, where six megahertz is the best band for reception. She recited poetry to herself in whispers.

Along with the hiss of the water, some other sound abruptly insinuated itself into Nadia's ears. A moment later, her mother began to talk, in tones of warm respect, yet without any audible reply. That was when Nadia realized that the other sound had been the phone ringing.

No point hurrying, Nadia told herself. *He can fly but not through the phone. I'm to wash my hair well.* She thought of the unseen days when Ida had pulled out her hair and when Johnny had grown his matted beard. She reached for a can of used coffee grounds that her mother kept on a corner shelf. These were for proper scrubbing of the scalp, shining of the brown hair, and (perhaps) shading of the grey. *Worst case, I'm going to smell like smokes and coffee. Who knows, maybe the Lieutenant Colonel will too, at the end of his day.*

By the time Nadia came out of the shower, Katya was doing more listening than speaking. Nevertheless, she had her say. "So much responsibility," she interjected, "is costing you your health. I've seen you."

Seen what? I wonder… though you could just as well be warning Grandpa Lev, were he not already dead. Near the stove, Nadia hesitated for a moment but she decided to press ahead, not to eavesdrop.

"Nadia is here now," Katya said into the telephone. "Would you like to…? Oh, then you must go. Yes, go instruct your aide. Yes, goodbye until then." She hung up and glanced at Nadia's hair.

Preempting any further grooming instructions, Nadia asked, "How soon will he be here?"

"Now he's on duty till midnight Moscow Time," Katya reported, "to handle any further crisis—be it ten-storey tsunami, nuclear missile, UFO landing, falling space station, asteroid, or anything else that shits on us from above. His Sunday night off, he has to cover for a general who has 'taken ill'. Men are sickly in the evenings; remember that, my gentle one." Katya marched out to the kitchen to wrap the pan of meatballs in tinfoil and stick it in the oven on low heat.

She wants a moment alone out there, Nadia surmised from the banging and the crushing and the banging.

"Well, then," Katya breathed as she marched back to the sofa, "if everything is to be a disaster, let it be a fucking great disaster! Then, at least, our clever men, who lord it over us, might have to admit it happened." She sat, crossed her arms, and glared in the direction of her vacant dining table and vacant bedroom.

"Are we still waiting for him?" Nadia asked.

"Yes," said Katya.

Nadia's stomach grumbled. "Can we eat?"

"No. I'll get the laundry," Katya said, "and see what needs mending. You find something to read to me."

Nadia went to her old bedroom and checked that Tentser was still breathing, where once Gramma had snored. *"This feather stirs; he lives!"* She covered him up again. She got *Great Expectations* and her partial translation and returned to the sofa, where Katya was choosing thread to go with the plaid shirt of red, black, and yellow. A couple of buttons were dangling on account of fidgety buttoning and unbuttoning, the cuffs were fraying and the elbows were thinning from gymnastics and heavy lifting, and Tentser had left claw-marks around the breast pockets and collar, where he would brace his paws as he climbed.

"That shirt is Ida's favourite," Nadia said.

Katya replied, "She told me she wanted you to have it in Moscow, to wear over your pyjamas on winter nights."

"Oh." Nadia turned away from the sofa to adjust a lampshade and she wiped a nascent tear from each eye.

"Read to me," Katya requested.

"Yes, Mama," Nadia said as she settled into the sofa once more. "I'll read you the latest from my translation."

"Good." (Katya knew bits of this opus, almost by heart, from her recent phone calls to Kiev.) "Have you done more on the visit to the manor house where he's made to play cards?"

"Yes. Do you want to hear that?"

"Yes."

Nadia started to read.

"What was the house called?" Katya interrupted.

"Satis," said Nadia, "Latin for 'Enough'."

"Ah." For a while, Katya listened silently and, at times, paused her sewing to stare far away. Then, she requested a reading of a different part and a different one after that.

Nadia obliged, sometimes having to translate from the book on-the-fly, until she grew tired.

At last, Katya whispered, "Very good, my clever one. Anyone would think you had spent a lifetime listening to ladies and ruffians and all sorts in between. You sleep a little now."

So it would be. Katya took Nadia's work from her hands and set it aside in the safety of a folder of sewing patterns.

"I'll put the radio on," Katya whispered, "to help you sleep."

The classical music continued.

Are the ants marching to the wedding feast that Gramma crashed?

At some point, the music blipped to a stop, making way for a report on breaking news in America. A passenger jet had crashed in Los Angeles after a collision with a private plane. Wreckage had landed on a row of houses and a playground and a conflagration was spreading…

Katya got up to turn the radio off.

"Mama," Nadia mumbled, "is it past midnight … Moscow Time?"

"Yes. He'll come," Katya said, "as soon as he's able." She sat, finished stitching up a rip above a pocket, and started to reinforce the top corners.

"Should you call…?"

The doorbell rang. Katya leapt up.

Here we go, Nadia told herself as she pushed her weary body from the squashy sofa once more. *For Mama, I shall race to the door alongside her to greet Lieutenant Colonel Sokolov of Naval Aviation. A few weeks ago, he seemed such a prominent enigma. Now, he just seems late. Everything seems late and unready and I am sick with worry that has nothing to do with this man.*

Nadia was present, gazing attentively from a place beside the refrigerator, when Katya answered the second ring of the bell.

That's a bit cheeky, Nadia thought, *to do a double-ring.*

On the doorstep stood a young man in black naval uniform. After a moment, Nadia recognized him as the driver who had waited for her at the station a few weeks ago. He handed an envelope to Katya and said, "Lieutenant Colonel Sokolov sends his regrets." Then, he turned, strode out the garden gate, shut it behind him, and got in his car to drive away, all before Katya could conjure a question.

Shutting the door and staring at the envelope, Katya muttered, "I've told him his driver doesn't like me."

I doubt he's enamoured of me either, after the caper of my disappearance from the station. To seek and solve mysteries seems an unlikely sideline for a sailor who serves as a pilot's driver. Nadia followed her mother back to the family room.

Katya lowered herself into the depths of the sofa. Her hands were shaking as she half mouthed the words of a hand-scrawled message. Suddenly, she refolded it, put it back in the envelope, and pocketed it. She extended her hands towards her daughter and said, "He isn't coming tonight."

Nadia clasped her mother's hands and sat next to her. "Okay, Mama," she said. "I'll meet him another time. Try not to be disappointed."

"My dearest," Katya whispered, "it's another disaster."

"What?"

"He sends terrible news. He must have wanted to tell me first, in case it's people we know or if later he's silenced…"

"Tell you what?"

"A thousand people are drowning. Our cruise ship, the *Admiral Nakhimov*, has sunk."

"Just now?"

"Forty minutes ago. Forty minutes before he wrote the letter. He wrote it in the car on his way out and that was as soon as they got orders to scramble and that was forty minutes after she sank."

"Where was this?"

"Near Novorossiysk. He says he'll be in the group who take up the secondary search in the morning."

"He must dread it," Nadia said. She imagined the forlorn task of seeking missing bodies between the pitiless lines of waves, cliffs, and beaches. "How interesting that at a moment when he needs courage, he stops to write a letter to you."

Katya drew in her breath and let it out in a disconsolate scoff. "He's certainly lost if he's looking for courage in me."

"Well," said Nadia, "he'd do no better to look in me but … courage, empathy, it comes to the same place, maybe. From what you've said of him, he's a kind man…" …*even if, like an albatross, he eludes us on land. All things considered, perhaps it's for the best.* She thought of Baudelaire's albatross. *"His giant's wings prevent him from walking…"* …*or from coming to dinner, as the case may be.*

"Yes." Katya rose and walked to the kitchen. This time, she made little din as she moved the meatballs.

Nadia nuzzled into the back of the sofa and tried to think clearly about the present nightmare. *See how the sand shifts in the minute-glass, when this toy of a world is turned upside down. The engines are running, life grows cold. With such a wailing all around, a man might slip from one fate to another. Only so many manhunts and so many rescues can go on in one night. If ever Johnny can scrounge a pass to freedom, it is now. Then Papa will have saved a man. Avel, perhaps, will have got away with something too.*

Some version of these thoughts must have been transparent to Katya, for she returned with Misha's lunchbox, which she placed in her daughter's hands. "Now, my quiet one," said Katya, "if you scurry, the meatballs should stay warm in the foil. I put four or five rubles change in there too. Find a taxi. I'm sure your Papa will want to hear the news."

Nadia nodded. "Yes, Mama."

"Have the taxi drop you somewhere … not quite where you're going."

"Yes, Mama."

"Misha hasn't made you do anything crooked, has he? That, I couldn't forgive of him."

"No, Mama," Nadia said, "I promise you. Papa is doing this for me. I asked him. He's helping someone get out to start a new life."

Katya looked away to read the patterns in the rug on the wall. She whispered, "I understand now, my dearest. Your grandmothers would respect the action that you and your father are taking. Perhaps, yes, perhaps this will set things right for all of us."

They exchanged a swift hug, of the kind given in war movies.

"Go now," said Katya. "Tell them the news."

15: Awakening

When Tentser emerged from his nap under the quilt, he found himself alone. He cried and Katya brought him half a meatball to quiet him.

16: Death and Life

As Nadia raced along the promenades of this Baroque misfit of a city, words crashed in her head. *Odysseus lives, yet his whole crew dies, and here we are tonight, furnishing one more ship to float this soul on the chaos of the sea.* At a lamppost halfway down the Stairs, she stopped to catch her breath. Her hand touched the painted iron and a realization came to her: *Mama thought I meant a new life for Ida.*

About the Author

Joseph Howse lives in a Nova Scotian fishing village, where he chats with his cats, crafts his books, and nurtures an orchard of hardy fruit trees. When he can, he goes roaming in a pair of old work boots, which have lasted twelve years on six continents, though the soles have twice been replaced.

As a computer scientist, Joseph is known for his books on computer vision or, in other words, the ways a machine can "see" and interpret waves of light, radiation, and sound.

The Girl in the Water is Joseph's debut novel.

To learn more about Joseph's work, go online:

- **Nummist Media:** nummist.com

    - **Novels, Stories, Book Club Guides**: nummist.com/stories

- **Facebook**: @josephhowse.author
- **Twitter:** @CatsAndMonkeys
- **Goodreads:** goodreads.com/author/show/2835685.Joseph_Howse
- **Flickr:** flickr.com/josephhowse